DEATH SCENE

J.J. FRANCESCO

Scene, chapter, and cover film strip designs by freepik.com

Cover photo by Melanie P. Smith

Cover models: Devin and Jansina

Death Scene
Rivershore Books
Copyright © 2016 Jonathan Francesco
All rights reserved.
ISBN: 978-0692679210
ISBN-10: 0692679219

DEDICATION

For all the lives impacted by the evils of kidnapping and human trafficking, you are loved and you matter.

And he that stealeth a man, and selleth him,
or if he be found in his hand,
he shall surely be put to death. (Exodus 21:16)

CHAPTER 1

Wayne Tempest locked eyes with the terrified child one last time as he threw himself behind a stranger's Ford Transit parked by the diner entrance. Two bullets buried themselves in the driver's door as another shattered the window.

Wayne rolled out with his Glock in hand to return fire, but the SUV was already speeding out of the parking lot.

He fired a shot to blow a tire but missed.

Attempting to read the plates was virtually useless. The light from the flickering sign of the "Tunney Family Diner" only allowed him to see the first character, a "G."

"Damn," he muttered as he picked the blue envelope out of his shirt pocket. He pulled out the picture from inside. It was just like all of them, only this time he was here. Could it be a taunt or just plain coincidence? The picture was a candid shot. The boy and his father outside of a church. But it was unquestionably them. The boy's almost metallic dark hair and calm brown eyes would've stood out under normal circumstances, but the melancholy stare in the photograph definitely matched the somber child he'd just met inside.

He hadn't even planned to work the case tonight. For the first time in months, Wayne Tempest allowed himself a night out to get a real meal. The boy and the dad seated next to him seemed pleasant enough. The father introduced himself as a nondenominational pastor. Jeremy Garret. And his son was named Aaron. The boy didn't talk much. Barely even made eye contact. He didn't even protest when his father ordered broiled flounder for the both of them. What kid would willfully eat that?

Wayne had considered abuse for the briefest moment. But the boy didn't seem afraid of his father at all. Likewise, the father seemed legitimately gentle with his son. In his years as a private investigator and prior involvement with law enforcement, he'd developed a knack for spotting an abuser's front. He'd have known if the boy was being mistreated.

Still, the boy was troubled by something deeper. Something a lot more real than the petty complaints most eleven-year-olds hurled at their over-scheduled parents. Wayne had learned to pick up on these things as well. But for all the tension, the two appeared to be living a normal life. There wasn't any reason to pay attention.

If he'd only known. Within half an hour, the case that had been bothering him for years and this quiet pastor and son would collide before his eyes.

This damn case. It'd taken over his life for over three years now.

It was always the same. People would randomly vanish without a trace. The instances would've all seemed irrelevant if not for a single blue envelope left behind at the scene. Inside, there'd be a recent candid shot of the victim. Likely taken within days of the abduction. Glossy finish, but only moderate image quality. Wayne had tracked over fifteen separate abductions over the past few years alone.

Family members filed reports, the police had investigated, but they never came up with a viable suspect. Some had even written it off as disgruntled individuals trying to start fresh. But how would that mesh with the photographs left behind? That screamed to be the signature of a serial offender. Clearly, evidence rarely got in the way of a convenient theory.

Wayne took out another envelope. He'd carried it with him since he'd taken this case. Inside was a picture of a woman, 20-something, blonde, fierce blue eyes, and a smile that was innocent with a splash of sly. Therese . . . Her family had hired him to find her after the legal search went cold. He'd theorized all the usual possibilities: runaway, abusive boyfriend, drugs, even witness protection. Never could he have realized how many other victims she'd be connected to. A parish priest who disappeared after morning Mass, an elderly woman taken from a retirement community, now the quiet boy and his father. So many more, some of whom he may not even know about. How something so huge could fly almost totally under the radar of the authorities. Was this some human trafficking ring? A forensically savvy rapist? How could so many people disappear without a trace?

Even years later, not one body recovered. Could all of these victims be alive somewhere? Wayne dared to hope from time to time, but his senses quickly squashed it. More than likely, whoever was behind this just had a sophisticated disposal method.

Regardless, Wayne had made a promise to find answers for Therese's family. For all of those families. Even if that answer was confirmation of death. Closure was closure. Even if it hurt. He'd promised them. And he was failing.

Wayne walked to the edge of the parking lot. An eerie silence swept over the dark, country road. Even the sounds of distant traffic seemed to dissipate. Two people were kidnapped at gunpoint and not two minutes later all was returned to a quiet suburban night.

Then the blare of a siren cut through the night. Wayne saw the distant flashes of red and blue coming toward the diner. Apparently, one of the few people inside actually had heard the commotion and notified the authorities. For all the good that would do. Wayne had seen what they could offer.

He needed something more.

He took out his phone and highlighted her number. Even five years later, it was still in his contacts. Maybe it wasn't even current, but he had to try. This case couldn't be completed on his own anymore. With this latest abduction, things had escalated too far. Now he needed his old partner. She was the best then, and with her name all over the local news these past few months, he knew she still was.

Over the summer, a serial killer had terrorized their community. He'd violently slaughtered entire families and posed them after paintings he'd made. The Blood Chain Killer. The depths of his depravity had been unmatched, but she brought him down and restored a feeling of peace to the community. She made a name for herself, but Wayne knew that she wasn't all hype. She was the only one on the force he still trusted.

Wayne's stomach knotted as he dialed. Memories flooded him. He remembered working case theory hours after dark. Chasing suspects through crowded highways. Slamming perpetrators into their cells. Meeting those hilarious little twin boys. Holding his crying partner as she broke down after one of them was killed by a drunk driver. That bitter final confrontation when he'd had enough of the badge failing people. He remembered every moment so clearly.

That flowing blonde hair. Piercing eyes that could see into the deepest corridors of the soul. He'd never intended to see her again, and yet here he was, calling up Detective Julie Martel. If anybody operating under the sanctity of the badge could help him, it would be her. Her name meant "hammer," and right now, Wayne knew that was exactly what this case needed.

CHAPTER 2

Pastor Jeremy Garret nervously clenched the steering wheel of the stranger's SUV. A car had always represented freedom to him, but as he stared at the masked man with a gun to his ribs, it felt more like a prison.

He could almost hear Aaron in the back seat, shaking. He couldn't imagine how terrified Aaron was now. Jeremy himself was terrified and he'd stared down the barrel of a gun more than once in his life already. Aaron had been through enough for an eleven-year-old. He didn't need this.

"Dad!"

Aaron's voice, weak and trembling.

"Aaron!" A jolt in his chest. He struggled just a moment to keep the car steady in the lane. "I'm here, Aaron."

"Where are we going? Dad, I'm scared."

Jeremy took a deep breath. "I don't know, son. I wish I did." He glared at the man seated next to him. No reaction. Then into the rearview mirror at the second one in the back seat, a gun pointed to Aaron's head. "Don't worry, Aaron. We'll be okay. We just have to trust in God. Okay?"

"God can't help you now, Pastor." So casual. So matter-of-fact. Did what he was doing even phase this monster?

The pastor in him wanted to challenge the Godless fool seated next to him, but he knew now wasn't the time for a theological war of words. He didn't care what happened to him, but he couldn't risk them hurting Aaron. If he'd been alone, maybe he'd chance trying something. Crashing the car, running, fighting for one of the guns.

Jeremy shot another glance at the rearview mirror. Aaron was shaking. He was trying not to look at the gun. He'd seen them on TV but never in person, but Aaron knew what happened when they went off.

"Please, don't kill us." Aaron's voice was shaking now.

Jeremy could see tears running down his son's cheeks. Those glimmering eyes were like knives to his soul. Nothing he could say seemed anything other than a church cliché.

"Calm down, kid." The one in the front shot a half scowl to Aaron. "We won't kill you if you do what we say."

"What is this about?" Jeremy turned to the one in front. "If this is about money, we can work that out. There's no need to hurt the boy."

"They always think it's about money." The goon chuckled. "You'll find out when we get where we're going." He raised the gun to Jeremy's head. "Now shut up and drive. We don't have all night."

Jeremy picked up speed. His sweaty palms clenched the wheel tighter. "So how much farther?"

"Not far. In fact, our exit is coming up in half a mile."

Half a mile. Not nearly as far as Jeremy had thought. Where the heck could they be going? And for that matter, how could he escape once he was there? Jeremy prayed hard to keep his faith alive. In all his trials in life thus far, he'd always had a clear path as to what God expected of him. Now he didn't know anything for sure other than that God would be with him. For the first time ever, that didn't seem to be enough. He was completely in the dark and he desperately was trying to find a light to make sense of it all.

A limo pulled up to Zander Park. Its headlights broke through the shrouding darkness, joining with the dim glow from the waning crescent moon.

The driver stopped by the fountain directly in the park's center. The silhouette of St. Anthony was still barely visible. He put on a pair of gloves and opened the trunk and pulled out two zipped body bags, which blended into the night. One was significantly larger than the other.

He unzipped the first one and revealed the dead body of a woman. He brushed her curly black hair away from her face. He took her body out of the bag and carried it over to the fountain and set it down gently before it. Arms folded at the chest.

Returning to the car, he unzipped the smaller bag. A young boy, about nine. Hair color the same as the woman's—his mother. He had a large, bloody gash across his throat, a contrast to the seeming lack of wounds to the woman.

He gently stroked the boy's cheek, just for a moment. One last fleeting glimpse of dignity for somebody who never stood a chance. He placed the boy a few feet away from his mother, resting the head next to her chest. Even in the poor light, the peacefully arranged bodies created a grisly sight. The man fought the gurgle of vomit. He couldn't chance leaving DNA.

Hurrying back to the car, he gathered the empty body bags with him before shutting himself inside. The limo sped off into the night, leaving the corpses to whatever fate awaited them. Now, it was beyond his control or worry.

Aaron couldn't believe how large this mansion was. He didn't even know such fancy homes existed anywhere near his community, let alone believe he'd ever actually be kidnapped and taken to one.

He looked back at the large black gates they'd just entered. They were probably as tall as the mansion, if not taller. Nobody could see this house from the street. Maybe that's how these people wanted it.

There were also a lot of trees. Tall, menacing, creaking trees. It wasn't a particularly windy night but the trees were swaying as if a storm was coming. Shadowed by the moonlight and already stripped of most of their leaves, they seemed an appropriate thing to find at such a scary place.

But why would somebody bring him here? None of this made any sense.

The man next to him handed him a blindfold. "Put it on."

"Why?" Aaron clenched the rough fabric in his hands. "I already see where we are. You're not going to let me get away."

The man took his gun and gently pushed aside Aaron's black locks from his forehead. "Did I imply that this was negotiable?" He pressed the cold black metal of the barrel against Aaron's clammy skin, just barely above his nose.

"Aaron!" His father. Aaron could see him a few feet

away. The other thug had a gun to him too. "Just do what they say, son. Okay?" He put his own blindfold on. "Just listen to them."

Aaron nodded. He fought a tear. He had to be strong. He wrapped the blindfold around his eyes. As if by instinct, his hands thrust out to feel his way around. But they smacked his hands down and shoved him forward. He stumbled but regained his balance and slowly took a step.

His foot caught the hard edge of something.

He tumbled forward.

The thug behind him grabbed him by the shirt. "Watch your step. Can't have you messing up your face. The boss would kill us."

He whimpered. A last pitiful attempt to stuff down a full-blown cry.

The thug grabbed the back of Aaron's neck. "Don't be a wimp. The boss doesn't like wimps."

"He's just a little boy." Aaron could hear his father come closer. "Have some compassion."

"Brat's gotta grow a pair sooner or later."

"Don't fight with them, Dad." Aaron took a deep breath as he was pushed further along. "I'm fine."

The loud creak of a door.

They were shoved inside. The smell of elegance overwhelmed him. It wasn't like anything Aaron had ever smelled before. It wasn't sweet or stinky, just rich. Even without seeing anything, Aaron could almost picture the glimmering valuables.

Footsteps approached them. Starting at a whisper and then a clanking echo.

"The pastor and his son, I presume?" The voice was slightly high-pitched but still fierce and manly. Just the sound of it fired a sharp chill through Aaron's neck.

"Yes, sir." The thug pushed Aaron forward.

The blindfold was ripped off.

Aaron still couldn't see anything. It was too dark. He looked over and could make out his father standing a few feet away, looking back at him with concern.

A hand grabbed his chin.

Aaron squinted. He could just barely see a face. Examining his. But it was too dark to make out features beyond the moonlight reflecting off of silver glasses.

Aaron broke free of the man's grip.

"Strong. Very good."

The man moved on to his father and did the same.

"Nice, very nice." The man turned to go. "I think they're going to look great."

"What do you people want?" His father struggled in the goon's grip. "I'll give you anything I have if you just let my son and me go."

The man turned around. "I realize it's dark but surely you see that I want for very little. Do you honestly think you can buy your way out of this? Or do you want to bless me into letting you go? Save my soul? Answer your altar call, Pastor Jeremy? Introduce me to my savior, perhaps?"

"Please, I'll do anything." His father fell to his knees. "At least let my son go."

"Anything, you say? We'll see about that." The man pointed to what seemed to be a staircase. "Take them to the stars' wing. Make sure they're comfortable. Can't have the newbies throwing a fuss. We want them well rested."

The shadowed man then walked away.

"You heard the man. Let's go." The thugs pushed Aaron and his father deeper into the house.

Aaron could make out a fine, carpeted staircase. He struggled to climb it in the dark. There were many more steps than he had at home. Thank God the carpet cushioned his feet some. Yet, he was still gasping for breath by the time he reached the top.

He could hear his father wheezing too.

"Keep moving." Another shove. "You're almost there. You'll have all night to sleep this off."

Aaron heard a bang. Like a body hitting the wall or a kick to the back. But he didn't feel anything.

His father grunted.

"Dad! Are you okay?" Was it over? Were they about to be shot?

"I'm fine, Aaron. Just keep walking."

They were led down a hall, to a locked door at the end.

One of the thugs took out a key and unlocked it. He quietly pushed it open.

He grabbed Aaron and shoved him inside. He hit the ground with a loud thump.

A stab shot through his entire front.

His father fell beside him, holding his side.

Aaron crawled over to his father and wrapped his arms around him. "Dad? Are you okay?"

"Yes." He took Aaron in his arms. "How about you?"

The door closed. Then the click of a lock.

Aaron stuffed in a wail. "Yes."

"You sound hurt. Are you okay? You can tell me."

Aaron groaned a bit. He touched his arm. It ached a little, but not too much. "I'm fine."

His dad helped him to his feet and the two looked around.

Moonlight was coming through the windows. It seemed ironically elegant. Not like downstairs, but like a nice hotel. Thick drapes, fancy chairs and sofas, fine carpets, and various odds and ends decorating the quarters. What kind of kidnappers would keep their captives in such a nice room?

Should Aaron be grateful? Everyone kidnapped on TV was kept in filthy basements and cages. Maybe these were nice kidnappers after all? Aaron gave himself one minute to believe this. They weren't going to hurt him. Then the burning in his intestines returned and his legs again threatened to break beneath him. Somehow, the nice things started to make him even more afraid.

"Where are we?"

"I don't know." His father pulled him close. "But stay close to me."

Footsteps broke through the piercing silence.

A shadowed silhouette walked toward them.

Aaron gasped and clung close to his father.

His father wrapped him tighter. "Who are you people?"

"We're not with them." A sweet and gentle feminine voice. "Not by choice, at least."

The shadowed figure stepped into the moonlight coming from the window, dimly illuminating her face.

Aaron looked over her. He'd never met her before, but somehow she seemed so familiar.

"Who are you people?" His father moved him closer.

"You two have been through a lot." She didn't even blink. This all seemed so routine to her. "You should probably get cleaned up and changed. I know those guys aren't very accommodating when they take you. But for all the crazy stuff that goes on here, we live pretty comfortably. For the most part. There are three full bathrooms in this wing. Freshen up a bit. The showers are warm. There are closets in each of the bedrooms and there are lots of clothes that people left . . . that aren't being used anymore. I'm sure some should fit both of you."

A shower sounded good right about now, but not at a strange place. Not even a nice one.

"Why are we here?" His father approached the woman. "What do they want with us?"

"Are they gonna kill us?" Aaron didn't even wait for her to answer his father. "Are we gonna die?"

The woman's expression turned downward. "When I first came here, I asked all these same questions." She swallowed hard. "I don't mean to sound cold. I understand how confusing this must all be to you. I know it's scary. But I don't want to lie to you either. So for tonight, let's just try to get you settled in. Get through tonight. Then tomorrow. That's how you live through this. One day at a time."

She took Aaron by the hand and led them toward one of the rooms. "We do what we can for each other."

She pointed out each of the three bedrooms. "The men have one room. The women another. The third one is for the kids. But you two can stay together tonight, if you want." She walked away toward the women's bedroom. "We'll talk tomorrow. Try to rest tonight." She disappeared into the room.

"Dad, what should we do? This is all so . . . what kind of place is this?"

His father shook his head. "I really wish I knew, but this is as confusing to me as it is to you."

Aaron took his father's hand. He could feel the sweat on his palms slipping on the sweat from his dad's. His father didn't usually scare very easily. He was a pastor. Fearless. God's warrior. He didn't let things bother him. If he was scared, then things must be really bad. Like with his mother.

"It's going to be okay, Aaron. God will take care of us."

"You don't have to pastor-talk me, Dad. I'll be fine."

"Maybe you'd be more convincing if your hand wasn't holding onto mine so tightly."

Aaron shifted his gazed to their hands. His father was right. He was still shaking. He tried to stop it, but his body wasn't listening to him. Maybe if he kept telling himself that everything was going to be okay . . . that he and his dad were going to be okay, he'd start to believe it. Maybe it would start to become true.

CHAPTER 3

Julie Martel stared in her bedroom mirror. She carefully applied just a touch of makeup to hide the traces of another night of nightmare-laced sleep. It'd been several months since the Blood Chain Killer terrorized her and stolen her closest friends, and nearly her son. Her Patrick was safe, but the nightmares of losing him still persisted in slowly wearing her down.

Autumn temperatures were finally beginning to drive out the intense rage of summer heat waves. If only the changing of seasons could really give her a fresh start, freed from the pain of those July murders.

"Patrick, you ready for school yet?"

Patrick pushed open her bedroom door. Was he waiting in the hall for his cue?

He was dressed in his tan and blue school uniform. A navy clip-on-tie hung from his neck. He swung his backpack over his shoulders.

"Yes, Mom, I'm ready. But I don't think you are."

She laughed. At least he still had a sense of humor. She'd worried she'd never see it again, but it was slowly returning. "Well, I can't help it that I'm a woman. It takes us longer to get ready."

"I understand longer. But three times as long?" He

raised an eyebrow.

"I can't just step into my clothes like you can, kid." She stuck out her tongue. "I may chase bad guys all day but I'm a woman. I like to look good doing it."

He seemed to buy her little stretch. The last thing she needed was Patrick knowing about her not sleeping well.

"All right, kiddo, let's go."

"Sure you don't mind driving me to school, Mom?" He strolled down the stairs.

"Of course not." She grabbed her keys from the coffee table. "If Jacob isn't walking with you, there's no reason I shouldn't drive you. How's he feeling anyway?"

"He's fine. The doctor says he'll be on his feet again in a day or two. He just needs to stay in bed until the leg heals. That's what's killing him."

She chuckled. "I'm sure he'll be fine. He's been through worse."

"Don't remind me." Almost sarcastic. For once, his speaking about what happened over the summer didn't carry a somber veneer. Progress.

Julie couldn't remember the last time she'd driven Patrick to school. He'd always walked with a friend. It was good to have those extra five minutes with him.

As she turned the corner to his school, she asked, "So, got anything good going on at school today?"

"I think we gotta make one of them silly diorama things tonight."

"Silly?" She shook her head. "I remember doing them in school. They were a blast."

"Yeah, but we gotta do it on whatever theme they give us. It's no fun if I can't choose something cool like rock music or anime. And you think they're going to let me pick something cool like that? I'll probably be stuck doing it on John Adams or the small intestine."

"Oh, please. I'll help you."

"Doesn't make it fun."

She smiled. "Well, you'll still get it done anyway. Got it?"

Patrick sighed. "Yeah, yeah, I'll try."

She stopped as she pulled up to the school. Patrick quickly hopped out of the car. Julie rolled down the window and the two exchanged a cheek kiss before he ran up the driveway to the line of kids waiting outside the door to be let inside. She watched until he safely got in line. A part of her never wanted to let him out of her sight again, but he deserved as normal a life as possible.

The station was its typically noisy and bustling self as she walked through the doors. She barely got five good steps in before one of the officers informed her that her father wanted to see her in his office.

"I didn't even have my second cup of coffee yet." She groaned and gummed her lower lip a moment.

Her father was behind his desk waiting for her. Chief Kevin Martel, in all his sarcastic glory.

"There's my tardy daughter." He flashed her a smile.

"Being a couple of minutes late is not tardy when you're a mother. Getting kids dressed and off to school makes most of them late."

"Don't pass the buck to Patrick. I know for a fact that boy could go from zero to wedding approved in five minutes max. Gotta do better than that."

She smiled and took a seat. "So what kind of degenerate is making life in New Jersey difficult today?"

"Well, your desk phone rang last night. You'd already long since gone home but I was here so I answered it."

"Who calls my desk anymore? And why were you

here so late?"

He rolled his eyes. "Don't start with that. Anyway, when I picked up, it was an old friend. He'd brought something to my attention and I think we might have a legitimate case on our hands."

"An old friend?"

He pointed to Wayne, casually seated in the office's sofa.

Julie crossed her arms. "Tempest! Wayne Tempest?" Maybe ten pounds heavier but otherwise exactly the same as the day he stormed out of the precinct. "Well I'll be . . . what brings you back? I mean . . . I knew you'd be back. One day." She caught herself smiling but tried to stuff it down before he noticed. "I'm just curious. What finally made you come to your senses?"

Wayne rose to his feet. "Don't get too excited, Jules. I am not here because I have changed my views about the force." He walked over to Kevin's desk. "I'm here because I believe that there are still noble people on it. Namely you and your father." He swallowed hard. "And because this case is getting too difficult for me to handle by myself anymore. It's just escalating far beyond anything I could've predicted."

"A case? You mean one of your silly little private investigator gigs? I read about the lost pig you returned in the papers a few years back."

He shook his head. "Still as headstrong as ever. I'll have you know that my cases are often much more intense than the guys you regularly have to bust. Oh sure, every now and then you get a Blood Chain Killer to beat. But most of the time, you end up busting junkies, abusers, and cheating politicians."

"You realize I am a homicide detective, right? They

don't typically call me without a body? Plus, if you want to play that card, you end up catching men cheating on their wives at sleazy motels and finding lost dogs more often than anything. Face it, Tempest, this job is much more exciting."

"And much more restrictive." He clenched his hand into a fist. "So much so, it lets most of the bad guys go free."

"Don't start that again, Tempest."

He pulled up another chair and sat down. "I didn't come here to discuss that. I've been investigating the case of a missing woman for three years now, but I've come to connect her to several other likely victims as recently as last month and going back at least eight years. Two more people were taken last night. Right in front of me. They were kidnapped right in front of me and I couldn't do a damn thing about it or see anything. All I could do is clutch this damn envelope the perps left behind." He tossed the envelope on the desk. "Just like all the other ones. Old, young, white, black . . . Nothing about these people is similar. Just this stupid signature connects them."

Julie froze. She knew full well that feeling of powerlessness. She knew she couldn't hold it against him. And there was this desperation in his eyes. She'd recognized it from seeing herself in the mirror every day when the Blood Chain Killer was on the loose.

"I remember hearing a little about that case." She nodded. "You came here three years ago, when you were hired to find that missing woman. We looked as good as we could but we couldn't find any leads. We had to move on. There was no proof any foul play had even happened. No witnesses. No evidence. Not even a motive. For her or any of the people for that matter."

"The pictures in the blue envelopes are the kidnapper's MO. I don't know what he does with them but you deal with serial killers all the time. Leaving things behind that have no other apparent merit other than to serve as a calling card is common behavior. There were two guys this time, and they seemed more like hired muscle than masterminds. So maybe they've been used this entire time. I don't know. All I do know is that whoever is behind these kidnappings leaves these blue envelopes with a candid shot of the victims behind for every victim. Usually at the last place the victims were seen. You're smart enough to know that's not a coincidence. That's a solid link. And last night proves this guy is an active offender. Counting last night, since I got on this case alone, at least ten people have been taken. And that's just the reported missing. God only knows what the total number is."

"Other than what you saw last night, what's changed in terms of evidence? What more can we do?"

Wayne shook his head. "This isn't the Julie I know. The Julie who'd use the tiniest clue to find a lead. The one who I read about all summer."

Julie went to reply but stopped herself. He was right. If this were Patrick missing, she'd never be making excuses like this. "I understand. These families deserve answers. I just am not sure where we start if we don't even have a body to go on. No DNA or sightings. Like I said, I'm a homicide detective. Even if it's tiny, I still need evidence to find something. What do you want from me?"

Wayne locked eyes with her. "I want you to be the woman who brought down the Blood Chain Killer. I want you to be the fierce cop I remember, the one who would find the culprit no matter how steep the odds. Together, I think the three of us can find whoever is doing this. And maybe we can save the lives of these good people. They deserve a happy ending. They deserve to have those who are capable fighting for them. They need us."

Kevin waved Julie aside. "We haven't had a serial since the summer, Jules. I understand that after what happened with Falcon, you're hesitant. You don't want to put Patrick in danger. You don't want to let these people down. You don't want to wade back into those hellish waters. But Patrick is safe. And caring about these people is why you're so good at what you do. Don't let Falcon have the last laugh by taking a good detective out."

Julie looked away. Her father reading her like a book could still make her feel like a little girl again. Yet what was her fear making her but just that? Tempest had a legitimate case, with real lives at stake. And she was looking for reasons to not get involved.

Kevin motioned for them both to pay attention. "Just before Julie got here, I got a call. I wanted to tell you two together so we're all caught up and on the same page. I already have men on the scene and we'll be joining them."

"What the hell are you talking about?" Wayne looked to Julie.

She shrugged. "I'm as in the dark as you."

"Early this morning, I got a call about a murder report filed by two joggers." Kevin slid over photos to them. "Two bodies found in the park—a mother and her eight-year-old son. Cora's already been to the scene and the bodies are already down at her office. I wouldn't be telling you this if she hadn't called me and told me the identifications. They match two of your missing persons. Sally and Billy Corbett."

Wayne froze a moment before slowly sinking into his seat. "They're dead?"

"I'm afraid so."

He twitched and held himself. "We never found any bodies before." A tear welled in his eye. "Not once. I thought maybe there was a chance they were all still alive."

"Maybe some of them still are." Kevin gathered the photos. "These two were found out in the open. Nobody tried to hide them, so maybe these are the first. I don't know. But with these bodies, this case is officially being made a priority again."

"Do we know how it happened? When it happened?"

Kevin held out his hand. "Give Cora a few to do her thing. She'll call you down to do her usual. In the meantime, I want you guys to go the scene and see if there's anything there to discover. Maybe you'll see something they missed."

Julie said, "What do you mean 'you guys'? I don't need Tempest to do my job. I realize he brought us this case, but he's not even a cop. If we're on it, he can stand aside."

"I am not standing aside." Wayne thrust his finger at Kevin. "I promised to see this case through and I am not letting her just kick me off."

Kevin rolled his eyes. "Jules, whether you need him or not isn't of consequence. I'm ordering you to work with him."

"Dad . . ."

"He may not have a badge anymore but he's good at what he does and he has experience in this case that could prove beneficial. You're bringing him."

Julie flashed Wayne a scowl before storming out. She turned back and locked eyes with Wayne through the open door. "I'm leaving in three minutes with or without you, Tempest."

Wayne chased after her. "Excuse me, but your attitude isn't helping anyone.

Julie continued walking.

She had already started the car by the time he got outside.

He jumped in the passenger's side. He barely buckled his seatbelt before Julie sped out of the lot.

When they were on the road, Julie turned to Wayne. "So the prodigal comes home. What's it been, five years? Six?"

"I'm no prodigal. I just figured the force still has some principle left that isn't concerned with protecting the bad guy. You. For all your stubborn loyalty that totally conflicts with your 'get things done' way of doing things, you actually care about the people involved and not just about saving face with the media. I'm willing to put up with your attitude if it means you can help me bring these people home."

"You were a good cop, Wayne." She shook her head and bit her lip. "One of the best. Why throw it all away? Just because you couldn't satisfy your bloodthirsty cravings?"

"Wanting child molesters and murderers to not go free due to technicalities or shady deals is not blood thirst. You can't tell me it doesn't piss you off when our hands are tied to truly stop these crooks."

"It does piss me off. But I try to find ways to work the system, whereas you just gave up on it completely. When we get the badge, we take an oath. I take that oath seriously. You tossed that oath and your badge away to become some vigilante."

Wayne shook his head. "I still take my oath seriously every day, badge or no badge. I am a private investigator, not a vigilante. There's a difference."

"What? You get paid to do it? I might work the system but I have respect for the badge and what it stands for. The fact that you come back to us the moment the case you took gets rough just proves me right. You didn't get any closer to solving this case on your own than you would have with us. If anything, not having a badge means you'll be less able to help with this."

Wayne stared at the park coming into view. "We'll see about that. But we're here, so how about we put our differences aside so we can do this?"

"You don't have to worry about me, Tempest." She parked the car as close to the roped-off scene as she could. "I take what I do very seriously."

Julie stepped out of the car. "I'll ask the questions. Okay?"

He slammed the door shut. "Yes, ma'am. I'll be a good little lackey."

Lackey? Jerk was definitely pushing his luck.

The two approached the cop-infested scene. Julie caught a glimpse of the chalk outlines. They seemed to fuse together into one.

Julie approached the cop overseeing the crime scene. A younger guy than she was used to seeing. Probably newly promoted. She flashed her badge. "Detective Julie Martel. Homicide."

The cop stopped a moment and eyed her tag-along. "Who's he?" The cop pointed to Wayne.

Julie shot Wayne a smirk. "Along for the ride."

His nostrils flared a bit. He went to retort but she cut him off.

"He's consulting."

The cop nodded. He slowly started toward the fountain, keeping an eye on Wayne.

Julie kept a pace behind him. "So what are your findings so far?"

The cop led her to the outlines. "Not much. Not much at all. Sometime last night, these bodies were left here. No witnesses. No DNA traces so far. There are tire tracks we're analyzing but no matches yet. Whoever did it was careful."

Julie knelt down to the chalk outlines. Upon closer inspection, she could make out the outline of the child. He was nestled so close to the mother, like she was holding her sleeping child close. Like their future wasn't violently ripped from them. She felt her knuckles begin to shake. She tensed her fingers to crush it. She couldn't afford such a display now, especially not in front of him. He'd seen her fall apart once, after the accident. If he was to respect her, he couldn't see her flinch. "A pair of joggers found the bodies?" She stood up and looked around at the park, at the roads and entrances visible from this spot.

"Yeah. Call came in around 6 or so. We interviewed them but they didn't see anything. Just cried a lot about how it was so sad and all."

Wayne stepped closer to the scene. "Well, it does tell us a bit." So much for him not talking.

He closed his eyes and began to pace. "Whoever left the bodies here wanted them found. They picked a place that would get fairly heavy traffic come dawn. The way the bodies were left together? Sort of tender. It's posed, but not in any particularly noteworthy way. Just had them nestled together. Could indicate remorse? At the same time, doing it at night and being careful not to leave anything incriminating behind. That indicates he isn't ready to be identified either. Now we know that whoever is behind this uses hired muscle. So we can't even be sure that the killer is the same person who left the bodies. If one of his hired guns did this, the remorse could've been his and not the actual perpetrator's."

The cop shot Wayne a confused stare. "I'm not sure what your point—"

"These people were missing for fourteen months. Without a trace. Now, they turn up freshly killed. This killer hasn't left bodies publicly like this before. There are several suspected victims and yet only two bodies have been recovered? Killed recently and left publicly? Something just doesn't add up. Why start leaving bodies after all these years? Why these two victims? It's definitely a break for us, but it tells us little and leaves us with even more questions than before."

Julie circled Wayne with a grin. "Hitting the procedurals a bit hard, Tempest?"

He chuckled, but his eyes betrayed his indignity. "You act like you aren't thinking the same thing. These are valid questions."

"I didn't say they weren't." She patted him on the back. His face-saving was almost cute. "I just never remember you analyzing much. You were more the 'go right for the nearest throat and apply pressure' kind of guy."

"From what I hear . . ." He leaned in close. "You do the same now."

"I don't have to go for the throat." She pulled back with a sneer. "I have other tactics."

The cop walked between them. "I'm not sure what you two have going on, but I don't think it's appropriate to be hanging it all out here."

Julie blushed and moved aside. Her teasing guard was up and Tempest could probably see right through it. Like he always did. "I apologize. Old habits. I think we've seen all we can here, unless you have something else."

"I wish I did. I'm used to sloppy impulse kills. I hate not having anything to go on."

Wayne nodded. "That feeling sucks. And when you have a book tying your hands, it makes it even more hopeless." He pocketed his hands and started a slow pace back to the car.

Julie watched him a moment. He seemed legitimately concerned. For a brief moment, she felt his words sting her. But she quickly thrust them out of her mind. The last thing she needed was Tempest trying to brainwash her into justifying his abandoning the badge.

Wayne signaled for her to get in the car. There he was, trying to call the shots again. He lost that right when he went rogue. But he had a point. Staying there wasn't going to be productive.

She walked to the car and slammed the door shut as she took her seat. She sat frozen a moment, her hand on the key.

"Something the matter?"

She caught Wayne starring at her. He almost looked like he was concerned. Maybe he was. She always suspected he liked her. All the more reason to not show him any vulnerability.

"That was a waste of time." She revved up the engine. "We didn't learn much of anything, as you said. And don't start on your anti-law stuff again. We're going to crack this case and we're going to do it by the book. Okay?"

"Are you trying to convince me, or yourself?"

She turned to him. "Care to elaborate?"

He shrugged. "It's just that I've heard of some of your

stunts. Locking a suspect in his cell and slipping him a laxative? Getting personally attached to victims and families of victims when you're supposed to remain objective? Don't feed me a line of bull about how the badge means everything to you. You know just as well as I do that sometimes you have to go outside the parameters of what the job allows. You do it all the time. Your dad's a chief, so you have more wiggle room than most to maybe cover those facts up. Live in denial a little while longer. But don't try to convince me that you have this deep-rooted love for due process. I think we're a lot more alike than you would ever admit. Why do you think I wanted you on this case?"

Julie started for the exit. "I'm going to see if Cora has anything for us yet."

"Way to change the subject."

"It's not changing—"

"You don't have to convince me." He winked and turned away.

Julie squeezed her lips closed. Wayne had a lot of nerve trying to profile her. Her emotional investment may not be standard procedure, but it didn't make her anything like him. Maybe he was just trying to convince himself that he made the right decision in walking away. She couldn't pay him any mind. She had a case to solve.

"So how's the family?"

"I thought we weren't talking," she said.

"I didn't vote on that. You going to answer or just nurse your chip?"

She almost let him see her chuckle. "By family, you mean Patrick?"

"Right. I'm still used to you . . ." he stopped himself a moment. "Yes, I meant Patrick. How is he?"

"He's doing good. Still a bit shaken up from everything that happened over the summer, but he's getting by. I think we're going to make it."

"That's good," he said. "That's very good. I hope you guys continue to work through all of this."

"Thanks, Tempest."

Wayne had forgotten how much he hated the medical examiner's office. Not that it was a place to be liked, but even upon entering, he felt every hair on his arm stand on end and his stomach seemed to fight a repellent magnetic force trying to push him out. This place also had a distinct smell. Faint and almost unnoticeable, but present.

"They don't tend to make these places really flashy." He caught Julie watching him. "People are dead inside after all."

"That doesn't make me like it any more." He shivered a moment and tried to tense his muscles to seem calm. Images of being on the force flashed like a slideshow in his mind. A young woman had been raped and butchered by an angry boyfriend. A father of four was run down in a dark alley. A young man on his way to college was gunned down in a drug deal gone bad. The circumstances were all so different, and yet so much the same. The Y-shaped cut down their bare chest. That same pale complexion across their rigid skin. For all the variance, the deaths he'd investigated were all so much the same. This visit was definitely not something he'd missed.

He stood frozen outside the door a moment. He tried to will his legs to move but it was almost as if he was outside himself.

"You don't have to go in, Tempest. None of us enjoy this part. We'd all skip it if we could. There's no reason for you to come in."

"I can't just sit the hard parts out, Julie."

She nodded. "I understand. But you're not abandoning this case by not going in. You'll still be privy to anything this investigation uncovers from the autopsies. You'll still be bringing them closure."

"I've been looking for them. I was only hired to find the one girl, but I made it my mission to find each and every one of them. I'd sacrificed lucrative clients just to have more time to bring these people back. Now two of them are dead because I couldn't find them sooner. I can't just skip the hard parts."

"Understood." She opened the door and stepped inside, holding it open for him. "If you need a moment, take it."

The snarky wench from earlier was gone. Even when they'd worked together as cops, Wayne hardly remembered her ever being this soft with him. She always saved it either for her boys or the families of victims. He'd always admired her fire, but something about this gentle side was an oddly fitting complement.

He went in behind her and immediately saw Cora, the medical examiner, standing over the pale mother and son.

Cora looked up a moment. "I was just about to shut them away and call you." Classic Cora attitude already locked and loaded.

"Good morning to you too," Julie said, covering just a bit of annoyance with pleasantry.

"What's with the sexy shadow, Jules? You seeing someone and not telling me? Or is it just 'bring your hunky neighbor to work' day?"

Wayne folded his arms and remained silent to allow

Julie to answer. If only out of his own curiosity.

Shooting Cora a grin, she said, "I lost a bet." She watched amused as Cora eyed Wayne head to toe. "You remember Detective Wayne Tempest, right?"

"Of course I remember." She circled him with a sensual grin. "I also remember he quit." She hit him with the report file, suddenly fuming. "Became some private investigator to get things done on his terms. Not that I've heard his name in the news for busting bad guys. No, Jules, that was you."

Wayne fought the urge to lecture her. Now wasn't the time to defend his honor.

"Well, regardless of all of that," Julie said as she snatched the files from Cora, "he does have a relevant role to play in this."

"If you say so." Cora flashed Wayne a sneer.

Wayne turned to Julie, impressed that she defended him. Sort of.

Cora eyed Julie as she read the report. "The boy died quickly," Cora said. "His carotid artery was severed by the knife. He bled out very quickly."

Wayne stared at the body a moment. He'd only seen the boy via a candid shot of him and his mother licking ice cream outside a parlor. The boy looked happy enough. Normal. His mother looked caring. Fun. He could've walked right by them that very day and never paid either any mind. Two good, healthy people weren't supposed to end up like this.

Julie asked, "Do you think he felt any pain?"

"Probably some. A little." She pointed to the jagged path of the line. "The death was almost instantaneous, but not quite. There was some slight hesitation at the start. Unfortunately, that likely dragged out his suffering, if only by a few seconds. Might seem insignificant but I imagine for the kid it definitely wasn't."

Julie rummaged through the file. "Any signs of sexual abuse?"

"Not a one." Cora folded her arms. "That's actually what's so interesting. Aside from the wound and blood, the boy's totally clean."

Julie's eyes narrowed. "What do you mean, clean?"

"I mean clean. Well bathed. Hair and teeth well cared for. Well fed too. His stomach contents included a burger and fries. Honestly, he doesn't look like somebody who's been kept a prisoner for eighteen months. I'd venture to say he seems more physically well cared for than I'd expect a boy his age to be. The mother's pretty much the same way. Even their clothes . . ." She picked them up from evidence. "Slightly worn. Bloodstained from the wound but other than that, overall good condition."

Julie walked around the tables examining the two. "How long have they been dead?"

"Based only on the rate of decomposition, I'd guess no more than about twenty-four hours."

"So he was alive all this time." Wayne leaned against the wall and held his head a moment. "All these months, somebody had them. And they just died. That means everybody else could still be alive too." He approached Cora. "What about the mother? How did she die?"

"Two to the stomach. But I think she's been dead a slightly shorter period of time than the boy has."

"That's interesting." Julie scanned the bodies. "Why would you say that? Decomposition rate?"

"That's part of it, but I think the body might've been frozen."

Julie said, "You think the boy was frozen after being

killed? But not the mother?"

"She was too. I just think he was dead a few hours longer before he was frozen than she was. Regardless, this would make the exact times of death a lot harder to determine. Still, even factoring that in, I don't think they've been frozen for too extended a time, so they were still killed fairly recently. That said, as bloody as they were, I don't think torture was an issue. Whoever did this wanted it done pretty quickly."

Wayne and Julie exchanged a look. He turned back to the bodies. "The more we find out, it seems the less this all makes sense. Is there anything else? Some detail that maybe could help us?"

"Wish there was." Cora shook her head. "I hate not knowing too. The kills are just so basic. Simple slice to the throat and a boom, boom to the stomach, and the typical expected injuries resulting from them. The gun used to kill Miss Corbett was a basic handgun. The knife that sliced the boy's throat is a common switchblade. It's all very basic stuff. Almost too basic. It's almost sophisticated how unsophisticated this all is. Maybe I'm just thrown off my game from how depraved Artie was. After decapitations and broom javelins, this is just so common. We do have to remember that most kills are like this. But, I don't know . . . something just feels off about this guy's MO."

A grim moment of silence took over the room. Wayne saw the women staring at each other, and him. Like they were waiting for one of them to break the ice.

Julie closed the file. "Well, thanks for all the information." Of course it was her. "Hopefully we can use this to find a lead."

Cora shut the mother and son away. "Just try not to get so personally involved this time. I don't want to turn on the evening news to find out you had another standoff with a killer with a gun to Patrick's head."

"Don't joke about that." Julie approached Cora with a slightly clenched fist.

"Sorry, Jules." Cora took a step back, almost a bit frightful of Julie.

Wayne took a step between them. "I think we've spent enough time here. If there's nothing else, we should go."

Julie was already halfway to the door before he could finish. "Thanks, Cora. Sorry about biting your head off."

"Forget it. You have a lot of slack left when it comes to that case."

Julie opened the door. "Coming, Tempest?"

Wayne stood a moment. "Just one more thing. You can go out. I'll be out in a minute. It's not really relevant to the case. Just . . . personal."

"Just make it quick."

When he heard the click of the door, he turned to Cora. "Just one question. As you probably heard, it's not really relevant. I just want to know."

"Shoot."

"I only saw them in the picture from the envelope. And they're looking down so I can't really tell. I gave a brief interview to some family but I never really got a good look at them. And here, their eyes are closed and . . ."

"Just spit it out."

"What color are their eyes?"

Her eyes widened. He could see her thinking he was strange for asking such a question. But if she answered, at least a moment of awkward embarrassment would be worth it. "I just like to have a good picture of what the people I help look like. Maybe it's just some weird idiosyncratic tick. I just want to have a face to go with the names, the case details. It helps me always remember that these were people. Not that I can forget. Maybe it's just a hangup."

"Hazel. Both of their eyes were the same shade of hazel."

He allowed himself a faint smile. "Thank you, Cora." He turned to go.

"It's not as weird as you think, Wayne. We all have something we do to get us through. Even me. I never even told Julie this, but before every autopsy, I take the person's hand and hold it a moment. I don't say anything. I'm not even sure what I believe about the soul yet. So I don't know if they feel me. But it helps me. So I get it."

Wayne turned to her and smiled. "Thank you for telling me. I was beginning to think I was just not cut out for this anymore."

Cora shook her head. "Maybe you're not, but not because of that." She smiled.

He shook his head. "Had to get that in, huh?"

"Wayne? Don't let Julie scare you off. She puts up walls because she's lost a lot. But I think she could use somebody new who gives her a reason to lower them."

Wayne kept silent. He opened the door slowly, thinking over her words a moment.

As he stepped out, he saw Julie standing next to the door. He'd thought she was at the car already. She was staring at him almost with a tear in her eyes. Had she heard?

Wayne didn't want to hash anything out with her here. Not now. "Let's head back to the station. See what your dad's uncovered." He started off ahead of her. He could feel her watching him a moment before he heard the clink of her footsteps behind him.

Julie and Wayne didn't even get a chance to utter one word to Kevin upon entering the station. He was waiting for them by the door and began talking immediately. "Evidence just brought something to me. Apparently they found it on the body but took it to evidence before we had a chance to see it."

Kevin was off to his office before he even finished talking. He signaled for them to follow.

Wayne rushed behind him. "And you guys call me unprofessional."

Julie ran ahead of both of them. "What kind of evidence? Slow down for a second, Dad."

Kevin held out a DVD in a sleeve. "For all the lack of DNA or evidence, our killer is apparently quite proud of his work."

He signaled for them to follow him into his office. He was already starting the scene when the two of them caught up. The screen lit up with a title card, "The Good Die Young."

The scene opened on Billy Corbett.

He was walking around a dark hall.

Julie's eyes widened. "Wait, that's our vic."

Wayne hushed her.

"Hello?" Billy called out. He looked around. Like he was lost, or someone was following him. Maybe both. Dramatic music accompanied the scene. Audio quality was fairly crisp for a home movie. Julie almost thought she was imagining it, but it grew louder as the scene progressed. Classical violin and cello. A cliché cheesy horror movie score.

Billy walked until he reached the end of a hallway. There was a door there. Open. He stopped a moment and gulped audibly. Like he wanted to make sure somebody heard him. But he was shaking. Julie recognized that trembling from experience. No matter how good the child actor, no movie could truly capture that raw fear a child has when truly terrified.

A large man stepped out from the door. He was big. Not so much fat as very well built from years of hard work rather than workout routines. His face was characterized by a thin, uneven, gray beard, but without even the slightest trace of a mustache.

The boy tensed upon seeing the man. He shut his eyes a moment and clenched a fist. He made the slightest twitch like he was going to run, but he didn't. He just took two steps back and began to breathe heavily. He looked down.

There was a few seconds of silence. Even the music paused.

The man eyed the boy, and then let out an agitated "ehem." As if he was expecting the boy to say something that he wasn't saying.

As if snapped out of some daze, he thrust his head up and said, "My name is Evan. I'm looking for my mom. Have you seen her anywhere?" His voice was shaking. His words a borderline slur.

The man knelt down to eye level with him. "I know exactly where she is."

"Could you take me to her? Please?"

"Yes. I can."

The man took the boy's hand in his and led him away. The boy's tiny hand looked like an infant's in the man's. The two disappeared into the darkness of the hallway as the scene ended.

"What the hell is this?" Wayne leaned in closer. "It's like some bad amateur movie. And that boy's name is Billy. Why is he calling himself Evan?"

Julie shook her head. "He's talking like he's reciting lines. Both of them are, but the guy is better at it. More practiced."

Kevin pointed to the screen. "Keep watching."

The next scene was composed entirely of the man talking to the boy about a hunting trip his dad had taken him on as a kid. Billy didn't say much of anything. He didn't do much of anything. He just walked beside the man with his hands in his pockets.

Eventually, they reached a small cabana by a pool.

Billy turned to the man. "Where are we?"

The man patted him on the shoulder. "We are where your mother is. She's inside."

"Really?" His faux excitement seemed apparent even to the man.

The man held out his hand. "Why don't you go inside and find out?"

The boy stopped a moment. He took his steps slowly.

The man gave him a slight shove.

The boy sniffled. He went to the cabana door and carefully opened it, turning the knob so slowly it seemed like he was dreading what came next. Then he walked inside.

The cabana was dimly lit, but a woman was visible on the floor on a thin mattress. Billy's mother.

"Mom." The first words Billy had said that seemed real. A genuine emotion besides pure fear. Not just strings of sentences fearfully strung together.

Billy ran into his weeping mother's arms and the two

embraced.

"I thought I'd never see you again." He buried his head on her chest.

She stroked his hair. "I thought the same thing about you. I'm so glad you're okay."

The man folded his arms and rolled his eyes. "I hate to be the bearer of bad news, but we aren't here for you two to waste a day hugging. We have a task."

The man yanked the boy away from his mother.

He took out a gun and shoved it in the boy's hands.

He leaned close to Billy's ear. "You have to shoot your mother, Evan. You have to kill her."

Billy froze a moment and began to cry harder. "No. I don't want to. He never told me . . . we were just supposed to find each other and hug. That's what it said. I thought maybe me but . . ."

The man shrugged. "He wanted this to be a surprise. Now do it. You know what not doing it means."

The man raised the boy's hands as they clenched the gun. He steadied the shaking hands. He aimed the gun at the mother and said to Billy. "See? You don't need good aim. All you have to do is squeeze the trigger."

Billy shook his head. "I don't want to."

"It doesn't matter." He squeezed Billy's shoulder. "All that matters is that you do what he says."

"No. I won't do it," he said. "I won't kill my mom."

The man took out a large switchblade. He placed it against Billy's neck, applying just a little bit of pressure.

Sally screamed.

The man himself began to shake. Ever so slightly. "Evan, do it. Or I will have to kill you."

Sally crawled closer to them. "Please Billy, just do it. It's okay. Mommy says it's okay."

The man clenched his teeth "You mean Evan?"

"Right!" She wiped aside tears. "Evan, just do it. It's going to be okay."

The boy shook his head. "No, no, no." He began to cry. "I won't. I love her. Mommy! I love you. I'm bad sometimes, but I won't do it."

The man shook his head. "Damn it, kid. You're not leaving me a choice."

He slashed Billy's neck with the blade.

One split second of hesitation followed by a single, ruthless swipe.

Blood splattered on his face and on the cabana ceiling.

Sally screamed.

He stepped back.

The blood flood continued to pour.

Sally ran to Billy and caught him as his body crumpled to the floor.

He flailed and gasped for a few seconds, gurgling as he tried to say something but his body refused him one last word.

In a single instant, he went still. Silent, relentless, stillness. Even his eyelids didn't move to cover those hazel irises.

Sally screamed. She pulled her little boy close, his open wound still spilling out blood.

"I'll leave you two alone a moment." The man left out the door.

She didn't even lift her eyes. She couldn't look away from her little boy. She brushed his hair aside from his face and kissed his cheek.

Julie turned her head away. This was too much. Too much like too many murders she'd seen. Why did people hurt innocent children in such ways? This death scene in any theatrical movie would've been controversial.

Knowing it was real made it unbearable.

The movie then collaged the following twelve hours in a few seconds.

Sally slid her little boy's eyelid closed.

She sat his body aside, covering it with her bed sheet. All the modicum of respect she could offer.

She tried to sleep but couldn't, tossing and turning just feet away from the remains of her child.

She tried to look away, but she kept returning to her child.

She started talking to him, telling him stories. Singing him lullabies.

When morning came, she hadn't slept. Just singing to him.

The man returned with the gun.

He didn't say anything.

She rose to her feet, almost in submission. Acceptance. Maybe even anticipation of being reunited with her little boy. But she still kept singing, softly, her hoarse voice barely audible.

He fired two rounds in the stomach.

She fell silent and crumpled to the ground.

The man watched for a few seconds until she was dead.

He reached down and closed her eyes with a sigh. "I'm sorry it had to be this way. We do what we have to do . . . what he asks us. To survive."

He walked out of the cabana alone.

The dramatic music intensified as the shot faded out and credits rolled. Most of the credits seemed a mere stunt until the lines "Billy Corbett as Evan" and "Sally Corbett as Evan's mother" came across the screen.

Once the credits rolled, the video stopped.

Kevin shut off the television after a complete minute of silence.

Julie held her head a moment, crying. "Did I really just see that?"

Wayne stood up and walked to the window. He stared out at the sunlit day. Somehow, seeing the sun seemed wrong after what he'd just seen. "We clearly saw who killed them, but it was presented like a movie. That guy must be seriously twisted."

Kevin sat down at his desk. "That guy might've been the one to end their lives, but they all kept talking about another person." He clicked a pen a few times before tossing it across the room. "For all we know, that guy is an actor too. Just doing what he was told. The one actually behind all of this is probably somebody off camera. Like a true coward."

Wayne shook his head. "I don't recognize that guy as one of my missing people. Maybe this guy is just unafraid for us to see his face and this is just a taunt . . ." He scrubbed his head. "Then again, God only knows how many people have been taken that I don't know about. I don't know."

"I looked close at his body language," Julie said. "The guy's detached but there's still a hint of hesitation. He doesn't want to do this. He has to. Toward the end there, I don't think that was scripted. That felt more improvised, like it was really what he felt."

"And he just decides to kill a kid because somebody tells him to? That's extreme, even by survival standards."

Julie ejected the DVD and returned it to its sleeve.

"God only knows what these people have been through. But looking at the video, I don't think this is the first home movie they've made. And did you see all the different camera angles? There had to be some sort of crew there. I don't think this operation is just one guy or even just a guy and hired muscle. Whoever is behind this has the resources for a fairly sophisticated operation." She looked through the reports of the crime scene. "This wasn't just filming a murder. It was some sort of snuff film. Before they got to the cabana, Billy seemed to be reciting lines, albeit against his will. He's making movies, but the death scenes are real, and the people he's kidnapped . . . they're his cast."

"But then where are the other bodies?" Wayne stared at the dark screen. "If he's just another actor, that guy was too casual about that. He'd done it before. And for that matter, where is he keeping all of these people?"

Julie nodded. "If he's been taking people for years, he's likely been making movies for years. Having his cast killed for years." She held out a DVD. "But why have we only just found a body now? With a DVD hidden on the person? Is he bragging? Maybe he finally wants somebody to see his work."

Kevin leaned back in his chair. "We saw what the desire for an audience did for the Blood Chain Killings. If this guy is some crazed moviemaker, he could be another Falcon. And he probably knows that we can't tie anything to him based on the footage on that disc. So why not send it? He's just the man behind the curtain. The director."

Wayne punched the desk. "Well, we may not know who he is yet, but this is a hell of a lead. This time yesterday, nobody knew much of anything about this case. Now we at least have a working hypothesis as to what this guy's game is and what he's doing with the people he takes. That gives us a place to start looking." He smiled. "I finally have a real angle to help these people."

Julie approached Wayne a moment but pulled back. "But we'd better get on it. Odds are he's already planning his sequel to this, and that means trouble for anyone he hasn't already killed. The boy and his father taken last night? They could be the replacements for these two."

Wayne rushed for the door. "I won't let them end up like those two. I can't."

Julie nodded. "Neither will I."

"Mind if I hang on to the DVD?" Kevin extended his hand to Julie. "I want to take a closer look at something. Maybe there's a clue we didn't see the first time. Something not obvious. The ones who filmed it might have even overlooked something. I'm gonna check every frame."

Julie handed it to him. "I hope you're right."

"I hope I am too. You'll be the first to know if I find anything."

Julie handed him the disc. She didn't know if it was just in her head, but she felt true evil radiating off the disc. The end of two lives was captured on it as mere data. Real murder treated like a play. She never thought she would live to see somebody even come close to the depravity of the Blood Chain Killings. She should've known better. As she followed Wayne out of her father's office, she felt her stomach tighten with that same dread she'd finally gotten used to not having. How many more bodies were out there undiscovered? How many sick home movies like this were out there? Worse yet, how could so much of this be going on for so long and nobody in law enforcement knew a thing about it? For one split second, she began to understand Wayne.

She wanted to say something to him, but she didn't know what. She knew how heavy the weight he had to carry was. And she knew only closing this case could help lighten it even a little.

A man stood outside the door of the 'cast wing' of the mansion he'd been forced to live at for so long, he'd stopped counting the months.

One of the hired thugs approached him carrying sheets of paper. "Here's your next scene. He wants you to know it by the morning."

"Maybe one day the big cheese will deliver them personally instead of using one of his hired bitches to do it." The man laughed. The thug did not. "He's giving me that long? Must be in a good mood." The man took the papers and scanned over them. "A script where nobody dies? That's new for Lincoln Prescott."

The thug smacked the man with the barrel of his gun. "Cut the sarcasm. Mr. Prescott doesn't call for a death scene that much. Plus, you know he likes to give the new ones a chance to settle in before giving them the meaty material. He has to write ones best suited for them. You can't rush genius."

"You'll have to get me whatever it is you use to keep your lips from adopting the stench of his ass. People who don't know you might not believe you spend most of your time licking it."

"Here I thought you'd like a chance to have a break from killing. You are one of the only ones with the balls to do it. I think you are Mr. Prescott's favorite. He always raves about 'that Drake Harrison,' the best actor in his cast."

Drake laughed. "I do what I have to in order to survive. Not to help his pathetic attempts at movie productions be any less than the putrid horsecrap they are." He stuck up his middle finger. "Give the boss my regards." He returned to the quarters prepared for the cast. The door automatically locked behind him.

CHAPTER 4

Aaron opened his eyes to a bedroom lit by shade-filtered sunlight. Everything looked so dark the night before but in the daylight, the blue room actually looked very bright and nice. It would've made a nice bedroom if he weren't being kept prisoner here.

No amount of lavish accommodations would make him stop longing to go home.

He pulled his feet out of the covers and noticed the navy pajama bottoms just about his wiggling feet. They weren't his and didn't remember changing into them. In fact, he didn't remember being put in the bed at all. The thought of a stranger tucking him into bed made his stomach knot.

He closed his eyes and tried to recall what had happened after he and his dad met Therese. He had vague flashes of a shower and the faint traces of lavender in his hair confirmed that. He sat up and looked over the matching pajama top on him. They were very comfortable, if a little large for him. But how did they get on? Did his dad dress him?

He looked around. Where was his dad?

"Don't worry. He's just in another room."

Aaron turned around to see a girl sitting on a bed

against the wall a few feet away from his. She had long dark hair and was smiling at him in a way that made him a bit uncomfortable at first.

"Other room?"

"You were so tired." Did she even hear his question? She scooted closer to him. "You practically fell asleep in the shower last night."

Aaron suddenly felt a little underdressed and pulled the covers back over himself. He looked around at the room. It looked almost inviting. Nicer than his own bedroom. Yet there was something about it. A thickness in the air that made it hard to breathe. Maybe it was just his own heart gnawing at his chest to find a way home. He'd prayed the night before was a nightmare but the light of dawn doused any traces of hope.

The girl hopped off her bed and jumped next to him. "So, what's your name? You conked out before I got to ask you." She leaned in close, eager eyes flashing at him. He could almost feel her breath on him. He wanted to nudge her back but refrained to keep from hurting her feelings. If she was kidnapped like him, maybe she was just happy to see a new friend. Or maybe girls were just weird.

"Aaron." He curled his legs against his chest. "Aaron Garret."

She held out her hand. "Dinah Kramer. You look close to my age. How old are you?"

"I'm eleven. Almost twelve."

"Well, I'm thirteen. Almost." She winked. "So we are close in age." She wrapped her arm around him. "We can be friends."

Aaron moved away a moment and let her arm fall away. Having a friend here was good but she didn't have to get so touchy with him. Still, he forced a smile. Just be nice and maybe she'd ease up.

He looked her over. She seemed comfortable here. Too comfortable. Did she see this as her home now? Maybe she'd be able to help him understand. "Um . . ." He cleared his throat. "Do you know why I'm here? Why did they take me and my dad? What are they going to do with us?"

Dinah sighed. "You must be so confused right now." She stroked his cheek. She tried to sound adult, but he saw a childish gleam in her eyes. "You're going to be okay. I won't let them hurt you."

His eyes widened. "Hurt me?"

"We're at the mansion of Lincoln Prescott. He's rich and kind of a jackass. His dad is some big cheese and owns politicians and stuff. So nobody bugs him and he just lets Lincoln take people and keep them here. Like us."

"Wait, he's a kid?" Aaron raised an eyebrow.

"Not Lincoln. He's grown. Even if he usually acts like a bully."

"What does he want?" Aaron's hands tensed. He linked them together and counted slow beats. "I remember there was this guy over the summer who did things to kids and my dad had a talk with me and . . . is this guy going to—"

"Hell no." She rolled her eyes. "Lincoln Prescott is whacked out of his mind, but he's not the pervert."

"What do you mean 'the' pervert?"

She froze and her mouth hung open. "I mean . . . you don't have to worry about that. He's dangerous, but not like that. He once walked in on Therese in a bath towel and started freaking out. I seriously thought he was gonna start yammering about cooties. The dude has serious hang-ups." She took Aaron's hand. "But like I said, that's not something you have to worry about."

Her hand was so cold and sweaty on Aaron's. She seemed so calm. Why did her hands feel like his did when he was scared?

He looked up at her, hoping his eyes weren't tearing as much as they burned. "How long have you been here?"

"Just two years." She shrugged. "Not that long."

Not that long? How was two years not that long?

"You're eleven, right?"

Aaron nodded.

"I was your age when I first came here. I was scared too, but you get used to it. You don't worry about what you used to be like. It's not so bad here. We get good food and can even have some fun. I think you're gonna fit right in."

"But two years is a really long time . . ." Chills shot through his body. Life as he knew it might be over forever. If people could be here years without ever being found, then so could he. Even if people knew he was missing, if nobody here was ever found, he could spend the rest of his life trapped here. "Doesn't anybody look for us?"

She looked away. "I'm sure they look. But why would they look here? It's a big place, you know. You can't even see the road from any of the windows. And they're rich. If somebody found us, they could probably just make them go away."

Aaron wanted to cry, but his eyes remained dry. "We just stay trapped in this place forever?"

She hopped off the bed. "Let's not worry about that right now." Her solemn stare exploded into a beaming grin. "We got all the time in the world to worry about that. I wanna know about you. What do you like to do?"

"I really should go find my dad." Aaron hopped off the opposite side of the bed and started for the door. "Thank you for telling me about this place."

Dina blocked his way. "What's the rush?" She placed her hands on his shoulders. There was just a tiny grip but it sent chills through his spine. Her long hair draped just a little too closely to his. "Your dad's probably still sleeping. He was even more tired than you were last night. Give him a few more minutes to sleep, and talk to me." She moved him back to the bed and sat him down.

Aaron noticed some force in her push. And the way she gripped his hand? Like she never wanted to let it go. Did she like him? She did have that weird swoon look girls got when they had a crush on the one boy at school good at soccer. Or maybe she was more damaged by this place than she let on.

She smiled and pulled him a little closer. "Tell me about your life. I like finding out about people's lives. I find their stories so interesting."

Aaron looked away. It couldn't hurt to tell her something. It wasn't like any of that mattered anymore. "Well, my dad's a pastor. I like anime."

"What about your mom?"

"She died." Aaron's chest throbbed. "I was only seven. I think it was some kind of cancer. She was so sick . . . I always kept a picture of her with me so I wouldn't forget what she looked like." He reached for his pocket before realizing these weren't his clothes. It wouldn't have mattered if they were. He'd left it at home this time. Maybe his dad had his still. "Dad and I weren't supposed to be out long and we were in such a rush to get to the church.

It took all day so we stopped for dinner. That's when . . . I wish I brought that picture with me yesterday. I want to see her right now."

"I think that's so interesting." She smiled and sat back. Didn't she hear about his mom? He didn't want her to hug him but was she even paying attention at all?

"My family was Jewish. I had a lot of Christian friends at school, but no kids of pastors. I think that's so cool that your dad's a pastor."

"Can I go find my dad now?" Aaron hopped back off the bed, keeping an eye on his strange new friend.

Dinah sighed. "He can't help you escape. You might as well get to know me. 'Cause we're roommates until . . ." She stopped herself and looked away.

"Until what?" He walked closer. Was she finally going to tell him what she'd obviously been trying not to?

"Just go find your dad." She looked down. "I lied when I said he wasn't up 'cause I wanted to talk to you. He's in the living room with everybody else."

"Everybody else?" A droplet of sweat rolled down his back. "How many people are here?"

"There's usually about seven or eight of us at a time. Sometimes a little more. Sometimes less. But right now, you and your dad make eight."

"Then there must've been others here before me and my dad, right?" Aaron tried to catch his breath. "What happened to them? Is it going to happen to us too?"

"Aaron, just go to your dad." She went back to her bed and sat down. "And take your housecoat." She pointed to the violet housecoat hanging up on the door. It had a white stripe on the bottom of it and on the sleeves.

"I have a housecoat already?" He walked to it and pulled it off the door. It was soft. "How do you have clothes that fit me?"

"You're pretty normal size. It wasn't hard. We have a lot of clothes here. He's rich after all."

Aaron put the housecoat on. It fit even better than the pajamas did. It was warm too. But there was something weird about it. A slight feeling, maybe even the faintest smell. Aaron held himself a moment. "I'm not the first person to wear these, am I?"

Dina remained silent, avoiding eye contact.

"What was his name? What happened to him?" Tears rolled down his face now. "Did he die? Did they kill him? Is he going to kill me too?"

Dinah began to cry too. "It's complicated. I'm sorry that you're here, but once you know how everything works, you can't go back to having peace of mind. You still can have that. You're going to find out sooner or later how things around here work, and then you'll wish you hadn't."

Aaron was silent a moment. He took deep breaths until he didn't hear his own sobs anymore. He turned to Dinah. She was still crying. He held his hand out to her. "I'm kind of scared to just walk in there alone. They're a bunch of people I don't know. Can you come with me?"

She looked up at him with narrow eyes. She moved back from him. Did she not believe him?

"I'm sorry about pulling away from you earlier. I'm just scared. Yesterday, I was with my dad and everything was normal. Then some guys forced us to drive here and it seems bad things can happen to us here. I don't want to hurt your feelings. You were just trying to help. So please, come in with me. Maybe you can help me learn who everyone is."

She smiled and took his hand. "You got it."

Jeremy stared at the strangers in the room. Such an odd bunch, yet they seemed to be comfortable enough with each other. He felt the urge to speak up and start conversations, but he surprised himself with how silent he chose to stay. Back home, he'd be the first to learn the life story of any stranger who walked into his church. He'd met with pastors from all over the world and spoke at other churches on a regular basis. Why was he all of a sudden at a loss for words? Sure, he was kidnapped, but could something he always considered a dominant character trait in himself really be undone so easily?

Maybe it was the fancy furniture. Or maybe it was knowing that all of these people were also here against their will. No matter how comfortable they appeared, this was their prison.

But he still listened. Looking for hints about what was going on, if there was any way out. Anything to give him an idea of how to protect Aaron. He thought he picked up the gist of things, but everything still felt a little jumbled and confused. He had to ask outright, but which one was the best? Could these people even be trusted? What if they had Stockholm?

One of the men locked eyes with Jeremy. The man's commanding yet gentle eyes and boyish bowled blond hair made him seem probably ten years younger than he actually was.

The man walked over and took a seat next to him. "You have the same look in your eyes that I had when I first came here."

Jeremy cracked a smile. He could only imagine how ridiculous he looked to these people. "How long have you been here?"

"About twenty months now. Give or take a few weeks." The man leaned back onto the sofa. "It feels longer. Time used to go so fast before I got here. One time just after Christmas, when I was helping take down the decorations at the church, I remembered asking God to slow it down. Just a little. Be careful what you wish for, huh?"

Jeremy chuckled. "I guess so. I think I know better than most that God has His own unique way of tackling answers to questions."

"Why is that?"

"I'm a pastor. It's a small church but the congregation is loyal. Most have been there for more than two generations."

The man smiled and extended his hand. "Father Jake Doyle, associate pastor of St. Augustine's Catholic Church. Or at least I was. I'm pretty sure I've been replaced by now."

"Two men of God? That's a bit overkill, isn't it?"

Father Doyle shrugged. "Maybe he's planning to get rid of me soon. It would be his style."

Jeremy froze. "Kill you? Because of me?"

"Sorry. I don't mean to alarm you." Father Doyle folded his hands. "You're still trying to make sense of this all. You don't need the burden of worrying about me. God's got me, whatever happens. You and I both know that whatever happens here, Jesus is Lord. We have to be the spiritual leaders for them because hope is something they all need right now. We may not agree on all theological points, but right now we have to stand united to help them."

Jeremy nodded. "Right now I'm not so sure I'm in any shape to be leading anybody."

"I feel that way every day. It's so easy to lose yourself here. Lose who you thought you were. It's been almost two years since I've been able to say a Mass. But I did manage to hide away a few things from them. My collar, my confession stole, and even my Divine Office prayerbook. Maybe he knows and just doesn't care. But to me, they mean so much to remind me of who I still am. Even if I'm cut off from everything else."

Jeremy sighed. "I hope my church can survive without me. I suppose they can send somebody else, but we're a community. We thrive off of each other. If they send in somebody who doesn't understand that . . ."

"God will provide." Father Doyle put his hand on Jeremy's shoulder. "Right now, I think you need to focus on staying alive. How is your son taking to this?"

"He's probably still asleep." Jeremy shot a glance toward the bedroom. "I'll let him be a little longer. Maybe he can dream that he's still at home. Things have been a bit hard for us. I've felt more and more unable to reach him lately."

"He is approaching that age."

"It's deeper than that. Aaron's never quite recovered from losing his mother. Sometimes I think he's slipping into depression and I'm not going to be able to pull him out." Jeremy quickly wiped away a tear. "Aaron doesn't deserve to have to deal with this. He was still struggling with enough."

Father Doyle nodded. "These are the times he needs his father more than ever. Maybe this is a chance to reach him. To push him into finding a reason to live again."

"I overheard them talking about the people we replaced." Jeremy shook his head. "Nobody leaves here alive, do they? It's only a matter of time until whoever this guy is kills us."

Father Doyle looked away. "I choose to keep hope alive. I don't know who's investigating our disappearances. Somebody has to notice all of these people going missing. Somebody has to stumble upon a lead. I don't believe God would just abandon all of us. I can't promise either of you will survive this. But there's always a reason to keep hoping. Keep praying."

"How often does somebody die?"

"There's no telling how often." Father Doyle folded his hands. "Depends on what his movies call for."

"Movies?"

"Sick, huh? We're his cast. He writes scripts, has a crew to film them, and forces us to act them out. I suppose it wouldn't be the end of the world if he didn't have a twisted bloodthirst. He likes violent deaths in his films and they're not staged. If he scripts your death, the general rule is that you die. If somebody doesn't want to participate, he'll have them killed for disobedience."

"You're kidding, right?"

Father Doyle shook his head. "If only I were. Every day I pray that one day he'll realize how insane all of this is. I don't care what happens to me but seeing what he pushes good people to . . . it's almost worse than any torture. If you don't wind up dead early, you'll end up spiritually wrecked from all the murder you either witness or take part in. There's no getting out of this unscathed. You should know that now. Whatever happens, Aaron's going to need your strength and you're going to need him. Dying is sad, but losing who you are is the real tragedy. If he takes that from somebody, he's really succeeded in destroying them."

"So, he's just going to bump off me and my son."

Breath caught in his throat. "Like we're some stupid movie character?"

"Some of us have been here awhile." Father Doyle pointed to a gruff man with gray facial hair whom Jeremy had noticed giving him a scowl all morning. "That guy over there? He's been here five years. Drake Harrison. Not the most pleasant guy and usually the one who ends up being the killer in the movies. He does make a convincing bad guy, but he's also one of the only ones consistently willing. He's the biggest example of what happens to you here. I sense he used to know his humanity but he's long since abandoned it in order to survive. I'd say don't piss him off, but chances are he'll be the one to kill all of us in the end."

"I guess it's best not to make friends." Jeremy tensed and sunk a little lower into the sofa.

"Drake doesn't do friendship." He shook his head. "More than anything, I worry about his soul."

Jeremy nodded. "Who are the others? What's their story?"

Father Doyle pointed to the older lady working in the kitchen. "Maude Lacey. She's been here for four years. She's kind of like the mother figure to everyone. Even to me, if you can believe that. She prepares a lot of the food. Tells the kids stories. I never really knew what her life was life before this. She never talks too much about it. I gather she had a family once. There's a sadness in her eyes that you have to look really close to see." He then pointed to Therese. "That woman has been here for about three years. Her name's Therese Wilder. Maude teaches her a lot. She's very kind to everyone but she's got an angry side. I can't say I blame her. There's a lot she doesn't share with us. I've tried to talk to her sometimes. It's not healthy to bottle things up like she does, but I still can't reach her." He then pointed to a little girl playing with dolls in a corner. "Little Emily Bradley. She's only been here for eight months. Her mother was here with her too. Prescott had her killed three months ago. Poor girl hasn't slept a whole night since."

"How does he pick who to kill?"

"Usually, it's just those who don't cooperate that die quickly. But I should warn you that he does like to turn families against each other. Parents against children. Children against parents."

Jeremy shot the priest a nervous look. "I will not hurt my son. No matter what."

"Of course not. I can't say I haven't done things I will have to answer for here, but I try to have standards. Even if one day they cost me my life."

Jeremy watched the little girl play. She almost looked like a normal little girl, immersed in her imaginary worlds. He could only imagine the pain she was trying to escape from, hiding behind dolls and plastic blocks. "Why does this guy do this? Is it some sort of sexual gratification?"

"I don't think it's sexual for Lincoln. He smugly sits in a director's chair and just directs it like it's some indie movie. If he doesn't get his way, he throws a tantrum. He's a spoiled child who never grew up, even though he's thirty-two years old now. I used to think his father was a pushover but I think he gets something out of this too." Father Doyle glanced at the women. "I can't prove anything yet, but I have suspicions."

Jeremy shot Therese a look and returned his gaze to the priest. "Do I have to worry about anybody coming after Aaron?"

He shook his head. "I don't think so. For whatever

comfort that brings."

Jeremy bit his lip a moment. "Is there nothing we can do?" He thought of Aaron's teary eyes the night before. These men could take him away with a single word. How could he keep his son safe when he wasn't even sure what he was up against?

Father Doyle smiled. "There's always something we can do. We may not understand the answer, but we know we're being heard."

"The priest schooling the minister." Jeremy forced a smile. "Don't tell my congregation that."

"I think your secret is safe." He chuckled.

Jeremy again gazed out at his fellow "roommates." They were all facing the same fate. He might have to kill one of them. Or they might have to kill him. They looked like ordinary people.

All the advice he would've given himself a day before was out of reach. He knew evil existed. He'd experienced it. Yet, looking this nightmare in the eyes left the book of solutions blank. He'd always had all the answers, wrapped in a neat little bow with a Scripture verse attached. Not anymore.

Images of Aaron bleeding out in his arms taunted him. No amount of willpower could vanquish them. If they weren't going to go away, he had to use them. As motivation. As a warning. No matter what, he wouldn't let them come true.

He always strived to bring lost sheep back into the fold. Now he was the one lost. And he wasn't sure where his shepherd was. Only that somehow, beyond all the fear and uncertainty, He was still there.

Dinah walked Aaron into the living room where about

six other people were around doing various things.

Aaron instantly locked eyes with his father. He spent a minute looking around at the others scattered about the room. He could see an older woman cooking breakfast. It smelled pretty good.

Aaron walked into his father's hug. Aaron could feel a tear wet his hair. Seeing his father like this made him even more scared. His father must've known because he threw on a smile and stroked his cheek. "Remember, Aaron, God will take care of us. You don't ever have to be afraid. But it's okay if you are."

Aaron had heard his father say these words so many times. He knew he believed them, but sometimes they felt so empty. Especially when his mother was dying. And now? He wanted to believe them so much.

"What's going on, Dad?" Aaron gulped. "What's gonna happen?"

His father then proceeded to explain to him about how they'd be forced to make movies. His vagueness worried Aaron. His father usually was big on details. Aaron could see in his father's eyes that he was keeping something back. If his father would keep something back, it must've been really bad.

Jeremy gently rested his hand on the boy's shoulder. "It's just like at home, Aaron. Home movies." He kissed Aaron's forehead. "God loves you. And so do I. No matter what happens, remember that."

A large man approached the two of them. "Don't lie to the kid. It's best that he be prepared for what's happening. The fact is that sooner or later, I'm probably going to have to kill him." The man turned to Aaron. "You see, kid, the guy who took all of us? He likes us to make movies and we gotta do whatever he tells us to. So if that means killing somebody here, that's what it means. Usually he makes me do it 'cause I'm the only one with enough balls to do it. So don't bother trusting in some silly 'God will protect you' idea. Know what to expect and you'll be prepared when it comes."

Aaron looked away, afraid to see the man's dark eyes scowling down at him. He pictured the man snapping his neck. Leaving him dead on the floor. The man's arms were thick and rough. They could break every one of his bones at once. Aaron took a step behind his father, ashamed that he probably looked like a wimp.

Therese stormed over to Drake. "Damn you. We weren't going to tell him yet. He just got here. He didn't have to know that."

Drake settled into a chair and put his feet up. "Oh, and you think I should've waited to tell him until I put the gun to his head? Yes, that would've been the best time to tell the brat."

"You're way too proud of being a murderer."

He thrust himself out of the chair. "I'm not the only one who's killed." He stabbed her shoulder with his finger. "I just do it without flinching. Without excuses. It's not like I want to hurt the kid. I'm just not giving up my life to spare somebody who the boss will plug on his own anyway. The kid looks old enough to deal with reality. Barring some highly unlikely miracle rescue, he is going to be killed here. Maybe not for a few years, but it's going to happen. To him and to all of us. So excuse me for thinking enough of the kid to give him the truth."

Aaron came out from behind his father. He had to face Drake now. Without fear. If he didn't do it now, he'd always be afraid. He stepped toward Drake, catching the man's eye. He could feel himself shaking. He could see in the man's hard eyes that he probably looked pathetic. He took a deep breath. "Thank you for telling me the truth." He tensed his lips and tried to not let a tear slip out. "I'm glad you were honest with me." He turned to head into the kitchen. "But you're wrong. God can still help me."

"Think what you want kid." Drake shook his head and shot down another of his dismissive glares. The man's face was so far above his but Aaron could still see those large nostrils flaring right at him. "Then you'll only have yourself to blame when you're let down." He sat down in a huff and turned away from Aaron.

The old woman came and took Aaron aside. "Don't listen to him, child. He's just trying to upset you. You're a good boy for praying to God. I've been here almost as long as he has and despite all the bad things that have happened, I still see God working every day. So you keep believing."

She reminded Aaron of the kindly women at church who said nice things to him after his mother died. Even if they didn't know him. Even if she was just an old lady, he felt safe with her. Like she'd protect him.

"Thank you, ma'am." He hid his arms behind his back. "Sometimes I don't really believe. Not like my dad. Like right now, I keep thinking that God left me to die here. Does that make me a bad Christian?"

She smiled. "I think it makes you human. But you know the truth. You wouldn't have said it otherwise. We often let feelings get in the way of what we know, don't we?"

He nodded.

"By the way, I'm Maude. I hear your name is Aaron, right?"

"Yes."

"Well, Aaron, I don't like to toot my own horn but I think myself a fairly decent cook. Would you like some breakfast? Everyone's eaten but you and the girls."

"Thanks, but I'm not really hungry." His stomach gurgled. He held his stomach a moment and blushed. "Well, I guess I am a little hungry. I'm just a little queasy too. Sometimes I get stomach pains when I'm scared."

"Well, just try a little then. I think you'll really enjoy it. Maybe once you try it, you'll feel a little better."

She escorted him to the kitchen table and sat him down. She then signaled for Dinah and Emily to come over. "Dinah, Emily! Come make Aaron feel at home."

The girls rushed over, each taking a seat next to Aaron,

He felt a bit awkward sandwiched between two girls. Especially with both of them staring at him.

Then they both grabbed his closest hand.

The little girl swung his hand a bit. "We have to pray first."

Aaron smiled at her. "Of course we do."

Dinah stared at him with a relentless focus. Maybe she did like him after all. "Aaron, you're a pastor's son. And you're new. New guy always has to pray." She pulled his hand close.

Aaron remembered his failed attempts to speak in front of the class and winced. His words always came out bad when put on the spot like this, but he was a pastor's son and leading people in prayer should be something he could do. So he took a deep breath and tried to remember what his father always said over their meals at home. "We thank You Father, for giving us this great bounty in which we are about to partake . . ." His mouth hung open a moment as he searched for the words. He looked to his father for a hint. His father seemed ready to take over for him. To rescue him again. Afraid of everyone thinking he couldn't do it by himself, Aaron shut his eyes and tried to let memory take over. "And we pray that You will continue to provide for all of our needs in the times to come. We ask this through Christ, Our Lord, Amen."

Wait! Dinah was Jewish. He hoped he hadn't offended her. He wasn't ashamed of being a Christian but his father had always taught him to respect what others believed.

He turned to Dinah to apologize.

She held out her hands. "Aaron, really. It's fine." She sounded convincing, but Aaron wasn't sure about her.

Emily swung her hand away from Aaron's. "You're going to love the stuff Miss Maude cooks. She's the bestest cook in the whole world."

Maude laughed as she brought the pan over. "I don't know about that, Emily, but I think I can hold my own."

Maude used a spatula to give each of them a healthy portion of egg and then added some cubed potatoes to the side.

Aaron stared at the food. The food looked so good. It looked like the food his mom used to cook. His dad tried, but he just wasn't as good. It smelled good too. How could being held prisoner feed so well?

He tasted the egg and then the potatoes. His eyes widened. Delicious. The best he'd ever had. This woman should be working at a world-class restaurant. If she cooked at a restaurant, Aaron would get a job there just so he could have her food every day. He was almost crying. For one moment, he almost felt like he had a mother again.

Maude patted him over the head. "Pretty good, no?"

Aaron swallowed. "Very good. Thank you so much,

ma'am."

"You're very welcome. And stop with the ma'am. I have a name."

"Yes, Maude."

"Better." She smiled. "Hopefully you'll get to taste a whole lot of my recipes soon."

"I hope so."

Emily grabbed his hand with one hand and held her fork with the other. "I like you. I want you to be my big brother."

Dinah reached over and unlinked their hands. "Easy, Emily. Aaron's still settling in. Maybe you gotta give him a chance to do that before you adopt him."

Aaron picked Emily's hand back up. "No, it's okay. She's just playing pretend. I don't mind being a big brother at all. I always wanted a little sister."

Emily grinned. "We're going to play a lot of games. Like dress up and castle and princess. It's gonna be sooooooo fun!"

The little girl was almost angelic. The girls at his church were so loud compared to her. And they never even really noticed him. Aaron didn't know many games, but he liked to play along with what others wanted when he got the chance. He liked making them happy, and he was pretty good at most games he'd tried. As long as they weren't "adult" games. But being a temporary big brother to a little girl who belonged at home with her mommy and daddy? It finally gave him something important to do.

Dinah scowled at Emily. "Aaron, why don't you just let her play by herself? You're too big for little kid games. You have somebody your own age to hang out with. You don't have to humor a needy little girl."

Aaron smiled. "Nah, I don't mind. You can join us too if you want."

Dinah's eyes filled with disappointment. "No thanks. If you'll excuse me." She pushed her plate aside and left the table.

After the hungry children had licked the last morsels of food off the plates, Maude cleared them away and began to wash them.

Emily took Aaron by the hand. "Let's go play."

Drake stood, blocking their way. "Actually, we got a bit of work to do first."

He took out a few pages of a script. He handed a copy to Aaron and then some to Jeremy.

Jeremy looked through them. "What am I supposed to do with this?"

"Read it, moron." Drake grunted as he took a seat. "Boss already has your first movie scripted. Don't worry. Nobody's dying yet. The boss never kills too close together. He likes to give the new ones a chance to ease into the profession. But he does want us to be ready at ten o'clock sharp to film those scenes. Translation, learn those in the next hour. It's only a few scenes so don't bitch that it's not enough time. We work fast around here."

Jeremy scanned the script. "This stuff is so amateur. The dialogue is cheap. There's no point to it."

Drake chuckled. "There's a good reason that despite the loads of cash he could fork over, he never made it big in the industry. Prescott sucks balls as a screenwriter. He's too damn self-centered to realize that. So since no studio worth their weight will provide him with actors to talk out this drivel, he has his goons take people he thinks look the part."

"So we're just his playthings until he decides to kill us

off?"

Drake winked. "Maybe you're not as dumb as you look. Be warned that he also forces us to improvise on a lot of scenes. Likes natural reactions. If I were you, I'd make a point of it to start learning how to be really good at your new job. It's how I survived this long when most of the others didn't. The goons will be up soon. I'd start looking those sheets over."

He then walked off to the bedroom.

Jeremy flipped through the pages, hands shaking. "It all seems . . . simple enough. I guess." He looked to Aaron with a smile. "Like on TV. Just like TV." He forced a smile, but Aaron could see that his father didn't believe it either.

Aaron looked at the script sheet. The language was simple enough, but he had never been strong at memorizing. What if he messed up? Would this guy kill him?

Emily popped her head between him and the script. "I'll help you."

"Don't listen to her." Dinah walked over to them. She pulled Emily aside. "She gets half of her lines wrong. I'm the one who is good at this. Just follow my lead and you'll be fine."

Dinah was starting to get on Aaron's nerves. She was too rough with Emily. Dinah was older and should know better. He wanted to say something but he couldn't fight and learn his lines at the same time. Maybe Dinah would cool off once he wasn't so new anymore.

He returned his focus to the script and prepared to get into character, or at least try to be good enough not to get killed.

The goons showed up right on time. They escorted

everyone downstairs. It was the first time Aaron had seen the rest of the house in daylight. It was even more breathtaking.

As they descended the staircase, Dinah leaned in to Aaron. "Don't try to run. The last guy who tried to do that ended up with a bullet in his back."

Aaron gulped. He was just thinking of doing just that at least once on the way down. She'd probably just saved his life. Maybe that alone merited giving her a second chance.

They were led into the parlor. It was already fixed up as a set with props like a kitchen table.

Two suited men were standing in the middle of the room. Their dress was in stark contrast to the black suits the thugs wore. One was an older man, early sixties, who wore a professional brown suit. A younger man stood next to him. He scowled at the group and was tapping his foot. He wore a flashy, blue suit. He tugged at his shades. "Gosh, these people are slow."

The elder man stepped forward first. He adjusted his tie. "It seems we have two new faces today." He looked at Aaron and Jeremy. "Hello, my name is Bradford Prescott." He pointed to the other man. "This is my son, Lincoln Prescott. Do as he asks and you'll be treated very well. It's really that simple." He looked at the rest of the group. "Everyone else, good luck today." He then excused himself and left them with Lincoln.

Lincoln approached Jeremy and Aaron. He circled them a few times. He reached into Aaron's hair a moment and measured their heights against his own. "You two look good." He grabbed Aaron's face and stared into his eyes. "So cute. Nice eyes." He cracked a smile. "Perfect face for the camera." He let go and took a step back.

"How was your first night with us? I hope everything was to your liking."

"I wanna go home." Aaron gasped. He didn't want to piss off somebody like Lincoln. The words had just fallen out of his mouth. He took a step back.

Lincoln patted him on the head. "But this is your home now. You'll adjust soon enough. All the others did. They wanted to leave too when they first got here, but now, look at them." He shot them a stern glare before walking to the corner of the room and signaling to the other man with a large camera and microphone. "Anyway, let us get started."

He snapped his fingers.

A team of butlers rushed in with a director's chair. He settled his bony frame into the chair and crossed his legs. "Everyone but the newbies clear out. I wanna film their scenes first today."

They had to go first? Aaron wanted to see the others do it first to warm up. He felt like when he was called first in gym class. Everyone was going to be staring at him, just waiting for him to mess up and get yelled at.

He looked around for some visual support but the others were already well on the other side of the room. They must've learned to move fast or else.

Lincoln then got up and escorted Jeremy to the kitchen table. He shoved him into the seat.

He patted Jeremy on the back. "Relax." He massaged Jeremy's back a moment. "This is a simple scene. I'm not a tyrant. You're still new at this. I don't expect an award-winning performance out of the gate. But I do want you to do one thing that isn't in the script."

"Something not in the script?" Jeremy clenched a fist. "I just barely memorized this. I don't want to get confused."

Even Aaron could hear how phony his dad sounded.

Lincoln whispered into Jeremy's ear.

Jeremy's mouth dropped. "No. I will not do that!"

Lincoln grew tense. He clenched a fist and grabbed Jeremy by the neck. "Did you just refuse to follow the director's orders? That's not the best way to learn."

Aaron could feel the fury radiating from Lincoln from several feet away. He folded his hands. His dad couldn't be killed. Whatever Lincoln wanted him to do, he should just do it.

Jeremy looked at Aaron and back at Lincoln. "Okay, I'll do it. After the scene is done . . ."

Lincoln exhaled a deep breath. "That's fine with me. It actually works best that way." He began to smile again. "Alrighty then, let's get to work."

He signaled for Aaron to come over. Then he had one of his butlers hand him a bowl with steaming hot cereal coming out of it.

"You two think you remember the scripts?"

They both nodded. Even though Aaron was only half sure.

He took his seat. "Then without further delay, lights, camera, and action."

The camera started rolling.

Aaron stepped right into the role he had read on the script sheet. He had never acted a day in his life but anything to stay alive. To not make this guy angry.

He tried to visualize the script. He took a deep breath and carried the bowl toward his father. He was shaking. What if he messed up? What if his shaking got Lincoln mad? Then again, the script called for him to be afraid of his father. Maybe being scared of Lincoln would work just as well. Maybe it would actually make him more convincing. Aaron prayed this was the case, and began to tremble even harder.

He came to his father and held the bowl out. "I made you some breakfast, Dad. Oatmeal. Just how you like it. With strawberries."

Jeremy pointed to the table. "Put it down then. Let me see if you did it right."

Aaron carefully set it down and stepped back as Jeremy dipped his spoon carefully into the creamy breakfast.

He raised the spoon to his mouth and slurped off the steamy, creamy oatmeal, chewing it a bit before swallowing.

Jeremy almost looked like he enjoyed it. It did look good, so why wouldn't he? But Aaron remembered that the script didn't call for the father to enjoy it. Was his dad going off script?

"This trash is terrible." Jeremy turned to him. He raised his fist. "You call this food?" Aaron thought his father's tone wasn't convincing but maybe Lincoln would be convinced. "You'd have to work hard to screw this up, but then again, that's all you know how to do."

Aaron's lips tensed a moment. "But I worked so hard on it. I did everything the recipe said. It should taste good."

Jeremy stood up. "You think I care what you think, you little asswipe?"

He swung and landed a strong punch on Aaron's face.

Aaron was thrust several feet back and crashed to the ground.

He heard gasps all around. That wasn't in the script. Was this what his father didn't want to do?

Aaron tried not to but tears spilled out. His face

throbbed with agony, but even if his father was only doing what he was told, being hit by him stung.

He looked over at Lincoln. He was clapping with a big smile on his face. Freak.

Jeremy yanked Aaron to his feet. "Next time you try to cook, make it edible. This couldn't have tasted worse if you cooked it in your own piss. Now get out of my sight."

Jeremy's eyes welled up.

Aaron could see what this was doing to him. He tried to tell himself that this was all an act. No matter how easy it felt to forget the difference, his father didn't really mean what he was saying.

Aaron hopped to his feet and clutched his sore cheek. He could already feel a little swell. He tried to remember the script but his mind went blank. All he felt was the pain.

He ran back toward the stairs, still crying. He recalled reading something like this in the script. Maybe it was what Lincoln wanted all along.

Therese and Dinah both called out for him to stop.

Aaron continued running anyway. Maybe they'd shoot him dead right there but right now, he just wanted to be away from this.

Lincoln shot to his feet. He clapped and then did a small dance. "Cut! And print. That was absolutely amazing." He ran to Jeremy and put his arm around him. "One take? One take, I tell you. The boy is a natural. I could feel the emotion. It was so beautiful." He turned to Jeremy. "You were a bit slow to start but when you got to the good part, you really let loose. So impressive."

Jeremy turned away to hide his disapproval. He didn't want this maniac to see how much he hated him. He looked at the staircase Aaron had just run up. He could still hear some of Aaron's wails for just a second before they too vanished.

He turned to Lincoln. The creep had already moved on. He was directing his crew on their new positions.

There were several more pages he'd been given they had yet to film. It was going to be a rough day.

Aaron ran through the upstairs halls until he was out of breath. He bent over a bit and took deep breaths.

He looked around. Nothing looked familiar. Then again, he was still a stranger here. All parts of the hallway looked similar. At this point, he just wanted to find where he'd stayed at night and crawl back into bed. At least he'd felt a sliver of safety there.

"I'm such a baby." He dropped to his knees. His father had never hit him before. There was something more to being hit by him now than just the pain. Aaron didn't quite understand, but it cut deeper than just his skin. He just wanted to hug his father and hear how much he loved him.

He took a deep breath. His chest began to hurt a little bit less. His face too. Now the problem came with getting back. What if Lincoln just shot him dead the moment he saw him? Or what if he accidentally stumbled onto something he wasn't supposed to see? Aaron felt his chest pounding again. Getting lost in this kind of strange place was definitely not a smart decision.

He looked around and tried to determine the way back. Maybe he could slip back unnoticed. He almost couldn't believe how far he'd come without knowing where he was running.

Should he risk calling out? Maybe one of the workers there would help him without turning him in. On second thought, better not to risk it. If they were even a little corrupt, they could get Aaron good and dead with just a few words to the nut boss.

He tried to retrace his steps, checking each door before he passed by to make sure it was closed.

"You really shouldn't be in here." A voice behind him.

His limbs locked up. This was it. His life was about to end in a loud crack.

He stood like that for a few seconds. Then he replayed the voice in his head. It was softer and higher than he'd expect. Not a man's or a woman's. It sounded closer to his voice. A boy's voice.

Aaron spun around.

A boy locked eyes with him. They were strong, distinctive, brown eyes. Older than the rest of him.

The boy stood a few inches taller than Aaron, but they still made direct eye contact without tilting their heads. The boy had short, brown hair with a slight spiked effect that Aaron thought was cool.

Aaron went to speak but nothing came out. He took a step back.

The boy didn't even flinch.

Aaron took a deep breath. "Who are you?"

"Does that really matter right now?" The boy raised an eyebrow. "You should get downstairs."

"I don't know how." Aaron shifted his eyes a bit. "I think I'm lost. I wasn't paying attention when I ran up here. I was . . ."

"I know what you were doing." The boy folded his arms and took a step toward Aaron. "I was watching from another room. I know how scary all of this must be for you. So I decided to come and find you before my dad or his goons do. Trust me, you're damn lucky I found you and not one of them."

"Your father?" Aaron's eyes widened. "That guy is your father?"

The boy nodded. "I ain't proud of it." He pocketed his hands. "I hate the stuff he does. I wish every day he could be a normal dad and not some crazy freak. So try not to think I'm a jerk just 'cause he is."

Aaron nodded.

The boy looked behind him and then back around. "But you'd really better get out of here." His eyes narrowed a moment. He reached out and touched Aaron's face where he'd been hit.

Aaron flinched. "Ow." He reached up to grab his wound.

"What happened?"

Aaron rubbed his swollen cheek. "My dad hit me, but I know he did it 'cause he was told to."

The boy stared at it for a minute. "Come with me." He waved Aaron on. "We'd better get some ice for it. That's what I always use when I get hurt." He carefully looked around. "Coast is clear. Follow me. We'll go to my room to get you some ice."

The boy's room was big. At least twice the size of the room Aaron shared with Dinah and Emily. It was almost too big. Much more like a living room than a bedroom. As nice as it was, it wasn't very cozy.

A man stood in the boy's room. He was dressed in the same uniform as the thugs who brought him there.

The boy pointed to his bed. "Sit down. I'll get you an ice pack."

Aaron took a seat on the bed. It was softer than his

bed either at home or in his new quarters. But it was cold. "You got your own freezer? In your room?" Aaron eyed it. It looked as big as the fridge and freezer at home. All for just one kid.

The boy shrugged. "My family's rich." He groaned and shook his head.

Did he not like having all of this cool stuff?

The boy reached into the freezer and took out a pack to hand to Aaron. "Here, put it on your face."

Aaron took it and pressed it against his face. It stung when it made contact with his raw skin. He flinched. After a second, the pain eased a bit and it just felt cold and numb.

Aaron turned to the boy. "Thanks. It's feeling a little better."

The boy sat down next to Aaron. "Don't worry about it." He flopped his head down on his pillow. "Just don't let my dad find out. He doesn't like me having friends over."

"Trust me. I don't want to tell your dad anything." Aaron pressed the ice pack a little harder. Another flinch. "Just make sure you get me back to my room when we're done, okay?"

The boy chuckled. "Sure."

Aaron lowered the ice pack a moment. His skin was beginning to feel like an ice cube. And his arm hurt. "So, you're the creepy director's son . . . what's your name?"

The boy laughed. He swung his legs in the air and somersaulted onto his stomach. He pushed himself up to eye level with Aaron. "You actually care what my name is?"

"I just wanna know who's helping me." Aaron held out his hand. "I'm Aaron."

"Ryan." The boy smirked and knocked Aaron's hand away. He initiated a fist bump instead. "My name's Ryan."

Jeremy became familiar with Lincoln's short attention span before the start of the second scene. The creep didn't even seem to remember Aaron during the next hour. He threw himself into every scene like it was a passion project. Harping on random errors and letting others slide. He even rewrote two of them halfway through and forced a reshoot. Jeremy tried to piece the scenes together into some coherent plot but few storylines seemed anything but a random mess.

Lincoln also seemed to be quite unoriginal with his characters. Almost every character seemed to be an exact replica of the portrayer. Drake played an emotionless, sarcastic jackass. Therese played a sweet and sensitive young woman. Maude played a kind grandmotherly figure. Jeremy wondered why his role was the only one not reflective of his true personality. Maybe it was how Lincoln saw him.

At about three o'clock, Bradford Prescott returned to the room. He quietly called Lincoln aside and whispered something in his ear. The two then left the room.

Jeremy could tell that Lincoln wasn't pleased with what he had been told. He worried about what Lincoln being upset would mean for them. Lincoln didn't seem the type to be above taking out frustrations on his captives.

Jeremy turned to Father Doyle. "Does that happen a lot?"

Father Doyle shook his head. "No. That's new to me. Usually Bradford just stays in his office all day."

"Does he really not care about everything going on

here?"

Drake stomped between the two. "Of course he doesn't care. He's got money coming out of his ass and he wants to make his son happy. He's probably compensating for the fact that he was a substandard father. The man wouldn't bat an eye if he witnessed his spoiled ass of a son cutting off all of our heads." Drake lay down on the floor and rested his head on his arms. "I suppose it could be worse. The little bitch could be raping us, right?"

Therese twitched a moment. "You're such an optimist." She turned to Jeremy, "There's so much to be scared of in life but you're still alive."

Father Doyle nodded. "You could still spend years here with your son. We're not guaranteed tomorrow even when things seem to be at their best. This isn't where any of us want to be, but as long as we're alive, that's something to be grateful for."

Jeremy nodded. He knew this. He'd been telling himself this since he'd gotten there. But he couldn't shake those voices in his head. The pounding fears that refused to be silent even in the dead of night. What if he killed them quickly? There was no promise they'd last as long as the others here had. What if he only killed one of them? Aaron couldn't handle losing a second parent. And Jeremy sure as heck couldn't handle losing his son.

Therese gently took his hands in hers. "Hey. If you ever need to talk, about fears. Or anything. Don't be afraid to talk to me."

"That would be a real role reversal for me." He chuckled and blushed a bit. "I usually give the advice."

"You're still a person, Jeremy," she said. "Especially in this place, we all need somebody to talk to. If anything, this place reminds you of your own mortality. Before I came here, I was wasting my life. I've been here for over three years and I still haven't been here one day for every regret. But here, I had a lot of people to talk to. It helped me stay sane. To not just let the regrets define me. So please. Don't be afraid to talk to me about anything. Same goes for Aaron."

Jeremy smiled. "Thanks." His lips tensed. "I might take you up on that."

"I hope you do."

Drake kicked his feet together. "Hate to break up the schmaltzy love fest but you two should probably be ready to film as soon as the walking suit gets back. I don't want him getting in one of his hissy moods because you two love birds are shooting the breeze."

Maude kicked him. He didn't even flinch. "Relax, Harrison. You don't always have to be a little trouble-maker."

"I've never been a little anything." He grunted and locked eyes with Jeremy.

Jeremy could feel disdain radiating off the man's thick skin. It was bad enough being held by a psychopath but this curmudgeon was starting to become just as worrisome.

"What do you mean they found two of the bodies?" Lincoln stamped his foot and began to pace. "I preserved all of the bodies. They were supposed to be secure. How the hell did one wind up somewhere the cops could find it?"

Bradford poured a glass of bourbon. "Does it matter? You got sloppy. Somehow, they found two of them and made a positive identification. I have contacts at the department. Apparently some private investigator has been looking for everyone you've taken and now has the cops making this a priority. I told you leaving those envelopes was a dumb idea but that thick skull of yours doesn't register any ideas but your own."

"Damn it." Lincoln swiped the glass from his father and downed it. "Those bodies were supposed to stay in my hall of fame forever." He slammed the glass down on the table. "No cops were supposed to get their filthy little hands on them." He turned to his father. "I suppose the real question is what are you going to do about this?"

"And what is it you want me to do, Lincoln?" Bradford filled another glass and sipped it. "If I start poking around, it could arouse suspicion and lead right to us. I've kept your activities from them this long. As long as you don't screw up again, I can keep doing it. But you have to start seriously thinking about taking a break from this. I have clout in this town but one more sloppy mishap like this and even I may not be able to keep those roaches away." Bradford clenched a fist and leaned in close to Lincoln, giving the slightest tug on Lincoln's clip-on tie. "And I am not going to jail for your proclivities. That's where I draw the line."

Lincoln held his hand up and nudged his father back. "Whatever." He resumed pacing. "I just don't know who could've done this? Who would be stupid enough? It has to be one of the crew, but who?"

"I don't know. I don't care." Bradford set his glass down. "What's done is done. But get rid of them, Lincoln. End this soon. I won't let your little hobby bring our family down. Do you understand?"

Lincoln half-nodded. "I knew this couldn't last forever. I felt too alive. But it's too much of a risk to keep it up." He tapped his foot at a rapid pace. "But I can't just let them all leave."

Bradford cracked a smile. "I wasn't implying you let them leave. Just get rid of them."

"I'll start writing them out of my scripts."

"Do it quickly." Bradford stood up. "If cops start to piece things together, I don't want them to have something to find here."

"Just a couple more weeks." Lincoln took deep breaths. "Then this will all be over. I'll make this movie the last one." His worry turned into a grin. "And what a grand movie it'll be. No survivors." He smiled. A movie where the entire cast died? It was his best idea yet. Maybe the best idea he'd ever have. "This might actually be a lot more fun than I thought. I always did enjoy a good challenge."

CHAPTER 5

Another dead end. Julie watched the hands of the clock race around the hours. She went through the files of every missing person, grasping for the tiniest clue that could serve as a lead. A witness statement that gave a hint to the perpetrator's identity. Some tiny detail to connect the victims and their selection. Even online reports of potential sightings. Anything to give this mess of a case some direction. Nothing.

She looked over at Wayne. He'd been remarkably quiet for hours now. But as he muttered to himself tearing through each file, she could see that he wasn't faring any better.

Julie sat back from her desk a moment as the faces of the abducted stared back at her from photos of their former lives. "How the heck can so many people go missing and nobody sees a thing?"

Wayne slammed a folder down on the desk. "You'd be surprised what can happen without anybody noticing a damn thing."

She glanced at the photo of Aaron and his dad. "Do you really think any of these people are still alive?"

"I don't know what to think." Wayne picked up the crime scene photos of Billy and his mother. "Up until today, I kept this faint hope that not finding bodies meant that they were all alive somewhere. Just hidden. I talked myself out of it, but in the back of my mind, I prayed that was the reason. But now we have two bodies. So I'm not so sure of anything anymore. My worst fears about it all were probably on the money."

The anger in his dark eyes knotted her stomach. When the day began, they seemed brighter. With every passing hour, they grew emptier and emptier. "I'm still trying to wrap my head around this guy filming his murders like a movie. It's a pretty sick MO."

"You've dealt with sick before." He flipped through another file without even looking at it closely. He'd looked at that one at least twice in the past hour. "None of this should surprise you."

Images of her best friend with a mop through her chest flashed in her mind. Her best friend, her godchildren, gone in one horrible night. "I can't seem to take the shock out of it. No matter how much evil I see, every new case is a fresh shot of hell. I try to cling to the notion that most people are inherently good. But every day, there's a new reminder of how cruel and demented people are capable of being."

Julie replayed the events on the DVD in her mind. Billy's forced dialogue, his meeting with the man, his murder. So staged and yet its consequences so real. "Let's consider the guy on the DVD a minute. Even if he's not the one in charge, he's the muscle. Why is he willfully participating in this?"

"Seems like a no-brainer to me." He shrugged. "There's probably somebody off camera with a gun to his head. It could be just survival."

"But to kill a child so violently . . ." She flashed Wayne

the autopsy photos. "How many people would actually do that, even to save their own life? It takes a lot of mettle to slit anyone's throat, much less a child's. Some people would die before doing that. Clearly this guy's been desensitized enough that he could do it with barely a flinch."

"Well, the guy in the video wasn't on my list of victims." Wayne rolled his chair back a bit and locked eyes with Julie. "Maybe he works for the killer. Like you said, he would have to be pretty depraved to agree to murder a child in such a violent manner. He doesn't match the descriptions of any reported missing persons, so I don't think I just missed him. We've checked him against every database in the country three times. If he were just another hostage, wouldn't somebody know?"

That was it. Julie's eyes widened. What if they hadn't been digging deep enough? "Maybe he was a victim and you just missed it. For the same reason we've all been missing it."

"How could I miss it?" He threw his hand at her. "Julie, I know you don't think a measly ole private investigator can be thorough, but take it from me, I went over every facet of this case. I tracked down every reported disappearance I could find with that calling card. Even if there wasn't a witness, nobody can just disappear without somebody noticing."

Julie nodded. "Usually. But look at the most recent victims. Jeremy and Aaron Garret don't have any nearby family. If you hadn't been there to see the calling card, it could've easily been thrown away and then nobody would've noticed."

"Not quite." He held up a finger. "Just this morning, I heard that one of the church staff reported that Jeremy hadn't shown up for an agreed-upon meeting. And he never misses an appointment without calling. Ever. So even somebody who you'd think could easily go missing, didn't. Plus, if it hadn't been them, it'd have been Aaron's school. You'd have to be living very far off the grid to not have somebody notice if you disappear."

Julie leaned in. "That's my point. It's unlikely, but it's possible. What if this guy did live off the grid? He doesn't look like the kind of guy who works nine to five and punches an office time clock. And who knows, maybe somebody did notice but never got to file a report? Do you know how many kidnappings go unsolved because somebody didn't report it in time? The smallest reason could keep people from making that trip to the station, let alone bigger ones. Never underestimate how easy it is for something to fall through the cracks."

Wayne scrubbed his face a moment. "Look Julie, I appreciate how you've taken on this case and made it personal to you. That's what I wanted when I called you. But I don't want to waste time with these huge stretches and miniscule facts that won't lead anywhere."

"One thing police work has taught me, Tempest, is that most cases live and die by the subtle. Those little details even many cops overlook because they just didn't seem relevant. A receipt for ice cream. An identifying dent on a van. A sarcastic quip about where your little boy is." Her chest convulsed for just a moment before she willed it away. "Somewhere out there is one of these little details for this case. Something that can lead us to who is behind this. Maybe we already even have it lying around right in front of us. But something tells me that finding out who this guy is might be one of those little details. Little details can add up quickly to become some very big pieces of evidence. I think this is one detail we have to press.

We have to find out who this guy is."

"Okay."

Julie froze. "You're not going to protest anymore?"

Wayne shook his head. "Take a shot at it. I came to you because I trust your instincts."

Julie allowed herself the faintest of smiles. "I'm glad I have your permission." She turned to walk out.

Wayne's cell phone rang.

He checked the number. Then a huge grin replaced the gloom.

Julie stopped and hid just outside the doorway. She poked her head in.

"Hey, Lucy." Wayne settled into his seat and leaned back. Julie had never seen him relaxed before, but all traces of his anxiety about the case seemed to melt away.

"That's great, honey." He switched the phone to his other hand. "I knew you could do it. I told you that you didn't have anything to worry about."

His daughter. Julie remembered her beautiful brown hair and eyes just like her father's.

"Hey, you know what they say about artists. They are their own worst critics. I've heard you play and you can play circles around most adults, let alone other eighth graders. And now you can take it to the bank 'cause the school agrees with me." He chuckled. "I'm grateful for that. Thank you, sweetie. How's your mom doing?"

He shot to his feet. "Dating a loser? He isn't hurting you is he?"

Wayne let out a whooping laugh. "Elevator music? Are you for real? Ouch. I really hope those headphones I sent you still work."

He sat back down. "That's my girl." His smile faded just a little. "Well, it was nice talking to you. Thank you for calling, Lucy. It means a lot. I love you too."

Julie tensed her lips but she couldn't muffle her snickers. She hadn't remembered laughing like this since she was in college.

Wayne stormed over to her. "What the heck are you doing here?" He stuffed his phone in his pocket. "I thought you had stuff to look up."

"You should remember that I pawn that stuff off on my underlings to save my stamina for the real work." She stuck out her tongue.

"I remember the opposite, actually." He leaned against the doorframe. "You never trusted the eyes of somebody under you."

"Let's talk about you." She smacked him on the shoulder. "So the great Wayne Tempest isn't all brute and thirst for justice. He does still have a soft side."

He shifted his eyes and leaned in close. "Don't let word get around."

"And here I was planning to put up a billboard." She winked and walked out, signaling for him to follow her. "I barely even remembered you had a daughter. I only recall meeting her once or twice."

Wayne nodded. "I always kept my personal life and the job pretty separate so the risk of anybody targeting my family would be minimal."

Julie spun around and grabbed his shirt collar. "Are you suggesting that I intentionally put my son in danger?"

He took a step back, out of her grip. "Defensive much? I wasn't suggesting anything."

He was right. Julie cursed herself for overreacting again. Two times lashing out over the same kind of comment was too much for something that wasn't true. The awkward silence dragged a little too long. Time to steer this ship back. "So, you have a family?"

"I had one." He pocketed his hands. "But I lost them."

"Seeing as I heard you talking on a phone and not some spiritualist device, I think you might be overstating that."

"I met a girl fresh outta high school. We immediately hit it off. Maybe a little too much. We barely knew each other a month when she told me she was pregnant. I did what I thought anybody in my situation was supposed to do and proposed to her. She turned me down. She didn't love me. I was lucky that she let me see Lucy whenever I wanted. I was a big part of her life. Until I quit my job here. All of a sudden, my ex thought it was time to give our daughter a better life. Away from me. She took her away. I thought about filing for joint custody, but I didn't want to put Lucy through that. I've only seen her a few times since. She calls a lot. We email. She even friended me." He cocked his head with a faux grin that faded into an empty stare. "I had so much grander visions of what being a father would be like. Something like what you have with Patrick."

"You still have her. You can still build that." She shuddered. "What I wouldn't give to have just one five-minute phone call with Petey again. I love Patrick with all my heart, and I am so glad I still have him in my life. But I still miss Petey every day. So much of my heart was still buried with him. With Seth. You still have Lucy. Fight to know her better."

"Would you stop making sense? You're making it really hard for me to find comebacks."

Good. His comebacks were becoming tiresome.

He took a few steps ahead of her and then blocked her way. "Speaking of Patrick, you'll have to take me by to see him one day. Maybe when this case is done. I doubt he remembers me, but I remember him. I haven't seen him since the top of his head reached my knees."

Julie laughed. "Why wait? You can come over for dinner sometime this week. We can talk about the case some and you can see Patrick. Sometimes taking a breather can help clear your mind and allow you to approach the case from fresh eyes. Plus, I really think Patrick would enjoy having somebody else to cook for."

"He cooks?"

"Cooking is a pedestrian term for what Patrick does. Kid's gifted."

"Detective Martel, isn't it highly inappropriate to be asking me out on a date in the middle of an investigation?" He stuck out his tongue. "Very unprofessional."

A date? Just when she was beginning to like him. She focused on his teasing narrow eyes. He wanted her to get upset like a schoolgirl.

"I'm a woman of results. Professionalism is overrated." She could almost hear her father's voice as an echo.

He laughed. "But in all seriousness, I'd love to take you up on it. I just don't like knowing that a bunch of innocent people are being held by some lunatic who might force them to die to make some stupid movie. I want to know who he is so I can stop him. And even if it's not a quote-unquote date, I still feel awkward enjoying myself while their lives are in jeopardy."

Kevin burst out from his office. "Whatever you two are talking about, forget it right now. I think I might've found us a clue."

"What kind of clue?" Wayne met him halfway at the water cooler.

"I took a second look at this video. Closer this time."

He held up a finger. "I think we might've missed something the first time around 'cause we were so concerned with what was happening onscreen." He waved them over to his office.

Kevin took a seat at his desk and called up the video on his computer. He fast-forwarded the video to the point to just before Billy's throat was slashed.

Kevin then played the scene again.

Julie fought the urge to vomit. This image was already burned into her brain. She didn't need another viewing.

Kevin asked, "Do you hear that, the screaming?"

Julie closed her eyes a moment. "The mother screaming as her child is brutally murdered in front of her?" She opened her eyes again. "Yes, I hear that."

"No, not her." He pounded at his keyboard a moment. "I did some tinkering with the audio and I caught a little something in the background. Somebody else is screaming in the video. I amplified it so we can get a better listen." He replayed it.

"No! Don't kill him." A boy's voice. Not Billy's. Somebody else. "He's my friend."

A high-pitched manly voice said, "You should've known better than to get attached, Ryan. You'll suck at life if you worry about friends like this."

Their voices were just a little distant. Like they were watching from the same room, away from the microphones.

Kevin paused the video.

Julie fell into a chair. "Somebody was watching from off set. Another kid. Maybe another captive? Who was the adult? The guy behind all of this? And what he said to him? What was that all about?"

Wayne looked at the paused screen. "How did you

find that on the original video?"

"After about the tenth time, I picked up on a faint background voice. I thought I was hearing things at first. I may be approaching old koot status but I've always been a bit of a techy. Almost anything in a video, even the quietest of sounds, can be made audible if you know what to do. Who wants to bet our killer director didn't realize the microphones picked him up? Sounds like he might be the 'him' they were referring to. Now we just have to figure out who the other kid is and why this guy seems set on using Billy's death to teach him a lesson."

Wayne shrugged. "His friend is being brutally murdered. That's why he's upset. Seems obvious."

Julie held her chin a moment. She'd heard that tone before. In Patrick. When he found out his best friend was dead. "Clearly, they were friends. Maybe they shouldn't have been. Maybe this guy doesn't like his captives making friends? Then again, maybe this kid wasn't just another captive." She sat back in her chair. "Oh my gosh. I think this Ryan kid might be the son of the guy making these movies." She shot to her feet. "The voice we heard was definitely our guy. But he didn't sound like he was just talking to some random kid he's kidnapped. The tone, the word choice. That's how you talk to your kids. The way he said it sounded like Billy's death was a punishment. Maybe some twisted attempt to discipline. He wants his son to man up by losing his best friend, who he probably shouldn't have been making friends with anyway."

Kevin nodded. "If our guy has a kid, it's not surprising that he'd eventually befriend one of the male victims around his age. This guy probably wouldn't be happy about that. So he makes him into a man by forcing him to watch his new friend slaughtered. Maybe even make him feel like it's his fault for being friends in the first place."

Wayne grunted. "But why wait so long? Billy and Sally Corbett have been missing for a year. Why kill them now? Then send us the video? Even if the theory sounds right, there's too much here that doesn't make sense."

Kevin shrugged. "It's a working theory. We're still a ways off from this making sense."

Julie began to pace. "Well, from the looks of things, our killer seems to be a kind of director. Using some form of threats, he directs his captives into filming the scenes he wrote. In order to pull all of this off, he'd have to be pretty wealthy, wouldn't you say? The cabana alone looks more expensive than the average house. Certainly more than mine. And I imagine he has more movies than just this one given the number of people missing. If he's been keeping numerous people hidden and sustained for over a decade, and on top of that has the resources to do that while also making these films, he'd need not only considerable financial resources but a large and secluded property as well. He has the money to live out this fantasy without attracting attention."

Wayne said, "That does make sense. But if he's wealthy, then odds are finding true evidence on him is going to be hard. We can't go to a judge and ask for a warrant to search the property of every wealthy person in the state."

"What about the name we heard the man use, Ryan?" Julie replayed Ryan's plea in her head. So much terror. "Is it safe to assume that our killer's son is named Ryan?"

Kevin said, "I doubt he'd use an alias unless he planned for us to hear that and judging by what we heard, I don't think he did."

Wayne tensed a bit. "But he did leave the DVD on the body. Maybe it was all planned and he just wants to distract us with unimportant details."

Julie went for the door. "Well, planned or not, it's something. More than we had five minutes ago. It can't hurt to rule anything out. And with any luck, having a name could be the break we've needed."

Wayne rolled his eyes a moment. "Our lead is to search every rich person who has a son named Ryan?"

Julie smiled. "We know this guy has to have a good source of income. He's keeping these people alive to be his stars, at least until he kills them off in his movies. Billy and Sally Corbett were pretty well dressed and well nourished before they died. That doesn't strike me as being kept in some underground bunker. So I am thinking he has a nice house, maybe even a mansion. This is where he keeps them. Somewhere big enough to keep any outsiders from seeing the people he took. He probably would need a good deal of security to ensure nobody gets in or out. All of that would require a lot of money, much more than just a comfortable income. Not many people get into that income bracket, and adding in what else we know about him could actually produce a more compact list than you'd think."

"I see what you're saying. I don't disagree with your theory." Wayne held his words and tensed his folded arms. "But how the heck is looking up every rich guy in the tri-state area with a son named Ryan going to lead us to this guy?"

"It's a starting point. Look closer at men with connections to the film industry, maybe?"

Kevin nodded. "This is starting to make a little bit of sense. Let's see what you can dig up."

Julie returned her gaze to the paused screen. It was frozen on the clip where Sally caught Billy's bleeding body. If a child witnessed that in person, Julie could only imagine the trauma he'd be carrying because of it. If he really was the child of this monster, they just found one more person they needed to rescue.

Wayne strolled into Julie's office.

She was pounding away at her computer, looking up her theories in the database.

"What happened to delegating?"

"Who says I'm not?" She motioned him in without looking up. "I've been trying to narrow down potential suspects using 'Ryan' as jumping point."

"How's that coming along?"

She shrugged. "Well, so far I've found about twelve hundred rich guys with sons named Ryan in this state alone. Even more if I factor in bordering states. I knew Ryan was a popular name, but this is ridiculous."

Indeed it was. Had she ever looked through a baby name book? "Can you at least narrow the list down?"

"Luckily. I'm trying to eliminate those without the means to pull off something of this caliber. Income doesn't always equate to property assets. I'm also trying to eliminate those without connections to the film industry but that's proving more difficult than I'd anticipated. I guess they don't keep very good records of failed screenwriters."

"If search engines fail, we can always start banging down over a thousand doors." His smirk met her scowl. "What?"

"Somehow it doesn't surprise me that you'd do that."

He settled into a seat next to her. "And you wouldn't?"

She smiled. "Did I say that?" She winked at him.

He tapped his fingers against her cherry wood desk. "I feel like I've been chasing this guy forever. Three years of doing little else and it took until now to come up with any real leads. And even now, he still seems to be so well guarded that taking him down is a pipe dream."

Julie turned to him. "I know that feeling all too well."

His eyes watered just a bit. He tried to blink away any droplets of tears before she saw. He wasn't an emotional wreck like her. A single tear slid down his cheek. Too late. "Even Therese's family told me to move on last year. They made peace with never knowing, I think. Maybe if it was just her, but there were so many. So many lives without closure. I wasn't in this for a client any more. It was bigger than that. I couldn't let this go until there was some resolution. Some justice."

"That's common ground between us. You should know I'm committed to this case. No matter how hard a time I give you about it. I'm going to find them, Wayne. I don't know what we're going to find when we do, but at least we'll know. Their families will know."

Julie's cell phone blasted a classic rock ring tone.

Wayne looked at it petrified a bit for a moment. "It's like something straight out of fiction. You make a broad comment. Then bam! You're either proven very right or very wrong."

Julie picked up her phone. "You know what they say about confusing coincidence for something bigger, don't you?" She raised the phone to her ear, hands shaking. Did she even buy what she'd just said? "Hello?"

Wayne studied Julie's face for any clue of what was being told to her. For a few seconds, she kept it remarkably still. He almost went to snatch the phone from her hands and ask himself.

Then her mouth dropped.

"What?" He shot to his feet. Had they found something?

"How long ago?" She began to breathe heavy. "I'll be right there." Julie slammed the phone shut and jammed it into her pocket. She took off for the door, holding her mouth.

Wayne chased after her. "What was that about? Julie?"

She stumbled and almost fell.

He grabbed her. "Easy there." He helped her steady herself. "What's wrong? Was that about the case? Did they find something?"

She shook her head. "It's Patrick." She cried harder.

"Patrick? Is he hurt?"

"I don't know. They didn't tell me much."

Wayne took the keys from her. "Well then, let's go. Let me drive you. You shouldn't drive in your condition."

She pushed him away. "I'll be fine. I just have to get to him. You stay here. Work the case."

"Kevin can handle the case for an hour." He took her hand. "I'm coming with you. That's not negotiable. You're only wasting precious time trying to fight me on it."

She gave up. She almost fell into his arms as they both made a mad dash for the door. Wayne prepared for the worst. Was Patrick hurt? Taken? Worse? If only he'd heard at least some of that conversation, he'd know if she was right to worry or if memories of nearly losing him were amplifying something minor in her mind.

Maybe it didn't matter. Her child needed her. And he was going to get her to him.

Julie burst through the doors of Patrick's school. Wayne kept pace a second behind her.

She stopped a moment to catch her breath.

He held her shoulders a moment. "Easy, Julie."

It was almost five o'clock. The final bell had rung hours ago.

A few scattered kids roamed the halls. They flashed her scowls as she dashed past them for the nurse's office.

She burst through the door.

To the nurse's desk.

A graying woman half-glanced up from a report. "Ms. Martel."

Julie caught her breath a moment. "Where's Patrick? What happened?"

"He's lying down in the other room." She pointed. "Calm down. There's no need to get upset."

"Calm down?" Julie clenched a fist. She pressed it against the desk. Clocking Patrick's nurse would only cause him unneeded grief. "You called me and told me to pick him up right away. That something happened and he wasn't doing well. Now you want me to relax?"

"Ma'am, let's not overreact."

Maybe Julie would clock her after all. She held her hands down even harder.

Wayne put his hands on Julie's shoulders. "I think you might've just misunderstood what she said." He turned to the nurse. "She almost lost him over the summer. I think you scared her."

The nurse looked at Julie. Her mouth dropped a bit. "Oh, I know who you are. I'm sorry if I frightened you." She bit her lower lip and scooted back a bit. "He threw up after his cooking class. I thought it was just some indigestion but he's really getting sick, and he does have a slight fever. Pretty serious chills too. I see this at least three times a semester. I don't think it's serious, but I'd get him to a doctor. Probably picked up some kind of virus. There's never a week when something isn't going around a school."

Julie took a few deep breaths. Patrick was okay. She tried to let the visions and fears wash away before she saw him. He didn't need to see her panicked. "Thank you for calling me. But in the future, please try to . . ." Better not to say anything. She didn't have the time or the strength.

Julie rushed in to the exam room.

Patrick was lying on the sofa. Groaning and turning about, grabbing his stomach.

She walked over to him.

He didn't even look at her. His face was covered in sweat and his hair was drenched. Maybe she was right to worry after all.

"Sweetie? Mommy's here." She knelt down next to him. She stroked his face. "They told me you got sick."

He struggled to open his eyes. He tried to sit up but quickly fell back down. "Opening my eyes makes me dizzy." His voice was barely there.

"It'll be okay." She kissed him. "We're going to get you to the doctor's and see what's up. Then he can fix it."

Wayne gently picked Patrick up. "Here, I'll help you get him to the car." He cradled him snugly in his arms.

Julie couldn't take her eyes off of her son. He'd never been this weak before. Even after the accident, he was still more aware. Didn't he even wonder who Wayne was?

Food poisoning.

It was barely six thirty when Wayne pulled up to Julie's house, but it was completely dark. Julie was still getting used to the shorter days of October. An hour of waiting at the doctor's for him to spend two minutes with Patrick.

Something from his cooking class must've been tainted, but there hadn't been any other reports from his classmates. Maybe he'd just been unlucky?

A few days' rest and Patrick would be back to normal, but now Julie would be kept home for most of the remainder of the week to care for him.

These people needed urgent help, but her son had to come first. Somebody else would have to take up the case.

Patrick woke up for a minute as Wayne carried him through the front door of Julie's house. "Are we home?"

Julie ruffled his hair a bit. "You bet. Just go back to sleep. The doctor said you need rest more than anything else."

He was asleep again halfway through her sentence.

"How could the school let this happen?" She slammed the door, catching it before it closed. "Don't they make sure the food is safe for their students?" She quietly pushed it closed. Waking up Patrick wouldn't do him any good.

"Schools can be negligent." He offered a smile to lighten the mood. Failure. "At least the doctor prescribed something to take the edge off this thing. We're just going to have to ride it out." He slowly ascended the stairs with Patrick in his arms.

Julie followed him up. "I'm the one who has to ride it out with him. What's with the 'We'?"

He turned to her at the top of the stairs. "I'm sticking around to help you take care of him." He looked around the hall. "Now which one's his?" He walked further down. "Nevermind, I think I can figure it out."

"Since when did we decide this?"

He chuckled. "Now who's using first person plural? We didn't decide anything. I decided I am going to stay to help you out since you're going to need it." He set Patrick down on his bed.

"Wayne, you came to me to help on your case, not to take care of my sick son. Don't you want to keep on this case? We don't have the time for both of us to put it on hold."

"I'm not putting anything on hold. Right now all we're doing is rummaging through names. I can do that here. Should something more concrete come up, that's different. But he's going to be sleeping most of the time so we'll both have more than enough time to keep investigating."

Julie sighed. "This isn't a time to be making sense." She swallowed hard. "Don't get any ideas. Okay?"

He rolled his eyes. "Like I would expect that." He took a sniff. "You think you want to wash off some of that smell?"

She pulled the covers over him. "In the morning. No use doing it now. He's only going to throw up again." She ushered Wayne into the hall and took out a basin from the linen closet. She placed it beside the bed. "Goodnight, Patrick." She kissed his forehead. His skin was even clammier than before. She closed his door all but a crack. Just so she could hear if he called her.

Wayne was waiting for her in the hall.

"You really can go, Tempest. I've taken care of him before. I know how to handle sick children. I'm not new at this."

"Has he ever had food poisoning before?" He raised

an eyebrow.

"Well, no. But he's been sick."

He shook his head. "I had food poisoning when I was about the his age. Trust me. I know what to expect and it isn't pretty. You're going to need all the help you can get. Plus, I know tricks to help keep him comfortable that you probably don't."

"If I need help, I'll call my dad." She leaned against the closet door. "Wayne, I hadn't seen you in years before today. We're not exactly close friends."

"Your dad needs to stay on top of this case. And we're not exactly strangers either. Or did you forget all the time we spent together back in the day? Late nights working theory. Long talks on stakeouts. You were even going to have me babysit once before I had to cancel at the last minute. I hope you're not planning to pull the 'you're a man' card. You know I am not the kind of guy who'd ever take advantage of you."

She scratched her head and ran her fingers through her hair. "Why are you so insistent on helping him? Why are you so insistent on helping me?" She took off for the stairs.

He groaned. "Why are you so insistent on making this difficult?" Wayne followed her downstairs.

Julie stretched her shoulders a moment. Her chiropractor would be glad to see her soon. She wondered if life would ever give her a break.

Wayne came up behind her and attacked the knot in her upper back with knuckle pressure. "It's a little known secret that I am quite the knot slayer."

"Thanks, but really . . ." She felt the tension thrust through her sore tendons. "I'm just a little tired. Patrick gave me a big scare today. I know I overreacted but after coming so close to losing him, it doesn't take much. He trips or just bumps his head and I'm ready to . . . I'm so afraid of losing him."

"You're his mother. Of course you're worried."

"I do appreciate your help. Really, I do. I just don't want you to feel obligated or feel like I can't handle it. I've taken care of him all his life. I'm going to be okay, Tempest."

"You women really are stubborn aren't you?" He patted her on the back and sat her down on the couch. "I'm sticking around to help."

"You know, some people might take a guy refusing to leave after he's been asked to the wrong way." She flared him a sneer.

He shrugged. "Well, some people can kiss my ass."

"Such a gentleman." She laughed. "You're something else, Tempest."

"Would you mind if this something else made you something to eat?" He stood up and walked to the kitchen. "Between the case and Patrick, it'd be easy to wear yourself down."

She grinned and leaned into a pillow. "Since when can you cook?"

"I can't." He stuck out his tongue. "But I can open a can with my bare hands, and my eyes closed. It's a gift."

She smiled. "Well, that's definitely something." She threw the pillow at him. "Let's see what you got."

He caught the pillow and bounced it back at her.

She caught it with a laugh. For just one second, she could forget that people were missing. That Patrick was sick. For just the briefest of moments, she felt young again. She'd give herself just this minute to let her mind entertain possibilities.

CHAPTER 6

"Is he really going to kill all of us?" Aaron pushed a baseball back and forth from one hand to another. "I mean . . . he hasn't killed us yet. Maybe if we do what he wants, he won't. Right?" He kicked his feet together, trying to remember what it was like to be free. When getting caught doing something bad meant being grounded instead of being shot.

Ryan leaned back over the side of his bed and stared at Aaron with his head upside-down. "Don't worry about it." He rolled onto his stomach. "If you think about it too much, it'll show in your scenes. Better to just focus on your acting and make it look convincing."

"Does he make you do acting too?" Aaron tossed Ryan the ball.

Ryan caught it. "He makes me do worse." He threw it back. "He wants me to be just like him. Even though I don't want to be anything like him." He lay back down with his hands behind his head. "Try not to hate me 'cause he's a prick."

Aaron sprung to his feet. "Dude, you're allowed to talk like that? My dad would ground me for a week if I said that word. Especially about him."

Ryan pulled Aaron onto the bed. "Lame."

Aaron pushed himself away, fighting a smile. "Well, it's true."

"Your dad's a pastor right?" Ryan raised an eyebrow. "Yeah?"

He chuckled. "Well, my dad kills people. And records it so he can watch it again. Don't you think that makes him a prick?"

"Well . . ." Aaron leaned back against Ryan's pillow. He knocked his knees together. "I'm just not used to hearing the word much, even if it is true. Dad's pretty big on talking like I'm in church even when I'm not." He sighed. "But he's great. He's a good dad. It must suck to not have a good dad."

Ryan shrugged and jumped off his bed. "You get over it." He pointed to a man standing in the corner of the room. "But he gave me a cool butler. That's this guy. Say 'Hi,' Roy."

The man stood stonefaced.

Aaron glanced over him. The man was tall and thin. He wasn't as scary as the other men. He'd wondered why he followed Ryan everywhere. But since there was always a guard in the house, he just assumed it was another goon.

Ryan shook his head. "My dad isn't here, Roy. You can say something."

Roy gave no reply.

Ryan rolled his eyes. "My dad doesn't let him talk to you guys. Another of his stupid rules. Roy's a really cool guy but he does whatever my dad says. He needs to lighten up."

"You have a butler. That's cool even if he doesn't talk much."

Ryan nodded. "Yeah, Roy is probably the only guy who works for Dad who doesn't suck. Good thing for me 'cause my dad makes him follow me everywhere. And I mean everywhere. So it's a real good thing he's not an asshole like my dad."

Aaron recoiled a bit at the thought of somebody watching him do everything. No privacy at all. It would be the worst. "That is not fun at all."

Ryan patted Roy on the back. "I'm used to him. He's been there since I can remember. Frankly, he knows more about me than my dad does. We're tight. So if he has to be there all the time, at least we're close."

"Wait a minute." Aaron looked back at Roy and over at the door. "When I saw you in the halls, he wasn't there. He was in here when we came in."

Ryan's eyes widened. "Well . . ." he chuckled. "That's another thing you don't wanna tell my dad. Roy isn't as quick as he used to be." He shot Roy a sneer. Still no reaction. "I've learned how to lose him without Dad finding out. It's not like Roy will tell him. So Dad doesn't have to punish either of us."

Ryan's smiles were so relaxed. So unlike the frowns Aaron always felt on his own face. He was fun and outgoing. He almost made Aaron want to try to be like that too. For a moment, Aaron allowed himself to daydream of a world in which he and Ryan could be best friends. Going to school together. Playing video games. Building forts in the summer. Crazy killer snowmen in the wintertime. The best friend he'd never had, even before his life started to suck. How could he be friends with the son of the guy who was keeping him here? What would Ryan's dad say to that?

Aaron turned to Ryan. "What if your dad finds out we've been talking?"

Ryan reached out and patted Aaron on the shoulder.

"Well, we can try to be careful so he won't."

Aaron looked deeper into Ryan's eyes. Upon closer look, the dark brown seemed to hide the slightest hints of fear. Of sadness. Of loneliness. That same look that had greeted Aaron in the mirror since he could remember. Behind that smile and fun act, Aaron felt a painful tension in Ryan. Something else that maybe would make them friends. As differently as they dealt with it, maybe they were really the same.

But was he really the first person Ryan ever talked to who'd been there? There was so much about this place that he didn't know. Maybe Ryan was just the person to ask.

"There were others here before, right?"

Ryan froze. "Yeah . . ."

"Did you know any of them? Like, the kids. Did you ever talk to them like you're talking to me?"

Ryan's smile faded into a grimace.

Aaron knew he'd touched a nerve. "I'm sorry." He took a step toward Ryan. He extended his hand a moment to comfort him but quickly pulled it back. He didn't know what Ryan had been through. Maybe it was best to not get too close. He really didn't know Ryan at all. What if he got violent? But the pain in his eyes was real. Aaron knew he had to do something. "I had no right to ask you that. I should mind my own business. Please forgive me."

Ryan threw a smile back on. "Relax, will ya?" He clapped Aaron on the back. "I'm not going to have you killed because you said something I didn't like."

"I didn't think you were going to kill me."

Ryan shook his head. "Yeah, right. I know that 'oh crap, I shouldn't have said that' look."

Aaron opened his mouth to say something but he'd

been had. What else could he say?

"Look." Ryan took a step toward him. "I know my dad is bad and that he hurts people. He's hurt a lot of people here before. Some of them were even my friends. And maybe he will hurt you too. Okay? I can't lie to you about it. He's dangerous and scary and whacked out of his mind. But you don't have to worry about me. When you're with me, you can chill. I'm not going to hurt you. Piss all over the carpet for all I care."

Aaron giggled.

Ryan did too. "Do it. Heck, I might do it just to tick my dad off."

Aaron decided to laugh with him. It felt good to laugh. It made the fact that he was kidnapped, that he might be killed by some crazy maniac, a lot less scary. At least for a few minutes. Aaron couldn't remember the last time he'd really had another kid who he could call a friend. Maybe Ryan could be a real friend. He seemed to want it.

A few seconds of awkward silence followed. Not cool between friends. Aaron had to break the ice somehow. He turned back to Roy. "So does he talk? Like at all?"

"Only to me." Ryan shook his head. "Dad's orders. His rules suck."

Aaron rubbed his tender cheek. It still stung a little but it wasn't as puffy as he'd thought. "I think my face feels a little better now. I'd better get back. I've been here too long. Thanks for helping me. It's great to know that not everyone here wants to see me dead."

Ryan went silent a moment. His serious look came back.

"You don't, right?"

Ryan shook his head. "No, it's not that. It's just . . . nevermind. Come on. Follow me. I'll help you get back before somebody like my dad notices and goes bonkers."

Ryan turned to Roy. "Stay here."

Roy hesitated as to whether to speak. He cleared his throat. "You know I can't leave you alone."

Ryan grunted. "I'm your master too and I say stay here."

Roy sighed. He took a reluctant step back. "Just hurry up before your dad finds out. We're both in trouble if he knows I'm letting you wander around with one of his guests alone."

"I know how crazy Dad is. I'll be fast."

Ryan led Aaron out of his room. "Like I said, great guy. But he needs to lighten up."

Aaron followed Ryan through back halls of the house.

When they stopped, he recognized the door as the wing they'd stayed in the night before. The cast's wing. Their prison.

Ryan looked both ways. Nobody around. He quietly opened the door.

Aaron was surprised it was unlocked. Maybe it was only locked from the inside. Or maybe it wasn't even locked at all. Maybe it didn't need one if there were guards by all the doors outside.

He waved Aaron to follow him inside. He propped the door open with his foot.

It was quiet and empty. Everyone else must've still been filming downstairs.

Aaron turned to Ryan. "Thank you for not freaking out that I was freaking out."

"Please. You're doing pretty good. Give yourself a break."

Aaron peeked outside. "You should go. If somebody sees, you might get in trouble."

Ryan looked out into the hall. He tapped his foot nervously. He looked back at Aaron. "I don't want to go." He swallowed hard. "I don't get to go out. I never get to see anybody. Just the staff. And everybody but Roy sucks. You're the first person who I can just hang with since . . . a long time." He checked the hall again. Then he stepped inside and let the door close. "Don't worry. I can open it again. They won't lock it during the day." He strolled over to the couch and plopped down on it. "So let's play something."

Aaron cautiously sat down next to Ryan. "What if you get caught?"

He tackled Aaron to the ground and began to grab his arms. "Darn, you talk a lot. Shut up and fight me."

Aaron threw Ryan off of him. He found himself laughing. He'd never gotten to play rough as a kid. But it felt good. For once in his life, he could just be a boy. He prayed a moment that nobody could find out, because despite being somewhere that scared him so much, he was actually having fun. Maybe being here didn't have to be all bad.

Jeremy carried a small paper bag with concealed contents inside. He kept it away from his body but close enough to hopefully fool Lincoln. He could see the grinning idiot out of the corner of his eye. He was ordered to keep it close to him. And this was close enough.

He carried it over to Father Doyle. The priest was dressed in layman's clothes at a table. He could hardly see the fear in his fellow clergyman's eyes, even though he knew the good father was still as terrified as he was, even after all this time doing this. He'd just developed a knack for hiding it. Probably why he was still alive.

Father Doyle took the bag from him. "Is this it?"

Jeremy groaned and nodded. "Everything you asked for. And a little more as an incentive." He leaned in close. "So now, how about what I asked for?"

Father Doyle smiled. "Why even ask? Don't you trust me?" He pulled up a suitcase and plopped it on the table. "The cornerstone of any good business relationship is trust." He slid the suitcase over to Jeremy.

Jeremy opened up the suitcase. There was ten grand in cash inside. Actual hundred dollar bills. Not prop money. What a waste of wealth.

Jeremy slammed the suitcase shut. "When somebody's buying the kind of stuff you are, trust isn't on the table. I get you the goods. You give me the money or I take my product to somebody who will. No trust required. You can take your business elsewhere if you're looking for trust."

"Easy. I was merely making a point." He pointed to the suitcase. "To prove my good faith, I gave a bit more than you were asking."

Jeremy yanked the suitcase off the table. "Don't act like tipping me is some great act of generosity." He stormed off the set.

"Cut and paste." Lincoln hopped into the scene. He clapped Father Doyle on the back. "You're improving every day, padre. I love it." He turned to Jeremy. "You are already so amazing. You're going to go so far if you keep up the good work. You two are brilliant indeed."

Father Doyle got up and pushed in his chair. "I'm not sure making a convincing drug dealer to you is a compliment."

Lincoln had already moved on. He was muttering something to the cameramen.

Therese stepped onto the set. "I don't know why you boys insist on antagonizing him."

Drake walked onto the set and sat down on one of the prop chairs. "I say we should let him sass the boss. Maybe he'll finally let me kill him and we can stop having those annoying sermons."

Therese rolled her eyes. "Those sermons are only annoying or preachy if they show you how wrong the things you do are."

"What things?" Drake sat back in the chair and stretched his arms. "I don't rape anyone. I don't beat the brats for getting on my nerves. And I make every effort to kill everyone quickly. I think I'm quite a good person."

Lincoln stepped between them. "You can fight when you're off the clock. We still got a few more scenes to film today." He pounded his fist. "And we ain't gonna get it done by standing around arguing. Let's move, people." He waved them to take their places and returned to his glittery director's chair. Then he grabbed his megaphone. "Everyone to the patio."

Jeremy approached Father Doyle. "I don't know whether the fact that he actually seems to buy this director act makes him more or less dangerous."

Father Doyle chuckled. "Sometimes the wolves come in a monkey's clothing instead of sheep's."

Jeremy cracked a smile. "Good one. Mind if I borrow that for a sermon? If I ever get out of here, that is."

Father Doyle took a step toward the patio. "A Protestant minister using something from a Catholic priest in a sermon? Don't let me stop you."

Jeremy followed the others outside to the patio. It

overlooked a beautiful pool that seemed to glimmer like crystal. The autumn temperatures were chilly, but the fresh, crisp, evening air was still a welcome comfort.

Jeremy could see Maude and Emily standing a few feet away by a fancy cabana. Maude seemed to be comforting the girl over something. Jeremy couldn't tell if it was a serious issue or a flicker of normalcy in a child crying over something silly.

Lincoln shouted for everybody to focus their attention on him. "Places. Come on, people. The sooner we wrap this, the sooner we can all get to dinner."

Jeremy, Drake, and Therese were ordered to the sidelines.

Maude, Father Doyle, and Emily took center stage. Then the cameras began rolling at Lincoln's command.

Father Doyle approached Maude. He held out the paper bag Jeremy's character had sold to him in the previous scene.

Emily began playing with an inflatable fish by the pool. She put her feet into the water as she sat on the edge. The cold didn't seem to bother her much. She splashed her feet around and giggled as she flicked some water droplets toward Maude.

Father Doyle handed Maude the bag. "This is what you asked for. I told you I could get it."

She took it and stuffed it inside her blouse. "I am most grateful."

He turned to the girl. "I hope you don't ever have to use it. I don't want a repeat of last time. I'm not going to always be there to clean up the mess, old lady."

Maude smiled and turned to go. "Don't worry, boy. I think I finally got the hang of it. Of course, maybe if you stopped by more often . . . an old lady needs company sometimes."

"You have plenty of people to keep you company." He pointed to the girl. "Why do you need me?"

"Intellectual stimulation, I suppose." She winked. "Not all company is created equal."

He chuckled. "Well, well, well. Maybe I will come around more."

As they were talking, a blow-up ball was dropped into the pool outside the scope of the camera. It slowly floated over toward Emily. When it was just within reach, she stretched out her arm to grab it.

Her fingers brushed against the ball but it repelled further out into the pool. She tried to reach again but the same thing happened. Almost like it was planned.

The girl didn't even seem to realize how much of her body she had stretched over the pool until gravity was too much to hold it up any longer.

She collided with the cold autumn water with a loud splash.

Father Doyle and Maude rushed to the side of the pool.

Jeremy went to do the same but Drake held him back. "Don't get into the scene uninvited. It will only make it worse."

"I won't just let her drown."

Jeremy glanced up at Lincoln. The creep was smiling. This was exactly what he wanted. But Jeremy remembered the script. This wasn't a part of it.

Father Doyle and Maude looked at each other and then at Lincoln. This wasn't rehearsed.

Lincoln didn't seem to be in any hurry to direct them either. He sat on the edge of his seat, tapping his foot. He was waiting to see what they did on their own.

Father Doyle jumped into the water.

Jeremy broke free of Drake's grip. "Let him shoot me in the head. I'm not just going to sit here and watch a little girl drown." He rushed to the pool and was in the water before anybody could try to talk him out of it.

He recalled being told about the deaths in Lincoln's movies. They were real. He'd almost wanted to tell himself that it was a cruel joke. Hyperbole to scare him into compliance. But a little girl was sinking into cold, October water. This was real. She could drown and it would be real. Permanent. And all Lincoln cared about was getting it on video. Maybe this is what Lincoln wanted. Or maybe this was a test. Either way, it didn't matter. When lives were at stake, the right thing to do trumped this screwball's stupid script.

Jeremy popped up in the water. He inhaled a sharp breath.

"Are you okay?" Father Doyle was at his side.

"Don't worry about me. Find her."

They both looked around. Emily was nowhere in sight. Could she be on the bottom of the pool already?

"Help." Her voice. Shaking from fear.

She was flailing in the middle of the pool, where the water was deepest. Her head and tiny hands were barely above the surface.

She screamed again.

Then the water washed over her head. Her form vanished beneath the murky surface.

Jeremy hadn't been in water for years. He hadn't had a swimming lesson since he was Aaron's age. But it didn't matter. He had to try to remember. Circular dashes. Remember to breathe.

Jeremy took a breath and dove down.

Father Doyle was already under. Searching. How could she disappear so quickly?

Jeremy saw a shadow. He looked up and saw her small body sinking deeper into the depths.

He shot after her and threw his arms around her. His body almost completely covered hers.

He went to say something to comfort her, forgetting for just a second that he was under water.

Water shot into his lungs like a bullet. He felt his consciousness begin to fade before he even realized. All he knew was that he had to get her to the surface. Even if he drowned.

He closed his eyes and made a dash upward.

Then he felt arms around his body.

Air. Precious air. It hurt like hell. He felt himself violently coughing, but he was breathing. He was alive. He looked over and saw Father Doyle pulling him out of the pool.

Then he looked down and saw Emily cradled in his arms. Unmoving.

Was he too late?

He said a quick prayer as he felt himself gently placed against the cement. God couldn't let this effort be for nothing.

Then the sound of her dainty cough broke through. She was breathing. She was alive. He looked over and saw Therese and Father Doyle steadying her and helping her cough up the water. She was going to live.

"Thank you." His words barely escaped as a whisper but he knew God heard them. He pushed himself to his knees and crawled over to her.

"Are you okay?" He gently caressed her damp arms.

She nodded. "I'm okay. You saved me."

He smiled and playfully touched her nose. "God saved you." His eyes met Father Doyle's with approval.

She smiled and grabbed his finger. "Your hands are so big. But not as big as Mr. Drake's."

Jeremy laughed and gave her a little tickle. Already making jokes. He took a deep breath and told himself that she was going to be okay.

He looked over toward Drake who was scowling with folded arms. He shook his head and turned to go.

Maude and Therese swooped her up in their arms, cuddling her close and drowning each other out with their comforting parent talk.

Lincoln approached Jeremy and extended a hand.

Jeremy stared up at him a moment. "You're going to help me up?"

Lincoln grabbed him by the arm and pulled Jeremy to his feet. "That was a pretty bold move you made there. All to save some kid you don't even know."

Jeremy broke free of Lincoln's grip. "I don't have to know somebody to know what's right for them. Maybe I'm just the new guy and so I haven't just resigned myself to people dying in your little movies whenever you find it most convenient to write them off." He watched Drake disappear back into the house. Then he looked over at Father Doyle who was catching his breath. "But apparently I'm also not the only one here with a sense of right and wrong either. I don't know what you expected to happen but if you're going to kill us, don't expect all of us to just go happily along with it."

Lincoln smiled and patted Jeremy on the shoulder. "You think I'm some kind of monster, don't you?"

"If the director's hat fits."

"I'm hurt." Lincoln took a step back and adjusted his

glasses. "I'm a filmmaker. I believe motion pictures have the potential to connect us on the deepest of levels. Sometimes even deeper than we can in personal conversations. There's a certain honesty to the script. We're allowed to actually act out fantasies and fictions that otherwise could never be. In every film, there's a deep and personal emotional investment. I try to infuse every second of my films with this. Granted, the reaction from small-minded businessmen hasn't been receptive. But that's only because all they see is how much money a film can make. Money is no problem to me, and so my films can be more honest. They can explore things on a more unbiased and unrestricted level. Heck, sometimes the best of scenes can come completely unscripted. Like what happened with you and the girl."

Jeremy shook his head. "Maybe that's what you tell yourself every night so you can sleep with what you've done to innocent people. But you'll have to excuse me if I don't believe you."

Lincoln smiled and shook his head. "Give me a little time. It's still your first day. Before you realize it, I'll have you right where I want you." He patted Jeremy on the back. "We're through for today. You should rest up." Then he disappeared into the house.

Jeremy looked around for Emily. Maude and Therese must've already taken her inside. He wondered if Lincoln even cared a little whether she died by accident or not. If it even was an accident. How could he be so indifferent to another human being's life, let alone a child's?

Father Doyle stepped in front of him. "Somewhere behind all that philosophical film jargon, there is a human being. He's chosen his lot in life, and I make no excuses for him. But in the time I've been observing him, I've come to know that he needs prayers more than anything. There's a pitiful sadness to the effect his choices have had on him. He could've really made a difference if he'd not been so full of himself."

Jeremy recoiled a moment. "It must take a long time to see that because all I see right now is a megalomaniac."

Father Doyle grinned. "Well, you're not wrong. Not at all." He waved Jeremy on. "Let's go inside. We should dry off and maybe get a change of clothes. Evenings after work are one of the few peaceful times we get here so no use wasting it thinking about him."

Jeremy followed Father Doyle inside.

He turned back to look at the pool. So calm. Such a contrast to what almost happened mere minutes ago.

"What happened to Emily, do you think he planned it?"

Father Doyle sighed. "There's no telling with him. It would be in his wheelhouse to arrange something like that. Whether by accident or by plan, if she did drown in there, he'd have been elated. I'm sure us saving her is a great consolation prize, but that man likes death scenes. And if he was after one today, not getting one is only going to make him crave another one sooner rather than later."

Jeremy swallowed hard. He couldn't let anyone else get hurt. Not Aaron. Not anybody. He tried to stuff down the bile of powerlessness that backed up into his throat but no amount of self-reassurance seemed to calm the acidic fear.

Aaron didn't know what he was more impressed with, the fact that Ryan knew the location of an old chess game set hidden under the couch or that he was so good at it.

Aaron recalled his dad teaching him the game when he was six. He was always pretty good at it, even if he only won half the time. But Ryan was on a whole different level. He seemed to be thinking more moves ahead than there were game pieces.

They had spent well over an hour playing five games. Most of them only lasted a few minutes. Aaron had lost all but one, and he was sure Ryan threw that last game out of pity for kicking his butt so thoroughly three times in a row. Now seven minutes into the fifth game, Aaron could feel that Ryan wasn't about to do it twice.

With a swift move of his Bishop piece that nearly made an entire diagonal span of the game board, Ryan smiled and plopped his piece down against the wood. "Checkmate again, dude."

Aaron recoiled in shock. "How did I not see that? I was thinking three moves ahead of you."

Ryan snickered. "If both people are thinking three moves ahead of the other, they'll be chasing each other and will end up being at the same place. I let the other guy think ahead while I come in for a sneak attack."

"That's dumb. You'd get creamed with that plan if I was a better player."

Ryan stuck out his tongue. "Well, I guess it's a good thing I'm playing you then, isn't it?"

Aaron made a fist. "You asking to get your butt kicked?"

Ryan turned around and shook his butt at Aaron mockingly. "Go ahead. Let's see how good your aim is. Bet you can't do it."

Aaron grinned and shook his head. He was a good Christian boy. He didn't get physical. Even if he would totally kick this skinny rich kid's butt.

The door creaked open.

Both boys froze, unsure of whether to run or hide.

Ryan lost his balance and crashed into the chessboard, sending the wooden game pieces flying.

Aaron prepared to lock eyes with Ryan's dad, or one of his goons. He wasn't sure which would be scarier.

Dinah and Emily walked through the doors instead.

"What are you doing here, Ryan?" Dinah approached him and dragged him to his feet.

Ryan opened his mouth to say something but only a drawn out "Ahhh" popped out, followed by a mouth-drooping silence. "Room service?" He threw on a grin.

Dinah folded her arms and shook her head. "You know you're not allowed here. You trying to get Aaron killed?"

Aaron stepped between them. "He was just making me understand how things work around here. That's all."

Ryan shoved Aaron aside. "No, I'm playing with him. Screw lying. I'm almost thirteen. I can do what I want. And today, I wanted to play with someone. Especially when it's a guy and he can actually be cool. It's not like you're any fun."

Emily ran over to Aaron, shouting his name. She pulled him into a hug. "I missed you so much." She planted a kiss on his cheek.

Aaron laughed and picked her up. "You didn't even know me yesterday. And you just saw me this morning."

"I still missed you." She laid her head against his chest.

Dinah rolled her eyes and tried to grab Emily away. "She's just still shaken up from being a little scaredy cat."

"I am not." Emily slapped Dinah's hand away.

Aaron felt Emily's curls brush against his skin. They

were wet and darker than the golden ones he'd seen that morning. "Wait, did something happen down there?"

Emily pouted and looked away. "I made a booboo."

Dinah turned on her best "gossip" tone and took a seat on the couch. "That little klutz was trying to reach a ball that was too far into the pool and she fell in and almost drowned. Or so I'm told. I was doing something else but I saw them carrying her in like a little cripple and got the story from Therese."

Aaron shot to his feet. "That's not right. Somebody should've been watching her. She could've gotten killed." He pulled her close to him. "I'm just glad she's okay."

Dinah folded her arms and put on a pout like Emily's. "Aren't we lucky that your dad was there to be the hero?"

"My dad saved her?" He looked her over to make sure she was okay. "Like, he really saved her? For real?"

"Guess so." She hopped off the couch and took Emily by the hand. "I guess the pastor in him just makes him try to be a Good Samaritan when he gets the chance." She tried to lead Emily to their bedroom.

Emily threw Dinah's hand off of her. "I don't want to go back in that water. I'm scared." She hugged Aaron tighter.

She was so cute, so needy and vulnerable. Like the little sister he'd always wanted. Before his mother was taken away from him, he'd always dreamed of what being a big brother would be like. Having somebody look up to him, somebody he could protect. Maybe he could do that for Emily now. They weren't related but if they were both here together for God only knew how long, they were family.

He stroked her hair. "It's okay. The water isn't going to get you." He kissed her forehead. "You're safe now."

She rested her head on his shoulder.

She could almost disappear next to him, and he wasn't even that tall yet. She was still so little. It dawned on him that it was a much greater evil that somebody would take her than him. He was almost twelve now. He was big and would be a teenager soon. He could handle this. He had to be strong for her.

"I'm glad you're my big brother now." She smiled and tugged him to sit down on the floor with her.

Ryan gathered the chess pieces. None seemed to be damaged from the fall. He stuffed them in their proper compartment on the board, and then slid the board back into its hiding place under the couch. He then hopped to his feet with a smile. "Well, I'd better be going back to my room. But I'll try to stop by tomorrow."

Aaron nodded. "I hope so. You've been cool today. Thank you. I like having a friend."

Ryan looked down and turned to go. "I like having a friend too." He snuck out the door with a wave and gently closed it behind him.

Ryan didn't see anybody in the halls. He could hear the guards downstairs chatting on their rounds. He could get to his room.

He proceeded down the hallways, staying close to a wall in case he needed to duck into a room. His hand dragged against the rough red wallpaper as he paced toward his bedroom.

A hand grabbed him by the shoulder and threw him against the wall.

He shielded his head with his hand but a sharp throb pieced through his shoulder.

"Dad!" He tried to appear natural but even he could

hear the trembling tone in his own voice.

Lincoln Prescott was a bit gaunt and short. Like Ryan, but older. But he was still Dad. Hard and terrifying. Not only ready to punish at a moment's notice, but willing to have somebody taken away and never brought back. It only took one stare to convey everything he wanted from Ryan.

And as Ryan stared into his father's eyes, that stare was menacing back at him.

He pulled Ryan closer to him. "Well, it looks like you've had quite an afternoon." Lincoln smiled. A stranger might think he actually cared.

Ryan gulped. He linked his hands together behind his back. His father's collected tone scared him almost more than an outburst would. Lincoln got mad very easy over small things. It's when he took the time to think through a punishment and implement it slowly that it was really a sign that it was designed to cut deep. And Ryan knew his father wouldn't even spare his own son the cruelty of his enlightened discipline.

Lincoln led Ryan to his bedroom. He locked his eyes with Roy as they walked in.

Roy seemed to twitch just a bit. Ryan rarely saw him afraid but Roy knew full well that Lincoln could get rid of him at a moment's notice. For good.

Lincoln sat Ryan down next to him on the bed. "Ryan, you know you're not supposed to make friends with the actors. For any reason. And you're not supposed to ditch Roy." He shot Roy another cursory glance. "I'm disappointed in you."

Ryan scooted away. "Dad, I'm almost thirteen years old. Normal kids have friends at my age. Friends our own age, not some guys hired to follow me around." He turned to Roy. "No offense."

"But he's not staying long." Lincoln placed a firm hand on Ryan's shoulder. "You remember what happened to Billy. How it destroyed you. Do you want that to happen again?"

Ryan felt a tear slip down his face. "Can't you just let him live? He doesn't have to die."

"That's the business, Ryan."

"Just because I'm friends with him?"

Lincoln shook his head. "It has nothing to do with you. He's not going to go just because you like him. He'd be going either way. But if you like him, it hurts more."

Ryan shook his head. "I don't believe you. You've kept some of them around for a long time. You take the ones I like away sooner. You have a big house to hide all of them. You could let them stay here. You could let me have a friend but you don't. You want me alone because you want me to be like you."

Lincoln shrugged. "Doesn't every parent?" He pulled Ryan into a hug. "You always end up burning out. The key is to not get attached." He kissed Ryan's head. "You got attached to Billy and when he died, you fell apart."

"He was my friend and you killed him for no reason. Just like . . ."

"It wasn't me who killed him."

"Yes it was." Ryan pushed his father away. "You killed him. Every bit as much as if you were holding the knife yourself. I was there. I saw you tell Drake to do it. I felt you hold me back from saving him. You don't want me to get attached? Well, I'm not heartless like you are. So I do get attached. He was just a kid. Just like me. He was my friend. Maybe if you really cared about me you would let me get attached. You wouldn't kill anyone."

Lincoln sighed. "You know I love you, Ryan. I care deeply what happens to you. And that is why I make these rules. Each and every one of them is for your own good."

Ryan laughed through his tears. "You cut his throat open. Right in front of me. How is that for my good?"

"Because it makes you stronger." Lincoln rose to his feet. "It detaches you from frivolous things. I used to be like you. Grandpa gave me everything I wanted. I had more money than any other boy for miles. But I wasn't satisfied. I wanted friends. I wanted to show my friends my movies." He wiped a tear from his cheek. "When you are detached from things that hold you back—like friends—you can become truly successful. The only people that should ever matter to you are yourself and your family. So you and Grandpa? You are the only two people I care about. Grandpa believes the same. That is why we are successful. That is why we are strong."

"Murdering people doesn't make you successful. It doesn't make you strong." He sniffled. "It makes you a monster."

"You're young. You don't understand yet. As you grow up, you'll see that I was always right." He patted Ryan on the head. "We're different than they are. We have success. They don't deserve to do anything more than I let them do."

"I'm not different than them." Ryan grabbed at his shirt. It tore at the sleeves. "Take off these nice clothes and I'm just like them. I'm not different. We're all the same. The only thing that makes you different is you kill them. Because you're just evil. That's the only thing that makes you any different than them and I don't want to be anything like you. Ever."

Lincoln landed a hard slap on Ryan's cheek.

Ryan recoiled against the headboard of his bed.

Ryan held in his tears more. He couldn't let his father see him hurt. He tried to ignore the sting on his face. That made it hurt worse. But he wouldn't raise his hand to ease it. He wouldn't cry more. He stared down his father even more. Hating him even more.

"Never say that to me. Ever." Lincoln stepped away. "You are better than them. That is why you shouldn't become friends with them."

"I like Aaron. He's cool. He's fun to be around. He's my friend. No matter what you do. Why can't you just let that be?"

Lincoln groaned and threw his hands in the air. "Do I have to repeat myself? Why must you be so defiant? I never backtalked my father. You're just like your mother. You need to learn to listen to me."

"Not until you start making sense."

Lincoln sighed and held his head a moment. "If you want to become friends with Aaron, go ahead. I'm not going to punish you just because of that. Or even write him off sooner than I planned. But he's not here for good. None of them are. When it's his time and you find yourself watching another friend die in front of you, don't come crying to me." He then put on a smile. Just like that. "Dinner is at six. Be at the table five minutes early."

He walked out of the room. He left it wide open so Ryan could see him walk away.

Ryan grabbed a pillow and threw it across the room. It knocked his writing lamp off his desk and sent it crashing to the floor.

Roy walked over to it and picked it up. "Don't give him any more reason to be mad."

"Well, I'm mad. So I don't care." Ryan folded his arms in a pout.

Roy sighed. "I know. I'm not saying you have to agree with him. Or even listen to him. But you should know by now that arguing with him doesn't work. Just let him think you're giving him what he wants." Roy returned to his post without another word.

Ryan curled himself up and buried his head in his knees, sinking further into his tears.

Evening. It was getting dark earlier now but there was still just a hair of sunlight left visible through the living room's sole bolted window.

Aaron was surprised that everybody ate together. Gathered around the table like any other family.

Father Doyle moved his plate of just steamed greens from the head of the table to a seat further down. He signaled for Jeremy to take the place, with Aaron at his right side.

Dinah had to sit two seats away from Aaron since Emily insisted on sitting next to him. And he was all too happy to let her.

Dinah grunted as she watched Emily do a song and dance as she sat down. Aaron thought she liked the girl. Emily seemed to like Dinah and feel comfortable with her. Surely she wouldn't want to be around her if Dinah had always treated her this way. Maybe Dinah just liked being around him. Maybe she just wanted a brother too. Somebody to keep her safe.

Therese sat on Father Doyle's left, with Drake next to her. Maude took the other head of the table.

Aaron's nostrils were treated to a buffet of fine aromas

that helped him block out the grim realization that he was kidnapped. Thick slices of roast beef smothered in a fine gravy, a side of creamy mashed potatoes, and a dish of asparagus that actually looked decent enough to stick it out and try. Restaurant-quality cuisine.

Jeremy eyed his finely prepared plate. "Do we always eat like this?"

Father Doyle nodded. "Almost. Despite the circumstances, we have much to be grateful for. Lincoln likes us well fed. Thinks it makes us do our job better. And I suspect he thinks giving us lowly people such food is charity." He chuckled. "True wealth redistribution, huh? We'd be so lost without him."

Jeremy nodded. "I know, right?"

"Of course he and everyone else eat much better than this. Not that rich food has ever appealed to me. I'll take the meat and potatoes . . ." He looked at his own lowly plate. "Or steamed vegetables." He smiled. "Any day over the fried calamari sticks or the cold soups with foreign names that even I can't pronounce."

"Same here."

Father Doyle folded his hands. "Why don't you join me in leading the blessing?"

Father Doyle extended his hands over the food.

Jeremy took Aaron's hand.

Aaron took Emily's.

Emily tried to take Dinah's but the girl smacked her hand away.

Drake had already begun eating.

Father Doyle said, "Bless us, O Lord. And these Thy gifts, which we are about to receive. Through Thy bounty."

Jeremy added, "Bless this food, and bless those of us

who partake in it. Draw us closer to You and help us to be grateful for what You've given us, even if we are scared and don't understand why we are here. Help us to trust that You have a greater plan in mind."

Then in unison, "Through Christ Our Lord, Amen."

Then they dug into the dinner.

Aaron cut a piece of beef and dipped it in the potatoes. He forked it between his lips. "Wow, this is really good." He then cut a piece of asparagus and dipped it in the meat's juices. He slowly lifted it to his mouth and took a reluctant bite. It was actually good. "It's all really good. Thank you, Miss Maude."

Therese smiled and shot Maude an approval nod. "I think the reason the food is so delicious is less because Lincoln gives a damn and more because we always have Miss Maude here to make it all."

The old woman blushed. "Oh, please! It's not that hard."

Aaron said, "Well, it's still really good."

"Thank you, child."

Emily munched on a spoonful of the potatoes. "I like the mashie. They are all soft and fluffy, like clouds. The green sticks taste bad."

Maude blushed and thanked the girl.

Drake grunted and shot an eye roll at Maude. "You are too easily impressed." He chugged a mouthful of ice water. "You're not helping her toughen up to survive here."

"Can't I cherish innocence?"

Drake slammed his glass down. "Can't I have a day go by where you aren't cooing over something stupid that one of those brats does?" He blotted his face with a napkin. "You did it with that brat Billy, you do it with the girl, and I am sure you'll do it with the new kid." He shot Aaron a scowl as he plucked a stray beard hair. "You are not helping them. They need real life skills. Firm discipline. That's their only hope. What you're doing is just making them weak."

Maude shook her head. "You're a sad man, Drake. What could've possibly happened to make you so jaded? There must've been a time when you didn't see the glass as half empty."

Drake pushed his chair back and stood up. "I'm the guy who sees the glass as containing however many ounces of liquid it currently has. I don't complicate it beyond that with semantics." He pulled down his sleeves and stormed off to the living room.

Maude stared at him a moment as he plopped himself into the recliner. "Pitiful fool."

Everyone returned their focus to Emily as she told an exaggerated recount of her rescue from the pool. Even Dinah seemed to allow herself a moment to be enthralled. But she kept her gaze focused on Aaron.

Aaron forced a smile at her, even if her clingy nature was beginning to become more unnerving than welcoming.

Aaron focused on Emily as she obviously embellished the facts. It didn't really matter if she believed them or not. Her story made her happy, and in such conditions, it was a good way to end the day.

Aaron was woken from a shallow sleep by the loud crack of the storm overhead. One last hurrah of summer air making a grand exit.

Aaron glanced at the digital clock on the dresser. 22:11.

Aaron heard footsteps.

"Who's there?"

"Aaron." Emily's groggy voice. She stumbled over to his bed and crawled inside. She pulled the covers over her head.

Aaron caressed her arm. "What's wrong, Emily?"

"Aaron, I'm scared. The thunder's loud. Can I sleep with you?"

Aaron smiled. He remembered being scared of thunder at her age. Heck, he still felt his heart jolt at every monstrous flash or blood-curdling crack. Having her here actually made him feel safer too. "Sure." He planted a kiss on her head and gave her a hug. "Try to get some sleep." She wrapped her arms around him and was asleep in minutes. Even asleep, her grip was stronger than her size let on. But it didn't matter. If it made her sleep better, it was a small inconvenience. Feeling her heartbeat actually relaxed Aaron some. They were both alive. Whatever horrible visions of what could be, they were both still breathing. Slowly. Steadily. With hope. Maybe one day they could both go home again.

Jeremy sat up late alone in the living room. He watched flashes of the storm light up the dark room. He prayed to God for direction. Just one night ago, he didn't know what to expect. Ransom? Sexual predators? Some angry screw up with a hatred of single fathers? Either way, he'd half expected him and Aaron to be lying dead on a patch of grass by a sparsely traveled highway by now. For all he knew, they'd be there tomorrow. But none of his fears seemed to be the case.

They were both still alive. In the clutches of a deranged filmmaker, but alive. Safe. As long as they did what they were told, maybe they'd stay that way. Jeremy thanked God for keeping them thus far. It could be so much worse. At least there was time for the police to find them.

Jeremy thought of the private investigator who'd spoken with him in the restaurant that night. He'd showed him a picture of a missing girl. He hadn't made the connection at first but he could see it so clearly in his mind now. She looked just like Therese. Probably was. What were the chances for Aaron and him to be taken by the same people who took that girl, just minutes after they'd been told about her?

He closed his eyes and remembered the shouts of the private investigator. The gunfire. He'd witnessed them taken. He knew. Maybe he could help. Maybe he was already trying to find them.

Footsteps.

Jeremy thrust his eyes open and turned around.

Therese stood frozen. "I thought everyone was asleep."

Jeremy nodded. "So did I. What are you doing up?"

She looked away and fidgeted with her hair. "I just have to do a few things for Mr. Prescott. Silly little housekeeping things. Why hire a maid when you have us, right?"

"In the middle of the night?"

She shrugged. "We're filming most of the day." She forced a giggle. "But I'd better get it done now or else it'll be morning. You should get some sleep. I'll be back soon."

With a slight wave, she walked out the door.

Jeremy stood watching a moment. Something about her story didn't ring true but he was still so new here.

There was still so much about the way these people lived he had yet to learn. Everything seemed to be like a walk on glass, with the ground ready to shatter and draw blood at any second. And the last thing he wanted to do was be the first crack in their foundation.

Dinah sat up in her bed.

Aaron was fast asleep with Emily tucked under his arms like a little doll. They looked so cute together. But Emily didn't belong there.

She did.

She closed her eyes and pictured herself swaddled in Aaron's embrace. She'd always pictured a man like him rescuing her from this place. Maybe she only knew Aaron a day, but he was everything she'd ever pictured. The dark hair and eyes, the young limbs and voice, just at the cusp of manhood with so many years ahead of him. He was hers. Pathetic or not, she embraced her fantasy.

She rose out of bed and approached the two of them. She pretended that Emily wasn't there. That Aaron had decided that his pajamas were too hot. That he'd ask her to get in and cuddle close. That they could run away together and live alone in a forest cabin where nobody could ever hurt them again. No more violations. No more movies. No more competition. Just Aaron and her.

As she snapped back to reality, Emily's form returned to her vision. Why did Aaron like her better? Dinah tried to think of how she could make herself more endearing to the boy. He hadn't yet developed, so seduction wouldn't work. She'd have to be cleverer than that. Or maybe not. He was almost twelve. Maybe it would work. But only if they were alone. Not an easy task in a house full of people. But she was willing to wait for her chance. Aaron had just gotten here. Billy was there awhile before Lincoln had sent him off to be killed. There was still time.

She lifted Aaron's arm from Emily. He turned on his other side and scrunched his body up a bit tighter.

Better now. At least she could just focus on Aaron.

She sat down on the bed and stared at him a moment. Just a little while longer until the storm was gone.

CHAPTER 7

Sunrise found Patrick hugging the toilet bowl.

Julie stood behind him, steadying him.

This was the third round since he'd gotten home. Somehow, he'd managed to get four hours or so of sleep between each episode. But his strength was still non-existent.

Patrick took deep breaths. He felt like he needed food but even the very thought of swallowing his saliva gagged him. Without food, he felt like his body was starving.

He pulled away from her and lay down against a folded up towel that acted as a pillow.

He felt so dirty and sweaty.

The tub was just a few inches away. So welcoming. He imagined soaking in the warm water, but he couldn't even move or sit up. All he'd been able to take was a damp washcloth that never stayed warm for more than five seconds. Useless.

In between breaths, he could hear the faucet drip like it always did. Drip. Drip. He recalled the shower two days before. He'd felt clean. Alive. Now he felt dead. This must be what people about to die felt like.

He groaned and held his stomach. Relief was a long ways away. The day had just started and already he prayed for tomorrow to come.

Tears mixed with sweat as he opened his mouth to speak. "Just let me die already."

Julie scooped him into her arms like a toddler. "Now that's no way to talk."

He could feel his limbs sagging over hers. He couldn't even lift his head an inch to look her in the eyes.

"Mom, when is this going to get better?"

She sighed. "You're going to have to let it run its course, Patrick."

"You mean let it kill me?"

"Patrick, the doctor says you're going to be fine. It's just food poisoning. He prescribed some medicine. It'll take the edge off. You're going to be okay."

"I don't feel it."

"Give it a little time, Patrick. I know it's horrible but we're gonna plow through it."

She returned him to his bed. The room was still kept as dark as possible by the shades. Good. The light hurt his eyes.

He was asleep again as soon as his head hit the pillow.

Julie smiled as she stroked his clammy cheek. "Feel better soon, Patrick." She kissed him and quietly closed his door behind her.

Wayne was waiting for her downstairs. "How is he?"

She shrugged. "Like you'd expect."

"I could hear . . . even down here. Poor kid. You sure he doesn't want me to pick him up something to settle his stomach?"

She shook her head. "He couldn't keep it down any-way." She settled into the sofa and held her head in prayer.

"He hasn't eaten this little since he had that infection as a toddler. I'm worried."

Wayne placed his hand on her shoulder. "He's acting just like I did when I got it. Don't worry. He'll be fine."

"I hope so. I hate seeing him like this."

"Hopefully he'll feel better later." He pulled her to her feet. "But right now, you gotta focus on keeping yourself healthy. I made you some breakfast."

She smiled. "Thanks Wayne, but I'm really not hungry."

He tugged her to the kitchen. "Are we really still playing this game? Stop arguing."

Julie sighed. "What did you make?"

"Well, I knew smells would get Patrick sick so I made something without much smell, a biscuit chicken sandwich."

"How does that not have a smell?"

"It's an instant breakfast thingie. I'd have whipped up some sausage and eggs but then it would smell like a five star restaurant and get Patrick sick. Plus, you're out of eggs. Don't you ever go shopping? So yeah, I made you that. It's almost entirely chemical and probably will kill you if you eat it every day. But it'll keep you from fainting from one of your 'I'm fine' hunger strikes."

Julie fought a grin. Silly man. "Okay fine, I'll eat it. But just this time."

Wayne smiled and held out his hands toward the kitchen. "Ladies first." His faux proper tone didn't fool her.

Anime themed eight-ounce glasses with orange juice were set next to the small plates. A warmed and slightly misshapen breakfast sandwich was the centerpiece of both of the plates.

"I hope you don't mind I made myself one too."

Julie chuckled. "No, not at all." She leaned against the fridge." It's not as if Patrick's going to be wanting them any time soon."

"Then let's sit down to breakfast, my lady." He grinned as he pulled out a chair for her.

She knocked his hand off the chair and sat down. "I don't need to be treated like a baby. I'm not a princess."

Wayne rolled his eyes and took a sip of the juice. "I never said you were. I just have an old fashioned side. Sometimes, I believe a woman needs to be treated like a lady. You hear that? A lady, not a baby."

She turned away. "I'm sorry. I don't mean to snap at you. I'm flattered. I just—"

He held out his hand. "I get it. Let's just eat."

Taking a seat opposite her, the two each said a prayer silently to themselves.

"These things are never as good as you get in the fast food places." Wayne set his sandwich down and dabbed his fingers with a napkin. "But as frozen boxed food goes, these ain't half bad. Must be my magic touch."

Julie smiled. "You're either very easily impressed or very full of yourself. Probably both."

Wayne downed the rest of the sandwich in less than two minutes. He brushed the crumbs aside. "So have you ever considered dating somebody again?"

Julie quickly swallowed the food in her mouth to avoid choking. "Excuse me? Did you just hit on me?"

"What? No." He placed his plate in the sink. "I was just curious. If you got married or started dating again, I might have somebody to watch the games with." He quickly washed off his plate with a dot of soap. "I'm seriously tired of doing it alone or in sports bars. It's pathetic."

"You want to know if I'm going to find another guy so you can have somebody to watch football with?" She raised an eyebrow.

"Well, baseball too."

Julie chuckled. "Good. For a second there, I thought you were trying to get me to date you."

Wayne laughed. "Date you?" He paused a moment. "You should be so lucky."

"And what is that supposed to mean?" She sat back and folded her arms.

"I got some very strict standards, you know." He turned off the water. "I've always wanted to settle down, but I guess work has always been a great distraction. You gotta remember that I was the only guy on the force not constantly rotating significant others."

"Yeah, I know. Some of the guys used to think it meant you were gay." She shot him a playful sneer.

"In their dreams." He smiled and took a seat. "I just take relationships seriously." His flippancy melted into a solemn stare. He almost seemed earnest. "If I were going to date you, you'd have to be just as into it as me or it'd be a waste of both of our times. And I wouldn't do that."

They locked eyes a moment before Julie looked away. She tried to recall the last time she tried to date. She'd been set up once or twice since Seth died but nothing serious. She'd never been interested. But maybe she was missing out. She missed having a strong hand to hold her. Somebody she could fall apart with. She suddenly realized that the past day made her feel like she had Seth again. Having somebody who wasn't just a friend. But was it just memories?

She looked back at him. He was staring aside a moment. Almost like he was thinking the exact same thing she was.

He went to speak to break the silence, but Julie's cell-phone beat him to it.

She hushed him with a single index finger.

Kevin's hyper voice greeted her. "Any leads yet?"

"I've been a bit preoccupied with Patrick, so no."

"How is he?"

"Fine, but he's kept me up all night. I've barely thought about the case since we left."

"Well, we might've gotten a break anyway. I just got back the results of the first search you put in. The one for similar reports of crimes involving a man whose description matches the one in the video. It took a bit of refining, but I think I might've come up with something. It's just shaky."

"The last time you had a shaky theory, you were right." She rose to her feet. "If you think you have something, you probably do."

"There was a missing persons report filed for this guy. About five or so years ago."

"Then why didn't it show up sooner?"

"It was never taken seriously."

"Why not? Police aren't usually in the business of just ignoring reports." She caught Tempest shaking his head. She waved him off and turned away. "Even if they felt he'd run off of his own will, it wouldn't have just been ignored outright."

"The only witness to it was a mental patient. I don't know. Whoever took the report probably just dismissed her story as fantasy. This thing was buried so deep that I don't think the guy even lifted a finger to look into the matter."

"Hold on, there was a witness? And they dismissed

her?"

"I think so."

She groaned and shook her head. "Is this witness still alive?"

"Yeah, and still at the same mental hospital too. I hate to ask this with Patrick being sick, but could you go down there and question her?"

"You're asking me to leave Patrick? Why can't Tempest do it? Heck, why can't you do it? Why can't one of the many other cops in the station do it?"

"Tempest isn't a cop."

"He's a private investigator."

"He doesn't have the authority to go there alone in an official capacity."

"He's taken this case. He has a license."

"Jules! He left the force. He just came back to us when he needed us. I need more time before I trust him. I'd send somebody else but you're the best. It was some lesser cop taking her statement the first time that caused it to be dismissed outright. You could pick up on things the other guys wouldn't. And I am the chief here. I can't just up and leave. I got the D.A. breathing down my back over a whole slew of cases. I am still your superior and I'm not asking you to do much. Just ride over to the mental hospital, ask her a few questions, and then get back home to Patrick. It's an hour's work. Tops."

"I can't just leave my sick son, Dad." She nervously twirled her hair around her finger. "You know that. He needs me."

Wayne raised his hand. "I could stay with him. I know what to expect from a food-poisoned kid."

Julie muted her phone's receiver. "I can't ask you to do that. It's not even right. I don't know you that well."

Wayne rolled his eyes and grabbed the phone from Julie's hand. "She'll be right there." He hung it up.

She grabbed the phone from him. "Don't ever do that. Who do you think you are? Coming back into my life after five years and making demands and acting like we're besties?"

"We weren't just acquaintances. We were partners. And you know what? Maybe we joke about it, but let's stop pretending for a moment that the idea of 'us' as a thing isn't something both of us have been thinking about from the moment we saw each other again."

"Speak for yourself, Tempest." His eyes were piercing into her soul. She refused to look at him. "Look, it's not that you're a bad guy . . ."

"Do you think I'd hurt him or something?" He threw his hands in the air.

"No. That's not it."

He took a step toward her. "Then what?"

"I know." She swallowed hard. "You've always felt something. From the first time we met. I could sense it. You were a gentleman about it, but . . . I was married. I loved my husband. I respected my husband. I would never even dream of even entertaining the thought of being with anybody else but my husband. Forsaking all others. That was my vow. I meant it."

"Until death do you part."

"That doesn't give you a right to assume I'm wide open the moment my husband is in the ground."

"Is that what you think I did?" He held up his hands and took a step back. "We didn't even kiss. It was just a moment. You felt the same thing I did in that moment. It was almost a whole year later. And the moment I sensed you were uncomfortable, I broke things off because I respect you."

"And then you left." She turned away. "I didn't see you for years. You just wrote us out of your life. I know you say it was the limitations of the job getting to you, and maybe that's somewhat true. But I always felt like maybe there was something else."

"Gosh, Julie. Why are we even still talking about this?" He settled into a recliner. "I'm not here to pressure you into starting something. I'm not even here to suggest it. Regardless of any potential feelings then or now, we were friends. We trusted each other. Why is it suddenly such a foreign concept for you to trust me now? I like Patrick. I know how to take care of a sick kid. And I'm not some monster out to hurt him. We both want this case solved, don't we? Well, questioning this woman could accomplish that. If your dad would let me do it, I would. Heck, a few days ago I'd just have done it anyway. But I brought you guys into this case. It's your case too now. And I'm going to respect his authority on the matter. And he picked you. So go. Patrick will be okay for one hour. They might not be."

Julie turned away in silence, cursing herself for not having a counter. How could she let him get away with being so right? She walked to the front door and called her dad back. "You forgot to give me directions."

A crash.

Patrick had made it eight steps to the bathroom but tumbled to the floor right outside of it.

The thunder of feet rushing up the stairs.

He turned to see an out-of-breath Wayne.

"Hold it there, kiddo." He went to help Patrick up but

the boy knocked his hand away.

"I don't have time to wait for you to help." He hastened his pace to the toilet and suspended his head over it. Two seconds of horrid silence. Then the next wave came.

Wayne turned his head for the briefest instant then was at Patrick's side, holding him up firmly. "Easy does it."

"I'm fine." Patrick pushed Wayne away and pulled himself to his feet. "It was just a little this time." He flushed the toilet and closed the lid. Then he sank onto the porcelain seat and leaned back.

Sharp piercing hammered in his head and the room spun but he felt it spin a little slower than last night. "Thanks for checking on me. But really, I'm fine."

"Do you want to go back to bed? I can help."

Patrick shook his head. "No, I've been in bed too long. The longer I stay in bed, the worse I feel. I'm starting to feel like I'm dying from all this lying down."

"Okay then." Wayne held out his hands. "You don't want to stay in bed and I doubt you want to sit on a toilet all day. So, you want to go downstairs?"

"I do." Patrick looked outside the bathroom. He could see the top of the stairs. "I just don't know if I can make it."

Wayne helped him to his feet. "Well, that's what I'm here for."

"I'm not letting you carry me again."

Wayne rolled his eyes. "You're your mother's kid all right. I'm not going to carry you. I'm just going to help you walk. That a fair compromise?"

Patrick nodded. He followed Wayne into the hallway and to the stairs.

The eleven steps down the stairs seemed like a sky-scraper of staircases. But to his surprise, each step made him feel a hair better. Not much, but he felt like he could maybe sit up for a few minutes.

Luckily, there was a bathroom down there. So even if he had to throw up again, maybe he could stay here at least until the evening.

Downstairs, Patrick looked ahead at the sofa. "Mom always wraps the couch in a sheet when we're sick." He swallowed hard. "So we don't contaminate it." Why didn't he think to mention that upstairs? Wayne was kind enough to help him and he didn't want to make him rush up and down stairs all day.

Still, Wayne took it like a trooper. He disappeared upstairs and returned in a minute with a blue sheet. Patrick hadn't even seen it before but it looked soft enough.

Wayne threw it crudely over the couch, covering it just enough.

"Okay, have a seat. You don't want to push your strength too much."

Patrick stumbled over to the couch and crashed to it with a thump. He buried his head in a pillow and groaned a moment before turning on his side. "Thank you."

"So . . . um. Is there anything I can get you? Some water maybe? Or some hot tea?"

"Mom always says ginger ale helps." He pointed to the kitchen. "I think we have some in the fridge."

"Ginger ale it is then."

Wayne strolled into the kitchen. There was a lot of noise for just getting a drink but after five minutes or so, he came in carrying a glass filled with the fizzy beverage. He even put in a green bendy straw.

"This okay?"

"It's fine. Thank you." Patrick took the glass and took a sip. Then he set it down on the coffee table.

A minute or so of awkward silence passed a moment before Patrick sat up. "Can I ask you a question?"

Wayne took a seat on the recliner. "Sure thing. What is it?"

"Who are you?"

Wayne sat dumfounded at Patrick's question. All this time and he didn't even know who he was? Poor thing must've felt worse than he thought.

But they hadn't been formally introduced since Patrick was a little kid. With that in mind, it was shocking that Patrick didn't say anything sooner.

Wayne stared down Patrick a moment. The boy's stare was quite intense. Wayne started to say something three times before mentally nixing it.

"It's okay. I'm not scared of you or anything." Patrick cracked a smile. "I trust my mom wouldn't let somebody crazy stay with me. If she thought you were dangerous, you'd be in jail. I was just curious."

Wayne nodded. "You know your mother well. Why don't you tell me what you know already?"

Patrick shrugged. "You were with my mom when she picked me up yesterday. And you're here now so you must've stayed the night to help her take care of me."

Wayne took a deep breath and nodded. "You were pretty sick last night. So we didn't really have time to get introduced. I'm surprised you even remember it." He extended his hand. "My name is Wayne Tempest. I'm a friend of your mom's."

"That's a really cool name." Patrick cracked a grin.

"Thanks." Wayne tapped his fingers together a moment. "Do you remember me at all? You were pretty young when I knew you."

"A little. You used to work with her, right? But then you didn't."

"It's complicated." Wayne tensed his lips. Then shook his head. "There were a lot of reasons that I quit being a cop. You don't have to worry about any of them. But I remembered your mom was the best at what she does and I needed her help to find some missing people. So we're working together to bring them home safe. She had to go do some official stuff about that but she's coming right back. Then you'll have me out of your hair."

"I don't mind if you stay. You seem cool. And Mom could use a friend too."

Wayne chuckled. "I'm not sure she'd agree with that. At least not out loud."

Patrick shrugged. "She thinks she has to be really strong and tough to take care of me. Sometimes I think she doesn't think about what she needs. Maybe even after you crack this case, you can still be friends again?"

"You should just worry about getting better."

"About that . . ." Patrick took a sip of his ginger ale. "Did you really have food poisoning before?"

Wayne nodded. "Unfortunately. Not something I recall fondly. It sucks a lot but tough guys like us can take it."

"How'd you get it?"

"Great Aunt Bessie's crab salad. No question. My grandmother forced me to try it. It didn't even taste good." He laughed. "But it was the last time anyone forced me to eat anything."

Wayne then noticed Patrick staring off into space. "Is everything all right, kiddo?"

"I'm just thinking. About you and my mom."

Wayne raised an eyebrow. "You don't think I'm lying about how I know her, do you?"

"I think you two look cute together. She likes Chinese food a lot, in case you ever wanted to ask her out."

Wayne choked on his saliva. He bent over and knocked his chest a moment. "I think you might have the wrong idea. We're just working a case together."

"Sorry. Didn't mean to get you mad."

Wayne shook his head. "No. I'm not mad at all. It's just . . . your mother and I have some disagreements. And I don't think she sees me as somebody she'd ever like to be friends with in the way you're thinking."

"Mom can sometimes get lonely. She doesn't think I see. Maybe she thinks I'm still too young or that she hides it better. But I know she misses Dad. I just wish she could find somebody one day who could make her happy like that again."

Wayne reached over and gave Patrick a pat on the head. "I'm sure she will. She's a good person."

Patrick turned on his side. "She is. But you seem like a good guy too. I think you'd have a chance." He scrunched down and turned on his side.

Faint snoring in seconds.

Wayne paused a moment. Was Patrick just being nice or did he really believe what he said? It had to be the stomachache talking for now.

Wayne watched Patrick sleep a moment. Wondering about a life where what Patrick said could be reality.

The mahogany gables of St. Lucy's mental hospital made it stand out even several blocks away in the Seaside

Point shore community. A Toyota Lexus cut Julie off as she turned into the parking lot. Then the driver stormed into one of the nine spaces explicitly marked as belonging to one of the doctors on staff. A red-haired woman in shades stepped out and flipped Julie off before heading inside. Not even through the doors and already pissing her off. With every other space reserved, Julie was confined to a dollar-per-hour parking garage a block down the road.

Once inside, Julie did a quick look around for something to justify the saintly name. Nothing. Not even a stray crucifix above a doorway. So much for a religious institution. But there were plenty of artificial flowers and well-polished Victorian furniture.

Eyes still fixated in all directions, she made her way to the front desk.

A secretary was tapping away on a keyboard, stopping only to sip a steaming beverage with so much foam that it smelled more like milk than coffee.

"Can I help you, ma'am?" The woman didn't even turn her head up.

Julie glanced over and saw a novel open on the desk.

She cleared her throat. "I'm here to see a patient."

"I'm sorry, visiting hours don't start for another half-hour."

Julie took out her badge and dangled it in front of the computer screen. "As I said, I'm here to see a patient. Are you able to assist me or do I have ask somebody higher up?"

The woman eyed the badge with a blank stare. "Um . . ." She slammed her book closed and called up a window on the computer. "Which patient would you be wanting to see?" She flashed a toothy smile.

"Macy Harrison."

"Macy Harrison?" The woman peeked up from the keyboard. "You sure you're looking for her? She hasn't had a visitor in five years. Can't imagine what business you'd have with her. She's pretty fragile and I don't think she'd be up to some interrogation so maybe you should—"

"I'm sure she's the one I need to see. The fact that she hasn't had any visitors in five years only strengthens my suspicions. Don't worry. I'm not here to give her trouble. I just need to ask her a few questions. She could hold some information that could be key to saving several lives. Now, please, can you tell me where her room is?"

"Room 316." She pointed. "Take the first elevator to your right to the third floor. Last room in the hall on your left."

"Thank you." Julie took back her badge.

As the doors opened on the third floor, Julie felt like she was in a different institution. No plants. Any visible furniture was worn and tarnished. The floor was clean but cheaper and darker.

She made her way down the hall, passing a few open doors. One had a woman screaming at a male nurse. Cliché and stereotypical, but right in front of her eyes. She gulped a moment, considering that Mrs. Harrison could be in a similar state. Getting information from her might not be as easy as she thought.

Room 316.

She took a deep breath before knocking. The door was open so she stepped inside.

A woman in her late fifties sat by a table playing Solitaire.

The woman appeared stable enough, but sometimes the most unstable of patients were the quiet ones.

"Hello?" Julie took a few steps more into the room. "Mrs. Harrison?" She gave a polite wave.

Macy Harrison looked up from her game and locked eyes with Julie. She smiled. "They took my Kings. And my Jacks. How can you play Solitaire without a full deck?" She giggled. "Cards are always much more fun when you have a second person to play with. But nobody comes to see me. The nurses are nice enough but they are always so busy and if they ever do play with me, they let me win. Bad food and solitaire. Such a boring life. I miss that doctor show that used to be on TV. That one doctor would've played with me."

Julie nervously took a seat next to the woman. Clearly the woman wasn't here unjustly, but maybe she was still lucid enough to give an answer.

"My name is Julie Martel. I'm with the police." She took out her badge but quickly put it back inside. Too intimidating. "I'm here to ask you a few questions."

"You're here about my husband." She shuffled her deck.

"How did you know that?" Julie leaned in a bit closer.

The woman pointed to the television on the wall. "They put it on for me every night so I can watch those people try to win money. I always see the end of the news. The new anchor isn't as good as the old one."

"Did you see something about your husband on the news?"

"He's been gone for five years. I don't think the news would be talking much about him anymore. But I saw about the boy and his father. Kidnapped at gunpoint from the Tunney diner. Drake took me there once. Chicken was a bit undercooked. I figured you cops might finally believe what I told you way back then and would be paying me a visit. Can I interest you in a card game?" She held out the deck.

"If it's okay, I really don't have much time—"

"Nonsense. Good card games don't take much time." She began to deal the cards to Julie. "Let's play a game. You can ask whatever you want while we play."

"I don't know any card games." She shrugged. "I was never a poker gal."

"Me neither. Always liked to make 'em up as I went." She dealt herself five cards. "We each got five cards. We add up the total number of the cards. 'Queen's' as a twelve, 'Ace' as a fourteen. For each hand you win, you get a point. Best of three rounds wins. Sound good?"

Julie took a deep breath. There wasn't time for this but she didn't see any other way. "Very well then." She grouped her cards into one stack.

Mrs. Harrison looked over hers then glanced over at Julie. "Aren't you going to pick them up?"

"I don't have to." She cracked a sneer. "I'm confident that I won."

"Is that a fact?"

"Just a gut feeling. But first, you answer some questions about your husband."

Macy grinned. "Drake was a good man. He didn't do anything to deserve the hand he was dealt."

"He was taken away from you. Doesn't sound like you got dealt a good hand either."

Macy tugged at one of her cards. "You didn't know me way back when. Slept with any guy who'd have me. Anywhere. Didn't matter if they were married or not. Which of course quickly made me a bit of a town pariah. Sad thing is I didn't care about any of that. Least not until some of the guys started fighting back. Started realizing what I was doing wasn't right but didn't quite know how to stop. I figured any beatdowns I got was punishment. If only that was the only punishment I got. I always knew there'd be something worse one day."

Julie reached out and took her hand. "What happened worse?"

"Drake saved me." The woman nodded. "I'd be dead if he didn't find me that night. Bleeding out in an alley after one of my partners had a little too much to drink and didn't like my choice in perfume. Felt disrespected. Drake was the bartender that night. He came out back and clocked the guy something fierce. Took me to the emergency room to get fixed up. He stayed with me. And we fell in love." She held her chest and laughed. "He was a good man. A bit of a hothead with other guys, but never with me." She shook her head. "He was always gentle with me. A perfect gentleman. We were married a year later. It was a beautiful ceremony. He even got a promotion at work. Managed the whole saloon. Made it the hottest spot anywhere for five miles." She laughed.

"Sounds like a great life." Julie smiled. She flashed to when she met her husband. She was still at the academy and he held the door for her at a church concert. She almost didn't return his call the next day, but one of her classmates encouraged her. Wayne.

"We wanted children so badly." Macy's smile faded. "When three years went by and we didn't get pregnant, we went to see a specialist. Turns out both of us had medical conditions that contributed to it. They said it wasn't impossible, but they encouraged us to not get our hopes up. Maybe consider other options. But then a miracle happened. It was Mother's Day. I had gotten sick that morning. Drake thought we should buy a test just to see.

So we went to the dollar store and bought three. They all came back positive. We were going to have a baby. A little baby boy. Chase. We named him Chase. He was perfect. Eight pounds. Blond like his father. Big brown eyes. Such a blessing." She started to cry. She took out a handkerchief and dabbed her eyes.

Julie flashed to when Patrick and Petey were born. How perfect they were. But time was running out. Macy was getting emotional and still hadn't given her anything relevant. Did she even know anything or was this a red herring after all?

"We knew from a young age Chase was special. Just a year old and he was talking full sentences. Having conversations with us. Do you have children, Detective Martel?"

"I have a son." She smiled. "Patrick."

"Just one?"

Julie paused a moment. Her heart sank. It had been years but even the thought of it still stabbed fresh. "He had a twin brother. Petey. We lost him in an accident when they were six. Their father too."

"I am sorry." She reached out and touched Julie's arm. "Still feels like yesterday? You still sometimes think you hear his voice and for one second expect to turn around and see him standing there?"

A tear slipped onto her hand. She quickly wiped her eyes. "I imagine you've been through a lot too."

"Drake loved that boy." She stared at a photograph of a young boy on her night table. "One look into his eyes and you knew he was just so much smarter than you. I always knew my boy would be the smartest kid in the world to me but when other people started using words like 'prodigy' I knew it wasn't just my mama's bias. He was able to do fifth grade work by the time he was five.

He was doing algebra like a pro when he was seven. I have no idea where he gets it. Drake couldn't tell a polynomial from an acronym if his life depended on it, and I only barley passed algebra in high school."

"Some kids are just born smart," Julie said.

"Well, Chase was one of them if I ever saw one. He was winning state championships in spelling, and math. He was so smart. I thought for a time that there was nothing he couldn't ace. I was convinced he'd be in college by the time he turned fourteen. We had to send him to a private tutor because he had outgrown his entire grade school."

"Wow, that's impressive."

"I know. Drake was so proud. I remember when they wanted to promote him to high school work. It was in February. A few days before his birthday. He was turning nine. Drake took him out for dinner to celebrate. I never saw Drake take us to such an expensive restaurant but he was really happy and proud of his little boy. The bill was almost a hundred dollars and he didn't flinch. Even left a twenty-dollar tip. Drake doesn't do that. So you can imagine how happy he was with his boy."

"I'll bet Chase was happy too."

"He was." She picked up the picture and pressed it against her chest. "He loved doing schoolwork, but I never saw his eyes sparkle brighter or his smile happier than when Drake put his arm around him that night and told him that he was the proudest father in the world because he had the world's best son, not just because he was smarter than everybody else but because he was his. I think Chase only cared about that last part. And I still remember clear as day when he said 'I love you, Dad' to him, telling both of us that he had the best parents in the world."

"I'll bet that made you even happier. We always want to feel like we're not letting down our kids, and it's hard to match the feeling when they themselves confirm that you're doing a good job."

"Yes, Chase did that a lot. He never let his smarts go to his head. He knew he had a lot of intelligence and that it made him special, but he was never arrogant about it. He was a true humble genius. He had so much potential. I have no doubt he'd be nationally renowned today for something special."

Julie stared at the picture still clutched in Macy's arms. She hesitated but knew she had to ask the next question. Even if it would hurt. "What happened to him?"

Macy picked up her hand. "Why don't we get back to the card game? I have a '6,' a "4," a "2," a "10," and an "8." That is thirty for me. What do you have?"

Julie turned over her hand, revealing a "9," a "7," an "Ace," a "5," and a "2." "That's thirty-seven. I win this round."

"Lady luck is with you, young lady." She dealt them each a new hand.

She breathed heavily as she looked over her cards.

Julie set hers down without looking at them. "I'd really like it if you continued your story."

Macy slammed her cards down. "We're playing a game. Why do you want to talk about things that shouldn't be talked about?"

"You wouldn't have started to tell me if these things didn't need to be talked about." She gently took the picture from Macy and looked over the curly-haired boy it depicted. "Chase's dad. Drake. Help me find him. Wouldn't Chase want it that way?"

Macy wailed and buried her head in her hands.

Julie got out of her chair and kneeled down next to Macy. She lowered Macy's hands and looked her in the eyes. "Children need your help. I need to bring them home. Help me."

Macy shook her head. "Nobody could bring Chase home to me."

"What happened?"

"It was just about a week after that dinner. Chase and I were at the clothes store. He really didn't want to go but I promised him we'd stop at the bookstore on the way home if he waited quietly. He did. For over an hour. Just so I could try on a dress I'd never wear anyway. But it was fifty percent off." She gulped. "I think he counted ceiling tiles. Or hangers on a rack. He was always counting something. I was almost ready to leave, but he had to go the bathroom. That was always his weakness. He had a tiny bladder. Couldn't even sit through *E.T.* without pausing three times. I really didn't like him going alone. He was small for his age. I used to take him in the ladies room, but he was long since past that. His dad was at work and he couldn't wait until we got home. So I let him go in alone. It was a small store. He'd be safe. But he didn't come out. After twenty minutes, I went in to check on him. It was empty. I called for him. He wasn't there. I checked every stall. Twice. Maybe he was hiding. Or passed out. But he was gone. My little boy was gone."

Macy began to breathe heavy.

Maybe Julie should call a nurse. Maybe this was a mistake.

"It's okay, Macy." Julie pulled her into a hug. "It's okay. If this is too much for you, I'll stop asking."

Macy shook her head. "No, you have to understand it

all." She pulled back. "You were right before. I just need a minute."

"Take all the time you need."

Macy took a few deep breaths. "I called the police. I called Drake. He was there in five minutes. He worked on the other side of town. The rest of that day is a blur. Hell, the rest of that week is a blur. All I remember clearly is that empty house. His empty room. His desk still had some biology homework on it. Cottonheart was on his bed. He was Chase's teddy bear. He was a genius, but he still loved that bear. I walked to his bed and just laid there. I pressed that bear to my chest and cried. Maybe this was the punishment I was dreading for years. I just had this stab in my chest telling me . . ."

"It wasn't your fault. Every parent blames themselves." Her throat burned. "It doesn't make sense but we do it."

"They looked for a week with no trace of him." She shook her head. "It was a Thursday afternoon. They were searching a small wooded area behind a local church. Off the highway. Drake was the one who saw him. Rested against a tree. Our Chase. His eyes were wide open and he didn't have any clothes on. I was right behind him. I just stood there. Drake picked him up and cradled him like he did when Chase was a baby. They told him not to contaminate the scene but he knocked them away. Then, he cried. He cried so hard. I never heard him cry like that before. Or ever again."

Julie felt a sharp pain in the pit of her stomach. She remembered that smoking car. That broken glass surrounding her little boy and the man she loved.

"When he saw me, he tried to hide the body. But I could see everything. One look and I knew. My baby was gone. I didn't have to wait for any autopsy report to know what some monster did to my little angel. When they zipped him up, his eyes were closed. Drake must've done it when I wasn't looking. He didn't want me to look into those beautiful eyes when they were empty."

Julie nodded. "You don't forget a look like that." Milo. Damien. Nina. Her friends. Her godchild. Like family. Murdered in their own home.

"He was only dead five hours when Drake found him. That monster tortured my little boy for a whole week. He must've been so scared, and I wasn't there to protect him. He was a genius, but he was still just a little boy."

Macy wailed louder.

Julie hugged her tighter. She pulled Macy close to her. She'd forced a mother to relive her child's murder. All for a clue that may not even lead anywhere. "It's okay. It's okay." She didn't believe her own words.

"They told us to pick a suit to bury him in. We didn't want to do open casket but the director told us showing people he was at peace would help them have closure. Do you know how hard it is to pick a suit to help people forget that a little boy was slaughtered?"

Julie didn't answer. The truthful answer wouldn't help Macy.

"My life was over the moment they lowered his casket into the ground. Drake never smiled again. He barely even talked to me. He got fired after he gave up working and then he just did odd jobs around town. Mostly from friends who pitied him. We never ate together. We never decorated the house for Christmas again. He stopped going to church. We never even talked about Chase. If I ever tried to talk about him, Drake would yell and leave the house. The only time he ever talked to me was after I had a nightmare. But without coping together, the nightmares only got worse. Soon they escalated into nervous breakdowns and eventually I had to come here. It's been fifteen years now. Still no progress."

"Did they ever catch the guy who killed Chase?"

She shrugged. "They caught him. They convicted him. They let him see what happens in prison to guys who do what he did. Then they executed him. Justice was served. I'm glad no other child can ever go through what poor Chase did at that monster's hands, and the fact that he's burning in Hell right now doesn't keep me up at night. But Chase is still dead. I don't want for justice, but I still want for Chase. For Drake."

"If you don't mind my asking, if you were in here, how did you witness your husband being kidnapped? There's a report stating you saw him abducted."

"For some reason, every Mother's Day, he still came and took me out to the café down the street a bit. We'd walk there and he'd be somewhat gentle again. He never came any other time, but always on Mother's Day. He did it for a good ten years. The last year, though . . . he forgot to sign me out and nobody saw him take me out. When we were leaving the restaurant, they came up behind him and drugged him. They pushed him into a limo."

"Who did?"

"Two men in black outfits. I didn't get a good look at them. But I panicked. I ran. I don't remember what happened until the orderlies found me roaming the streets. It was dark by that point. I tried to tell them what happened, but they just assumed I was hallucinating because I was off my meds. I called the police that night but they took the phone from me before I could finish. I heard them explain and hoped maybe they would check into it just in case. But Drake never came back."

"Well, I can promise you, Mrs. Harrison. I'm taking it seriously." She took out a notepad. "Is there anything about the car you remember that can help us find it? Even the smallest detail."

"It was a limo. I didn't see the license plate. But Drake did call me about two months later."

"He called?" She shot to her feet. Could this be it?

Macy nodded. "Yes, that must be why nobody ever believed he was kidnapped. All he said was 'Columbia Court,' and then he was cut off."

"Did that mean anything to you?"

"I don't know. It sounded so familiar but I can't place it. But I always knew it was him telling me where he was. I tried to get them to listen. To tell somebody to check there. But they never did. By now, I don't think anyone will ever find him. He's with Chase now."

Julie bit her lip. Drake was probably still alive. Doing heinous things even if it was at gunpoint. "I'll find him. I promise you."

Macy smiled and looked down at her cards. "So what did you get this time?"

Julie slid the cards over to her. "Only thirty-five. I think you'll win this round."

Macy shook her head. "Think again. I got thirty-four. Looks like you win the game." She extended her hand to Julie. "I hope you find everybody you're looking for. Bring somebody's child home safe."

Julie shook her hand. "Thanks to you, maybe now I can."

As Julie walked out, Macy's story echoed in her mind. As a homicide detective, it was a story all too familiar. When would people learn to stop doing such horrible things to the most innocent people?

"Columbia Court." It wasn't much, but it was something. She kept repeating it in her mind, trying to figure out what it could mean.

Julie checked the time as she walked up to her front door. 4:30. Reporting to her father had taken much longer than expected. One point led to another and before she knew it, she was deeply engrossed in finding any information they could, all locations in the country with such a name. So far, they had a long and intimidating list that Kevin promised to have narrowed down by the morning. She'd offered to take half, but a sick son at home gave her a legitimate pass.

She pushed open the front door. "I am so sorry that I was gone so long. I lost track of time, but I think we got a good lead."

Wayne and Patrick were both asleep.

On the TV, a romantic comedy was concluding as the happy couple united in a passionate kiss to overly sentimental and bombastic music.

Julie shook her head. "Men." She turned the TV off.

Wayne shot up from the recliner. Awake. "Hey, I was watching that."

She smirked. "Well, well, well. Wayne Tempest, secret fan of chick flicks."

"Uh, I was asleep." He blushed and wiped his brow with his sleeve. "Must've come on after the other thing we were watching."

"If you say so." She winked and turned to Patrick.

Patrick yawned and pushed himself up. "Mom, you're home?"

Julie sat down next to him. "Yes, I am." She felt his

head. "How're you feeling?"

"Like crap."

She touched his cheeks. Then his chest. Not as clammy or warm. "Was Wayne nice to you?"

"He was cool."

"Did you eat anything yet?"

He shook his head. "No. I still feel like if I eat, I'll throw up. I think I should just wait until tomorrow. But Wayne gave me ginger ale, so that's helping a little."

"I'll let you off the hook today." She fluffed his pillow and nudged him to lay down again. "But tomorrow you need to try and eat something."

"I'm not cleaning it up when I throw it up." He stuck his tongue out.

Julie sighed. "Nice try, young man. But you should know your mother better than to think that would work on her." She stuck her tongue out, too, and ruffled his hair. "Get some more rest."

Patrick nodded and turned on his side. Asleep again in minutes.

8:30PM. Patrick had showered and changed into his pajamas. He even kept down a bowl of chicken noodle soup.

After carrying him to bed, Julie lightly felt his forehead. Better still than the afternoon. His color was returning. He still looked ill and far from his usual self, but she was beginning to feel like the worst was behind them.

She pulled the covers over him. "Sleep well. And feel better." She quietly closed the door and went back downstairs.

Before she even reached the bottom step, there was a loud pound on the door. "Did Dad lose his key again?"

She went to answer it.

Wayne stepped in front of her. "Actually, I think that's for me."

He marched to the door with his wallet in hand. He took a steaming brown paper bag from the man at the door and handed him a twenty.

"I bought us some dinner." Wayne held out the bag and signaled for her to follow him.

"Dinner? You mean you didn't just heat up one of those frozen burritos in the freezer?"

Julie followed him into the kitchen. Before he could even open the bag, the heavenly and unmistakable aroma that all Chinese food had filled the entire house.

He tore open the bag. "Okay, I got sesame chicken, egg foo young, pepper steak, pork and broccoli, wonton soup, lo mein, and two eggrolls." He also took out sauce packets, fortune cookies, and bamboo chopsticks and tossed them on the table. "Take your pick and dig in."

She grabbed a container and a pair of chopsticks and took a bite. "You don't pull any punches when it comes to dinner, do you?"

"I know a good place. Good specials and the owner gives me half off every time because I helped catch the guy who was robbing them every week."

"You better watch it. I might have you buying us dinner more often." She slurped a noodle. "How did you know I'm big on Chinese food? Or did you just guess?"

"Patrick told me." He gripped a piece of pork with his chopsticks. "He even told me what your favorite foods were." He dropped the pork but quickly caught it and threw it into his mouth with his hand.

She took a seat. "That's Patrick. Speaking of which, I want to hear about your day first."

He took a seat. "My day?" He raised an eyebrow.

"You spent a day with Patrick. You must have something to say about him."

"He's sick. He slept most of the time. But he's a good kid. Just like I remember. Polite. Respectful. Precocious. Pretty much me at his age."

She laughed. "You expect me to believe you were anything like Patrick at his age?"

He tossed a piece of broccoli into his mouth. "It's true. And I think he knows it too. He likes me."

"Really?"

"Yeah. He even said we'd make a cute couple." He winked at her.

"Kids and their imaginations."

"Yeah . . ."

She pushed her food away. "But before we get too distracted, we have a lot to talk about. We have a new lead and maybe some new angles to profile. I think Drake Harrison might've left us with the clue we needed. Columbia Court. It might be part of an address where he's being held, or maybe just a street adjacent. I don't know."

Wayne sat silent a moment. "You think it's legit? Not just some rambling or meaningless name?"

She shook her head. "It meant enough for him to risk calling his wife just to tell her. Maybe it's not a full address, but it's more than we've ever had. We're close, Wayne. We're going to find them. And we're going to bring them home."

He nodded. "But can we find them in time? Now that bodies are starting to turn up, maybe we're already too late?"

"Don't think that way." She reached out and took his hand. "You've given three years of your life to finding these people and bringing them back safe. You need to have a little faith that we'll do that."

He turned away. "I've spent so much time trading faith and doubt these last three years that I'm not sure which one is real and which one is the illusion anymore. Sometimes I just feel that no matter what I do, they've been doomed from the start and I've just been a meaningless footnote always one day too late to do anything. No matter how this ends, I want to feel like it mattered that I was involved. That all this time led to something good. If all that's left is a pile of bodies . . ."

He took another bite and closed his eyes.

Still, she saw a single tear slip out. He probably didn't even feel it. But it was real. His pain was real. And Julie knew she couldn't rest until everyone had closure. Including Wayne.

CHAPTER 8

Aaron and his father had been at the Prescott estate for one week. A painfully slow and frightening week.

Aaron recalled the days after his mother died. They were slow like this. When clocks seemed broken. When days were spent wishing for nights and nights spent wishing for morning.

At least he had friends. Emily. Ryan. Father Doyle. These were good people. They cared about him and he cared about them. If he had to wake up every morning fearful of dying, at least he knew he wasn't alone.

Every day they spent at least eight hours filming scenes that they could only loosely determine a connection among. Where they even for the same movie? They had enough for a three-night miniseries. Yet Lincoln had announced that they barely had an hour's worth of actual footage.

Every scene called for Jeremy to be abusive to Aaron. Verbally. Physically. It was just part of the act. The punches didn't mean anything. The curses were just scripted. Aaron told himself this with every tear. It was fake. But it hurt. Just hearing those words on his father's lips. "I hate you. I wish you were aborted." It didn't matter that they were fake. He couldn't unhear them.

After filming is usually when Ryan would sneak by. Sometimes those visits were the only things that could keep Aaron together. Ryan didn't seem to care that he was always crying. Maybe he got it. Ryan didn't ever cry in front of him. But Aaron could see in his eyes that he'd cried to himself many nights.

But Ryan always had a good way to distract Aaron from how bad things were. He made up games they could play with just fingers. Numbers. Playing cards. Old towels. There wasn't anything around Ryan couldn't make fun. It was like he'd spent his entire life looking for the good in even the most boring things. Maybe that was all he had.

Emily. Every evening, she hung on Aaron. Asking him to play with her. Hide and seek was her favorite. She wasn't very good at it. Every time he even got close, she began to giggle and he'd have to pretend not to see her just so he wouldn't find her too fast. At night, she'd always ask him to read her a story. The only books they had were a Bible and another Catholic book that Father Doyle had on him. They were too small to see well and Emily couldn't understand them well either. So Aaron retold her the Bible stories as he remembered them from the children's Bible he had as a kid. David and Goliath. Jonah and the Whale. Jesus healing the girl who had died. Emily loved hearing about these people as Aaron told them. And after every story, Aaron found himself loving them more too. Maybe telling them to somebody who hadn't heard them every day like he had painted them in a new perspective.

Father Doyle was a good man. Aaron hadn't ever known a priest before. He always just thought that they were like the Catholic version of his Dad who just wore fancier clothes. But Father Doyle wasn't just that. Every day, he always stopped what he was doing at least six times a day to read from his other prayer book. He called it 'The Divine Office.' Aaron didn't know what it meant but if Father Doyle did it every day, it must've been important. He also had a rosary on him at all times. He prayed that too every day. When he asked Father Doyle why, he said, "Because it's like holding Mary's hand. And if you're close to Mary, you're close to Jesus. Because Jesus is always close to His mother."

Aaron hadn't thought of that before, but it made sense. He thought of asking his dad but he didn't want to start any fights. But he watched Father Doyle pray every day. Every time he saw him praying, he said a prayer of his own too. Even if it was just "I love you, God."

Maude and Therese tried to keep things feeling as normal as possible. They cooked meals that reminded Aaron of his mother's cooking. They kept everybody tidy and on schedule. Being late for their scenes wasn't an option. After just a few days, Aaron felt like life had always been this way, and he didn't even need them to keep him on time.

Dinah was a strange girl. She always went out of her way to spend time with Aaron. She would always ask him questions about himself but never seem to really listen or care about what he said. As long as he was saying something to her. She was always watching just a little too closely. He wanted to say something but he never did. He didn't want to hurt her feelings, even if it meant feeling uncomfortable from time to time. She was probably just trying to feel close to somebody too.

Drake sat alone in silence most of the time. The only time he ever talked to anybody was to insult them or make a mean comment. Aaron never saw him smile. Not even once. Was he mad, or just sad? Aaron went to approach him one time but Drake rolled his eyes and walked away before he even heard a word.

Aaron felt his dad grow more distant as the week went by. He had fewer encouragements. Less cheer. In the beginning, he'd quoted him Scripture to comfort him. By the end of the week, he could barely touch Aaron. Maybe it was all the hitting. All the cursing. Those cutting words. After all he'd been forced to do to his only child, maybe he just couldn't look him in the eyes anymore.

Lincoln's antics became the norm. Impressed with a performance one minutes, enraged at a mistake the next. He could be gentle and encouraging and then cold and ferocious. There were moments where Aaron felt like Lincoln actually wanted him to do well and that he wouldn't actually hurt him. Other times his voice pierced so sharply into Aaron's chest that Aaron had to feel to make sure there wasn't already a knife cutting into his heart. Did Lincoln have any intentions to keep him around? Was he enjoying watching them suffer? Or did he simply not care? Or even notice.

One week imprisoned in the Prescott estate. Aaron was still alive. But a part of him inside was dead. The part of him that believed that people could still be free. That he could wake up in the morning without a relentless and nagging fear that he wouldn't be alive when the sun came up tomorrow.

CHAPTER 9

"I'm going to beat you." Emily's big blue eyes stared down Aaron. So innocent and yet there was a determined fire in them.

"No way. I'm going to win." His eyes burned but he had to make it look good when he let her win. He couldn't just blink too early or she'd know.

"I always win staring contests." She stuck out her tongue. "I beat out Dinah all the time. And I always beat Billy too."

"Billy?"

"He was a boy here before you." She frowned. "But he went away."

Aaron's eyes thrust close and he threw his hands over them. To hide the tear from her.

Emily jumped up and hugged him. "I win. See? I told you I would win." She planted butterfly kisses on his cheek.

"Emily, it's getting late." Dinah hopped off her bed and went to swoop up Emily. "You gotta get your bath and go to bed."

"I don't want to." She rolled away from Dinah.

"Emily, don't be naughty." She grabbed Emily by the arm. "You should be in bed already."

"I'm not being naughty." She yanked her arm back. "I just want to play some more." She hopped in Aaron's lap.

Dinah's face grew red. "Do you want me to tell Maude and Therese on you?" She leaned in close to Emily. "I'm not going to ask again."

"I'm being good." She stuck out her tongue. "You're not the boss of me."

Dinah threw her hands in the air. "Don't blame me when you get in trouble." She walked off, a slight stomp in each step.

Emily folded her arms and shook her head. "She's too bossy."

Aaron shrugged. "But you probably should get to bed." He put his arm around her. "You need your sleep if you want to get strong."

"But I wanna play some more with you." She leaned her head against his chest. "You're fun. And I never had a big brother before."

"What about Billy?"

"Well, he was kind of like one but he was always too scared to really play with me." She tapped him on the nose. "You're cool. You play with me. I like having a big brother."

"And I like having a little sister." He helped her to her feet. "But you still gotta do what the grown-ups tell you. It's kind of the rules of being a kid."

Emily shook her head. "I don't like being a kid. I want to be big like all of them and then I could do anything I want."

Aaron chuckled. "You'll be big one day." The lump in his throat began to throb. But he couldn't tell her the truth. Even if kind lies knotted his stomach. "But you're not big yet. You gotta do what you're told. So when Dinah comes back, you should go take your bath and then go to bed. We can play some more in the morning."

"Why don't you take a bath with me?"

Aaron laughed. "I don't think that's a good idea. You're a little girl, remember? Those are things boys and girls don't do together."

Emily pouted. "But Dinah never lets me make bubbles and she always makes the water too cold."

Aaron shrugged. "Maybe if you ask her really nice, she'll make it warm. I'll tell you what. I can read you a bedtime story when you get out if you want."

Her frown turned into a smile. "I love stories. Can you read me the one about Daniel again?"

He nodded. "But only if you're a good girl and don't give Dinah any trouble."

"What if the water gets me again? Who's going to save me? Dinah's not gonna save me. She'd let me get eaten by crocodiles."

Aaron laughed. "I used to think there were crocodiles in the bathtub too. I used to be so scared of taking a bath. But I never did see a crocodile. My mom used to say that if you think you saw a crocodile in the bathtub, just to ask Jonah to come and take it away."

"Jonah? Who's that?"

"He was the man eaten by a whale in the Bible. He didn't want to do what God asked him. So he got eaten by a whale and had to stay there for three whole days until he said he'd do what God wanted. Then God made the whale throw him up. And ever since then, anything in the water is scared of him. So whales, crocodiles, they don't go anywhere near you if you ask Jonah to take them away."

Emily threw off her shirt. "Okay. I'll take a bath. But

only a fast one. I still think there are crocodiles in there."

She strutted off to the bathroom.

Dinah walked back in to the room. "Well, they aren't going to help me. They coddle her all the time. She never has to do anything she doesn't want to do unless it's Lincoln making her do it."

Aaron pointed to the bathroom. "She's in there waiting for you."

Emily poked her head out of the bathroom. "Yeah, I'm waiting."

"How did you get her to go?"

Aaron stood up. "I asked her nicely. Maybe you can try being nice to her." He patted Dinah on the shoulder and started for the door.

"Aaron." Dinah grabbed his arm.

Aaron turned to her. "Yeah?"

Dinah froze. She released his arm. "It's nothing."

"Are you okay?"

Dinah nodded. "I'll see you soon. Let me go help her." She disappeared into the bathroom and closed the door.

Aaron watched the closed door a moment. He could hear the water running after a moment coupled with Emily's laughter. She had such a cute laugh. He wondered what Dinah's laugh sounded like. He hadn't heard her really laugh since he met her. Just fake laughs. The laughs she forced when she was trying not to tell him something. Not that she had to tell him.

It was almost midnight but Jeremy was still awake. He sat on the edge of his bed with the door ajar. Waiting.

Then footsteps broke through the silence.

He peeked out the door and saw Therese sneaking

out of her room. Just like she did almost every night.

She checked to make sure nobody saw as she went for the door. Her whole body was shaking, but she kept it controlled. Like she knew what to expect. Even if it still terrified her. He'd seen that look on so many of his congregation before.

He went to run after her.

A strong hand pulled him back.

He spun around. Drake.

"You really don't want to go after her." Drake let go of his arm. "And I'm not saying this just to be an ass."

Jeremy took a step away from the bulky man. "And why is that? None of us are just allowed to leave our chambers in the middle of the night, and you're not going to convince me that she's just an overnight maid service for Prescott."

"She has her reasons. If she's able to do it every night, it's probably a good one. None of us need you starting trouble by following her."

"Something's going on with her." Jeremy turned to the doorway. "I've seen people who are caught in something they don't want to be caught in before." He shot Drake a fierce scowl. "I'm a pastor for crying out loud. I work to help people like her."

"You're not a pastor anymore." Drake shoved Jeremy to the ground. "You're an actor. The sooner you remember that, the better."

"Does Father Doyle forget he's a priest?" Jeremy tried to get up.

"Unfortunately not." Drake shoved him back down again. He slammed his foot on Jeremy's back. "Frankly, him always making a racket every Sunday morning . . . every day really. And always having people run to tell him every little thing they've done wrong? It all pisses me off." He kicked Jeremy onto his stomach. "This might surprise you but I don't get off on hurting people. I'm just a survivor. And to survive here, you do what you are told and you don't call unneeded attention to yourself. You make yourself somebody Lincoln wants to keep around. If you do that, you live longer. If you make a pest of yourself, you don't. Now it doesn't make much difference to me what happens to you or the kid. But for your own good, get on Lincoln's good side and don't emulate the priest."

Jeremy struggled to his feet. "What happened to make you so bitter?" He grabbed the edge of his bed to steady himself. "Were you always like this or was there a time you remembered you were a person?"

Drake snorted. "I guess there was a time I was naïve like you. If I didn't grow up, I'd probably be dead by now. Life sucks. And you can't expect nothing out of it."

"That's a sad worldview."

"You call it sad. I call it practical."

Father Doyle appeared between them. Their fighting must've woken him up. "Keep the faith, Jeremy. I admire your concern for Therese." He turned to Drake with a stern glare. "Drake really doesn't believe any of what he told you. It's just what he tells himself to cope with everything that's happened to him. Bitter lies are sometimes easier to swallow than bitter truth. His lies give him the comfort of some meaningless mess of a world to avoid dealing with questions of why he has pain in his heart." Father Doyle took Jeremy by the shoulders. "I feel for him. Because of what was taken from him, but more so because of what he's thrown away because of it."

Drake grunted and returned to his bed.

Jeremy looked Father Doyle in the eyes. "Do you know where she goes every night?"

Father Doyle sighed. He nodded. "She does it to protect us. I've tried to talk to her. I don't know what to advise her anymore. She's so afraid. And she's not wrong to be." He wiped aside a tear. "They'd kill her if she didn't. But she's being destroyed by it anyway, in a much slower and more dangerous way."

Chills shot up Jeremy's limbs. "Where does she go?" He had to help her. Whatever it was.

Father Doyle looked away. "It's best that you don't know. There's nothing you can do to stop it."

"Why don't you let me be the judge of that?"

"I'm sorry. I can't." He placed his hand on Jeremy's shoulder. "You know I can't."

Jeremy threw the priest's hand away. "Then I'm going to go find out myself." He ran into the living room. Toward the door.

Father Doyle grabbed his shoulder. "You could get yourself killed."

Jeremy turned to him. "There's no greater love than to lay down one's life for one's friends."

"What about Aaron?"

"How could I look him in the eye if I let my safety keep me from helping somebody in need?"

Father Doyle let him go. He smiled. "You're a good man. And you're right. I'm ashamed. Sometimes surviving becomes so much the focus that we get too used to the status quo." Father Doyle led him to the door. "I'll come with you. I know the layout better."

Jeremy got between the priest and the door. "No. You stay here. You weren't wrong. This is dangerous." He gulped. "If anything happens to me, you can't let Mr. Sunshine be the only man here. You're a good man. A good priest. This is my fight. I'm the crazy new guy looking to make things better. I'll do this myself."

"May God be with you. And please be careful."

Jeremy nodded and looked around. "Alright, what can I use to bust out of this place?"

Father Doyle turned the knob and pushed the door open. "That seems a bit excessive, doesn't it?"

"You mean . . ." Jeremy took a step outside their quarters. Into the main halls of the house.

Father Doyle shrugged. "It's more of a test than anything." He stared down the hall. "And people like Therese have to get out." He turned to Jeremy. "But don't get any ideas about running. There are guards everywhere. You'd probably be dead before you could even make it down the stairs. Somebody made it outside once. A bullet flew through his head the moment his feet hit the porch. They don't lock this door because they don't have to."

"I understand. And thank you."

He turned to check for guards. Coast was clear. Then he quietly tiptoed off down the halls. Wherever Therese was, it wasn't somewhere good. He'd find her and put an end to it. Even if it meant a bullet in his head.

Father Doyle watched from the doorway until Jeremy disappeared around a corner. "Watch over him, God. He's a braver man than me. His son needs his father. Don't let his good deed cost them both their lives."

Father Doyle returned to the bedroom.

Drake was waiting by the door with folded arms. "You really just watched the dope walk to certain death."

"I have hope. So does he. Who am I to talk a man out

of doing what is right just because it's dangerous? What kind of priest would that make me?"

Drake leaned in close. "A not dead one."

Father Doyle sat on his bed and took out his Divine Office book. "I didn't become ordained to not die. And I doubt he became a pastor for safety and security."

Drake lay back down. "If Lincoln decides to make him watch his son get his throat slit as punishment, you both might be reevaluating your philosophies."

"Is making everyone else as miserable as you really all you live for? Do you really think that's what your son would want?"

Drake threw himself from his bed and tackled Father Doyle to the floor. "Screw you!" He placed his hands on the priest's throat. "You don't have any place saying what my son would want. You didn't know him. He's dead." A tear fell onto Father Doyle's face. "So what he wants doesn't matter anyway. I'm sure he wanted to come home to Mommy and Daddy, but he's still in the ground. So stop your pontificating about crap you don't know."

"I'm sorry, Drake. I'm sorry you lost the will to love."

"No loving God would've let my boy go through what he did. Don't you think I'd like the comfort of Heaven? Of thinking that there's somebody up there who gives a damn? But there isn't. I've been in hell since I found my boy under that tree. Knowing there isn't any greater good to it all." He loosened his grip.

"God never promised us that we wouldn't suffer in this life. He watched his son die by the most painful method of execution known to man." Father Doyle threw the man off of him. "Being Christian isn't a proposition for easy. The crosses we each have to carry . . . there's a purpose to them."

Drake returned to his bed. "More religious bull. Feeble attempts to make a world where everything is crap smell a little better."

Father Doyle stood up and brushed off his cassock. "Or maybe your sentiments are just doubter's propaganda to help cope with the fact that God allows bad things to happen on earth because this place isn't our permanent home. Some people just want to make earth out to be Heaven and they are the ones hit the hardest when the reality of a fallen world shows itself."

Drake grunted as he turned away. "As long as Reverend Know-it-all doesn't ruin things for the rest of us. If he does, I'll save Prescott the trouble of writing him a death scene."

Jeremy had made it around at least three turns in the labyrinthine upstairs of the Prescott estate before he had to stop and take a breath. How did somebody as simple-minded as Lincoln get from one place to another?

Jeremy looked around. Still no guards up here. He'd expected to have a lot more difficulty traversing about.

He walked by the stairs.

He could see the front door.

There was nobody there. Maybe it was like the door to their chambers. All a test. Empty fear.

For just one second, he was tempted to run. Even if it meant leaving Aaron behind. He'd have cops on the place before dawn.

But Lincoln wasn't that dumb. He could never have kept people here for years unless there was actual armed security. The fact that he didn't see it is probably what would get him killed if he tried something that reckless. This night rescue itself was already too big a risk.

He continued down the halls, looking for any trace of Therese. A lighted room. Whispers of a secret meeting. Even the swish of a mop on porcelain. But the house was so quiet that the floors didn't even creak much as he walked.

Then he noticed one of the doors was slightly ajar. There was a dim light coming from inside. Could this be it?

He peaked inside. It was a bedroom.

"You shouldn't be here."

He jumped back. He'd been discovered. A shadowed figure stood in the doorway.

He breathed in the hard, dry air to avoid shouting and giving himself away. But why? He was found out. In a matter of seconds, bullets would fly through his chest and take him down.

Five seconds later and he was still standing.

He opened his eyes and noticed that the dark silhouette in the doorway was short. Almost a whole foot shorter than him. Barely taller than Aaron.

He focused his eyes until he could see the face better. It was a boy.

"You're Ryan, right?" He took a step closer. "You know Aaron. He's been talking about you."

"Yeah that's me." Ryan looked around to see if anybody was coming. "Look, I don't know what you're looking for but you really shouldn't be here. Go back to your room before my dad finds you. He doesn't like it when people roam around. Not even me. You're lucky I saw you first and not him."

"I'm looking for somebody. One of the others. She left and I am trying to find her."

Ryan shook his head. "You gotta worry about you

and Aaron. Things like this are what get you killed sooner. Aaron needs you alive and he needs to stay alive." He gulped and looked around again. "I'm going to bed before I wake my dad up. That's what you should do. Now." Then the boy pulled his door closed.

Jeremy considered all the boy must've seen his father do. He knew things none of them did. Voices inside screamed for him to heed the child's advice. Play it safe and go back. If only for Aaron. But could he look his son in the eye if he chickened out? He knew he'd never get another chance like this. And could he trust the child of his captor? The boy seemed nice enough and Aaron liked him, but that could just make the kid much more dangerous. Maybe going back is exactly what would get him caught.

He ventured further down the hall.

He reached the end and stopped.

He heard noises coming from the master bedroom. Maybe muffled moans? It was too faint to say for sure.

He turned to the room and gently turned the knob. Unlocked? Carelessness? A trap?

Jeremy took a deep breath and pushed the door open. He went inside, prepared to be shot dead on the spot.

A light then switched on and he saw Bradford Prescott on top of Therese in bed. They were covered with sheets.

Jeremy charged the man. He grabbed Bradford and threw him onto the floor. "You pig." He went for the throat.

Therese screamed.

Two goons yanked Jeremy off of Bradford and slammed him against a wall, sending a painting of a lark crashing to the ground.

Bradford got to his feet and walked over to Jeremy.

"Now that was certainly rude." He leaned in close. "I was almost finished."

Jeremy spat in the man's face. "You are disgusting, raping a defenseless girl. So that's why you let your son get away with this. You do get something out of it."

Bradford wiped off his face with one of the bed sheets. "Did it look like I was raping her?" He shot the girl a stern look. "She is a consenting adult."

"Like hell she is." He looked at the mortified woman pressing the sheets against her chest. "What did you do? Threaten her life? Threaten the kids? She would never take you willingly unless she was afraid you'd kill somebody she cared about."

"Jeremy, stop it." Therese's face was wet with tears. "He's right. And I'm fine."

Jeremy shook his head. "No you're not. You can't lie to me. I've seen that look in your eyes before. I know, Therese."

"Daddy. I heard commotion." Lincoln bolted in wearing blue polka dot pajamas. "What the hell is going on?"

Bradford slipped into a housecoat. "I was just enjoying a lovely evening with this young lady here. When this arrogant jerk came storming in."

Lincoln turned his head down. "That's not good at all." He then took a swing and punched Jeremy in the stomach.

Jeremy winced. But he held in his screams. This creep didn't deserve the satisfaction.

Lincoln took out a knife. "I thought as a pastor you'd be a bit more abiding of rules."

"He's raping a defenseless young woman." He turned to her, still gasping for air but more nauseated over the thought of her letting that animal have his way with her.

"Any rule saying I can't defend her deserves to be broken."

Lincoln walked up to Jeremy. "Well, I'll show you how I deal with rule breakers." He placed the knife against Jeremy's throat. "I'll tell Aaron your character got cut."

Therese jumped up from the bed. She threw herself at Lincoln's feet. "Please, Mr. Prescott. It's my fault he's here. I told him to follow me. He did it for me. Punish me if you have to punish anyone. I was scared and he was new. He doesn't know the rules that well yet. Give him one more chance. You punished him. He's learned his lesson."

Bradford grabbed her by the arm "Don't defend him. He's not worth it."

"I'm not defending him." She pulled her arm free. "I'm telling the truth. Just like I was telling the truth about this being consensual." She shot Bradford a warning glare. "Let him go, please."

Lincoln pressed the blade against Jeremy's throat. "He attacked my father." He drew a small drop of blood. "He doesn't get to go on like he just tripped and knocked over a vase."

She wrapped her arms around Bradford. "You're his father. This is your house. You can order him to stop." She kissed his cheek. "If he and that boy die because of me, I might go crazy and do something stupid. Might get me killed."

Bradford sat down on the bed. "Very well." He raised his hand to Lincoln. "I'm your father, Lincoln. And I order you not to kill him. At least not tonight. The cameras aren't rolling, after all."

Lincoln took a deep breath and stepped back. "You're lucky the girl went to bat for you, Pastor." He pointed the blade at Jeremy's chest. "That's the only reason you'll wake up tomorrow."

He then took another punch. To Jeremy's eye.

Jeremy squeezed his lips even tighter to not scream.

The goons released him to crumple to the ground.

"I'm going back to bed." Lincoln kept his eyes on Jeremy. "Get both of them back to their chambers."

He turned and left, muttering to himself.

Bradford patted Therese on the shoulder. "Go back to your chambers. I'll see you again." He kissed her on the lips and smiled. "Thank you for a great night."

She turned away and ran to Jeremy. "Let me help you up." She extended her hand.

He took it and pulled himself to his feet. "You didn't have to lie to save me."

Bradford walked to his bathroom. "You really think you're saved, Pastor? Pity." He shook his head and closed himself into the bathroom.

Jeremy scowled as the goons stood watching him like stone statues. "Get dressed and let's get you home."

She threw on her robe and followed Jeremy into the halls.

"Are you okay?" She looked him over. "Did he break anything?"

"Am I okay?" Jeremy placed his hand on her shoulder. "You were the one raped."

She shook her head. "It's not rape."

"It's not love. If you told the cops, they'd say it was rape. What else can you call it?"

"Keeping us safe. By keeping him happy."

"And here I thought Lincoln was the psychopath and this guy was just some dolt bankrolling it."

"He can make things good for us. Or worse. He's done

both. Usually based on how much of a fight we put up."

"We?" He raised an eyebrow. "You're not the only one? Has he come for Dinah?"

They arrived at their room. She opened the door. "You're still new here. You still are operating on the way things worked out there. On justice. That's not the way things go in here. In here, you do what they say and they let you live longer. That's the only law that matters here. It's about dying verses not dying. Maybe I'm still naïve like you, but I think not dying is a lot better. No matter how much it sucks here."

He closed the door to their quarters behind him. "I'm sorry about coming after you. But I knew something wasn't right. You're worth more than that."

"We have it good right now. He likes me and if he likes one of us, he can keep Lincoln on a tighter leash."

"Lincoln kills people in his films." He sat her down on the sofa. "How is he on a leash?"

"I refused the first time." She shivered. "There was another guy here. My age. Strong. Wanted to protect everyone. The night after I refused, Lincoln wrote a scene where Drake put a bullet through his head. And they filmed it right in front of me." She pointed to the corner. "In this room." She swallowed hard. "I still have nightmares about it. Almost every night. Yes, he still kills us, but doing what they ask makes them kill us less. We have more time together."

"I'm sorry."

"Don't be sorry." She took his hand. "Sorry doesn't help. Just stay alive. For as long as we can, we have to stay alive."

Jeremy looked back at the door. Thinking of the halls on the other side. "Where does he put the bodies after he kills them? So nobody finds them or smells them?"

"There's a place. In the basement, I think. I've never been there. Usually it's just Drake. But he stores them there. To admire. His personal hall of fame."

"He's worse than I thought. He's a serial killer."

"The other day, just before you came, two of them went missing. Somehow. He wasn't happy about that. You and Aaron showed up that very night."

He took a deep breath. She was right. This was reality now. The Prescotts had enough money to shield themselves from public eyes. The law couldn't help them. They weren't free anymore. They were prisoners. But if Therese's innocence was the price of staying alive, maybe they should just let Lincoln send all of them home. Their real home.

"Well, hopefully they both calm down by morning." He winced as he touched his face. "And hopefully this stops hurting."

"Are you sure you're okay?" She looked over his wound. "Why don't I get you some ice? That's gonna be a shiner real fast."

"Ice never stopped a shiner for me." He forced a smile. "Plus, that guy hits like a girl."

"Girls can hit pretty hard." She smiled and leaned in close. "Don't be afraid to ice a wound 'cause a 'girl' gave it to you."

"I'm not." He laughed. "What about you? Does he hurt you?"

"Only if I give him trouble. That's why I don't fight. It's over quicker if I just do what he wants."

"You can't keep giving into him. Your body is sacred. God gave you the gift of sexuality for somebody special. A husband. Not that pig."

"It's a bit late for chastity. It's not like he was my first."

"It's never too late to start being pure."

She shot to her feet. "Look Jeremy, you're a great person. You mean well. And I appreciate the concern. But this is just something that I have to do. I'm used to it and I'm dealing with it. You know now, so you don't have to make trouble anymore." She wiped away tears with her sleeve. "It's about survival, Jeremy. I'm surviving."

Brutal silence.

He struggled as he pushed himself to his feet. "After tonight's stunt, I'm pretty sure surviving isn't a likely outcome for me."

"Don't say that." She shook her head. "Father Doyle caught me once. When he first got here. And he's still alive."

Jeremy shrugged. "It's a gut feeling I have. But just listen. If something were to happen to me, I'd want to know that Aaron was well looked after. I'm not saying that you have to take care of him yourself. I could never ask that. But can you make sure that somebody does? Somebody good?"

She nodded. "Aaron's a great kid. Anybody would be glad to take care of him. But that's your job. Don't talk like you're already dead. You and Aaron are going to walk out of this place together."

"I hope that you're right." His chest burned. "But I have to think about . . . I might not live to see that happen. So I need to make sure that Aaron has somebody to take care of him. Be it you. Doyle. Or maybe if we ever get out of here, somebody else. I don't know. I just don't want him to end up alone. I want him to have somebody who cares there to hold him. To comfort him. To make sure he becomes the kind of man I know he's meant to be."

"Jeremy."

"I have faith that God will protect Aaron. But I'm all he has left."

"What if I die too?"

They both froze.

Jeremy nodded. "Then you did your best."

"Is this some veiled attempt to get me to start telling Bradford 'no' for Aaron's sake?"

Jeremy chuckled. "I can't say the thought didn't enter my mind."

"And here I thought pastors weren't sneaky."

He smiled. "I've always been just a little bit of a rebel."

She smiled. "You trust that God will keep him safe. Trust that no matter what happens to us, God will make sure he's got somebody to care for him too."

Wise words from somebody so tortured. She was right. God would take care of Aaron. Jeremy just couldn't bear the thought of Aaron losing another parent. Being an orphan could damage a child and set them on a wrong path. He'd seen it too many times before. He prayed that wouldn't be the case for Aaron. Worse than seeing his son die would be knowing that he'd went astray and lost himself.

CHAPTER 10

A buffet of the most delicious and elegantly prepared food he had ever seen was set before Aaron on a red-draped table. The food was so beautiful, but better still was seeing everyone he loved at the table with him. His mother. His grandparents. His father. Ryan. Emily. Father Doyle. All the people, both alive and dead, that were important to him.

In the distance, he could hear muffled fighting. Two female voices, screaming. They grew louder and closer. Until they were right behind him. And overtook his happy dream.

He shot up from his bed and opened his eyes.

He tried to hang onto those images of the people he loved happily dining together with him. Trying to remember the conversations he was having with them. But it all was fleeing so fast. Before he knew it, it had vanished entirely into his subconscious. Leaving only the sting of loss.

Aaron looked around the room. Dinah and Emily were going at it over something. Again. He couldn't tell what. He rarely could. Usually by the time anybody heard them, it was already about something new.

"Why do you always have to be in my way?" Dinah shoved Emily aside. "I was trying to get dressed."

"I had to go pee pee." She smacked Dinah's arm.

"You were in there like five hours."

"You could've waited."

"Well I didn't." She folded her arms and sat on her bed. "You wouldn't have minded if Aaron did it." She stuck out her tongue.

"Shut it, you little brat." She went to slap the girl but held back when she locked eyes with Aaron. "You're not supposed to talk back to your elders." She lowered her hand.

"You're not an elder. You're a kid. Just like me."

"It doesn't matter. I'm older so you have to do whatever I say."

"Do not."

"Do too. So when I say you stay out of the bathroom, you stay out of the bathroom."

"I'm going to do what I want cause you aren't my mommy. Aaron doesn't tell me what to do. He's nice to me."

"That's 'cause Aaron's a nice guy. He doesn't want to tell you what an annoying little pipsqueak you really are."

"You're just jealous that Aaron likes me better."

Dinah grabbed Emily by the arms and lifted her up. "You really need to learn when to shut up."

Aaron rushed to Dinah and lifted Emily from her grip. "Hey, she's just a little girl. You can't be violent with her. If she's doing something wrong, discipline her the right way."

Dinah rolled her eyes. "Nobody here disciplines her because Lincoln might kill her. So she can just do whatever she wants and I'm supposed to put up with it. Well, I'm not putting up with it anymore."

Aaron turned to Emily. "Emily, you do have to listen to the grownups. And yes, even to Dinah sometimes."

Emily pouted. "But I had to pee. And she was just looking in the mirror."

"I was brushing my hair."

"For like ten hours."

"You don't even know how long that is."

Aaron pushed them apart more. "Would you two give it a rest? We're all stuck here so fighting isn't going to help. You're fighting over a bathroom. That's ridiculous."

Dinah folded her arms and began to pace. "No, we're fighting over boundaries. She came in during my time in there which is supposed to be private."

"And you come in there all the time when she's in the bath. We all do. And she doesn't mind."

Dinah exhaled an annoyed breath. "Aaron, she's not even six yet. She doesn't care about privacy. I do."

Aaron sighed. Privacy. He remembered that. He shook his head. "Do you think I like having to get dressed in front of girls? We're kidnapped. Together. Even if we might fight a little sometimes, we might as well be friends and try to help each other. Always screaming only makes it all worse."

Emily grinned and trotted to Dinah. "See? Aaron agrees with me."

Aaron shook his head. Emily probably didn't even understand a word he said.

Dinah recoiled and threw herself on the bed. "Everyone always takes her side."

"I'm not taking her side. I just think you overreacted. You were ready to hit her."

"She deserved it." Dinah thrust up. "What if I was doing something else when she came in?" She raised an eyebrow.

Aaron shrugged. "She probably would've run out

screaming? You can lock the door too." He wasn't getting anywhere. It was too early to referee a fight. "Dinah, I know you were mad at her. But I thought you liked her. Siblings get on each other's nerves a lot. Or at least I think so. If you get mad over something little, what about when something big happens? Like it or not, we're all like siblings now. So we gotta band together and work things out."

"You're wrong. Emily's not even close to being my sister." She raced out of the room and slammed the door behind her.

Emily laughed. "You showed her."

Aaron turned to her. "Emily, you know you shouldn't go into bathrooms whenever you want. People don't like other people to come in while they're in there."

"I know." She tapped her foot and frowned. "But she was taking too long and I had to pee."

"You could've asked Therese to use hers."

"I like this one."

"What if I was in the bathroom?"

"Boys go quickly."

He chuckled. "Maybe. But you gotta be polite to people. The bathroom is kind of a place where people like to be able to shut the door and be alone."

She whimpered a bit and gave him puppy dog eyes that he couldn't help but be charmed by.

He patted her on the shoulders. "Look, I'm not mad. You're just a little girl. I just hope next time you try to be a bit more polite. Can you do that for me?"

"I'll try." She grinned.

He patted her on the head and sent her on her way.

As she opened the bedroom door, he could see Dinah staring back, dripping with contempt. He knew Emily was in the wrong for what she did to Dinah, but Dinah's over-reactions were concerning. It seemed like she was mad about more than just privacy. Aaron couldn't help but feel responsible. The last thing he wanted was to be the cause of more fights.

"Good Morning, Aaron." Jeremy gave his son a hair ruffle. He flipped up the hood of Aaron's black hoodie.

Aaron laughed and pulled it down. "Good Morning, Dad."

"Sleep well?"

He went to tell his dad about the girls. His father always had good advice but it was better not to trouble him with something so stupid when they were prisoners of a crazy rich guy.

"Yeah." Aaron walked off toward the sweet smell of French toast that was filling the house.

Jeremy followed Aaron into the kitchen and took a seat opposite him at the table. Therese was already seated there, avoiding direct eye contact with either of them. "I asked Therese to sit next to us today. You two haven't really spoken much since you got here so I figured you should get to know her."

Aaron looked back and forth at the two of them a moment. Therese seemed nice enough but why did his Dad suddenly want them to get to know each other? "I guess that would be cool."

As Maude served them each a slice of French toast, Therese turned to Aaron. "So what's your favorite subject in school?"

School. It seemed like a flash of somebody else's life. Something he'd only heard about but didn't quite remember. It had only been a little over a week, but Aaron envisioned missing several grades in the time he'd been gone. He didn't have friends there. Would any of his classmates even notice he was missing? Would they even cry if they heard he was dead? And all the work he'd miss, he hadn't even thought of it once. Did his teacher even wonder where he was?

He clanked his fork against his plate. "Well, we don't really do anything in gym so it's like we get a free recess." His eyes met his dad's. His answer wasn't approved. He searched his brain to come up with something better. "And Math's pretty cool. No long lectures. We just see how it's done and then we solve the problems. So it makes more sense."

She nudged his shoulder and leaned in. "I liked P.E. best too when I was your age. It's a nice break from the typical monotony of school."

Aaron grinned. "Yeah. I guess," he said. Even if he wasn't totally sure what monotony meant.

"What about your hobbies?"

He shrugged. "I dunno. I don't really have too many. Some music."

"That's cool. I used to be really into rock music before . . . well, before I got here. I went to all the good concerts in the area. I loved seeing how all the instruments worked together. And breaking down what the words really meant. So much fun. But my family thought it was all trash. And my friends? They liked about two artists and anybody else was for nerds. So it was pretty much just me. But that didn't bother me because what everyone else thought didn't matter."

He nodded. "That's cool. I just like the way they sound."

"That's fine too." She laughed and took another bite.

Another silent spell. She sighed and picked up her plate. "Why don't I just let you two eat?" She carried her plate away and left Aaron and Jeremy alone at the table.

Jeremy stared Aaron down. "You shouldn't be rude to her."

"How was I rude?" Aaron forked another bite in. "I answered her questions."

"She wanted to talk with you. Really talk."

"I talked." He looked over into the living room. He met Dinah's shady eyes scowling at him. She pulled open the door to the main hallway and mouthed something to him, but he couldn't tell what. Then she was gone.

Aaron turned to Maude, who was washing dishes. "Is she allowed to do that?"

Maude turned off the water. "Lincoln sent for her. I think he had a script for her. He typically runs all the scripts through me or Drake. We're the seniors here, after all." She sat down at the table. "But sometimes he gives a one on one. Probably has something specific he wants to go over with her. That or he wants to train some new people to do it." She shot Drake a scowl. "We aren't going to be around forever. Only a matter of time until he writes one or both of us out."

Aaron took her hand. "Don't talk like that. Maybe he just wants to make things easier on you. So you can take it easier."

Maude chuckled. "Oh child, bless your heart. If only that were true. But I don't think making things easier on an old woman like me is very high on Lincoln Prescott's list of priorities."

What could Aaron say? Maude knew their captor better than he did. Maybe she was wrong. Lincoln was still a person. He had to have a heart somewhere. Maybe he'd find it just soon enough to show them a little bit of mercy.

Or maybe that was just the dumb kid in him. He used to think almost everybody could be good. But that was before. Things were different now. If Lincoln were good, everyone here would've still been back where they belonged. Back home.

Still, he didn't like that Dinah was having a private meeting with their captor. She was in a bad mood and could easily unload on him. If she was still angry and let Lincoln know it, it wouldn't end well for her. He prayed she knew how to hold her tongue, even if she was mad at him.

Dinah steadied her shaking knees as she walked into Lincoln's office. She'd never been here alone before. Lincoln had hardly said any words to her outside of his pompous directions. He hadn't even given her as many scenes as the others. Maybe he just didn't like her that much.

Lincoln rose to his feet when she walked through the door. "I am not used to seeing you with a smile on your face, pretty girl. You usually look as though you are mad at the world and just want to get your day over with so you can sleep."

Dinah took a seat. "I've got motivation today." She scooted it closer to the desk.

"Motivation?" He raised an eyebrow. "Pray tell, what could've flipped the position of your lips?" He linked his fingers together and leaned in close. "Oh wait, could it be that little sack of skin and bones that I brought in last week, Aaron?"

Dinah shrugged. "Maybe it's him. Or maybe it's just me. It doesn't matter. I'm here for a script, right?"

"Yes, you are. But . . ." he pointed to his computer screen. "I haven't printed it out yet. I was hoping you could help me make a few changes."

"Changes?" She looked at the screen. She could see the file open but couldn't read what it said from where she was sitting. "What kind of changes?"

He smiled and patted the seat of a chair next to his. Behind the desk. "Why don't you sit down and help me figure it out?"

Lincoln had never done this before. Since she'd been there, nobody had ever helped him write a script. He was the artist, not them. Why did he suddenly want her input? Could she trust him? If she couldn't, what difference did it make? Nobody there would miss her if he killed her.

But what if this was legit? It was a unique position. One she couldn't just ignore.

She smiled and happily took a seat besides Lincoln.

He put his arm around her and smiled back. "Let's get to work."

Aaron and Jeremy stood in the parlor.

Their characters were both scripted to be nervous. No acting required for that.

Drake walked into the room. He was dressed in a fancy suit. Aaron had never seen him in a suit before. It looked weird on him. Especially with a pink tie.

Drake approached the duo. "Is this him?" He took Aaron by the face and turned his head to have a look at him.

Jeremy nodded. "What do you think?

Drake paced around Aaron. "He's thin. Puny. Legs are shaking and I haven't even talked to him yet. He needs more work than you let on." He patted the boy on the shoulder. "But he's not unfixable."

Jeremy forced a smile. "Well, he's all yours. Once you pay the agreed upon price."

"Selling your own son?" Drake grinned and took out a moneybag. "That's a level of desperation most parents never reach. They'd sooner starve."

"Desperate for something of value. I don't keep assets around if they aren't useful." Jeremy shot Aaron an apologetic smile. "I am surprised you want him."

Drake grabbed Aaron by the neck. Applying just a little pressure to make breathing difficult. "As long as you're not trying to pass off a girl. He does look wimpier than most his age."

"If I didn't have to bathe and change the brat for two years, I'd have wondered myself. Take my word for it. He's a boy. It's not like I couldn't sell a girl to somebody else for just as high a price." Jeremy held out his hands. "Now hand over the money or else I'll just find somebody else to buy him. He's at the age where he's in demand for a lot of different jobs. You know I'd find a buyer. I'm just giving you first dibs as a courtesy."

Drake held out a stack of bills. "I trust you. It wouldn't be in your best interest to lie to me. I think we both know that." He dropped the stack into Jeremy's hand. "Buy yourself something pretty." He clapped him on the back.

Jeremy pocketed the money and shook Drake's hand.

Jeremy then gave Aaron a final pat on the back. "Do what he says. Maybe then you'll finally be a man."

Aaron didn't have to work to muster up tears as Drake led him away.

"Cut." Lincoln danced into the scene. Rambling like usual. Aaron tuned him out.

He made a dash for his father's arms. "I know that

scene was fake but I just needed to hug you, Dad."

Jeremy stroked his son's head. "I know. You know I'd never do that. Ever. Right?"

Aaron tearfully nodded. "I know. It's just hard to see."

"Just remember . . ." He pulled back and looked Aaron in the eyes. "No matter how bad things get here, I still love you. Always and forever."

Aaron forced out a smile as Jeremy stroked his cheek.

Drake grabbed Aaron and pulled him away. "Enough with the lovey dovey crap. Be professional and save that for the bedroom."

Jeremy rose to his feet. "Are you insinuating something?"

Drake rolled his eyes. "Don't take it personal, Rev. I'm only trying to help. Emotions only fuel the fanatic's ideas." He pointed to Lincoln with his thumb. "Show the tool that you love the kid and he'll make you hit him more in the next script. He's sadistic like that."

"He's right here, you know?"

Drake chuckled. "What do I care if he hears me? I don't have anybody here I care about." He rubbed his head and groaned. "Look, you're his dad. I get it. I'm not saying that you should enjoy smacking him around. But you have to live in reality. One or both of you is going to end up dead sooner or later. You're only making it harder on yourselves for when that happens. Turn off the feelings now. I don't care how, but work at it. That way, when he has me put one between your eyes, or his, the other will be able to survive it. Love doesn't last. In life, you're going to end up either dead or alone. It's how this world works. I had to learn that first hand. The hard way." He swallowed hard. Aaron could almost see the tinniest fleck of a tear in his eye. "I had a son once too you know. Before I came here. A long time ago. You'd two best learn to deal with life without each other. In this place, it's only a matter of when."

Jeremy pulled Aaron close to him. "Maybe you're right. Maybe Aaron and I aren't long for this world. But that's all the more reason to love each other now while we have each other."

"Even if it makes it cut deeper when fate yanks you both apart?"

"The memories we share will cushion any fall we have because of separation."

Drake chuckled. "You really are delusional aren't you? All that God stuff gives you a false sense of security. Well, don't say I didn't warn you." He looked down at Aaron. Then back to Jeremy. "Pray you go first, Rev." He pointed to Aaron. "He's young and naïve. If you die, he'll cry for a little bit but then ball up and face it. But if you're a man who still clings to these stupid ideas of love and parenthood, then you're just a house of cards waiting to be blown down by the big bad wolf. Pray you go first. You can't take the boy dying."

Dinah led Emily up a flight of stairs.

Emily looked around. "Dinah, where are we going? I never been to this part before."

Dinah waved her on. "We're filming something for Mr. Prescott. He's probably already waiting there."

"Are you still mad at me for earlier?"

"Of course not, silly. I'm not that shallow."

"Shallow?"

"Mean. I'm not mean like that."

Dinah didn't even turn around. She said she wasn't

mad but she must've been lying. "I'm sorry." Emily pouted. She liked Dinah. She didn't want her to be mad at her anymore.

"There's no point in being sorry."

"Why not?"

"There just isn't." Dinah turned around. "Besides, we're here." She pushed open a door.

A cool burst of wind embraced Emily's face. She smiled and looked up at a blue sky with cottony white clouds scattered about. It was so beautiful. Like one of her pictures. All it needed was a unicorn.

"Wow, I've never been here before." She jumped up and down and twirled. "It's so cool."

"It's a balcony just below the roof." Dinah paced around her. "I've never been here before either."

Emily looked over the balcony. She could see a few other big, beautiful houses. Red and brown, big and wide. Mini palaces. But not as big as this house. And the yards were so big that the houses were a lot farther apart than they were back home where all the houses were right next to each other. There were lots of trees too. They were tall and their leaves were red and orange. It'd be so much fun to play with Aaron in such a big yard. She could hear the wind rustle some leaves around. It was like a tiny fairy tale kingdom. And she was the princess.

Emily turned and saw Lincoln standing on the sidelines. His crew was there too. They didn't say anything or hand her papers to remember. They already had the camera turned on.

"What are they doing?" Emily cocked her head. "He didn't say 'action' or yell at us to take our places."

Dinah grinned and shook her head. "No, they didn't. But, they're definitely recording us."

"But we're not doing a movie right now."

"We kind of are." Dinah took a step toward Emily.

Emily looked at the camera crew and back at Dinah. "So what are we supposed to do?"

Dinah smiled and sat down on the ledge of the balcony. "We're going to talk a minute."

"About what?"

Dinah closed her eyes. The wind made her black hair do a dance. "It's about Aaron."

"What about him?"

"You were right." She turned to Emily. "About why I've been angry at you lately. I like Aaron. He's a good boy. And I want to spend time with him."

"But you do spend a lot of time with him. He's both of our friends. Because he's cool." She looked around. "Is Aaron here too?"

"You just don't understand. I want to do things with him that only big people can do."

"You mean like take a bath with him?"

Dinah smiled and took Emily's hand. "Yes, like that."

"What's so fun about that? The tub's small. You can't fit in there with Aaron."

She caressed Emily's cheek. "You're so young." She leaned in and kissed Emily's forehead.

"Why do you want to do that with Aaron?"

"Because he's a good boy." Dinah began to breathe heavier. "I was forced to play a game with a bad boy once. A bad man too. They would hurt me if I tried to not do it. It wasn't fun when I did it with him. But Aaron, he's a good boy. I thought all boys were bad, but Aaron's different. If I play the game with him, it will erase playing it with the bad boy."

"But you still played the game with the bad boy. Even

if you play with Aaron."

Dinah groaned. "But it'll be different. You'd understand if you were older."

Emily sat down next to Dinah. "So what do I do?"

Dinah placed her arm around Emily. "Well, Aaron's paying a lot of attention to you. With you always wanting to play with him, he doesn't want to play with me."

"I could ask him if he would play with you."

Dinah shook her head. "He wouldn't do it. Not as long as you're here. That's why you can't be here. If you're not here, Aaron will want to play with me some more. He'll give me the hope I've been wanting for so long."

Emily looked over Dinah's face. Why was she acting so weird? And talking about weird things. Aaron played lots of games. He'd play a game with Dinah if she asked him nicely. "Are you sure you can't just ask him? We can both ask him." She smiled. "If we ask together, he won't say 'no.' Promise."

"If you're not here, and it's just me and him, I think he'll listen to me more."

"But I am here, silly." She laughed.

Dinah sighed. "I know. But not anymore."

Dinah shoved Emily.

Emily screamed and fell back. Down to her kingdom.

One second she was sitting next to her. The next second her head was split open on the patio.

Dinah looked down at Emily's lifeless body. Even from high up, she could see the blood pooling in a halo around the brat.

"Cut." Lincoln clasped his hands together and walked over to Dinah. "Brilliant. So much tension and passion. It felt so real."

Dinah smiled. "There's a good reason for that."

Lincoln looked down and shook his head. "Well, we'd better get her to the freezer before she starts to stink."

Dinah held out her hand. "Give us a minute. Everyone has to know she's dead. I'd like to be the one to tell them. And can I ask you a favor?"

"That depends." He leaned in close. "What's the favor?"

"Don't tell them I did this. Wait until they see the movie."

He smiled. "It'll be our little secret." He giggled and walked back to his camera. "But hurry and tell them. We have a busy day ahead."

She turned to walk back down into the house. "Don't worry. I'm in just as much a rush as you to make sure I never have to see that annoying face again."

Aaron looked over Maude's shoulder as she mixed something in a bowl. He couldn't tell exactly what the watery substance would look like when it was all finished, but it smelled good.

"Where did you learn to cook so well?" He took a whiff.

Maude laughed as she shook in pepper. "Here, there, and everywhere. Being a good cook doesn't happen just from going to a cooking class. It comes from a mix of ability and lifetime of experiences."

"Wow, I wish I could cook like that one day."

She smiled. "Well, maybe one day I can teach you how to make a few things. You won't be a five-star chef but I'm sure you'll be able to impress your future girlfriend one day."

"A girlfriend . . . right."

"You don't think you'll ever find one?"

"Maybe if I wasn't kidnapped."

She whisked the mixture. "Well, I'm a prayerful woman. As long as you're breathing, I believe there's hope for rescue. You're a pastor's kid. You should believe that too."

Dinah burst through the door. Panting. Her clothes bloody. Dazed and confused and stumbling about.

Maude rushed to her and caught her as she fell. "What happened, child?"

Dinah wailed and cried as she muttered.

"We can't understand you. Slow down."

"She's dead. She was filming for him and . . . I don't know what happened. It wasn't supposed to happen. It wasn't scripted. But she fell and now she's not moving."

"Who?" She lifted Dinah up. "Who's dead?"

The word 'dead' attracted the rest of the captives to the room from whatever they were doing.

Drake, Jeremy, Father Doyle, and Therese all rushed to the kitchen.

Dinah turned to Aaron. "I'm sorry, Aaron. I know you liked her."

Aaron felt his insides collide with one another. He stomach knotted and exploded all at the same time. Nausea, burning, shaking. "Emily's dead?" He could feel his eyes burning with tears. Then he felt that burn dribble down his cheek in the narrowest stream and drop onto his shirt.

Dinah went over to him and threw her arms around him. "She's at peace now, Aaron."

Father Doyle rushed up to Dinah. "Where? Where is

she?"

"Outside. On the patio."

Father Doyle rushed out of the room to go to her.

Aaron threw Dinah away and chased after the priest.

"She was just a little girl." Therese covered her mouth and settled into a seat at the kitchen table. "It's so soon after the last one. He doesn't usually kill again this fast. I can't take all of this death."

"I don't know why he's doing this either." Maude sat down next to her. "Maybe something's changed."

Drake shook his head at them. "You two are really slow, aren't you? What's changed is that even those rich suits can't keep us all secret too much longer. Somebody's onto them. Probably left some clue when he took Rev or maybe it has to do with the missing corpses. Either way, if the cops are nosing around even a little bit, ole Papa Prescott may decide that his son's film career is over. In which case, the next step is getting rid of the evidence. A.K.A us."

Maude sneered at Drake. "Quite a theory you have going."

Drake leaned in close to her. "I'm observant. These walls aren't as thick as you'd be led to believe. You can learn a lot by listening. I learned their schedules and plans. Once, I was even able to make a call from their phone because I knew they'd be out of the room. It's those same thin walls that let me hear them coming back and I had to duck and hide and cut the call short. Shame the little tool forgot his latest z-movie script or else I could've gotten all of us sprung."

"If you can call out without them knowing, why haven't you tried again?"

"I realized that I'm better off here than I was out there. The dirty little secret is that we all are. Or at least those of us with the sense to learn how to survive."

The alarm to the patio door wasn't even set. Lincoln must've wanted them to see.

Father Doyle froze as he set foot outside.

There she was. Facedown on the stone. A halo of blood around her tiny body. He could see the gaping head wound even from several yards away. He looked up at the balcony. At that height, she never had a chance. Maybe she at least went home quickly.

He walked over to her and knelt down beside her.

He gently turned her over. Even with her eyes forever closed, she looked like an angel. He prayed over her and held her close as he cried.

He looked over and saw Aaron standing there. Frozen. Broken. He'd never seen such a look of utter devastation in a child before.

He made the sign of the cross over Emily's forehead and set her body down again. He looked to Aaron, knowing the boy was about to undergo one of the most traumatic experiences of his young life.

Aaron's whole body dragged as he approached Emily.

His father reached out for him but Aaron kept moving. He couldn't stay away. No matter how much it hurt.

He collapsed to his knees and lifted her into his arms, gently stroking her hair and bloodstained cheek.

He pulled back his hand. It was covered in her blood.

"How could he do this to you? You're just a little girl."

Last week, he didn't even know her. Now he felt like he'd watched her grow up from birth.

He pressed her face against his chest and tried to remember her voice. The feeling of her arms around him. Trusting him totally to keep her safe. How he'd failed her! When she needed him the most, he wasn't there. She died alone and he could never go back and change that. He could never go back and hold her hand as she fell into the arms of Jesus.

He lifted her hand to his lips and kissed it. His tears fell onto it and washed away some of the blood. "I'm so sorry, Emily. I'm so sorry."

Father Doyle placed his hand on Aaron's shoulder. "I don't think she suffered."

"She's still dead." Aaron's wails choked him a moment. He let out a scream that burned his throat but he didn't care. Everything hurt so much already. "This isn't fair. Who could do this? Why would somebody do this to her? What did she do?"

Father Doyle leaned down and looked Aaron in the eyes. "I wish I could answer that for you. I've never gotten used to this yet either. All I can say is that evil is real. People can choose to do evil. And somebody chose to do something very evil to Emily. Every day, my faith is tested with why God would allow things like this. In my head, I know. But when I see the results of evil choices, sometimes it's hard not to feel betrayed. But that just has to make our faith stronger because it's only in times when it's really hard to believe that our belief truly begins to mean something."

Aaron cuddled her close. One last time. "Wait for me in Heaven. You can dance with the angels now."

He laid her body gently down on the ground. Away from the blood.

He stood up and walked back to his father.

He saw Dinah standing there. Her hands were at her face and she was still crying. She held out her hand to him.

He couldn't look at her. After how she treated Emily that morning.

He walked over to Father Doyle again. "What do they do with her now? Where are they going to bury her?"

He turned his face away. "With everyone else. You shouldn't worry about it. It wouldn't bring you any peace."

Lincoln's voice pierced the silence of the patio. "Cut." That horrible phrase that haunted Aaron's nightmares.

He strolled onto the patio. Had he been filming all of this? Was Emily's death just part of his stupid movie? Didn't he care that a little girl was dead?

Aaron turned to their captor. He felt that fire in his chest again. But this time it wasn't the grief or pain. It was a burning anger unlike any he'd ever felt before. His father had always taught him that anger was wrong. But so was killing little girls. And being angry with Lincoln made him feel just a tiny bit less devastated. For just this one time, this was his to embrace.

He charged at Lincoln. He pounded the thin man's stomach. "Why did you have to kill her?"

Lincoln didn't even flinch at Aaron's frail fists.

He kneeled down and put his hands on the boy's shoulders "Why would we want to fake death in a movie? You can't truly feel what it's like to watch somebody die unless you are actually watching somebody die. Most directors aren't brave enough to go where I've gone, but I capture the real emotions of loss. I captured your real emotions. Every raw second. If Emily could just get up and walk away at the end of it, it wouldn't be real. The only way for it to feel real is for her to be really and truly gone forever."

"Liar. You're a liar." Aaron leaned in so close that he could smell Lincoln's cinnamon breath. "You don't have to kill us. You don't have to take us at all. You could've just left all of us alone. Why are you doing this?"

"Because I can. Because I want to." He stood up and turned away. "I make movies. And if others won't give me what I need, I'll take it."

"That's not fair." Aaron took a step after Lincoln. "That's not fair to us that we all have to die so you can make a movie." Tears now spilled out of him uncontrollably.

Lincoln shook his head. "I'd surely have expected more from the son of a pastor than to expect life to ever be fair."

He turned to Father Doyle and signaled to the body. "It's time to take her to the hall. That's where she belongs now."

Father Doyle turned toward Emily. "I'll carry her myself if you don't mind."

"Why would I mind?" He laughed. "I asked you, didn't I? I don't like carrying dead weight around."

He signaled for everyone to follow him. "You two should see this at least once. Maybe it'll remind you of where you'll end up if you get any bright ideas."

Jeremy and Aaron reluctantly followed after him.

With bodyguards by his side, he led them back into the mansion. Through a few rooms and to a staircase.

They descended the twisted flight. It was twice as long as Aaron thought. They must be pretty deep underground.

When they finally came to a stop, there was a large door before them.

Lincoln had his men unlock the door and pull it open.

A blast of frigid air pounded Aaron. It was a freezer.

Aaron and Jeremy stepped into the room of horrors. Dead bodies.

More than they could count.

Men. Women. Children. Lain out on a slab. The bloodstains and bulletholes still on the clothes they were dressed in when Lincoln filmed their last seconds alive. There was a nametag before each one. The only remaining reminder that these people had lives once.

Lincoln pointed to one of the empty slabs.

Father Doyle placed Emily's body there and then took a step back. There were a few other empty ones above and below her. Sure to be filled soon.

Jeremy said, "This is undignified." He walked over to the body of an elderly man. There was a knife wound in his chest. "People aren't meant to be kept in freezers like they're slabs of meat. They deserve proper burial and memorials."

Lincoln chuckled. "Being put in a box under dirt is better than permanent housing in my hall of fame? You make me laugh."

Father Doyle took Jeremy aside. "This is how it is here. Lincoln's set in his ways. There's no point in arguing."

Aaron looked around at all of the bodies. He wondered what their stories were. What they had felt. Where they as scared as him? Where they happy once? Did they have people still wondering where they were?

He looked at an empty slab directly above Emily. It could be his. His body could be there forever.

"Dear God!" he wasn't sure what to pray after that. So many murder victims in one place. He'd never seen so many dead bodies before.

Lincoln then ushered them out of the freezer. "Freshen up in your chambers. There'll be another scene filmed in an hour. Be ready."

As the goons escorted them back to their room, Dinah took Aaron's hand. "You can talk to me about it, Aaron. We can talk together."

He yanked his hand away. "I don't want to talk. Talking won't bring her back."

"But it could make you feel better."

"You yelled at her this morning. You were so mean. And now she's dead. She's gone and you just want to use it as an excuse to spend more time with me." His lips shook as he stared her down. "I know you didn't want her dead but I'm not ready to talk to you right now after how you talked to her. Not today. Maybe tomorrow."

Dinah turned away. "Okay then. Maybe tomorrow."

As Aaron continued his walk back upstairs, he felt Dinah's eyes staring at him. Piercing right through him. He saw tears in her eyes. But he didn't feel real grief. As sad as she tried to make herself look, he couldn't escape the suffocating vibe that she was happy that Emily was dead.

CHAPTER 11

Patrick was finally looking better. His color was back and he could keep meals down. More importantly, his signature smile was back in full force.

Despite being able to spend more time on the case, there still weren't any new breaks. Coming home to Patrick kept Julie's heart soft. Hopeful. Even as the prospects of finding anybody alive seemed to grow bleaker.

Dressed for work, Julie came downstairs to find Patrick already awake and on the sofa watching television. "You know, another day and you can probably get back to school. You haven't thrown up for two days now. I think you'd best be getting back to school before you get behind."

Patrick held up a book. "Jacob's back. He brought me my books the other day. I already caught up on most of what I missed."

She raised an eyebrow. "In one day?"

He shrugged. "School's slow."

A knock at the door. Wayne poked his head in. "All right if I drop something off for Patrick?"

"For Patrick?" Julie met him as he walked inside. "You've been helping me care for him all week. You don't need to do anything else."

He held up a gift bag. "It's a get-well gift. He's a kid

and he's been sick. A little trinket isn't going to spoil him."

"You got me something?" Patrick sprung to his feet and walked over to get it.

"Somebody's feeling better." Wayne handed him the bag. "I was beginning to think you might secretly be a cripple."

Patrick took the package. "Not cool to joke about crippled kids, Wayne." He winked at him and returned to the sofa. He peeked inside the bag and put his hand inside. Always trying to draw out the suspense.

"Thank you." Julie took him aside. "But really, you don't have to give him gifts. You didn't have to stay and help me. You're doing so much that you're not required to. You shouldn't feel obligated."

Wayne leaned in close. "I don't. I did it because it was right. It was nice. And Patrick has good jokes." He flashed her a silly grin.

She shook her head. "I don't really think of Patrick as comedic. He's usually so solemn. You must bring out the guy in my little boy. Because I never see him as bouncy as when he's with you. Once he's totally better, I can only imagine what you'll make him."

"Is that a bad thing?"

"Well, no. I guess not."

"If it makes you feel better, I honestly don't think he was trying to be funny when he spouts off a memorable quote. I actually think he's being seriously observant or giving heartfelt commentary. And as for the gift, he's a kid. Kids like gifts. I know I did. Sometimes good things do happen, Julie. You don't have to be afraid of them."

Patrick held up his shiny new video game. "This isn't even out yet." His wide eyes glittered as he examined the game case from all angles. "How'd you get it?"

Wayne winked with a grin. "A private investigator never reveals his sources."

Julie folded her arms. "This better not have anything inappropriate in it, Tempest."

"Relax." He patted her on the back. "Would I get him something inappropriate?"

"Yes."

"No respect."

Julie thrust concerns about the game out of her mind for a moment. It made Patrick happy for the time being. And seeing the contrast to the bedridden child from a week ago was a welcome change.

Her ringtone.

She took a look. Her father. Maybe he had a lead. "Yeah?"

"Julie, if you can, get down to the station with Wayne. I think I found something. And don't worry about Patrick. I already called in a favor to look after him. She should be over in a minute."

"She?"

He already hung up. Just as the bell rang.

Julie opened the door.

"Olivia."

Her nun sister stepped in with a filled tote bag swung over her shoulder.

Julie threw her arms around her. "I didn't know you were back."

"I got in last night."

"How was the trip?"

"Inspiring." She held her chest. "But Dad called me and told me Patrick would be needing somebody to look after him while you follow up on a lead? So here I am." She pointed outside. "And you'd better get going because he sounded kind of hyper and Dad only gets hyper when he has something."

"Thank you. I'll catch you up on everything later. But we've already lost too much time on this."

Julie waved goodbye to Patrick and rushed to her car. Patrick was okay. Now it was Aaron's turn. His and everyone held with him.

Kevin's desk was a mess of printed reports and maps. Julie eyed the mayhem. "Been busy?"

He grinned. "Nah. I'm mapping out directions to the boardwalk."

Julie and Wayne took a seat. She glanced over all of the papers on Kevin's desk as best she could. "So what do we have?"

"Well, I've been running that Columbia Court thing for days across the entire country. Nothing I found would be a good place to hide so many people. None of them would fit the bill of somebody as wealthy as our killer living there. But I tried a different angle. I tried to look for places that used to be named Columbia Court or that somehow have been nicknamed that."

Wayne asked, "Did you find anything?"

Kevin pulled up an old newspaper clipping. "Maybe. There is a match about twenty minutes away. The place is called Prescott Park. A small cluster of fancy mansions. There are no other human structures for at least two miles in any direction."

Julie nodded. "Sounds like the perfect place to hide a lot of people. Do any of the residents meet our profile?"

Kevin flashed her a dossier. "Some suit named Bradford Prescott owns the entire damn thing. He leases some of the homes but the largest and most secluded house on the property is his. He's an overstuffed prima donna. Could definitely be involved in this."

"It sounds like a good lead on its own," Wayne said. "But what's the connection to Columbia Court?"

"The mansions are actually only about thirty or so years old." He pointed to some yellowed documents. "In the thirties, there used to be a small housing development. It was named Kerwood Court officially on maps but it was built by a guy named Norman Columbia. He was a big cheese in the area back in those days so everyone who talked about his development of the homes called it 'Columbia Court.' It was a nickname but it kind of stuck in many people's minds. The land was seized by the government in the sixties to build an extension to a freeway. The entire development was demolished along with pretty much any building for several blocks. But the project never got off the ground. People protested. Alliances were changed. Politicians got replaced. Time went by and eventually the state decided to sell the land back to the private sector. Unfortunately, that was about the same time Bradford Prescott was coming into his own. The guy had built a corporate empire and was looking to build a small, gated community. Of course he had the dough to do it, and so Prescott Park was born. However, during that interim period where the land sat vacant, it became a popular spot for kids or young lovers to get away. This Drake guy and his wife are the right age to potentially have been among those who'd remember that. If they still thought of the land as 'Columbia Court,' it could be feasible they'd refer to it as such to each other."

Julie looked over an aerial map of the court. "There's only two other houses outside of the main estate on the property and nothing else for miles. And the three houses appear to be a few acres apart. Minimum. Add to that each house is gated off and the entire community again gated off from the road, and you could definitely hide people in any of them without anyone knowing. Not to mention ensuring that the people you're hiding have no viable way to escape."

Wayne flipped through Prescott's dossier. "Plus, if Prescott owns the place, he can evict any tenants who poke around too much. The only question is whether or not he's bold enough to hide them in his own home or whether he uses one of the others. One of the leases could be a front. Heck, all of them could be."

Julie stabbed the desk with her finger. "Either way, whoever lives in these houses probably won't be the most compliant people." She traced the distance between the homes and the road. "These are isolated homes. Not the kind of place you pick if you're into even moderate socialization. Who knows how many criminal activities could go unnoticed here? And with high-tech security systems, they'd be able to watch to make sure nobody unexpected shows up. This is the place. It has to be. It more than fits the profile. It is the profile."

Wayne pointed to the three houses. "So three homes. Is there an official record of who lives in each?"

"More than you'd think," Kevin said. "Bradford Prescott lives with a ridiculous amount of staff. He has an adult son named Lincoln who I am looking into. There's not nearly enough public records on him for somebody his age. That tells me that his daddy probably had a lot of it expunged. But the other homes have suspicious characters too. Harley Boris is one of the reported tenants. He had quite the criminal record until he moved into that home and now nobody's heard from him since. At least not officially. There's also a family who moved in a few years ago who have no record of having kids in the school system or any kind of doctor visits in the past three years. All utilities are paid through Prescott. A convenient way to hide a lot of secrets."

Wayne looked to Julie and then to Kevin. "So how do we do this? This is all nice theory, but it's not quite probable cause. Especially for somebody so well connected."

Julie stared at the scattered documents. It was all right here but Wayne was right. It was still just speculation. "You're right. We don't have enough to get a warrant. We're trapped." She caught Tempest giving her an "I told you so" glare. For once, she understood exactly how he felt. "We're not getting in unless they let us. And the chances for that happening aren't great." She scanned the maps again. "If the killer sees us and gets wise, he could eliminate the remaining hostages."

Kevin pointed to Julie. "You drive an unmarked car. They don't have to know why you're there."

Wayne shook his head. "If they catch us in a lie . . ."

"It doesn't have to be a lie." He rolled his chair back. "You're not a cop." He flipped his pointers at Wayne. "You're a private investigator. You could be looking up anything there. Just be careful who and what you ask and you might be able to find a lot out."

Wayne pushed himself to his feet. "I hope you have a good cover story."

Julie grabbed him by the arm. "You leave that to me. If we need them to be convinced we're selling vacuum cleaners, I'll make them believe it."

Prescott Park. Formerly Columbia Court. The houses

couldn't even be seen from the main street. Just a large, brick fence and a towering midnight steel gate.

Julie drove them up to the gate. It opened for them.

Wayne tapped his hand against the armrest. "That was a little too easy."

Julie signaled ahead. "Not quite. Each house has its own gate." She stopped the car in front of a fork that had three paths, each gated off. Three properties. She could see the houses off in the distance behind each gate. Each Victorian showpiece looked richer than the last.

Wayne stepped out of the car. "These homes look like glorified museums." He shut the car door. "Scratch that. Museums look dirtier."

Julie got out of the car. "Prescott's home is on the left. Since he's our most likely suspect, I don't think we should go right for him. Too forward. I say we talk to Boris. He's the closest in proximity. He might've seen something. Maybe some detail that can give us a warrant."

She walked up to the gate and flashed her badge. It opened for her.

Wayne stepped in front of her. "I thought you weren't going in as a cop."

She shrugged. "Yeah, I changed my mind. I ooze cop. They'd never buy that I wasn't. If we're caught in a lie, it'll blow our cover faster. So I'm improvising."

She led Wayne down the path. There were two running fountains, and large stone statues adorned the path to the front door.

A butler waited on the porch of the estate. "Can I help you?" He bowed to them.

Julie flashed her badge. "Could I speak to your boss?"

The butler examined the badge and eyed Julie. "May I ask what this is in regards to?"

Julie smiled. "We're looking into a series of home invasions in upper-class gated communities. A neighborhood a few miles south was hit last week. We got a tip saying a suspect matching the description was seen casing this neighborhood in a limo. Blends in well with this demographic. We're checking to see if anybody possibly saw anything that could help us apprehend this guy before he strikes again."

The butler looked down and tapped his foot. "I'll see if Mr. Boris is able to see you. If you'll follow me."

He led Julie through the front door.

The house had its own narthex with a two-story ceiling and a chandelier with more crystals than the local jewelry store. But that was where the expected elegance ended.

No paintings or fine artifact sculptures adorned the walls. Displayed in glass cases were a frightening assortment of knives, guns, arrows, and spears. Like trophies. Enough to kill somebody in a hundred different ways.

Wayne walked up to a rusted katana. "There're definitely a lot of movie props here. You think this guy is involved?"

Julie toured the showroom, glancing at each weapon. "He seems to treasure these things. Killing with them would risk defecting them."

An older balding man walked in. "How can I help you, officers?" He extended his hand. "My name is Bradford Prescott."

Julie's chest tightened. What was he doing here? She shook his hand. "Pleasure to meet you. But I thought this was the estate of a Mr. Harley Boris?"

Bradford smiled. "It is. Or it was. Mr. Boris recently decided to relocate to a state more friendly to his . . . political opinion." He held out his hand to the weapons on the wall. "Mr. Boris had quite the collection of fine weap-onry. Some valuable artifacts. He treasures them dearly. I tried to convince him to part with some, but they're his babies." He shrugged.

"Seems odd that he'd leave them here if he treasures them so much."

"Well, we do have a trusted understanding. He knows I'd never tarnish our relationship by allowing one of these to become victim to theft. That is why you're here, isn't it? The reports of theft."

"Yes, as I told the butler, I'm investigating a series of break-ins into wealthy estates and I have reason to believe that this neighborhood might be targeted. It may have already been targeted. Has Mr. Boris done an account of his collection to ensure that nothing's been stolen in his absence?"

Bradford smiled. "I assure you. Every piece is account-ed for. I was just here to supervise the packing of these items to ensure they get to him safely." He walked closer to her. "Not to mention the security in these estates is my top priority. These are my trusted clients. I didn't build my empire from underhanded tactics and back-room be-trayals. I built it on trust. On honor and respect for those I do business with. The tenants of these estates are my personal neighbors. I couldn't let them in here if there wasn't a deep-rooted mutual trust between us."

"I understand and I admire that. I just want to make sure the perpetrator responsible for these robberies is apprehended before he can take anything else. It's the lowest kind of low when somebody takes something that doesn't belong to them. Some people think that they are special. Above the law. But nobody is. Nobody has a right to infringe upon the rights of somebody else."

Bradford smiled. "I completely agree. You might want to consider a career in politics. With your charisma and views, I think you'd have the potential to go very far."

Julie threw on her most convincing grin. "I'm flattered, but I think I'm content on the sidelines. I think I see more that way."

"I can respect that view." He handed her a business card. "But if you ever change your mind, do give me a call. I always enjoy helping a fresh face get established. Spread the wealth around."

She took his card. Name and phone number. An address for an office downtown. Nothing useful. She stuffed it in her pocket. "I'll keep you in mind."

He placed his hand on her shoulder. "Shall I show you out?"

Julie stepped away. "Doesn't your butler do that?"

"You made a special trip. I can do the same."

He walked her and Wayne out to the porch.

He inhaled the fresh air. "I love this time of year. Especially out here. No noise. No pollution."

Julie turned to him. "So are you going to lease this building to a new tenant?"

He shook his head. "Not in the immediate future. As much as I did enjoy having the chance to meet some wonderful people, with Boris' decision to leave I think I will keep these properties vacant for the time being. I love the company but I also enjoy the solitude."

"Are all of the houses vacant aside from you and your staff's house? I thought a family lived at the other manor." She pointed to the third house in the distance. "Have they moved too?"

"You have to understand. These homes and this solitude aren't for everybody. The family who lived there had a lifestyle choice that required . . . privacy. They came here to practice it without judgment or inhibition. But it proved too lonely even for them. They missed their own friends. Their family. Going out. So much so that they moved back to the city where they have to essentially leave their lifestyle at their doorstep every day. We all want to be left alone. Until we are."

Wayne cleared his throat. "What about you?"

Bradford met his eyes. "What about me?"

"Other than your staff, do you live here alone?"

Bradford stood silent a moment. "My staff is family enough for me."

Julie hesitated a moment. Were they tipping their hand? But they had to press more. They might never get this chance again.

"Do you have any children, Mr. Prescott?"

He stared her down a moment. "I have a son. He's grown but he drops by a lot. Why do you ask?"

"Do give us a call if you see anything suspicious. Even if your security measures thwart it. The suspect may move on to another neighborhood. One less protected than yours."

He nodded and leaned in close. "If I catch anyone, you'll know about it."

Julie kept her eyes locked with his as she returned to the car. Even from the driver's seat, she could feel his eyes burning into her.

Wayne buckled himself in. "I don't think that went well."

She started the car and backed up out of the driveway. "I can't get a warrant based on tone. He's the one. He's gotta be. We just have to prove it."

She turned out of the gate and back onto the main

road. Then she stopped and looked back at the gated community. "Maybe there never were any other tenants. Or they got too nosey. Either way, he cleared them out, and that was before our little visit. I don't like that at all. Time could be running out."

"Maybe your dad found a connection between the film industry and him. Or with the name 'Ryan.' With the right judge, maybe we can still get a warrant."

Julie shook her head. "I just hope there's something left to find when we get there. He's gotta suspect something. If we don't get a concrete connection soon, we might've just killed those people. But we had to take this shot." She looked to him. "Right?"

Wayne looked away. Silent, but she knew what he was thinking. If he'd had it his way, they'd have just stormed the place. But she needed to do it by the book.

As she drove them back to town, the thought that this procedure could cost these people their lives stabbed at her.

As buildings came into sight again, Julie heard gunfire.

She slammed on the brakes and turned to see two men running from a convenience store. Each held a duffle bag in one hand and a gun in the other.

She shook her head. "Not a good day, perps. Not a good day."

CHAPTER 12

Ryan stared down from the window of his bedroom as the cops drove away.

He knew why they were here. Aaron. And the others. Kids missing made cops work harder. Always did. But how did they know where to look? His father and grandfather had enough money to make sure nobody saw anything. Maybe this time they messed up? Or maybe it was because they found Billy.

But they didn't come inside. They still couldn't prove anything. And now that his grandfather had seen them, they probably never would.

He tried to picture the cops coming in and taking everybody away. Aaron and the others would be able to go home. His dad and grandfather would go to jail. Along with everyone else who worked there. All the guards. The chefs. Roy. And what about him? He'd probably be sent to a home somewhere where everyone would talk about the evil things his dad did.

But Aaron would be able to go home.

Ryan would be able to go outside and see other people. Even if everyone hated him, he wouldn't have to live with this secret. With knowing all the people that died because of his father. He would be free. Maybe he could even be happy.

But he loved his father. His father hadn't once made him feel truly warm. Never once expressed to Ryan something to indicate that he truly loved him. Ryan's chest tightened with the thought that his father probably didn't love him at all. He was just a legacy chess piece, something for his father to display with pride. But the man was still his father. Despite all Ryan had seen his father do, the thought of seeing his father taken to jail forever scared him. But if his father didn't go to jail, Aaron would die.

Ryan knew it. He could see it so clearly. All the other dead people. Even some of the ones his father didn't think he saw. It was only a matter of when and how. He'd come for Aaron too.

Ryan stepped down from the window and sank to the ground. Aaron was his friend. Even closer than the others, or at least it felt that way. Ryan tried to picture what it was like to have real friends outside these walls. Of playing ball in the park. Running home from school. Wrestling, racing, swimming, laughing. But more importantly, somebody who cared enough to understand his heart. To understand what he feared, what he cried for. Aaron was that friend, and his father was going to kill him.

But if the cops came, he'd never see Aaron again anyway. But at least Aaron would be alive. That was all that mattered. Aaron had to stay alive. No matter what.

He swallowed hard and pushed himself to his feet. "I need to see him."

Roy stood aside with a subtle nod.

Ryan dodged the sight of his father's guards and strolled to the captive's wing.

He didn't see anybody. But he heard crying.

Ryan checked behind the couch and found Aaron curled in a ball, head buried in his arms.

Ryan took a seat next to him. "I heard what happened with Emily . . . I'm sorry. I know you liked her."

"How can your dad do that?" Aaron turned to him with bloodshot eyes and his face red. "She was just a little girl. She must've been so scared. That ledge was so high. The ground was so hard and there was so much blood. She was so small but there was so much blood."

Ryan turned away. He felt his own eyes burning. "My dad does that. He thinks making movies makes it different, like it's not his fault. But I know the truth. He's crazy. He's evil. He enjoys watching them die. And every time he kills somebody, I feel like my chest is going to explode. My dad takes somebody else's son or daughter and hurts them. If he's that kind of monster, what does that make me?"

Aaron touched Ryan's arm. "My dad always says we get to choose what we're gonna be. Your dad kills people, but you don't. You can't do anything to stop him. You choose the right things."

Ryan shrugged. What was the right thing anymore? "Grandpa is a bad man. Dad's a bad man. I don't think he was always bad. I think he used to want to do the right thing once. Like me. But now, look at him. Maybe I'm doomed to be just like him. Maybe I'm just as selfish as he is and I just don't know it yet."

"You're not." Aaron straightened his back against the couch. "If you were bad, I'd know. I'd see it. I see someone good. I see my friend."

"I'm sorry about Emily." Ryan wiped aside a tear before Aaron could see it. "I wish I could bring her back. I wish I knew how to get you all out without my dad seeing."

Aaron shook his head. "I know you can't do that. Nobody can. She's dead. That's not going to change. She's in Heaven. If I try to picture her in Heaven, maybe this won't hurt so much."

"Heaven." He sighed. "I guess."

"Don't you believe in Heaven?" Aaron raised an eyebrow.

"I'm not sure." He shrugged. He pictured what Heaven might be like. Then Hell. Then which one he belonged in. Then darkness. If his dad was evil, maybe darkness was the only thing he could hope for. "But it's great that you do."

"What's wrong, Ryan?"

Ryan threw on a smile. "I'm fine." He patted Aaron on the back. "You just lost your friend. Don't worry about me."

Aaron wiped aside his tears. "I can't be selfish. I see that you're sad too. Maybe I can help."

Aaron help him? Ryan couldn't help but chuckle. While he was only worried about losing Aaron, Aaron wanted to ignore his own pain to help him. Somebody like Aaron deserved Heaven. Aaron was a good person.

"You're a good person too," Aaron said.

Ryan froze. Could Aaron read minds too? Or was his self-pity that obvious?

"You can tell me." Aaron looked him in the eyes. "Just because I'm sad doesn't mean you have to pretend that you're not too."

"I'm just . . ." He felt a jolt shoot up his arm. He didn't open up. Not to anybody. But maybe he could this time. "I'm afraid my dad's planning something. Something bad." He turned away. "Aaron, I don't want you to die. Okay?"

Aaron nodded. "I kind of don't want to die either."

Ryan shook his head. "No, you don't get it. I don't want you to die, because you're such a good friend to me. You didn't hate me because my dad's crazy. You care about whether or not I'm sad when you're the one who should be sad. I don't want you to die because I don't want to lose a friend. Selfish, huh?"

Aaron leaned in close. "I don't want to die because I don't want to die. It's okay to not want to die. Most people don't. And it's okay to not want somebody you like to die. I mean, why is that a bad thing?"

Ryan held his lips shut. This wasn't how this was supposed to go. He wanted to comfort Aaron, not the other way around.

"Why do you think your dad is planning something?"

Ryan turned to Aaron. "I just do. I can't explain it. It's just a feeling I get in my stomach. Like a rock."

"Can you call the cops?"

Ryan shook his head. "He doesn't let me get near a phone. He knows I'd call. He knows I hate what he does. And I can't go anywhere without him planning every detail so I can't tell anybody. I tried to sneak out once. One of the guards found me and brought me to Dad. He hit me and then he stabbed Roy. Just in the shoulder, but he hurt him. Because of me." Ryan saw his arms shaking. He felt his breathing grow heavier. And faster. "I'm as trapped here as you are. He only treats me a little better 'cause he wants me to be like him. So he won't kill me, but that doesn't mean I have a good life."

Ryan looked up. And there was his father standing in the doorway.

When did he come in?

And why was he smiling?

Lincoln walked over to the two of them. "Having a

heart to heart?" He raised an eyebrow.

Ryan stood up and got between his father and Aaron. "I came here. I just thought he'd need somebody to talk to. That's all."

Lincoln rolled his eyes. "It's nothing I need to know." He shoved Ryan aside. "But there is business to take care of."

He yanked Aaron to his feet. "Everyone's waiting downstairs for you. Your next scene is ready."

Aaron sighed. "Okay, let's go."

The hopeless tone in Aaron's voice twisted Ryan's insides more. Even if his father didn't kill Aaron physically, he was destroying Aaron's spirit.

Ryan stood in front of the door. "He just saw a friend die. Can't you let him have the rest of the day off?"

Lincoln patted Ryan on the head. "You should come too. You'll want to see this."

"Great, you get to see me act." A tear streamed down Aaron's cheek. "Fun, right?"

As Ryan stared into his friend's eyes, he saw true and unfiltered pain. The same kind of darkness he saw in his own reflection every day. He had to stop it. Somehow, he had to save Aaron.

Aaron looked around in the basement. He counted faces. Everyone was here. His scenes usually didn't have this many people. They hadn't even been given a script yet. Why were they all here?

He looked over to Ryan, as if to ask him if he knew.

Ryan shrugged, as if he'd heard him.

Aaron had been down there once earlier in the week. He'd shot another scene where his father had to yell at him. More pointless drivel. But it was darker then. Now the lights almost hurt his eyes and forced him to squint just a bit.

He prayed this was another pointless scene. After watching Emily die, pointless drivel was about all he felt he could muster.

Lincoln walked to the center of the room and spun around to see his entire cast gathered round, each with one of his guards standing behind them.

He clapped with hands together. "I know I implied you all were going to film a scene, but really, only a few of you are going to be in this scene."

He signaled to his guards.

Then he pointed. "Padre." Then to Jeremy and Aaron. "Pastor and Pastor Junior." He waved them closer. "You guys come into camera view. Everybody else should get back out of the shot. But stay to watch. This is a really special scene. And I don't want any of you to miss it."

Aaron swallowed hard. He looked to his father but was met with only confusion.

He turned to Ryan.

Ryan went to come to him but Lincoln stood in the way. "This scene is especially going to be meaningful for you. But you should stay out of it. You belong behind the camera." He grabbed Ryan by the arm and shoved him back.

"What are you talking about?" Ryan pulled free of his father's grip.

Lincoln smiled. "You'll see, my son. Why don't you take a seat?"

He pulled up a second director's chair and gently eased Ryan into the chair.

Jeremy stormed to Lincoln. "So what are we supposed to do? We never got a script to study."

Lincoln giggled. "I'm trying something new out. Improvisation. I think it will make everything feel less . . . rehearsed."

Father Doyle shook his head. "You killed a little girl this morning and you think that felt rehearsed?"

"Don't backtalk, Padre." Lincoln flicked the priest in the face. "It's unbecoming."

Lincoln moved the men into position. "Now, you two are having another exchange." He handed Jeremy a package. The same packaged used before. "And yes, I know it is the same prop. I may be rich but why eat up the production budget?" He paused and eyed them for their response. Nothing. He sighed and stepped back. "For the scene, it's a different delivery of the same product. Play it out similarly to the last scene. You should be into your characters by now. Think of what they would say."

Lincoln nudged Aaron out of the shot and knelt down next to him. The man pulled Aaron closer to his bony frame. Aaron could feel the slight indent of his glasses against the back of his head and the man's hot breath on the back of his neck.

He felt sweat drip down the small of his back. "What do I do?"

Lincoln patted him on the shoulder. "I'll give you instructions when your cue comes up."

He ruffled Aaron's hair and strolled to his chair. "All right, El Padre de Doyle and El Padre de Aaron. Places."

The cameras started rolling. The scene played out the same as before. His father must've memorized it. But he still didn't look comfortable.

Aaron turned to Lincoln. On the edge of his seat. He wrote it. Didn't he know how it ended?

Lincoln waved him over after a minute. "Now you go

in. You yell at your father for selling you to that man and say that he hurt you."

Aaron nodded. "And then what?"

Lincoln smiled. "Then you use this on him." He took out a gun. Shiny and black.

He shoved it in Aaron's hands.

Aaron felt his insides crash into each other. He'd never felt a gun in his own hands. It wasn't as cold as he'd expected. But a lot heavier. His sweaty palms made the metal feel even worse in his trembling grip.

"I'm not using this. I can't. I don't know how." A tear dropped onto the barrel.

"It's easy. First, you aim." He then took out another gun identical to the one he'd handed Aaron. He pointed it at Aaron's head. "Then you squeeze the trigger."

Aaron struggled to inhale a breath. Should he try to turn the gun on Lincoln? No. He saw the guards out of the corner of his eye. They all had guns. They'd shoot everyone if he tried to do that. But he couldn't just do nothing.

Lincoln shoved Aaron into the camera shot. "You will do as you're told. Fire those bullets into your father." He pointed the gun. "Or I will fire a bullet into your head. And I don't miss. Ever."

Aaron couldn't move. He couldn't turn. He couldn't even blink. Everything in his body burned and his heart hammered to break free from his chest. His clothes were wet from tears and sweat and thinking of the loud crack of a gun amplified a headache.

He looked back at Lincoln. The man was serious.

This was it. The moment he'd dreaded for days. Somebody was going to die. He stared at the gun aimed at his head. He could see Lincoln's finger on the trigger, ready to squeeze. In just a few seconds, it would all be over.

Ryan stared wide-eyed as his father pointed a gun at Aaron.

It was just like with Billy. Almost like a mirror. Only now Lincoln held the gun.

Ryan jumped up from his seat. "Don't do it, Dad." He stood in front of the gun. "You're not going to hurt someone else. You have to stop."

Lincoln rolled his eyes and snapped to one of the guards.

The bulky goon grabbed Ryan and pulled him back.

Ryan struggled to break free but the muscular arms around him were too strong. He couldn't just stand there and watch Aaron be killed. There had to be a way to save him. He had to fight.

Lincoln shot his son a sneer. "The show must go on. Stay back and watch it. And learn."

Ryan shot a frightened glance to Aaron. He stared at the gun in Aaron's shaking hands. Aaron couldn't shoot somebody like that even if he was willing.

Aaron shook his head. "I won't do it."

Lincoln charged at him and smacked him with the butt of the gun.

Ryan started to scream but the guard blocked his mouth.

Aaron fell back but steadied himself. "Hurt me all you want. I won't do it."

Lincoln kicked Aaron. Into full view of the camera. Did he care that he was in the shot too? Or was this what he wanted?

Lincoln grabbed Aaron by the hair. "Now say what I

told you to say." He pulled Aaron to his feet and shoved him closer to his father.

Jeremy and Father Doyle stood frozen in place. One move and Lincoln would kill someone. Probably Aaron.

Jeremy took a hesitant step toward his son. "You leave my son alone, you hear? He's just a boy. I'm not going to stand here and let you kill him."

Lincoln screamed and stamped his foot. "You shut up, Preacherman." He began to giggle and wiped a bead of sweat from his brow. "You sold him to a creep, remember?"

"This isn't a game, damn it." With a deep breath, he took another step closer. "This is people's lives we're talking about."

"Specifically your life." Lincoln steadied the gun's aim at Aaron's head. "Now, Aaron, tell your father what you think of him."

Aaron tearfully shook his head. "No, I won't."

Lincoln fired a shot.

It skimmed just past Aaron's head and buried itself in the wall. "Say it, you stupid bastard."

Ryan bit the guard's hand.

The man yanked it back and screamed but kept Ryan imprisoned in his grip. "Let me go."

Jeremy held out his hands. "If you want to kill me, then have the balls to do it yourself. But leave my son out of this."

"Your son has to learn that in life, it's do or die." He spat at Jeremy. "You can't mistreat him and expect him to remain loyal to you."

Ryan stamped on the guard's foot and broke free. "Dad. Stop." He ran to his father and knelt at his feet. "If this is to punish me, I'll stop hanging with him. I promise.

If you let him live, I won't hang out with him again. Please just don't make him do this. Don't hurt him."

Lincoln shook his head. "I am giving him a choice." He shoved his glasses further onto his face. "He shoots his father, or I shoot him." He clicked the gun. "And I am not waiting all day."

Ryan looked toward Aaron. Then toward Jeremy. Then his father. There had to be a way out for Aaron. He could tackle his father. Tackle Aaron out of the way. But any sudden movements were too dangerous. There had to be another way.

Jeremy looked around the room. Father Doyle was a few feet away. He exchanged a glance with the priest but he only saw the same desperate stare he felt in his own eyes.

He turned toward Aaron. His own son couldn't even look him in the eyes. Aaron turned his head down but his muffled whimpers still echoed in the room along with each of his breaths.

Aaron's legs began to shake. He couldn't stand much longer. He'd literally collapse if somebody didn't do something.

He looked up. Guards blocked every way out. They outnumbered everyone here. Even if the others could or would help. And Lincoln's hand seemed tenser and tenser as he pointed the gun at Aaron's head.

Jeremy felt his insides collapse as it dawned on him. There was no happy ending to this. Either Aaron would die, or Aaron would lose his father. His life was about to be trashed no matter what. He'd lived through enough already. He didn't deserve more.

But better a wrecked life than no life at all.

Jeremy swallowed hard. He took another deep breath and stepped closer to Aaron. "Aaron? I just wanted to let you know that I love you. And I always will. Forever. No matter what happens today, remember that. This isn't the end."

Aaron looked up at him with wet eyes. "I love you too, Dad." He shook his head. "That's why I can't shoot you. You're my daddy."

"Do it." One step closer. Easier for Aaron to aim. "It's okay, Aaron. It's okay to do it." He smiled. "I won't be mad. I understand. You don't have a choice."

"It's wrong, Dad."

"I won't let him kill you, Aaron." His cheeks burned. "You're everything to me."

"You're all I have left. It hurt so much when Mom died. You remember. It hurt so much. I don't want you to die. I can't kill my own dad. Even if that means I have to die."

"Listen, Aaron, it's my job to protect you." He lowered his hands to his sides. "I'm ready to meet my Maker. I'm not scared for me. You're my son. If this is what I have to do to make sure you stay alive, then I do it with joy. With no regrets. So please, Aaron. Pull the trigger."

Lincoln leaned in close to Aaron. "You should listen to your father. Honor your father. Isn't that what you were taught?"

"Thou shall not kill." Aaron lowered the gun to his side.

No. Aaron couldn't sacrifice himself like this. He was just eleven. He had his whole life ahead of him. Jeremy struggled for a way to save him. He inched closer. Maybe he could jump between Lincoln and the bullet. But it was a risk. Lincoln was too close to Aaron.

Jeremy looked down into his son's eyes. He recalled staring at them the first time he'd held Aaron. Aaron had been a preemie and he hadn't seen his son's eyes for two days. But that first time he looked into them, he knew his son was a loving soul unlike any he'd seen. Gentle. Pure.

Then he remembered how broken and wounded that soul became after they lost his mother.

It was autumn. Late October. And twenty degrees below normal.

Family and friends gathered at Disciples of Christ Cemetery to mourn the passing of Cecelia Garret. Not even thirty-two years old. Half of the guests were told about her ovarian cancer diagnosis that day. She hadn't even been sick a month.

Jeremy remembered bringing her home after the diagnosis. She was still well enough then to fool most people. They even went to a party the next day and nobody knew anything was wrong. Then the chemo started. A part of Jeremy wondered why the doctors even bothered if there wasn't hope for a cure. The treatment seemed to kill her faster than the disease.

Aaron had always been quiet and reserved, but there was still always a light in his eyes. That light slowly faded with every passing day of Cecelia's sickness. It went out when she passed with Aaron next to her.

Jeremy had dressed Aaron in his suit the day of the funeral. Aaron had barely eaten a bite since it happened. He'd almost become catatonic.

He was only six years old.

Jeremy felt his heart ripped apart again when he saw Aaron standing before his mother's closed casket at the church. He was just above eye level with the casket. That was his mommy in there.

He knew what death was. To a point, at least. He had seen people die on TV. But this was the woman who read bedtime stories to him, bathed him, dressed him, kissed him goodnight.

"Aaron looks so handsome in his suit." Said at least three times by well-meaning relatives. Just trying to break the ice. It wasn't their fault it felt so inappropriate.

After the service, Aaron sat alone in the front pew. The casket was already in the hearse.

Jeremy sighed as he quietly walked up the center isle. He took a seat beside his little boy. "Everyone's ready to go. We're just waiting for you."

"I'm not going." He didn't even turn his head.

"You don't want to say goodbye to your mother?"

"I said goodbye. I can't watch them throw dirt on her."

"Her gravesite is beautiful. There's a tree over it. It grows beautiful purple flowers in the spring, every year. You know how much your mother loved those kinds of flowers. She'd be so happy there."

"She was happy with us," he said. "She wouldn't be happy away from us."

"But she knows that one day, we'll both be with her again in Heaven." He took Aaron's hand.

"Well then, I want to go there right now."

Jeremy smiled and put his arm around Aaron. "You can't. You've still got a whole life to live ahead of you." He pulled Aaron's head onto his shoulder. "You've got great things to do first. We'll all be together again one day."

Jeremy's words didn't seem to move Aaron at all.

Jeremy needed a new approach. "You know, she can

probably still see you. Do you really think she'd be happy to see that you're disobeying your father like this? And worse yet, doing it by refusing to be there when they lay her to rest."

Aaron shrugged. "Mom will understand."

"Maybe she'll understand, but she will still be sad." He stroked Aaron's still-moist cheek. "Don't you want to do this for her? She was so good to you, isn't this the least you can do in return?"

Sniffles broke through. Then louder cries. "I miss her so much, Daddy."

Jeremy couldn't hold his tears in anymore. "I do too." He hugged Aaron tighter. "It's okay, Aaron. It's going to be okay."

"No, it's not." He squeezed his father's arm. "Mom's dead. I'll never see her again."

He pulled Aaron back and looked him in the eyes. "You know that's not true."

"I don't want to wait until I go to Heaven." He shot a glance to the back of the church. They could see the hearse through the open doors. "I want her to sing me to sleep again. And hold me."

"She can sing to you from Heaven. And if you want, I can sing to you, and hold you."

Aaron threw his arms around Jeremy. "Daddy."

"I'm not going to leave you, Aaron. I know it hurts, but we'll get through it together."

"Promise?"

Jeremy smiled. "I promise."

He carried Aaron out of the church. He was going to get through it. With God, he could get through anything. Jeremy prayed that God would always give Aaron the strength to cope with loss. Always give him a stronger shoulder to cry on.

There was no miracle coming. Either the gun in his hand or the gun pointed at his head was going to go off. There'd be a dead body on the floor when the smoke cleared.

Aaron counted his heartbeats. They could be his last ones. One bullet and his heart would never beat again. He didn't want to die. Even if it didn't hurt.

But he couldn't kill his father.

Why couldn't this be just another nightmare? Where he could open his eyes before the gun went off and run to his father to dry his tears in the safety of their home?

"Time's a ticking, boy." Lincoln paced behind him. "Who takes the bullet?"

"Son, it's okay." Jeremy smiled at him. "I want you to live."

Aaron shook his head. "No, I won't do it. I won't kill you. I don't care if he kills me. Let him shoot me. I won't kill you. Not ever."

Aaron set the gun down on the ground. He kicked it away.

Aaron prayed getting shot wouldn't hurt too much. He turned to Lincoln. "I won't do it."

He wasn't sure what to do next. Should he squeeze his hands tightly? Turn his head down?

"No, Aaron!" Ryan's voice. "He's going to kill you."

Poor Ryan. He'd blame himself for this. He'd always remember this moment.

Aaron closed his eyes and waited for the shot.

Aaron was just standing there waiting to die. Why

didn't he fight? How could he just give up like that?

Ryan turned to his father. He grabbed his father's arm. "Dad, you don't have to do this. It's not too late."

Lincoln threw Ryan back. He steadied his aim at Aaron's head. "The script calls for somebody to die. Aaron or Jeremy. Aaron's made his decision."

"Screw the script." He looked over at Aaron and then at Jeremy. The man looked desperate to find a way out of this. Any way. "These are real people, damn it!"

Ryan swallowed hard. He couldn't let Aaron die.

Then he locked eyes with Jeremy. And it hit him. "What if Aaron's dad still dies? Can he live?"

Lincoln laughed. "Oh, and how do you propose that to happen?"

"Just tell me."

Lincoln shrugged. "Well, yes. I suppose if Jeremy did die somehow, Aaron could survive this scene at least."

Ryan brushed aside his tears. A deep breath. His sternest face to force himself to not chicken out.

He marched into the scene.

Aaron opened his eyes. "What are you doing?"

"What I have to." He shoved Aaron to the ground.

Then he swiped up the gun.

Ryan aimed it at Jeremy. He felt his eyes burn. No chickening out. "I'm sorry, Mr. Garret. I can't let him hurt Aaron."

Jeremy nodded. He even smiled. He almost looked happy, even though he was crying.

Three horrible cracks.

Three bloody holes in Jeremy's chest.

Jeremy clutched the wounds as blood spilled out.

Then he hit the ground.

Screams echoed in the room. Therese's. Maude's. Even Dinah's.

Aaron's mouth was open. He felt the stifled air of the basement shooting into his lungs. He wanted to scream. Everything in him was trying to. But not a sound came out. He couldn't breathe. Maybe he was shot instead. Maybe he was dead and seeing his new best friend shoot his father was just one last horrible dream of his dying brain.

The echo of the third shot faded.

Lincoln smiled and clapped. "That was beautiful."

Horrible seconds of silence followed as Jeremy hit the ground.

Aaron dashed to his father's side. He fell to his knees and threw his arms around his father's neck.

Blood streamed from his father's mouth. Aaron knew that was bad.

Jeremy reached up and caressed Aaron's cheek. He used his thumb to wipe away one of Aaron's many falling tears.

"Daddy . . ." Aaron took his father's hand in his. "Don't die, Daddy."

"It's okay, Aaron," he said. "I'm going to be with Mommy now. And Jesus."

"But who's gonna be here for me?"

"I never wanted to leave you an orphan. I'm sorry. I asked God to send you somebody. Somebody good and strong. Somebody who will show you love and help you be the man I know you can be. When this is all over . . . whoever it is. Know that I sent them for you. To take care of you for me."

Aaron shook his head. "No, I want you. Daddy."

Jeremy again wiped Aaron's tears as they fell. "I'm sorry all of this had to happen. I don't know what God's plan for all of this is. I wish I did. But I trust Him. I hope and pray that one day, you can find closure from all of this. I love you, Aaron. Forever. Always remember that. No matter how much you're hurting. Always remember."

Aaron felt his father's hand slipping from his tear-stained face. He caught it in his own hands. "I love you too, Daddy."

His father's eyes slid closed and his head turned away as one final breath escaped.

Aaron tightened his grip around his father's hand. He felt the strength drain as it became limp and heavy. He tried to stay in this moment. Where he could still feel his father. He tried to memorize the feeling of his father's hand. He never wanted to forget what it felt like.

Then he let it go.

It dropped down to his father's chest and slid to the side.

Aaron was an orphan now.

And he knew exactly who to blame for it.

First it was silent. And then it started. The loudest cries Ryan had ever heard. They stabbed him. Each wail. Each cry of complete and total pain. He'd hurt his best friend. He saved his life, but he hurt him so deeply.

"I hope you're happy, Dad."

Lincoln grinned. "Oh I am. This is great stuff. I hope you are happy, Ryan. You saved Aaron's life." He held out his hand. "Why don't you go ask him to thank you?"

Ryan stared at his father and for the first time, he hated that man. With such a deep and burning passion.

But he turned to Aaron anyway. He didn't want thanks. He wanted to help his best friend.

"Aaron?" He stopped in front of him. "I'm sorry. Are you okay?"

Aaron stopped crying. He slowly rose to his feet.

Aaron shot a punch into Ryan's face.

Ryan fell back. He struggled to keep his balance. He grabbed his face but felt he deserved the shooting pain.

"You killed him." Aaron shot him a scowl. "I thought you were my friend."

Ryan fought a tear. "I am your friend."

Aaron shook his head. "No you're not." He stabbed Ryan with his finger. "A friend wouldn't have killed my dad."

"You were going to get killed if I didn't." Ryan's eyes burned. "I did it to save you."

"Shut up." His voice grew louder. He shoved Ryan. "Just shut up." Again. "You murdered my dad." He grabbed Ryan by the shoulders. "You killed him. You." He cried harder and pushed Ryan back. "I hate you. I hate you so much."

The words felt like bullets in Ryan's chest. There was so much pain in Aaron's eyes. Grief. Anger. All aimed at him. Aaron was his friend.

But Ryan understood. He had just killed Aaron's father. Right in front of him.

Of course Aaron hated him. If Aaron picked up the gun and shot him dead right there, he'd understand. He'd even be happy for Aaron.

It was better than watching Aaron's blood and brains ooze out of his skull.

Ryan nodded. "I'm sorry, Aaron. I didn't want you to

die. But I know I hurt you. So if you hate me, then that's okay."

Aaron shot him a piercing glare. "I told you that you were a good person. I was wrong. You're not. You're evil. Just like your dad."

Aaron stumbled over to Therese, who was waiting with a tight embrace. She was crying too. He buried his head in her chest. He was crying so hard he felt like he'd run out of tears.

His legs caved in on him.

She caught him and held him.

Aaron turned to Maude. She met his eyes with compassion.

Maude approached Lincoln. "Are you done killing us for the day?"

Lincoln laughed and nodded. "Yes, for today. You can take him back upstairs and calm him down. I'll have the help clean up the pastor."

"God have mercy on your soul, Lincoln Prescott," she said. "Because you're definitely hellbound."

"You Christians and your Hell threats." He shook his head and left her.

Aaron turned to his father. He looked at his face one last time. As they carried him away, the face grew more and more distant. Until Aaron couldn't see him anymore.

Father Doyle and Drake lingered at the end of the group. Father Doyle said quick prayers over Jeremy before the guards took him away.

"Two of us in one day." Father Doyle clutched his rosary. "They weren't even connected. And so soon after the last one? He's escalating. Quickly. Why? I don't have a good feeling about this."

Drake chuckled and circled Father Doyle with folded arms. "I guess he's deciding that there are too many of us. Wants to whittle us down a bit." He clapped him on the back. "Toughen up, Padre."

Father Doyle felt a burst of pity. Drake was so cold. Even if he had suffered loss, such a callous view of life wouldn't help him.

The room was almost empty now. Just Ryan and his father.

Ryan fell to his knees. He looked over at the blood spot on the floor. He'd murdered somebody. A good man. His best friend's father.

Aaron's words echoed in his mind. "You're evil." They tasted horrible on Ryan's lips. Probably because they were true. Only evil people killed in cold blood. Maybe he was evil. If there was somewhere you went after you died, maybe he deserved the bad place. Aaron was good. He couldn't kill. Ryan didn't belong in the same place as him.

Lincoln patted Ryan on the shoulder. "Well done, my son." The words pounded his ears. "You're going to become a fine man. Because of me."

No. This hurt too much. Ryan didn't want to spend forever with people like that. With people who liked hurting others. He swallowed hard and shot to his feet. "I'd rather be dead than be anything like you."

He walked away, his head down, and Aaron's cries tormenting him.

"You'll come around, Ryan. I'll make sure of it."

CHAPTER 13

Aaron stared at a picture of him and his father, wallet-sized and well worn. His father's smile was so wide and warm. His own was more reserved, but still there. His father could always bring out a smile in him. His dad had carried this picture everywhere. Now it was the only physical thing Aaron had left of him.

Therese sat next to him on the sofa. "That's a beautiful picture," she said. "You and your dad both look so handsome. You're seven here?"

"Eight." He pressed the photo to his chest. "We take one every year. But this was my dad's favorite. My dad thought it was a good tradition."

"I agree with him." She caressed his shoulder.

"You don't have to watch me like a baby." He moved away from her. "I'm a big boy."

"I know you are," she said. "But I did promise your dad that I'd look after you if anything happened to him. We're still in this together."

Aaron shrugged. "I get it. But you don't have to."

Therese turned his head to hers. "Aaron, I know how it feels to loose somebody you love. I know it hurts and when it happens, there's nothing that can really comfort you or make any of this seem any better. But you can heal if you let yourself. And I'll be here to help you through it."

"I thought he'd always be here." He ran his finger across the picture. "Even after Mom got sick, I'd always have my dad."

"He wanted to be, Aaron."

"I don't know what to do now. My dad always had all the answers. He'd talk from the Bible or say something that made me feel better. He always knew what to say. Now he's dead. And I don't know what to do anymore."

"You know what he taught you. You remember it. You learned it well. I'm sure he's taught you a lot. Just keep thinking about all of those things. Live them. And it will help you."

Aaron leaned closer to her and rested his head on her shoulder. "I'm sorry I was mean to you," he said. "I know my dad would hate that. He always wanted me to respect everyone."

She stroked his hair. "I don't think you were mean. I know you're in pain."

Aaron looked up at her. "How do you deal with people dying? You must've seen so many people before me die. What do you do to make it stop hurting?"

Therese sighed. "There's really nothing you can do but pray. Do your best to just push on. You're right. I've been here for three years. I've seen so many people die. Little children. Mommies and daddies. Young people who were just starting to be an adult. I won't lie. It hurts. It never gets easier. I was naïve before I came here. I never really had to deal with death. Some great aunts and uncles here and there. My grandfather. Old people. I never really felt anything much. It just seemed like death was when you are really old and one day you don't wake up. I saw the news but it didn't feel real. Even when I grew up. Then I came here. Just when I'd get to like somebody and get to know them, Lincoln would have Drake kill them. Not to mention the fact that any day, he could kill me. Some days I still don't know what I fear more, dying myself or seeing somebody else I love die."

"So, is this it? Do we just hurt like this forever?"

"No," she said. "We fight to move on. Try to honor those we lost. We stand together as long as we can. That's what I'm going to do for you. As long as I'm alive, I'll do everything in my power to help you cope. And whether you know it or not, you just being here is going to help do the same thing for me."

"Really?"

"Really." She cuddled him closer.

"I'm glad you're here," he said. "It's nice to know that I still have one person left."

"I feel the same way."

Lincoln sat on a sofa in his room. The lights were turned out. Only the TV lit up the room some.

On the screen, a younger Lincoln stepped into the scene.

"How could you betray me like this? After all I've done for you. I gave you everything. And this is how you repay me?"

A woman in the bed with an unseen man rolled her eyes at him.

He then took out a gun and shot the unseen lover.

Then the woman shot Lincoln.

Pop. Pop. Fake gunshots and red paint filled the screen.

Lincoln cried as he watched the dramatic climax to

the film. A 50's movie score played over the end credits.

"Not as good as my newer stuff, but still the genius is there."

Lincoln then turned to notice Ryan had walked in.

Lincoln patted the seat on the cushion beside him. "Come here. Sit next to me."

Ryan reluctantly did as he was told. His father put his arm around him. The boy tensed up and pushed away just a little.

"This was the fifth movie I directed," Lincoln said. "It was supposed to be the one to make it big and take me along with it. The critics didn't quite agree. They called it transparent, unreal, fake. They laughed at me. Our family has enough money to finance several big budget blockbusters. And yet still nobody wanted to produce or distribute my work. Do you know how much that hurt me?"

"So you decided to make your movies on your own. Here, just for you." He turned to his father. "And to make it real, you actually have people die in them?"

Lincoln smiled. "Many centuries ago, plays had real victims. People died with their characters. I think it was the Romans that liked doing this. That's how some of the early Christians died. It's not like I made it up. But it makes sense. You can only act so dead. You can't totally stop breathing, remain totally still. Whether you close the eyes or open them, they flutter. Technology can fix it a little, but only so much. Death is one of the most important aspects of life. Movies need to truly capture the feel of it. And the only way to get a truly good video of what it is like to die, you need to see a real living person actually die before your eyes. That, my son, is a movie."

"But those are real people. They have feelings. Hopes and dreams. They have families and people who love them. They have real lives. Who are you to take that away from them?"

"I am better." He ruffled Ryan's hair. "And so are you. I hope one day you realize how worthless lesser people are. You can't get bogged down with trivial things like friendship. It's fake. Family is all that matters. Your family. And that is who I am. I'll teach you how to be great and how to make the world your playground. I have the money, and I have the skills. I will show you."

"How can you say friendship isn't worth it?"

"How can you say it is? Look at Aaron. You thought he was your friend. Yet the moment things go a little sour, he turned on you. He said he hated you. He called you evil. Just like all of my friends did to me."

"I killed his dad. He loved his dad and I shot him dead, right in front of him. I deserved what he called me."

"You saved his life. Doesn't that count for something? You're better than him. You were born better. He should be bowing at your feet that you even give him the time of day. You could kill him and he'd have no right to be mad at you."

"I don't see the world that way," Ryan said. "I can't. I can't hurt people like you can. I'm just not like that. I wish you'd try to change. Does killing people really make you happy?"

"It does." Lincoln shut off the television. "And it will do the same for you one day. I'm sure of it. I wasn't born like this, you know. There was a time I wanted friends. I wanted love. Your grandfather knew better than to make me chase after feelings. He never told me that he loved me. He showed me that I mattered by giving me what I wanted, giving me the tools to make my dreams come true. I didn't waste time on stupid things. But he also knew that pain would make me stronger. So he made sure I felt pain. Life had to kick me in the balls a few times before I realized I had to kick back. You'll realize the same thing one day. I'm a patient man. I'll wait."

"I'll never be like you." Ryan stood up to leave.

Lincoln gently pulled him back. He kissed Ryan's forehead. "That's what all sons say when they're children. Then one day they wake up, look in the mirror, and see their father. You can't escape your fate, Ryan. You will be like me, and I will be so proud."

Ryan pulled away. "I won't let it happen. No matter how much you try to hurt me."

Aaron lay alone in his bed. The tears had subsided, and now the real pain began. The silent, gnawing pain deep in his chest that he was completely and utterly alone. Both of his parents were gone. Ryan had betrayed him. Even little Emily wasn't here anymore. Crying hurt, but this silent hopelessness made it hard to breathe. It was like an elephant family had decided to sleep on his chest. Hours passed and he still couldn't sleep.

Therese checked in one last time before going to bed. She didn't say anything. She just smiled and waved him goodnight.

He turned on his side and saw that Dinah was not in her bed. She usually could be found staring back at him, but her bed was empty. Not even slept in. Maybe she couldn't sleep either. This was their first night without Emily.

But she could take care of herself.

He turned around under the blankets to get comfortable. He brushed against soft, unclothed legs.

He opened his eyes.

Dinah. "Aaron." She smiled at him.

"How long have you been there?" Aaron scooted away.

"Just a few minutes," she said. "I got in quietly. I didn't want to scare you."

"Where were you all night?"

"Getting ready."

"For what?"

She leaned in close. "For us to finally do what we were meant to do all of our lives."

He felt under the covers that she didn't have any clothes on.

He should have known. He knew she probably liked him. He caught her stares. Those subtle touches that lingered just a little too long. But he always brushed them off.

His father had given him a talk about this stuff. Sex. A friend showed him some horrible pictures. Aaron knew the facts, and he knew what he wasn't supposed to do. He couldn't do what she wanted.

"I've waited for this my whole life," Dinah said. "Other boys hurt me. They took advantage of me. But you? You're innocent. You're pure. Making love to you can undo all that they did to me."

"I can't do that." Aaron shook his head. "I'm only a kid. I'm too young."

"You're perfect." She leaned in for a kiss.

He dodged. "Please, put your clothes on. I don't want to do this. And I won't. My dad told me that it's a sin. And it is."

"That is so old school."

"He said that truth doesn't change, even if it becomes

unpopular. He was right."

"Look at us. We fit together like a puzzle. We were made to do this, Aaron. Don't listen to your father. He's dead. This is what you're supposed to do. Don't try to fight it. Trust me. Believe in me."

Aaron hopped out of bed. "Don't tell me that my father is wrong. Yes, he's dead. But I know what he told me, and I am not going to do what you want. Even if I was old enough."

Dinah began to cry. "It's me, isn't it? I'm not pretty enough for you."

Aaron sighed. He really didn't need this after everything that had happened that day. "It's not you. You're very pretty. It's not about that. It's about what's right. My dad taught me what Jesus wants us to do. Maybe you don't believe those things but I do. My dad was a good teacher and I'm going to listen to him. So please, get some clothes on. I won't look."

He walked to her things and retrieved her nightgown. He handed it to her and closed his eyes. Then he turned away.

She started to cry. Somehow he knew it wasn't really because he turned her down. Her pain came from a source much deeper than anything he could fix by holding her.

When she was dressed, he turned back around and saw the agony in her wet eyes.

"I'm sorry I can't help you," he said.

"I love you, Aaron Garret. Since I met you, I knew you were the one. I know I was ruined by other boys. But you were supposed to be my first real one."

"Dinah, we're still kids. Why can't we just be kids?"

"I'm sorry." She tearfully walked off to her bed and

buried herself in the covers. "But you're wrong."

Aaron stood and watched her for a minute. He thought he heard her sleeping but couldn't be sure she wasn't faking.

Regardless, his body ached. His eyes still burned from everything that had happened today. He went back to his own bed. He knew he had done the right thing for both of them. He was happy to know that both his father and God saw it.

Aaron dreamed of his father that night. The two spent another day together. Fishing, eating, and watching *The Waltons*. Aaron knew it was a dream. He knew it would end the moment he opened his eyes and forever drift to the back of his mind. Destined to be blips of memory. But for a moment, he had his father again. For tonight, that was enough.

CHAPTER 14

Hours wasted on a petty robbery.

"They didn't even have real guns." Wayne tapped a pen against the desk. "They were frickin' pellet guns."

Julie sipped a half-empty coffee. "We were on the scene. We couldn't just assume that. Besides, you got dinner out of it."

"Dinner." He chuckled. "Are you sure you don't want to go home?"

She nodded. "Patrick's okay. He's being looked after. After talking with Prescott, I can't rest until I know we got him. I need something to get a warrant. I've already tried two judges already. Nothing. We need more. A judge isn't just going to give it because we ask nicely. Prescott owns half the politicians. If he's behind this, we need something clear. Something solid."

"What if it's not him?" Wayne turned in his chair. "What if I got all of this wrong? Maybe this is just a human trafficking ring. Maybe these aren't connected. Or maybe it's somebody else entirely."

She rolled her chair over to his. "Since when do you doubt yourself?"

He shrugged. "I'm not sure of much of anything anymore." Memories flooded his mind. Faces he'd buried years ago. A burning feeling in his chest that was all too familiar.

"Did I ever tell you why I became a cop?" He met her eyes. "We used to have so many long talks, but it's been so long. I don't remember if we ever talked about it."

"We touched on it, but I don't think you ever gave specifics." She took his hand in hers. "I'm all ears if you want to tell me. I was so mad at you when you left but maybe because I didn't really understand it."

He nodded. "Powerlessness. That's what I've been running from for years. My mom ran out on us when I was a kid. Don't know why. Barely remember her. I never even bothered to find her. But my dad, he was a good man. He worked hard. So hard that he had a heart attack at forty, with no family history of heart disease. He tried so hard to take care of me." He linked his fingers back and forth. "I was ten. Not much younger than Patrick. And I was alone. Even my own grandparents didn't want me. So they put me in foster care. It wasn't all bad. Not like the stories you hear. I was lucky. I had good homes. But they always moved me around . . . and even the good ones never felt like places I really belonged. That was until I got placed with this retired cop. He was a good man. Pushed me, made sure I pulled my grades up. He didn't replace my father, and he never tried to. But when I graduated high school and I saw him looking back at me, I saw this smile that I knew couldn't have been brighter if I was his own son."

Julie nodded. "I remember you telling me about him. He sounded like quite a good role model."

"He was," Wayne said. He felt himself shaking. He took a deep breath. "The week before I was supposed to leave for college, we were walking home. Two guys came up and tried to mug us. He didn't have a weapon on him. So he just gave them his wallet, but one of the guys recognized him as the cop who busted him a few years back. They beat him and ridiculed him. They called him a traitor to his race. An Uncle Tom. Officer John Hollander didn't give two damns about race. If you were breaking the law, his job was to bring you in. Because they were still angry over serving time for crimes he busted them in the act of, they pulled out a gun and they shot him. They aimed a gun at his face and they pulled the trigger."

Julie's face went pale. She looked away. "I'm so sorry."

"I'm the one who's sorry. The entire time all I did was stand there. I hid. I ran. So they wouldn't kill me. That guy took me into his home and saved my frickin' worthless life and I stood there and hid while they murdered him in cold blood because I was a coward. I didn't think I could fight them and I didn't want to die. I was powerless."

"You were still a kid. They would've just killed you too."

Wayne shook his head. "You don't know that. I don't know that. All I know is that I resolved never to feel that powerless again. So I joined the academy. I became a cop. I would make up for my cowardice and make him proud. And I did. I made detective and I became a damn good cop."

Julie leaned in close. "You were a good cop. One of the best I ever worked with. One of the few I felt truly had my back. So what happened? Why did you leave?"

"Because of you."

'Because of me?" She leaned back.

"Well, your family. After the accident, we found out it was an ex-con who was joyriding drunk. The same lawyer who got him released early for his first crime got him four years for this." He pounded the desk. "Four years. He killed your little boy and your husband, and he only got four years."

A tear streamed down her face. "It was something. He paid a price. And he ended up committing more crimes in jail so he's still not walking free."

"It wasn't just that. It was the small value the law placed on their lives. And around the same time, one of the guys who murdered my father got out. He helped murder a cop in cold blood and we just let him back on the streets. A few months later, there was a guy who kidnapped a girl and raped her. He got off on a technicality. I couldn't do it anymore. Once again, there I was. Powerless. I couldn't help people. Murderers were going free and good people like your family were dying. So I left. I decided to become a private investigator so I could have fewer limits in bringing justice."

Julie shook her head. "Why didn't you talk to me? Why didn't you come to me?"

"You were grieving. You had to bury your husband. Your son. Patrick lost his father and his twin brother. You two had your own problems to deal with. You didn't need my baggage."

"We were friends. You could've come to me. Come to my father."

"I was a walking cliché. You think I was the first one to feel the way I did? I knew I wasn't. I knew it was mostly self-pity, but I didn't care."

Julie nodded. "Why are you telling me this now?"

Why indeed. Wayne stood frozen a moment. He thought of those missing. He thought of those he'd lost. He thought of walking out of that precinct, never intending to come back.

"Because here I am, once again. Powerless. I was doing well as a private investigator. Then I took this case and I couldn't solve it. There were so many people. And I couldn't help them. Then I saw that boy and his father taken. Aaron. I saw his face. I saw the fear in his eyes. He was so afraid and I couldn't help him. I failed him. I used to have the hope that I could bring them home but then we found those bodies. What if I've been fighting a losing battle this entire time? What if we find who did this and every single one of them is already dead? What then?"

Julie closed her eyes. "We take solace in knowing we stopped this guy from taking anybody else. And we move to the next case. It's the only thing we can do."

'That's just it. I can't just move on." Wayne rummaged through files on the desk and took out Aaron's case file. "I looked up Aaron's story. His mother died of cancer when he was just six. Now he and his father are in the clutches of somebody who very well may kill them. If he hasn't already. If we get there and they're already dead . . ."

Julie nodded. "I know how you feel. It's how I felt the entire time I was chasing the so-called Blood Chain Killer. I truly feared that he'd kill Patrick before I could stop him. And what would I do then? I'm glad that God spared me having to find out. But not every case ends like on *Criminal Minds*. Sometimes when you get the bad guy, he's already killed everyone."

Wayne scrubbed his brow. "This is your attempt at making me feel better?"

Julie shook her head. "This is my attempt at reminding you that this job rarely comes with absolute victory. Good people are going to get hurt no matter what we do. The best we can do is solve these cases as quickly as possible and pray for the best result. I hope we find these people alive. But even if we don't, we still can bring in the perpetrator. And to those who we may find alive? We can find other ways to help them. I guess my point is that we're not powerless. Even if we don't get the result we want, if we can bring about any good from these tragedies, then we're not powerless. Maybe we just saved countless future victims. Or maybe we just reach out to survivors to help them get through an unimaginable trauma. Maybe we even go home and hug the ones we love a little closer than we otherwise would have. But we're not powerless. Not in the least."

Wayne allowed himself a smile. He knew there was a reason he came back to her.

"Thank you, Julie."

She smiled and headed for the door. "Let me try out another judge. Keep looking through Prescott's records. He's not going to be easy to touch. If we can find a solid financial connection, maybe we'll get lucky."

"Why wait for a warrant? You and I can just storm the house and take the survivors."

"And go to jail as Prescott walks?" She raised an eyebrow.

He sighed. She was right. Even if he didn't like the book, Prescott wasn't the kind of person they could skirt it on. He had connections. They might've already tipped their hand too much. One wrong move and the people they had at that estate would be doomed

CHAPTER 15

For a split second as he opened his eyes, Aaron Garret forgot that his father was dead. He saw a slit of light coming into the window. He felt the urge to go greet his father. To go hug Emily.

Then the flashes pounded him. Ryan pumping three bullets into his father's chest. Feeling his father's hand go limp. Emily lying in a pool of blood.

They were dead. That was what was real.

Aaron held his head a moment. He couldn't leave the room with a tear in his eye. The stares of the others would already be hard enough.

He looked around the room. It was empty.

Where was Dinah? He recalled the night before. She'd looked so broken. So alone. He wanted to try and talk to her. Maybe try to make her feel better. Be a true friend.

He listened closer. He could hear her. Crying. It was coming from the bathroom. There was running water drowning it out.

Last night's attempt at seduction must've been her way of dealing with the grief of Emily dying. He wanted to go in there and help her not cry. But if she wanted to do bad things with him, it was probably better to stay away. She needed to get through this on her own. So he quietly dressed himself and snuck out of the bedroom.

He had only been there a week. Yet he'd had a routine that he'd become comfortable with. Greeting his father. Playing with Emily. Walking out to a painful silence cut him.

He saw Therese in the kitchen. She went to him before he could even make it to the living room.

"How did you sleep?" She knelt down to eye level with him.

He shrugged. "I was just thinking a lot."

"It's only been one night," she said. "It's going to be hard for a while. Now, why don't you sit down? Maude and I made some breakfast. You'll need to keep up your strength."

She pulled out a chair for him.

He took a seat. He looked to where Emily usually sat. Then his father. It looked so empty with only him there.

Therese signaled to Maude and Father Doyle.

They came in and took seats at the table. Therese sat next to Aaron.

"We all decided to eat together today."

Aaron gazed down at the bacon and eggs meal before him. He remembered it was one of his father's favorite meals.

Father Doyle said to Aaron, "Would you like to lead us in prayer?"

"I think you should do that," Aaron said. "You're the priest."

"You're a pastor's son. You did fine before."

"I don't really feel like it today." He squeezed his hands into a fold. "You can do it."

Father Doyle smiled. "Okay. I understand." He led them in the standard Prayer Before Meals, with a special mention at the end for the souls of Emily and Jeremy.

he ate, Aaron could see all three of them eyeing

As he ate, Aaron could see all three of them eyeing him. Waiting for him to break down and cry so they could hold him and tell him that he should stop crying or that it was okay to cry. That's what everyone always did after his mom died. But nobody dared break the ice themselves and say something. He didn't want to say anything either. So the entire meal passed without a word.

As Maude was clearing the dishes, the door swung open.

Lincoln.

"Bacon and eggs?" He held himself and snickered and strolled over to the kitchen. He sniffed the empty pan on the stove. "Here I thought I provided better for my actors than that. You really can't make anything a little better than that crap?"

"I never hear anybody complain." Maude picked up a wooden spoon. "Maybe we just aren't as spoiled as you."

"Or you just have no taste."

Father Doyle got between their captor and Maude. "Did you only come here to insult us?"

"No." He stepped aside. "I actually came here for a reason." He held up two pairs of clothes—white tee shirts and black shorts. He tossed one pair to Drake and the other to Aaron.

Drake examined the outfit. "And what the hell are these for?" He held it up to himself. "White? Are you for real? After all this time, you want us to put on tasteless costumes for your stupid little shows?"

Lincoln shook his head. "Crude, as always."

"Is that a yes?"

He sighed. "The scenes today require these. I suppose I could've also had you film them in the nude. But let's face it, mountain man. Nobody wants to look at your rear end, let alone have it preserved on film. So I decided to spare us."

Drake spat on the ground. "Alert the Vatican, we have a saint among us."

Father Doyle approached Lincoln. "Do we have to use those as well?"

Lincoln held out his empty hands. "Do you see any more outfits? Drake and Aaron are the only ones in this scene. He bought Aaron, remember? We're picking up from there. So I guess that means the rest of you get the morning off. You're free to watch."

Therese said, "I thought the last movie ended when Jeremy died."

Lincoln slinked around behind her and pressed his face next to hers. "All the best stories are heavily serialized. Gotta film every day or else we get rusty, and we can't have that, can we?" He shoved her aside and danced over to Drake. "Now get changed. Filming starts in ten minutes and my goons are waiting outside to bring you both down." He walked to the door. "Don't be late." He left with a giggle and slammed the door behind him.

Drake approached Aaron.

Aaron hopped out of the chair and stood up straight.

Drake grinned. "Aren't you the perfect little army cadet? It looks like we're filming together again."

Aaron could smell Drake's body odor and took a step back. "Sorry. I know you don't like me very much."

Drake rolled his eyes. "Don't take it personal. I don't like anybody. Now get changed. We don't want to keep our director waiting."

The clothes fit loosely and comfortably enough. Aaron and Drake were then escorted down the stairs to the basement. It was cleared out from yesterday and was now even more open.

The others followed behind and again were kept at bay by Lincoln's guards.

Drake looked around and circled the open space. "Well, this is new. Wonder what our jerk director is planning now?"

Lincoln strutted down the stairs and walked to his director's chair. Aaron saw that same gleeful sneer that Lincoln wore when he'd tried to force him to kill his father.

Aaron looked over at Drake. He seemed annoyed. He hoped he wouldn't take it out on him.

Drake leaned against a wall. "So what do you want us to do? Run around in circles? Or maybe do the chicken dance?"

Lincoln handed Drake a knife. "Is everything sarcasm with you?" Then he stuffed a knife into Aaron's hand. "Don't hurt yourself."

Drake juggled the knife and caught it by the hilt. "Giving the boy a knife? You're not getting a teaching job anytime soon. You going to have us gut a fish?"

Lincoln laughed. "Think less hunting trip and more *Fight Club*. The scene is this: Aaron is tired of you abusing him and has decided to fight for his emancipation. You, being the pompous asshole that you are, obviously, will not just roll over and give him what he wants. So the two of you will fight to the death. Whoever dies first doesn't get what they want. Sound simple enough?"

Therese tried to rush to the arena but the goons stopped her. "You gotta be kidding. Aaron doesn't stand a chance against Drake. He's just a little boy."

Lincoln knocked his head side to side. "Well, David killed Goliath with a little rock. At least Aaron has a knife."

"You're a monster."

Drake held out the knife to Lincoln. "Seriously, you're insulting me by having me fight this kid. You should've just had me slit his throat like I did for the last one."

"You're not thinking of trying to be a hero all of a sudden, I hope?" Lincoln pushed the knife away. "I thought this was more fun. The rules are simple. You two fight until the other is stone cold dead. No excuses. No reprieves. It doesn't matter how you kill each other. But I must insist that the knife must pierce the body, even if you just stick it in the corpse."

"You've come up with some doozies before, but I must say, this is your most ridiculous crap idea yet." Drake shook his head and took a step back. "But whatever. Game or no game, the result will be the same."

Aaron stared at Drake. The man was huge. Muscular. He could snap him in two without even trying. This wasn't a game. This was just a fancy way to kill him. Aaron was doomed.

He let it sink in a moment that he was about to die. It scared him. Where would Drake stab him? In the neck? In the heart? Would it hurt? Would he die quickly? Slowly bleeding to death terrified him. He felt his bowels stir inside of him and back up into his stomach.

His dad died for nothing now.

But he could see him again. And his mother. If he died, he wouldn't have to be sad anymore. He wouldn't have to cry. It would hurt, but then it wouldn't hurt anymore. Maybe he should just let Drake kill him. Maybe if he didn't fight, Drake would make it quick. Then he could be free.

No. His father wouldn't want that. He always taught him to fight. Even when the odds looked scary. He had to fight. Even if he couldn't win. Even if he would die anyway.

As he pictured himself dying, bleeding, he realized that even if it hurt, he wanted to live. He wanted to wake up tomorrow and see the sun rising again. Even without his mom or dad.

Aaron clutched the knife tighter. Maybe this was it, but if he was going to die now, he'd die fighting to live.

Lincoln clapped. "Places everyone."

The cameras began rolling.

The fight was to begin now.

Drake and Aaron stood three feet apart. They moved in a circle, eyes locked.

Drake held out his knife. "I'm sorry, kid." There was almost a look of compassion in his eyes and a slight hesitation in his grip on the blade. "I'll try to make it quick. Just cooperate and it'll all be over before you feel anything."

Drake charged at him.

Aaron moved away. He ran backwards, keeping his eyes on Drake.

Drake stabbed again.

Aaron jumped back.

Then between Drake's legs.

Aaron was surprised after a few minutes that he was still alive. Maybe he'd forgotten one thing. Drake was stronger, but he was faster.

But he couldn't keep running forever.

And what if he could? He didn't want to die, but he didn't want to kill either. All he could think of was to keep running until he saw a way out that didn't involve somebody dying.

Aaron heard Therese and Maude cheer for him. He felt a shot of adrenaline shoot through him. Like he could win this.

Drake swiped at him again.

Dodge.

"You're a quick little thing, aren't you?" He panted and stood in place. "Well, you'll tire soon. And then it's over."

They locked eyes again, circling each other, like two lions waiting to pounce.

"We can find a way out of this together." He tensed his lips and took a step back. "It doesn't have to end like this. We have knives. He doesn't. Maybe we can fight him."

"Don't you think I've tried stuff like that? Do you think I enjoy killing you all? This has always been about survival from day one. Nothing's changed. You're no different than any of the others. You all had stories. Stories all end the same. Everyone dies. The only question is how long you stay in the story. I'm not a monster. I've learned a lot here. I know where to cut your throat so you'll die immediately. You won't even know it happened. And you can't kill me, so you might as well stop running. You're only going to make it harder for yourself."

Aaron shook his head. "But I don't want to die." He dodged a jab.

Drake went to grab him.

Aaron rolled away.

"You think anyone here wants to die? None of us want to die. You don't think we'd jump at the chance to get out of this hellhole? At least you'd die quickly. That's more than my son ever got."

Aaron stopped a moment to catch his breath. He tried to picture Drake being a dad. The man seemed so cold, he couldn't imagine a kid ever going near him let alone calling him "Dad." "You had a son?"

"He wasn't much younger than you." Drake lowered the knife for a second. "A bad man took him from me and his mom. He did really bad things to him and hurt him really bad. When my son died, he was in so much pain. So humiliated . . . death was probably a relief. And what are you complaining about? You feel a pinch on your neck and then nothing. Then you're free. You don't have to worry about this place anymore. If my son had to die, I sure as hell wish somebody was kind enough to kill him before he had to go through what he did."

Aaron stopped moving. In that moment, Drake wasn't scary anymore. He almost looked like he had a tear in his eye. Aaron didn't think Drake felt anything. But now, there was something there. Pain. Actual loneliness and regret.

Any chance Aaron could see himself killing the man vanished.

"I'm sorry about your son." Aaron lowered his knife.

"I'm sure you are."

"But neither of us have to die." Aaron looked around to the guards. "Maybe it won't work, but we can try. We can fight. If we team up, we can escape."

Drake shook his head. "So naïve."

Lincoln stamped his foot. "Enough talking. Kill each other."

Drake lunged again.

Aaron dodged again. But his foot caught the floor and he tumbled to the ground.

Therese screamed.

Aaron rolled on his back to see Drake kneeling beside him.

He pressed his hand down on Aaron's chest and

pushed.

Aaron tried to move but he was stuck.

Drake held his knife to Aaron's neck. "Don't struggle. It could make me cut the wrong place and you'll die slower."

Aaron froze. He prayed to God a thousand different prayers. Save him. Make him strong. Take him to Heaven. Forgive Ryan. Don't let it hurt. Save him. Bring him home. Make it fast. Forgive Drake. Forgive Ryan. Don't let him die. Not like this. Not now. Jesus, help him.

Drake took a deep breath. "I don't know what will happen to you once I do this. I never quite figured out what I believed about the whole soul thing. Maybe you won't exist at all anymore. Or maybe there is something after this. Maybe you can be happy somewhere. You're a good kid, Aaron. Either way, I hope you find peace. This is the only ticket out of here. You're really the lucky one. But, if there is something after this, just do one little thing for me. Find my son. Tell him his dad still thinks about him."

Aaron felt a droplet hit his cheek. All this time he feared that Drake would kill him. And now Drake was about to kill him, and he wasn't afraid anymore. If only Drake had shown this side sooner.

Drake turned the blade to strike.

Then he stopped.

"Chase?" His eyes widened. He began to breathe heavier. "You look so much like him."

Aaron felt the knife still in his right arm. He tried to move his arm. It did. He didn't even remember turning the blade upwards. He didn't intend to swing up.

But he did.

The blade pieced Drake's neck.

The large man stood frozen in place.

Aaron swung the blade to get it away. It slashed more of Drake's neck.

Blood spurted from the room onto Aaron's face as Drake made a horrid gurgling sound as he hovered over Aaron.

Aaron saw the man's hand release the knife.

As the body fell, Aaron could swear he heard Drake say, "Forgive me."

Drake's dead flesh collapsed onto Aaron's.

Face to face.

Aaron could smell a fowl smell on Drake's lips.

He stared up in the open eyes of his opponent. They were so wide and still looking back at him.

He could feel his clothes become wet with Drake's blood.

Then he felt his underwear wet. He hadn't done that since he was four.

Aaron took a breath. He was alive.

But Drake wasn't. Aaron had killed him. He killed another human being. Taken a life. Just like Drake. Just like Ryan. Was he evil now too?

Aaron gasped for air. It was sharp and hot as it stabbed his lungs.

He threw Drake's body off of him, as heavy as it was. Then shot to his feet.

He threw the knife to the ground.

He looked down at his clothes. They were all red. There was hardly a spot of white left.

His hands. His feet. His neck. All crimson. Covered in death.

"We have a winner." Lincoln clapped and hopped off

his director's chair.

Therese ran over to Aaron. "Aaron, are you okay?"

Aaron was frozen. His eyes were wide and unblinking, his mouth agape.

Therese could hear his heart pounding even without getting in close.

Therese again called his name. Aaron only began to breathe heavier.

"So much blood." His voice a whisper. "There's so much blood."

Therese pulled him into a hug. "It's okay, Aaron. It's okay."

"No." He shook his head. "No. Blood. He's dead. There's so much blood. I killed him."

"Get him cleaned up." Lincoln pointed for them to leave. "Shame, my money was on Drake. Didn't think the boy'd actually pull off a win. Life's just full of surprises. I do love a good twist ending."

Therese hugged him tighter, trying to get him to breathe easier.

He pulled away. "I gotta get off the blood. There's so much blood," he whimpered.

"Aaron." She held him by the shoulders. "We'll get the blood off. Hold on."

He threw her away and held his head, screaming.

Then he took off.

He was up the stairs in a blink.

Therese, Father Doyle, and Maude quickly followed after him, but he was too fast.

Aaron scurried up the stairs. He didn't know he could run this fast. He didn't even try to run. His legs were moving. His body was shaking. He felt like he was still in that basement with Drake's blood draining onto him.

He went for his room. For the bathroom. He had to wash this off.

As he knelt down, he froze. No, not her too.

Submerged in water, Dinah lay there. Still, unmoving, wearing the very nightgown he had told her to put on the night before. Her eyes were closed and her complexion was pale.

He lifted her hand out of the water. The water flowed off. Her hand was so clammy and pale. Thick and limp.

He released it.

It dropped just like his father's hand had.

"No," he said. "You can't be dead too."

The room around him began to spin in all directions. He couldn't stand straight and stumbled about aimlessly as everything went red.

CHAPTER 16

Therese and Father Doyle found Aaron holding his head and knocking into the bathroom walls.

Therese turned and saw Dinah floating in the tub. "Oh my gosh." She covered her mouth a moment and sank to her knees. "How? When? Did anyone see anything?"

"It's my fault." Aaron's hands shook as he made a fist. "It's my fault she's dead."

"Don't talk like that." She went to comfort him.

"No." He threw her back. "I killed her too. I'm a murderer!"

"Aaron, please calm down."

"No." He violently twitched his head. "There's so much blood. So much blood."

Aaron shot like a cannon toward the door.

Therese fell into Father Doyle.

"Are you all right?" The priest helped her to her feet.

"We have to stop him." She chased after him. "He could hurt himself."

Therese searched the halls for Aaron. She followed the sound of his wails to the men's bedroom.

Then to the bathroom.

She tried the door. Locked.

She banged on it. "Aaron, let us in. We can help you."

He didn't even respond.

She tried to break the handle. "Damn it." She slammed her fist against the door. "We have to get this thing opened."

Maude caught up with them, out of breath. "Is he all right?"

Father Doyle took her aside. "Aaron's locked himself inside. Go get the key."

Therese picked up the bedroom lamp. "No time for that." She raised it over the doorknob. "Hang on, Aaron." She slammed it down on the knob. Nothing.

Father Doyle eased her aside. "Let me." He smashed the lamp against the knob. Then again. Then again.

Just as the lamp cracked, the knob detached.

Father Doyle reached in and undid the lock. "We're in."

They pushed open the door.

Aaron was crouched beneath the running shower, red water dripping from every inch of him.

Aaron grabbed a scrubbed brush and began to scrape his skin. Hard. "So much blood, make it go away." He scrubbed harder. "It won't come out. Why won't it come out?"

Aaron tore the shirt off and threw it.

He grabbed a bar of soap and scrubbed it. Up and down his skin. Faster and rougher. He screamed in pain but kept going anyway.

Therese ran to him. "Aaron, you're making it worse." She grabbed the soap from him and set it aside. "You're clean." She looked him over. His skin was red from the scrubbing but the blood was mostly washed away. "There's no more blood."

He ripped himself away. "No. It's still here." He grabbed the brush and slashed it against his neck. His face. His chest. "Make it go away. It's all over. It's everywhere."

Therese snatched the brush from his grasp and handed it off to Father Doyle. "There's no more blood, Aaron." She wrapped her arms around him. His skin was vibrating.

He knocked her down and took off out of the room. Screaming louder.

Glass shattered from the kitchen.

Therese chased after him. To the living room.

"Stop it, Aaron."

He ran around throwing things. No direction. He grabbed his head and ran in circles, leaving the carpet wet as his body dripped a puddle.

Therese trapped him in a corner of the room and restrained him against a wall. "You're going to get hurt. I know you're upset. I know you're scared. But you have to calm down."

He shook his head. "No, they're dead. I killed them. I killed them."

"You didn't kill Dinah. You know that. And you had to fight Drake. He would've killed you. It's all right. You didn't do anything wrong."

"It's not all right. Dinah died because I was mean. I was a bad friend. And I stabbed him. I did that. Not you. Not him. Not Ryan. I did it. I can't get their blood off of me. Not ever."

He struggled to break free.

She restrained him harder and wrestled him to the ground.

He was strong. Much stronger than he looked.

She squeezed tighter, keeping his arms pressed to his side.

She looked up at Father Doyle. "Find Ryan. He might be the only one who can calm him down."

"Are you sure? After yesterday, he could make it worse."

"I know, but we have to try. I can't hold him much longer. And at this rate, he won't stop until he's hurt."

Father Doyle nodded and disappeared out the door without a word. Thank God it was still open.

This was all too convenient. The unlocked door. The halls free of goons.

Father Doyle passed one. They locked eyes.

He braced to dodge a bullet, but the goon just walked on.

This had Lincoln written all over it. Was he watching them? Maybe he knew this was coming. If he was recording this, he must be loving it.

He tried to determine where Ryan's room was. He opened a door. A closet. Then another. An empty bedroom.

Further down the hall, he saw a room with a man standing outside it. He recognized the man as the one who'd always stood near Ryan. He'd heard the boy call him Roy.

Father Doyle stopped in front of the room. "I know you have orders, but I need Ryan's help." He tried a moment to catch his breath but resting only seemed to make them come faster. "It's an emergency."

Roy pushed him back. "I'm sorry, but you can't come in here. No exceptions. Master Ryan is not permitted visitors. Why are you out here anyway? You're not allowed around here unsupervised." The man looked around.

"It's dangerous. If he sees you talking to Ryan, we could all be in trouble."

"I know. I wouldn't be here if it wasn't an emergency." He said a quick prayer that Aaron hadn't hurt himself. "I need to see him."

"I can't help you."

Father Doyle clutched the small crucifix hanging from his neck. He turned to go and froze, eyes closed. He couldn't come back without Ryan, but he didn't want to start a scene with Ryan's guard and attract attention. He prayed for God to show him the way.

"What's wrong?" A boy's voice.

He turned to see Ryan standing with the door open.

"I heard you talking. You said there's an emergency. Is it Aaron?"

Father Doyle nodded. "He had to kill someone for your father today. It was kill or be killed but it doesn't matter. He's not taking it well at all. He went berserk. We're afraid he's going to hurt himself." His heart burned from seeing the concern in Ryan's eyes. He was a true friend. But was it enough? "We thought maybe you could help calm him down. I know after yesterday and the things he said to you, that maybe . . . what happened hurt so much because he considered you such a good friend. And I know he still does. If you could tap into that, maybe you can reach him."

Ryan closed his door behind him. "I'll try anything if it helps him. Let's go."

Roy grabbed him by the shoulder. "But Master Ryan."

Ryan moved Roy's hand away. "Aaron's my friend and he needs my help. I don't care what Dad says anymore."

Ryan then rushed off. He was practically at the room

before Father Doyle could even start. Youthful agility at its finest.

When Father Doyle caught up with Ryan, he found the boy standing there. Frozen.

"Are you going to go in?"

Ryan reached out and grasped the knob. "You're sure I won't upset him more? I killed the person he loved most. He's right to hate me for it. If he's upset, then seeing me could make it worse. I want to help him. I do."

Father Doyle placed his hand on Ryan's shoulder. "Whatever happened before, you're his friend. That's what he needs right now."

Ryan burst into the living room.

Aaron tore himself from Therese's grip and slammed his head into the sofa. He let out a scream and slammed his fists into the cushions. "Make it stop." He grabbed his head and yanked his hair.

Ryan didn't think Aaron was even capable of acting like this. Aaron was calm and quiet. He didn't go crazy. Ryan shuddered as he thought of what it took to push Aaron to this.

As Aaron went to take off again, Ryan lunged at him.

He knocked Aaron to the ground and pinned him down. "Aaron! It's me. Chill. Okay? You're safe. You're alive. Take it easy."

Aaron squirmed to break free. "I have to get it off." Aaron threw his hands at Ryan's face.

Ryan grabbed back and wrestled Aaron's hands back. "There's nothing to get off. Open your eyes, damn it. Look at yourself. There's nothing to get off. It's just your head. It's messing with you."

Aaron let out a hellish hiss followed by a horrifying spin of the eyes. It felt like he was possessed. Aaron was good. This wasn't him.

Ryan looked around at the adults. They stayed back, almost in fear.

Aaron threw him off.

Ryan crashed into the table.

He jumped up and headbutted Aaron in the stomach. "Sorry, man."

He reached back and landed a punch to Aaron's cheek.

Aaron went flying back and landed on the sofa.

Therese went to run to Aaron but Father Doyle put his hand out in front of her. "He needs it, Therese. Just let Ryan do this."

Aaron's breathing slowed and he slowly rose to his feet, clutching his red cheek.

Ryan locked eyes with him. Aaron's eyes were normal again. They were scared. Hurt. But they weren't crazed anymore. He was back.

Aaron struggled to his feet, holding his face where it had been punched.

He looked around at the turned-over chairs, the mess, the broken pieces.

He saw the others. Silent. Staring right at him with pity.

He turned and saw Ryan. "Aaron? You okay?"

"Did I really do all of that?"

"You weren't yourself."

Aaron tried to remember what had just happened. He remembered fighting Drake. He remembered killing him. He remembered finding Dinah. After that, it was like he was in a dream watching somebody else on TV with a picture that kept cutting out.

He felt cold. He looked down and saw that his clothes were gone. And everyone was looking at him. "Oh no."

He fell to his knees behind a coffee table and covered himself with his hands. His skin was soggy and cold. He felt a tear stream down his cheek. He couldn't believe he was acting like this in front of everyone.

Ryan knelt down next to him. "Somebody get him a housecoat or something."

Therese retrieved him a robe.

Aaron threw it over himself. It was long and draped over him like a tent. He tied it closed.

Ryan held out a hand and helped him to his feet.

After the adults straightened out the room, Ryan sat Aaron down on the couch. He put his arm around him.

Aaron turned to him. "Thank you."

One hour later. Aaron had changed into fresh clothes, but still kept the robe on. It was warm and he liked the way the blue cotton felt on his skin.

Dinah was taken away. Aaron had to turn away when they carried her out.

"You can look now." Ryan patted Aaron on the back. "They're gone."

Aaron opened his eyes. The fear and terror returned to it for just a second. "Why did she do it?"

Ryan looked down a moment. "Pain makes people do bad things. Like fear."

Aaron turned to him. "Like say they hate their best friend." He swallowed hard. "I'm sorry about what I said yesterday. I don't really hate you. And I know you're not evil like your dad. I know you're really a good person. You're my friend. And you did it so he wouldn't kill me. I shouldn't have said any of that, even if I was mad. And I'm sorry."

"Maybe you were right." Ryan looked down at his folded hands as a tear fell onto them. Razors shot up his arms. "You loved your dad and I killed him. How can we still be friends after that?"

"I killed somebody today." Ryan met Aaron's eyes. "He was alive and I stabbed him, and now he's not alive. You killed somebody, and I killed somebody."

Ryan shook his head. "But you had to do it."

"And you had to do it." Aaron held his chest and cried a moment. "If somebody didn't kill my dad, Lincoln was going to kill me. I hate it. I hate that my dad is dead and I hate that your dad made it happen. But you only did it to help me. Because you're my friend. Because you're good. It hurts so much. But I get it. I'm not mad at you. But I said all of those horrible things because I was mad. Can you ever forgive me?"

"What's to forgive?" Ryan forced a smile. Aaron didn't deserve to feel guilty for yelling at him on top of everything else. Ryan felt his chest hurt that he was still causing his friend pain. "I'm the one who destroyed your life. I took your father away from you. You can take back words. But I can't take back what I did. I can't get your father's face out of my mind. Every time I close my eyes, there he is. There's nothing for me to forgive. But what I did to you, you can't forgive that. It's too big."

"I do forgive you," Aaron said. "I know what it's like now. I can't hate you for what you did. And nothing's too big to forgive. God can forgive anything. I have to forgive too. But I want to forgive you. We're still friends, Ryan."

Forgiven. Ryan let the words sink in. He repeated them to himself in his mind. His chest hurt a little bit less. Maybe it was just feeling good that Aaron didn't hate him. Or was there something more to forgiveness?

"Can I ask you a question, Aaron?"

Aaron hesitated a moment. "I guess so."

"Why do you believe in Heaven?" He swallowed hard. "My dad never talked much about religion. The afterlife was kind of like a joke to him. He's all about living for today and being happy now. I used to think that when you died, you didn't exist anymore. You were like a robot that was turned off forever. Everything you ever thought, or felt, it would all just be gone. You were just . . . dead. And everyone is gonna die so you gotta hurry and have fun now. So I tried to have fun and be happy, which usually meant just doing whatever my dad told me so he'd be happy and give me stuff. But hey, I was rich. So if I stopped existing, at least I'd have been given a lot of money."

Aaron nodded. "What do you think now?"

Ryan shrugged. "I'm not sure. A couple years ago, I started seeing some preachers on TV. Some of them seemed so crazy with their funny talking and all the people clapping. But some made a whole lot of sense. If we can think and feel like we do, can all of that really just stop existing when our heart stops? Everything they said just seemed to make the idea of God so much easier to understand. I just don't think everything is an accident. But then I see dead people, and I see someone that was there and now they're not. Why would God let a good person die like that? And in so much pain? And I don't really know what a soul is. I'm me. My face. My hands. My brain. That's me. Where is my soul? It's all so confusing. And I couldn't ask anybody. Dad would never let me talk to the priest and nobody here believes in anything like that. I want to believe in it so bad. I want to believe that maybe God is real and that He loves me even though my dad is evil. But I don't know how to believe. Like you do. What makes you believe?"

Aaron looked up at the ceiling and leaned into the sofa. "I never really thought too much about it. My dad taught me about Heaven ever since I could remember. He used to tell me that Jesus was watching even when nobody else was. So if I was ever scared or lost, I just had to ask Him for help. He was somebody I could always talk to. And it always made sense to me. God made me. He made me, me. We all have hands and feet and eyes and ears. And we all can do really good things. And if we do good things, we feel something inside that just feels right. And when we do bad things, we don't feel right. I don't know. I guess I just always could feel God was real. I couldn't see Him or hear Him. But He was there. Whether I could make somebody else believe me or not. God was just there." He scrubbed his cheeks a moment and allowed himself a smile. "I'm not very good at explaining this, am I?"

"Actually, you're doing okay. You're just a kid, right? Like me. The grownups know more about that stuff than us."

"I hope maybe you believe one day." Aaron reached over and took Ryan's hand. "God's a good friend. Even better than me."

Ryan smiled. "Maybe God sent you to me."

"I think so. But even if I'm not here anymore—"

"I won't let my dad kill you."

Aaron closed his eyes. "Maybe we'll both live to be

one hundred." He smiled and opened his eyes. "But God's still the best friend we'll ever have. And if we know how to be His friend, we'll be even better friends to all our friends."

Ryan sighed. "Is God mad at me because I just killed somebody? If God's real, will I go to Hell now?"

Aaron put his arm around Ryan. "Nobody goes to Hell unless they're not sorry. I can see in your eyes. You're a good person. You're sorry for what you did. Just talk to God. Tell Him how you feel and He'll find a way to help. Maybe one day I can take you to church and you can get baptized. If we ever get out of here."

"Now you sound like a pastor." Ryan chuckled.

"My dad was a good teacher."

Ryan looked at the clock. "Well, I'd better get back to my room. I want to try and not piss off my dad."

Aaron nodded and they fist bumped.

"Thanks for coming. For helping me. I don't know what would've happened if you didn't snap me out of that crazy fit."

Ryan walked to the door. "You sure you're good?"

Aaron nodded. "I'll be okay."

He opened the door and went to walk out. He turned back to Aaron. "Aaron, I really am sorry. I'm always going to wish I found a way to make it so you and your dad could both stay alive."

"There wasn't anything you could do. You helped me stay alive. My dad wouldn't want to be alive if I died instead. Don't beat yourself up about it. Please?"

Ryan nodded. "I'm trying, Aaron. But I'm going to make it up to you. One day, I'm going to find a way to make it up to you."

"See you later, Ryan. Have a good night."

"Yeah, you too. See you tomorrow."

Ryan pulled the door shut behind him.

Aaron was alone now. He could hear his breathing echo in the silence. He felt his chest. His heart was still beating. He hated what he did to Drake. He hated that now Dinah was gone too. But he was still here. As long as his heart was still beating, he had a chance to go home. But even if he didn't, every moment alive was a gift. And he thanked God for them.

Ryan showered and changed into a collar shirt and dress pants. He even put on a belt. He didn't dress like this unless his father was having people over, which never happened anymore.

He walked to the mirror and combed his moist hair. He left a slight uneven tuft at the top. It added character. And he needed to look honest.

Roy came up behind him. "Are you actually voluntarily combing your hair, Master Ryan?"

Ryan turned and smoothed some stray hairs with his hand. "You don't have to look good to stay home. But you do have to look good to go out."

"Out?" Roy pulled him away from the mirror. "Mr. Prescott has not given us an itinerary for going out."

"No. He didn't." Ryan stepped aside. "I'm going on my own." He walked to his door.

"Master Ryan." Roy blocked the door. "I realize my orders are to do as you ask, but you realize that is limited strictly to what doesn't contradict Mr. Prescott's own rules. I already used up a lot of big favors with your last request. I can't just let you go out."

"You have to." Ryan grabbed Roy by the sleeves. "This is important."

"So was making sure young Billy received a proper burial." Roy bit his lower lip. "He did, by the way. I had somebody look up the obituary. His grave is next to his mother's. It's in a sunny spot of the cemetery, close to the road so everyone will see it as soon as they come in and they will know he's there." Roy kneeled down to eye level with Ryan. "Reports say you can't even tell how he died. He was buried with dignity. That's what you wanted, and I made it happen for you. But I can't keep doing things. One thing was close enough. If the cops had found out about your father because of it, we all could've paid dearly. I kept that one a secret, but if I do something else, your father could catch on."

Ryan smiled. "Thank you for helping Billy. Billy was a good boy. He was like a little brother. He was good like Aaron. But I couldn't save him. When they cut him, it was like they cut me. They killed him in front of me and I couldn't do anything to save him."

"I know that hurt you. I understand. But—"

"No buts." Ryan pulled Roy away from the door. "Billy died and I couldn't save him. Well, Aaron's my friend too now. He's suffered a lot. He had to watch me kill his dad. I've only known him a little bit but it's like we've been best friends since we were little kids. He deserves a chance to go back home and have a regular life. He's still alive. I can still help him. So I'm going out and I need you to make that happen for me."

"How is going out going to help Aaron?"

"I saw cops outside earlier today. They were looking in houses."

"That could've been for any reason. I heard your grandfather talking. He spoke with them. They were investigating burglaries."

"Maybe that was just a cover story." Ryan rolled his eyes. "Come on. The cops have to be looking for Aaron still. I saw on the news. They have something called an Amber Alert. That means they're looking for him, right? They know he's missing."

"And they have absolutely no reason to look here." He placed his hand on the back of Ryan's head and gently stroked. "You know the cops always check the family first and then look into men who might want to use a boy for some very bad things. After twenty-four hours, they tend to think the boy is dead. They probably think he's buried in the woods somewhere."

"Well then, I guess I'd better go set them straight. I believe those cops were here looking for Aaron. And I'm going to go tell them exactly where to find him."

"So you will turn your father in to the police?" He sat down on Ryan's bed. "Do you realize what will happen if they find him? You won't see Aaron again." He leaned his head against his hand as he shook his head. "You'll be taken away. Sent to God knows what kind of home. And your father? They'll lock him up and seize all his assets. Is that really what you want? Do you want to wreck your family?"

"I want Aaron safe." Ryan opened his door and peeked down. He pictured Aaron sitting alone on the sofa, still trying not to cry for how much his life was wrecked in the past week. The image stabbed Ryan's chest. "I'd rather never see him again and know that he's alive somewhere. My dad's not going to keep him alive if he stays here. The next day after I saved him, my dad made him fight somebody he thought would kill him. Aaron survived that too, but what's to stop my dad from trying something else tomorrow? He killed Billy. He'll kill Aaron too. He'll have more people taken. More parents. More kids. Then he'll make them scared for a while before he kills them too. This has to stop. I gotta get the cops here before anybody else gets hurt. They'll help Aaron and make sure he's safe. They won't let anything bad happen to him. Then it doesn't matter what happens to me."

"What if you make it worse?" He threw his hands in the air. "Your father has connections. Your grandfather has even more. Don't you think there have been close calls? Having the cops show up could just make them angrier and they'll take it out on whoever is still alive. You. Aaron."

"Roy, stop trying to change my mind." He wrung his hands together and took a deep breath. "I'm going out and you're going to help me. I gotta help Aaron and get the cops here. I can't just sit around and wait for my dad to kill him. I killed his father and I gotta find a way to make up for that. Somehow. Maybe saving him won't do it but it's a start. And it's more than sitting around."

Roy waved Ryan over to the bed. "Sit down for a minute." He patted next to him.

Ryan rolled his eyes and did as Roy asked. "You're not going to talk me out of it."

Roy put his arm around Ryan. He pulled him close to him. His strong arms were one of the few things that made Ryan feel safe. "You know, I remember when you were a baby and your father first assigned me to be your caretaker. I saw how your father was and I thought, for sure, that you were going to grow up to be some spoiled rich brat. Like him. But you didn't. Even when you were just learning to walk and talk, I noticed something about you. You were truly kind and you truly cared about what happened to other people. It wasn't just being a baby. There was something in your eyes. Something pure and special. You were destined to do great things to help people. And you've only gotten better as time's gone on. I'm so proud that you're willing to risk so much to help a friend. That's something your father would never do."

"Then why aren't you helping me?" He rested his head on Roy's chest.

"Your father will be mad if he finds out. He will punish you and I don't want to see you get hurt." He lifted Ryan's head up. Ryan could see his soft, brown eyes staring down. "I care about you just like you care about Aaron."

"I care about you too, Roy. You've been there for me when my dad wouldn't. You were there for me after Billy died." Ryan grasped Roy's sleeve and squeezed the fabric in his shaking hands. "You even risked your life to make sure he and his mother could be buried."

"I did that because I knew what it meant to you."

Ryan nodded. He hopped off the bed. "Then I need you to help me one more time. If this works, you'll never have to help me again."

Roy sighed. But Ryan could see in his eyes that Roy was coming around. Even if he still didn't think this was a good idea. "How will you find the police station?"

"I'll manage." He flashed money from his pocket. "I can walk to a bus stop. I remember seeing one not too far down the road."

"That's at least a mile."

"I'll walk it."

"You don't know your way around the city. You could get lost. There are people out there worse than your father. They could take you."

"I'll be okay, Roy."

"At least wait until the morning. This is dangerous."

"I can't wait. I gotta do this as soon as I can."

"I still say this is a bad idea." He groaned and shook his head. "But if you have your mind set on this, then who am I to stand in your way?"

"Are you saying that you'll help me?"

"I am." He smiled and stood up. "Just give me a few minutes to find a way to sneak you out. It's not exactly going to be easy."

Ryan grinned. "But if anybody could think of it, it'd be you."

Roy smiled and patted Ryan on the head.

Ryan threw his arms around Roy. "You're the best, Roy. You've always been the best."

Roy blushed. "Feeling's mutual." Roy opened the door and checked to make sure nobody else saw. "Start praying, Ryan. This is going to take some doing."

"Thank you, Roy. So much."

"It's my pleasure." He winked and closed the door behind him.

He returned in a few minutes with a blindfold. He put it on Ryan. "This is for your own good."

Ryan gulped for a moment. For just a moment, he considered that this could be a trap and he'd take off the blindfold to find Aaron hanging from the ceiling as his father laughed. But he could trust Roy. He knew that.

Ryan felt a cool breeze. Then he was put somewhere. A box? A trunk? He didn't know but he wasn't there too long. After a moment, he was moved to his feet and Roy took off the blindfold.

Ryan looked around. He was outside the estate. On

the road.

"Whoa." Ryan looked around at the trees. He held out his hands and spun in the wind. "It's so nice out here. How did you do it?"

"That's my secret. If this doesn't work out, I made sure your father could never find out from you." Roy pointed down the road. "The nearest bus stop should be a mile down the road. It's getting dark. Try to hurry. God only knows what's on this road."

"I will."

The two exchanged one final hug.

"I'll stall your father for as long as I can. Please be careful, Master Ryan."

"I will. This will all work out. You'll see."

Ryan turned to go. He looked back at Roy and waved.

Roy waved back and vanished back into the estate grounds. He prayed Roy could cover for him. If his dad found out he was gone, it wouldn't be good for anybody.

Ryan strolled along the road. He gazed up at the sky. The sun hadn't yet set but he could see the crescent moon amidst the fading orange and the beginning of starlights. He could barely breathe as he gazed up at them. He couldn't see them well from his bedroom window or even from the balcony. Out here, it was all so clear. So big. This was the world. Maybe Aaron was right. Looking up at this, Ryan just knew somebody had to design it all.

It took twenty minutes to reach the bus stop. He hadn't seen a single car go by or passed a single house. He never realized how far away from other people they were. No wonder nobody ever found them

As he got to the bus stop, he saw a bus approaching. Maybe God was trying to help him out.

Father Doyle and Therese were called away to film scenes just after dark. Aaron worried about them filming so late but he had to trust that they'd be okay. At least this time, it wasn't him filming.

Aaron could still remember his father wearing this housecoat a few days before. He could still smell his father on it and feeling it wrapped around his body felt like a hug from his dad.

He smelled something good coming from the kitchen. Maude was standing by the stove stirring something in a pot.

He walked in and peeked inside.

"Beef stew." Maude cracked a grin. "Smells good, eh?"

"Very."

Aaron noticed the pot was very small. Scarcely bigger than a bowl. "Is that going to be enough for everyone?"

Maude ladled some into a bowl. "This is just for you."

"Just for me?" Aaron smiled. "You made a dinner just for me."

"You had a tough day. I figured you deserved something a little special."

She set the bowl at the table with a spoon and glass of water. "Come, child. Have supper."

Aaron rushed to the table and sat down. He sniffed the contents as the hot steam warmed his face. The hearty cubes of potatoes, carrot slices, and tender chucks of beef looked right at home in the thick beefy broth. If it tasted half as good as it smelled, his stomach was in for a real treat.

He quickly said a prayer before digging in. One bite

and he was hooked.

Maude took a seat at the table and watched him. She leaned in close with a smile.

"This is really good." Aaron spooned another mouthful. "You must've been taught by somebody really good."

"My mother."

"Did you ever have kids to cook for?"

"I never really found the right man to marry. So no kids. But I did have younger brothers. Much younger. One was twelve years younger and the other sixteen. They really enjoyed my cooking. I think they were the only kids in school who ate their veggies by choice. And not because they were just so well behaved." She winked.

Aaron laughed. "If you can make spinach taste good, you must be the best cook in the world."

She smiled. "I am glad you think that. I love cooking for kids. I was a teacher for twenty years when I was younger. Then I volunteered at a soup kitchen. I had a lot of chances to cook for people. Even here, it's been one of the few things that keeps me going."

"Did your brothers ever have children?" Aaron sipped his water. "I'm sure they'd love having an aunt who can cook so well."

Maude sighed. "No. They never got the chance. They both passed away when they were little lads."

Aaron felt his stomach churn. "I'm sorry." He felt a wave sweep over him. She had to live all those years missing her brothers. Feeling sad for her must've been making him sleepy as he felt his eyelids growing heavy. He yawned. "You must've been so sad."

"It was a long time ago." She patted him on the hand.

"How did it happen? Was it an accident?"

Maude settled deeper into the chair and let out a sigh.

"When they were eight and four, they got really sick. It was a really bad flu going around. Everyone in my family got it, besides me. Daddy died fairly early on from it but the boys hung in there. Mama got really sick too so she couldn't take care of anyone. She got better eventually. But I had to work to take care of everyone. My brothers were good patients, though. They didn't whine or complain. Not much anyway." She chuckled as a tear slid down her face. "The last week, they even tried making jokes about school. They could barely lift their heads. That's when I knew they weren't going to get better." She scrubbed her face. "Poor things suffered so much. I could tell they were in a lot of pain." She stood up from her chair and stared off. "One morning, I came in to check on them. Their eyes were closed, like they were asleep. They looked so peaceful. But they weren't asleep. They were holding each other's hands. I think they knew. It was almost a relief. They weren't in pain anymore."

Aaron pushed his bowl away. "I'm sorry you had to lose them."

She smiled and wiped her tears. "Well, nothing we can do about it now. They're with their Maker and that's all one can really ask out of life anyway. You know, you remind me of them. Just a little bit." Her lips began to shake. "That sensitive sweetness for life. Those eyes. It's like I'm looking right at them."

"Everyone here has a sad story. We've almost all lost somebody we love."

"If you're alive long enough, it's bound to happen. But if we can talk about it, we can bond."

"I guess so. I'm glad you've all been so nice to me." Aaron yawned again. "It's made all of this a little bit easier."

"That makes me happy."

Aaron rubbed his eyes. The urge to sleep felt so strong now. "I'm never usually tired this early."

"You had a rough day." She collected his empty dish and began to wash it. "You should go lie down."

He took a sip of water. "Dinner was really good. Thank you so much."

"You're very welcome."

Aaron laid his head down on the tablecloth a minute. He could just fall asleep right there. Maybe he would. He was too tired to walk to the bed and this tablecloth was soft. Just for a few minutes.

Inhale. Exhale.

Maude watched Aaron sleep. Breathing slowly, then more slowly. Until his hand slumped from the table and dangled motionlessly in the air.

Maude walked over to Aaron and stood above him. A tear fell from her eyes onto his full, brown hair.

Her mind flashed back to an hour earlier. Just after Father Doyle and Therese had been called away.

She had just helped Aaron gently wash his face. He was still in his room.

She walked into the living room. Lincoln.

"Can't you let the boy grieve in peace?"

Lincoln patted the sofa and watched the dust particles. "This furniture is really cheap. I should buy new stuff."

"What do you want?"

"I heard the boy really had a fit after his little fight."

"Get to the point." She marched over to his face and shot him a defiant sneer.

He handed her a bag. That same damn paper bag prop.

"You want me to film a scene now?'

"In that bag is a vial filled with a drug. Tonight, you are going to empty that into Aaron's food or drink. It will kill him."

"What?" She froze.

"Did I stutter?"

"If you expect me to kill that child . . ." She shoved the bag back at him. "You're even more bonkers than I thought. You want to kill me if I don't? Go ahead."

"Don't act like you haven't done it before." He leaned in close. "Remember Old Man Maguire? Your little beau from two years ago?"

"That was different. He was old. He was sick. Aaron's a young, healthy boy."

"You're the one who gave me the idea. You see, I don't just take people at random." He breathed in her ear. "I make sure I investigate every little detail of their life. Details even the law doesn't know about. I leave pictures behind as a final memento of their former life. If I leave a picture behind, it's because I've so studied the life of the people taken that it's as if I wrote their story myself. That's how well I know them. That's how well I know you, Miss Maude."

"You don't know a damn thing about me."

He grinned. "I know you poisoned children before. Your little brothers? So sick and in so much pain. They had no idea you poisoned their dinner. They didn't feel a thing. They just went to sleep and you pretended to find them dead the next morning."

A chill shot up her spine. How did he know? She never told a soul. "They had such high fevers. Their bodies were shutting down. They were suffering. Aaron's not sick."

Lincoln smiled. "Isn't he? He's grieving. And by to-morrow, he'll be in a lot of pain. Tomorrow, I am killing off all of you."

"What?" She backed away.

"This operation is getting too risky. The cops are nosing around. My cast is becoming something of a liability. So I need to dispose of you. All of you. One day more." He held up a finger.

"That's why you've escalated killing us."

"Somebody's been paying attention." He patted her on the cheek. "Aaron didn't get shot yesterday. He didn't get stabbed today. It'd be a damn shame if he got shot or stabbed tomorrow. I am giving you a chance to spare Aaron that pain. Getting shot is a painful way to die." He placed the bag in her hand. "If you give him this, it will be just like going to sleep. He won't feel a thing. He won't know a thing. He'll think he's just tired from all the stress. He'll just close his eyes and die."

She shoved it back at him. "Why can't you do it?"

He shoved it back. "It has to come from you. He trusts you and won't suspect a thing."

He turned to go.

"You're a devil, Lincoln Prescott."

Lincoln opened the door. "Just give me a buzz when I can pick up his body for my hall of fame. The bed next to his father's is still open."

"Don't you like deaths to be recorded?"

Lincoln turned to her and winked. "What makes you think it won't be?" He waved with a giggle. "You never had any place to hide from me."

She watched as tears dripped onto the bag.

Now, not two hours later, it was done. She hovered above Aaron. He looked so peaceful slumped over at the table. The bag was in the trash now.

She reached down and felt his neck. Stillness. No warm breath from his nose.

She sat down next to him and took his hand in hers.

A sharp jolt shot through her chest. Maybe she was having a heart attack. She almost wished she was. After all he'd survived, to have somebody he trusted end his life. It wasn't fair. But it was the only choice. She couldn't let him suffer as he bled out. He didn't know. He was at peace now with his father and he never had to suffer the dread of dying.

"I'm so sorry, Aaron." She set his hand down. "Please forgive me. I didn't have a choice."

She flipped through every moment she'd spent with him. Every smile. Every tear. Every beat of his young eyes. Those eyes were closed now. She watched them. And as she watched them, she wept. Bitter, guilty, agonizing tears.

CHAPTER 17

A whole day and nothing. No judge would issue a warrant. No new leads from their data. Nothing that could nail Bradford Prescott to a wall and rescue the people Wayne knew he held captive behind the gates of his estate.

"All this time, they could be dead," Kevin said. "We have to prepare ourselves for that."

Wayne stared at a photo of Aaron and his father. "I've tried to prepare for that for years. It's tormented me day and night. But I can't use that fear as an excuse to stop looking."

"How about you use my orders as an excuse?" A sharp, feminine voice.

Julie and Wayne looked up. Kevin looked down with a groan.

She had brown hair down to her shoulders and was wearing a tan pants suit a size too tight. She wore a grimace and the wrinkled lines around her lips gave the impression she never took it off.

Kevin rose to his feet. "Cassandra Parnell, the big cheese herself."

"That's Madam Mayor to you, Martel."

"Oh, alliteration. So poetic."

"You think this is funny, don't you Martel?"

Kevin shrugged. "Every time you come here to bitch about how I run things, it is kind of funny. Since you aren't a cop."

She gasped and leaned in to yell more.

Wayne turned to Julie. "Who is this dame?"

Julie groaned and sank into her chair. "Gridlock in a pantsuit."

Cass shot around to Wayne. She held out her hand. "I don't believe we've met. Mayor Cass Parnell. Now, please tell me, who the hell are you?"

Wayne rose to his feet and slid his hand right past hers. "I'm a former employee who didn't like the way your kind ran things. So I quit."

"Yet here you are, in a police station." She looked at the files on the desk. "Working a case with my lead detectives with zero to no evidence."

Kevin took a shot of whiskey from a flask. "We got too freshly buried corpses that say otherwise."

Cass spun around to make sure all three saw her disapproving scowl. "So because two people are dead you think you have a right to go harassing political donors you have a gut feeling are involved? Yes, I know about Bradford Prescott. You're making a mockery of this department."

Kevin grunted and shot to his feet. "Funny, I thought I was trying to bring missing people home safe and sound instead of in body bags. But hey, you like people in body bags. Gives you a chance to cry to the media and increase your poll numbers. You'll never become governor unless there's a dead child to cry about on the eleven o'clock news."

"You know that is not true." She pounded his desk. "I just don't like you and your daughter going rogue and doing whatever the hell you want to do. Especially under the badge."

Julie got in her face. "I like how you bark orders while you sit behind your cozy little desk. While we're fighting crime, you're attending Planned Parenthood rallies and making empty promises to help the middle class with your new wage tax increase. Running your mouth on Sunday news shows is the closest you get to real danger. And yet here you are, trying to micromanage us the moment one of the wealthy donors you pretend to oppose is a suspect."

"You have a lot of nerve talking like that to somebody who can fire you."

Julie shot her a sneer. "Fire somebody with my record of closing cases? Go ahead. See what that does to your poll numbers. I'm not afraid of you. My job is to save lives, not back off from a viable suspect because the mayor is in his pocket."

Cass stabbed Julie with her finger. "You and your conspiracy theories. Your job is to protect constitutional rights."

"Since when do you give a damn about the constitution?" Julie paced around Cass. "I haven't violated anyone's constitutional rights. If I did, I'd have stormed that Prescott estate without a warrant and shot him dead the moment I saw one of our captives. You don't have any place talking to me about the constitution. Going by the bills you've signed into law, one would never know you even remember that a constitution even exists."

Wayne watched with a smile. Julie never did let anybody push her around. Not even a boss. She'd make a great private investigator.

Cass tugged at her suit. "I am ordering you to shelve

this case. Completely. Unless you get some concrete evidence. You are not cops to follow hunches. You are cops to enforce the law." She turned to Wayne. "And you are not even a cop. You shouldn't even be here. It's a disgrace to the badge to have you three working this case."

Kevin folded his arms. "What if I say no?"

Cass grinned. "We're a big town, Martel. There are a lot of cops I'm sure wouldn't give me hell. And I'm sure giving them a promotion would make them forever in my debt."

Kevin snickered. "Go ahead. Just know that both sides can go on CNN."

"You really do not want to push me."

"And you don't want to push me." Kevin leaned back in his chair. "I know where your skeletons are buried too. Given the killers we've apprehended in recent years, firing us wouldn't make that governor's seat you're eyeing very likely. Your approval ratings are already in the tank from the rising crime and unemployment in our town. The last thing you need for your image is firing cops for going above and beyond to make sure people don't die."

"That is not what I am doing. Police have a shaky public image in recent years. Police brutality is a hot issue. I would not be firing heroic child saviors. I'd be firing cops who used their badges to bully people they have no evidence are guilty."

Julie threw her hands in the air. "We have a profile. We have a witness connecting that area to the crimes. We have a reason to suspect Prescott."

"Your witness is a mental patient remembering a phrase from a phone call that can't even be proven to have happened. Legally, it's nothing. And you know I'm right. It's why no judge would give you a warrant. And this is not the FBI. You are not profilers." She pointed to the mess on the desk. "All you have is a bunch of unproven hunches and you're using them as if they were DNA evidence. I can't allow that."

Julie bit her lip. She was silent a moment. Did the shrew's words actually trap her, or was she just using the silence to make a comeback sting?

She leaned in close. "My hunches are what caught us Artie Falcon."

"So the end justifies the means?"

Wayne began to laugh. He caught Cass giving him the stink eye. "Are you always like this? I know the Martels are hotheads but I would think somebody who managed to dupe the people into voting for her—twice—could keep her cool a little bit better. Something tells me if we were harassing one of those radio commentators that make money by mocking you, you wouldn't be so upset. How much did Bradford Prescott contribute to your last campaign?" Wayne laughed. "Picture the headlines tomorrow." He wrote in the air with his finger. "New Jersey Mayor Fires Police Chief To Cover Up Bribery." He pointed to the floor. "Your poll numbers will be dropping faster than a snowman in July."

"I can't do this," Cass said. "You have my orders. Follow them or there will be consequences."

She turned to leave.

She almost bumped into a boy.

"What are you doing here, kid?"

"I have to talk to the police chief." The boy moved around her. He was dressed nicely, like he was going to church or a nice restaurant. He stuck his hands in his pockets and looked uneasy. "It's something really important."

"Isn't it past your bedtime?" Cass signaled for him to leave. "The police don't have time for your antics."

Wayne waved the boy aside. There was something about his eyes. This couldn't be a prank. "What's wrong? Is everything okay? Did somebody try to hurt you?"

The boy shook his head. He took a deep breath. "My name is Ryan Prescott."

Wayne's mouth dropped. Could this finally be God answering their prayers? "Ryan Prescott?" He raised an eyebrow. He met Julie's eyes. "Are you related to Bradford Prescott, by any chance?"

Ryan nodded. "He's my grandfather. My father's name is Lincoln."

"Ryan, how'd you get here?"

"That's not important. What's important is what I have to tell you about my dad. What he's been doing." He gulped. "For a very long time."

Julie sat him down in a chair.

Ryan took a deep breath. "My dad . . . he's kidnapped people. Lots of them. Since I can remember. I know you've been looking for them. I saw you outside the other day. They're in the house. Where I live."

Julie knelt down to eye level with Ryan. "How many are there?"

"There's four left, I think. But there were eight yesterday morning. He always has them killed from time to time, but never this fast. I'm scared he's going to kill all of them."

Wayne felt his stomach knot. In the time they'd failed to catch Prescott, four people were killed.

Julie rummaged through the desk and tried to find a picture of Billy from when he was alive. She found the boy's school photo. "We found this boy's body last week.

Do you know anything about him?"

"Billy." Ryan nodded. "He was my friend. Dad made me watch him die. Dad usually keeps them in a freezer under the house. He likes to go back and look at them sometimes. But I couldn't let him not bury my friend. My friend deserved to have a grave and be buried the right way. So I had somebody leave them somewhere you could find them. They deserved that."

"That explains why we never found anybody else," Wayne said.

Julie took Ryan's hand. "We found a video on the body. It shows . . . did you put it there?"

Ryan shook his head. "Maybe Roy did. He's the one I asked to leave them. I don't know how he made a copy but maybe he wanted to try and leave you a clue. Something to help you stop my dad. Roy worries about me. He pretends to go along with my dad but I know he wishes somebody would take him away."

Wayne leaned in close. "Why are you coming to us now?"

"I have a new friend there. His name is Aaron. I don't want him to die. He's a good person. He told me I could be a good person too. But I can't be a good person if I don't try to help him. You have to save him. He can't die too." Ryan began to cry.

Cass rolled her eyes. "Nice story, kid."

Ryan shot to his feet. "It's true."

"I know Bradford Prescott very well. He is one of the most respected members of the community. Lincoln is a bit odd but he's distinguished. They aren't common criminals. I don't even believe you're a Prescott. Lincoln Prescott has no record of having any child."

Kevin nodded. "That's true. We looked hundreds of

times for a child, a nephew. Anything. We didn't find any evidence of any child in the family."

Ryan's eyes narrowed. Wayne saw genuine bewilderment on the boy's face. "I don't understand." He shook his head. "How could there be no record of me? I'll be turning thirteen in a few weeks. I don't go places but there has to be proof I exist."

"Sorry." Cass shook her head. "I can't use the unproven testimony of a kid who lies about who he is." She turned to Kevin. "And I forbid you to do it. You leave the Prescotts alone."

Kevin grinned. He looked to Julie. "What do you think?" He raised an eyebrow.

Julie walked over to Cass. "I'm calling a judge. I will get a warrant. And you will shut up and let me do my job."

"I'll call every judge in the country first and tell them that an ex-cop is trying to get a phony warrant for a personal vendetta. I won't let you railroad the Prescotts." She then turned to Ryan. "Go home, kid. I'd throw you in jail if you were two years older. Consider yourself lucky." She left the room.

Ryan sank to his knees and began to cry. "You have to go get them. The longer you wait, the more chance he'll kill them."

Julie reached out to him.

He knocked her hand away.

"Ryan, we believe you," she said. "We just need a little time to prove it so we can issue a warrant to arrest your dad. We have to do this right so your dad can't hurt anybody ever again."

"They don't have time." Ryan grabbed her arm. "He's going to kill them all, and I'm going to have to watch another one of my best friends die. I told you what he did. You're the cops. Why can't you just believe me?"

"We do." Julie stroked his hair a moment. "We just have rules to follow." Those darn rules again.

"It's not fair."

He burst out of the office. Wailing.

Julie and Wayne chased after him.

"Wait up, Ryan." Julie went to grab hold of him but he was too fast. "We believe you. You need to stay here. We're going to save them."

He ran out of the building. Into the night.

Into the street.

In front of Cass' limo.

The driver slammed on the brakes as the headlights shined on Ryan.

Too late.

Ryan turned to see the car just before he went flying across the hood.

He landed on the ground, bleeding from his head.

Julie screamed and froze in the doorway.

Wayne rushed to Ryan's side. He checked for a pulse. "He's still alive."

Julie quickly took out her cell phone and dialed 911.

Cass got out of the car with her hands over her mouth. "We didn't see him."

"Of course you didn't." He took Ryan's hand in his. "You never see the people who don't fit your agenda."

"Are you saying I did this on purpose? That I had my driver run down a child?"

Wayne turned away from her and looked at Ryan. "Hang in there. Help's coming. For you and for Aaron."

Wayne tapped his foot in the hospital waiting room. He'd given statements and watched Cass return to her office cleared of any wrongdoing. He looked over at Julie, nervous mother face in full force.

"Do you need to call Patrick?"

"I have," she said. "He's at a friend's. Feeling back to his old self, apparently. He understands why I have to stay tonight."

Wayne shot a glance at the doors to the operating room. "Do you believe he's Prescott's?"

Julie leaned her head back against the wall. "I don't know. It fits perfectly with the tape." She scrubbed her face, pulling her hair back. "In theory, it works. But why is there no record of Lincoln Prescott having a son?"

"I think I can answer that." Kevin strolled down the hall waving his cell phone. "Just got off with the station. Legally and officially, not only does Lincoln Prescott have no son, but Ryan Prescott doesn't legally exist. But we did find something. Kimberly Clyde. She attended film school with Lincoln Prescott. There was word that they had a fling but there was never any proof. Things reportedly ended very bitterly. I made some calls to others from her class with Prescott. According to classmates, she got pregnant but denied that Lincoln was the father. She delivered the baby at home. Then the next day she drove her car into the bay and drowned. They found her body, but they never found a baby's. There was no car seat or anything fit for transporting a child. Just a baby blanket. Legally, the baby was never recognized. Friends tried to initiate a search for the baby, but no body was ever found. There was never any legal record of him." He held up a finger. "Coincidentally, Lincoln became a borderline recluse around this time. Who wants to bet that he kidnapped his son and staged his ex's death? Now, we can't prove anything by this alone, but it explains how Ryan could've totally been off our radar. Lincoln's been keeping him in this house all his life and never allowed him to have any official contact with anybody. That way he could have his son and never have to account for him to the law. Until now."

"I believe it," Julie said. "But will Parnell?"

"That woman doesn't have to believe a damn thing." He took a seat across from them. "She's irrelevant. We just have to hope the kid pulls through. Or we might never get answers. If he dies, not only do we have no testimony but it could make Lincoln go even crazier."

"But he isn't legally Lincoln's son." Wayne rubbed his chin. "Ryan doesn't have a legal next of kin. Why would they call Prescott no matter what happens?"

Kevin nodded. "True. Still . . ."

A doctor walked into the waiting room. "Are you the family of the boy brought in?"

Julie flashed her badge. "We're better. Can you tell us how he is?"

"He's going to pull through. His injuries were only minor. He's very lucky. But he will be unconscious until morning. It's best you wait to see him until then."

"That's good," Kevin said. "Then I'll be staying here tonight."

Wayne nodded. "I will too."

"That really isn't necessary," the doctor said.

Julie flashed the badge again. "Why don't you let us be the judge of that?"

The doctor was silent a moment before shaking his head and walking away.

Wayne glanced at the clock. Almost midnight. Tomorrow, this had to end. Just one more day. They only had to hang in there one more day.

CHAPTER 18

It was almost midnight as Therese returned.

The goon behind her smelled of beer and was even unsteadier than her tired legs. For a brief moment, she thought about making a run for it. She could take this guy. Then she remembered the guards pacing the doors, and the last time somebody tried that. There was a blood spot by the door the next morning and Therese never saw her again.

She turned her thoughts to Father Doyle. He tried so hard to keep them inspired. Lincoln had worked them for hours on some stupid dinner script. The poor priest had conked out from exhaustion at the table. Lincoln told her to leave him there. She prayed she'd see him again. With Lincoln's bloodthirsty appetite the past two days, she worried it was an excuse to get rid of him.

Aaron had calmed down before she left. She prayed he was able to get some rest. The poor kid had been through a horrible experience. She worried what the morning could bring.

She walked into the quarters. "Maude? You still up?" Silence.

She saw a light from the kitchen. Maude sat quietly at the table.

Aaron was slumped over in the chair next to her.

"Did he fall asleep like that? Kids. They can conk out anywhere. After the day he had, I'm not surprised."

Maude tensed her lips as she avoided eye contact.

Therese came up behind Aaron. "I should probably carry him to his bed. A table isn't exactly a comfy place to sleep."

"Might as well leave him there." Maude turned to her with downcast eyes. "Lincoln will come for him in the morning."

A sharp pain shot through her chest. "What are you talking about?"

"I'm sorry, Therese." She began to cry. "I had to."

Therese laid her fingers against Aaron's neck. Still.

She lifted him up and checked for breathing. "Aaron. Aaron, wake up." She shook him. No reaction. There was a heaviness to his body. She called him louder. Not even a flutter of his eyes.

"How did this happen?" She set his body down. "I don't see any blood. How did he die?"

"I did it," Maude said.

Therese felt her face and fists burn red. She walked closer to Maude. "You're going to have to repeat that. Because I don't think I heard you correctly."

Maude shook her head. "You heard just fine." She pushed herself to her feet with a grunt. "I killed Aaron. I put something in his food to put him down. He never knew what hit him. He didn't feel anything. He just fell asleep and passed."

Therese took deep breaths. She looked to Aaron and then to Maude. "Why would you kill Aaron?" A tear escaped her eye. "We were supposed to protect him."

"That's why I did it." Maude slammed the table. "Lincoln. He said he's killing us all tomorrow. All of us. He said after all Aaron survived, it'd be a shame for him to bleed to death in a lot of pain. I couldn't argue. He said this was a way for Aaron to go peacefully."

Therese twitched and threw her hands in the air. "He's going to kill us all? Maybe that was just another lie."

"Four of us are dead in two days. Don't you think that's a little much, given his usual patterns? He's done with us. He's probably going to shoot all of us. He said he didn't have a problem with shooting Aaron. Aaron didn't need a violent death after all he's been through. Would you really want Aaron's last memories alive to be bullets flying through his body? Or worse, screaming in agony as he slowly bleeds to death? The others died such horrible deaths." She held out her hand to him. "Look at him. See how peaceful he looks? He didn't suffer at all. He just closed his eyes and he was with his parents again. And God. He didn't have to dread it or be afraid."

"He's still dead." Therese charged at Maude and grabbed her by the blouse. "You murdered him."

"I did what was merciful."

"You poisoned him."

"Lincoln was going to shoot him."

"Maybe he wasn't." She shoved Maude back. "Maybe Lincoln made that up to get you to kill him. He's not above lying, you know."

"Do you really believe Aaron has a chance to get out of this alive? How many years have we all been here? Rescue's never come. Now Lincoln's done with us and he's getting rid of all of us. It was better for Aaron to just fall asleep instead of being snuffed out."

"You snuffed him out. If Lincoln wanted Aaron dead, why not just shoot him? Why have you poison him?"

"This is the guy who put a gun to Aaron's head and

told him to shoot his father. He gets off on watching us make the decision. We'll be dead either way, but if it comes from us, he has even more control. I hated giving him that. I resent it. But I did what I had to do. I did what was best for that boy. He's at peace now."

Tears spilled out of her. "I promised Jeremy I'd look after him. I promised Aaron I would." She turned to Aaron. "And now you've made a liar out of me 'cause Aaron is dead. You killed him, you old bitch."

"Hate me if it makes you feel better," she said. "I spared that boy the pain of a bullet."

Therese gazed at Aaron's face. She tried to remember the look in his eyes when she promised to keep him safe. Those eyes were closed forever now. Lincoln tried twice to kill him and Aaron survived. Now it was all for nothing. And it was because of Maude.

Therese charged at Maude and pinned her to the wall. "I don't care if you had good intentions. You had no right to kill him. You had no right to decide for him that he shouldn't live. He was another person, not some puppy. You can't just put people down under the guise of mercy. That's every bit as much murder as putting a gun to their head and pulling the trigger. You murdered Aaron, Maude. You. Not Drake. You murdered the boy we all were supposed to protect. And I can't forgive you for that."

Maude struggled to break free. "Let go of me."

Therese tightened her grip. "No, I won't let go."

Maude yanked harder. She broke Therese's grip.

They both tumbled to the ground.

Maude's head slammed against the point of the table. Hard.

She hit the ground with a thump.

Therese looked up. Maude was bleeding on the floor from her head.

Therese checked for a pulse. Nothing. Just like Aaron. Maude was dead.

She'd killed somebody too now. A friend. She was like them.

She returned to Aaron. He looked so pitiful seated there.

She gently lifted him from the chair. She was surprised his body wasn't heavier. He felt like a baby in her arms. She carried him over to the sofa and gently set his body down on it.

"Forgive me, Aaron." She stroked his cheek and hair. "I wanted you to be the one to live." She buried her face on his chest and cried harder.

She pulled back and took a final look at his face. She caressed it. His skin was so soft. He looked like he was just asleep.

She retrieved a sheet from his bed. She draped it over his body head to toe.

She said a prayer for his soul. He'd never get a funeral. Just stuffed into the freezer with everyone else. That thought stabbed her chest more.

She sat herself on a chair and stared at the covered body. All night. Maybe she fell asleep or maybe she was just delirious. But the next thing she knew, the sun was shining in through the window. If what Maude said had been true, Lincoln was probably already on his way to get her. To kill her.

CHAPTER 19

Father Doyle was astonished at how bright their quarters were this morning. He couldn't recall the last time the sun had been this majestic.

He rubbed his aching head as he opened the door to their quarters.

He locked eyes with Therese, who was seated calmly on the couch.

"Lincoln just woke me up with a song. I think he's losing it more. He told me there was something up here I'd need to see."

Then he saw Maude's body on the floor. A halo of blood surrounded her head.

Then he saw the covered body on the couch, with a boyish hand sticking out from the sheet.

He looked back and forth at the bodies and then to Therese. She seemed catatonic. "What happened?"

"Lincoln told Maude to poison Aaron. She did. Now he's dead." She tensed her lips and wiped aside a tear. "I confronted her about it. She fell." She pointed to the kitchen. "I think she hit her head. Now she's dead. You and me? We're the only ones left. And if what Maude said is true, Lincoln's going to finish us off today."

Father Doyle threw up his hands. "Back up a minute. Maude killed Aaron?"

"She said it was a mercy kill. He was sitting at the kitchen table, slumped over. She just stood there and watched him die. I covered his body to give him some respect. Maybe you should say a prayer over him."

A surreal heaviness overcame him. Standing became a chore. Two more senseless deaths. One of them a bright child with a great heart. He said a quick prayer to God for the strength to understand.

He knelt down next to Aaron and gently lifted the sheet of off his body. Aaron looked so peaceful compared to the other victims of Lincoln's madness. No blood. No wounds.

Father Doyle raised his hands over Aaron's body. Then he felt something. A slight wave of air. Like a breath.

"Therese, are you sure Aaron's dead?"

She nodded. "He wasn't breathing. He didn't have a pulse. He's stayed that way for hours. I'm pretty sure he's dead."

Father Doyle pressed his ear against Aaron's chest. He felt Aaron's neck. "That's just it, though. He is breathing. And I feel a pulse. It's faint. But it's there."

Therese's eyes widened and she rose to her feet and backed away. "No, he was definitely dead, Father. I checked. He was dead."

"I don't know what to tell you," he said. "Maybe it's a miracle. I don't know. But Aaron's definitely still alive."

She ran over to the body. She checked his pulse. "I don't understand," she said. "He didn't have a pulse last night. He was dead. I was sure of it."

"Of course you were sure of it." Lincoln. Behind them. "That was the point."

They spun around and met his piercing eyes.

Lincoln walked to Aaron and paced a moment. "Well,

I played a little game on the old lady and she fell for it hook, line . . ." He shot a glance at Maude's body. "and sinker." He giggled and leaned in close. "See, that drug I gave her? It doesn't really kill people. Rather, it puts them sort of in a state of suspended animation. The target loses consciousness and bodily functions cease to the point where you'd need to be an experienced doctor to detect the shallow breathing and pulse. Just enough to keep the body alive but low enough to fool most people into thinking that the subject is dead. A machine would've picked up on it. You would've too when hours went by and the boy wasn't stiff or cold, but I guess you were too busy being upset to really think that deeply. I take it the effect is wearing off. He should be awake soon. We'll all head downstairs after he comes to."

Therese charged at him. "You're sick, you know that?"

He pushed her into the wall. "I know. And to think, he's about to experience the very death the old lady was trying to save him from. Yet, she was willing to accept the death herself, but she'll be spared from it because you killed her for killing him. Talk about irony."

Father Doyle got between them. "Okay, we get it."

Lincoln smiled. "Doesn't matter much to me whether or not you get it. But I can't wait all day to get rid of you three." He swallowed hard. "I have to get rid of you quickly. Before anybody . . ." He turned to go. "You have one hour. My associates will be by to take you to me then. I suggest you say whatever prayers you need to now."

Father Doyle ran in front of the door. "Please, Lincoln. I'm begging you. At least let the boy go. He's a child. Nobody would believe him when he says where he's been. He hasn't done anything to you. Let him live. It doesn't have to end with death."

Lincoln patted Father Doyle on the shoulder. "You might wanna hear some of those confessions now. There won't be time once I shoot you."

Lincoln opened the door. Two goons were standing there. He pointed to Maude and they took her away.

Father Doyle stared at the closed door a moment. He slammed his fist against the door. "Oh God, I don't know what to do. I don't know. Whatever You will here, I need Your help."

Therese paced the room. "What good is his being alive if Lincoln's only going to kill him?"

"Every breath we take is a gift." He turned to her, trying to hide the tears in his eyes. "An hour is an hour. Some people would give anything for one hour."

Aaron sat up. He rubbed his eyes. "Is it morning?" He looked around. "I don't even remember going to bed."

Father Doyle and Therese looked at each other. Then at Aaron. It was like nothing ever happened. Just a normal night to him. He didn't even know Lincoln was going to kill him today.

Father Doyle went to him. "How do you feel?"

He shrugged. "Tired. My head hurts a little. But I think I'm okay."

Therese asked, "Do you have any memory of last night?"

He looked back and forth between them. "I had dinner. I don't remember anything after that. Is something wrong?" He looked around the room. "Where's Maude?"

Father Doyle sighed and looked away. He stroked the back of Aaron's neck. "Aaron, we thought you were dead. Therese didn't feel you breathing."

His eyes narrowed. "What are you talking about?" He took a deep breath. "I'm breathing. See?" Fear built in his eyes. He looked around. "Where's Maude? Why do you two look so scared? You're not telling me something."

"I was dead?" Aaron stared at the kitchen table. He didn't like thinking of what he looked like dead. He'd thought of it so many times since he'd gotten here. And it was almost like it really happened.

He stared at the blood spot on the floor. "And now Maude's dead?" He sniffled. They were even more alone now.

Therese shamefully bowed her head down. "I'm sorry, Aaron. I thought she killed you. I thought you were dead and I was so mad. We got into a fight and it just got out of hand. I'm sorry."

"I'm sorry I scared you." He gulped.

"It's not your fault, Aaron." She pulled him into a hug that caught him off guard. "I'm just so glad to see you alive again. I'd never thought I'd see those big, beautiful eyes again. Or hear your voice. You're a special person, Aaron. You don't deserve to die here."

"Well, we're still alive. Maybe Lincoln's done killing us for a little bit."

Therese's eyes turned down. "Aaron, there's something else. It's about Lincoln. We're not going to be here tomorrow."

Ryan opened his eyes. His head throbbed with agony. The sunlight was especially bright today and it only made it worse.

He groaned and rubbed his head. There was a bandage on the back. It itched and he ripped it off. He looked around. He was in a hospital room.

"I think the doctors want you to keep the bandage on." A woman's voice.

He sat up and saw a woman at the foot of his bed. Beautiful, blonde hair. A warm smile. Like how he pictured his mother.

"You're that cop from last night. Julie, right? What are you doing here? What am I doing here?"

She walked to the side of his bed. "What do you remember?"

"I remember you guys wouldn't believe me. So I left."

"Yeah." She chuckled. "Then you walked right out in front of a car and got yourself hit. You're lucky that you weren't killed."

Then he remembered the headlights coming for him and the pain of the car slamming into him. "Probably should've been paying more attention."

"Yes, you should have. The doctors say you're lucky nothing was broken. If the car was going any faster, you could have been seriously injured. Or worse."

"So did you arrest my dad yet?"

"We're waking up judges. We'll get one. And we'll get him, Ryan. Once we do, your testimony will ensure he goes to jail."

Ryan stared out the window as the rest of the night came back to him. "That lady said there's no proof I exist." He felt his arms and then his face. "What does she mean?"

Julie stroked his arm. "Your dad never let you outside much did he?"

Ryan shook his head. How did she know?

"Your father did some very bad things. He didn't want anybody else to know about you and so he made sure nobody ever did. But you do exist. Just because you

don't have some pieces of paper doesn't change that."
She tapped his chest. "You have a soul. God knows you
exist." She ruffled his hair. "I believe you, Ryan. I believe
everything you said. We've been looking for Aaron since
he went missing. My friend Wayne? Remember him?"

Ryan nodded.

"He's been looking for some of the other people there
for three years. We want to help them. We just have to
make sure your dad can't escape through a loophole so
we have to do this right. But we're going to get him. And
you're going to get a good home."

"Good, then I'd better get there." He went to get out
of bed.

Julie stopped him. "Hold on there, slugger. You aren't
going anywhere."

"I'm fine."

"Where are you going to go? You can't go home. It's
not safe for you to be in the house during a police raid.
Plus, you're still hurt from last night. You're staying here
until the hospital releases you."

"I've fallen down the stairs before. This is nothing."

She leaned in close. "You're staying."

Ryan felt the sweaty cotton of the sheets on his butt.
He looked down at his hospital robe. Then he smiled. "At
least let me put on some real clothes. This robe is drafty."

"Your clothes had to be cut off, Ryan. You'll just have
to wait here for a bit. I know what you're trying to do.
You need to stay here until we figure out what to do with
you."

"You say that like I'm some chore."

"No, but you're a factor in all of this."

"I don't feel like a factor." He threw his hands in the
air. "I just want to keep my friend from dying."

"And so do we. We're here to help you, Ryan, even if you don't think so. We just want to get this done without people getting hurt."

"That's what I want too." He looked at the door. It was closed and on the other side of the room. Could he do it? He had to chance it.

He ripped the IV out of his arm and hopped out of the bed.

"Hey." Julie got in his way. "Ryan, I'll get you some clothes but you have to stay here."

Just then, her phone rang. She answered it. Ryan could see it on her face before she said anything. They got the warrant.

She hung up. "I need to go. We got the warrant. We're going to go get your dad."

A doctor came into the room.

Ryan rushed for the door.

Julie chased after him. "Ryan! We're going to get him. You have to stay here."

Ryan ran down the hall. "I have to make sure Aaron's okay."

"Ryan, don't do this."

"I need to make sure nobody I love gets hurt."

An elevator door opened up and a man stepped out. Ryan quickly jumped inside.

He could see Julie running to catch him, so he pushed the button to close the doors.

They began to shut.

Julie jabbed her arm between them and they opened again. "Sorry, Ryan, I raised boys. I know these tricks."

Ryan shot out of the elevator just before the doors closed.

He turned and saw the elevator going down. He had a

minute. Nobody else in the busy hospital seemed to catch on yet.

He rushed down the hall. He ran into a room and checked the closet. Empty.

He ran into another. Nothing. He had to find something to wear besides this drafty hospital gown.

On the third try, he found a hoodie and pants. No underwear. Better than nothing, he supposed. He threw off his robe and stepped into the clothes. They were a little baggy but close enough. And the pants didn't fall off. They'd work.

Ryan rushed to the stairwell and hopped down them.

He peeked out the doors and saw Julie looking for him.

When her back was turned, he darted for the hospital doors and made his way outside. He saw a bus pulling up to the stop. He didn't have any money, but he'd worry about that later. He had to get home.

Ryan got off the bus at the same stop he was picked up on. Thank God it was the same route. He waved to the nice old lady who had covered his fare and started off for home.

He'd hoped by now the cops would've been there. By now, his father knew he was gone. He prayed to see police cars swarming the house. Julie said they got the warrant. They should be there.

But instead of cop cars, as he neared the front gate to the court, he saw his father standing there.

Ryan wanted to run the other way. Anywhere but here. But his father saw him. He couldn't run anymore. He'd started this. And now he'd finish it.

"Ryan." His father waved to him. "It's wonderful to see you. Imagine my surprise last night when I went into say goodnight to you and you're nowhere to be found."

"I had things to do," he said. "I'm here now."

Lincoln smacked Ryan across the face.

Ryan fell into a patch of grass. But he immediately shot back to his feet.

"You're just a pathetic little bastard. You don't know what business is. What were you doing last night, Ryan?"

"Just things." His father's eyes were narrowing on him. He had to lie better.

"Well, I had things to do as well." He signaled for Ryan to follow him. "Why don't I show you what I did while you were gone?"

"Do I really have to watch another lame movie?"

"For once, I'm not talking about my movies." He grabbed Ryan by the arm and dragged him to the house.

"You're hurting me." Ryan grunted and struggled, but his father was too strong.

He took Ryan to his room and slammed him onto the floor. Ryan screamed as he held his throbbing arm. The bruises from the car reignited and every area of his body shot with pain. "You want to beat me? Is that it?"

"Get over yourself." Lincoln turned Ryan around to the wall. "Open your eyes."

Ryan opened his eyes. His stomach turned.

Roy lay slumped against the wall. There was a bloody hole on his forehead and an eerie halo of blood on the wall around him.

"Roy." Ryan crawled over to him. He threw his arms around his lifeless caretaker. "I'm so sorry. I didn't want you to die."

Ryan heard his father snicker.

He shot around and got to his feet. "You killed him."
He lunged at his father. He wanted to curse him. Scream at him. But no words would come out. No words could work for how angry he was.

Lincoln shoved Ryan back. "No, you killed him, Ryan. I merely carried out the sentence you ordered when you asked him to help you break more of my rules. I could almost forgive dumping the bodies. But helping you betray this entire family? That is unforgivable."

"No, don't blame this on me." Ryan took deep breaths but they couldn't calm him or stop him from shaking. "You killed him. He was my friend. He was the only good thing about this crummy life you've given me."

"Crummy life? You had someone to literally wipe your ass. You had good food. You had a father who would indulge virtually anything you wanted to be. You had more money than you could count. Most boys would consider that life a hell of a good one."

"Well, money gets old."

"You sound like a Christian greeting card. These people you care so much about? They don't deserve you."

"No. I don't deserve them." Ryan thought of Jeremy. Of Aaron. How he'd destroyed them. "I am sorry I killed Aaron's dad. I hate that you forced him to kill or be killed. All of these people are good. And you made them betray that because you liked watching other people do evil things. But at least they are sorry. At least they want to be forgiven. You enjoy it. You enjoy hurting people. That's what makes you evil."

"This evil man gave you a dream world."

"More like a nightmare." He pointed to Roy as tears welled in his eyes. "And now you've taken one of the last things I had that was really good."

"Well, I guess you're going to hate what I'm going to do next." His father smiled. "I'm going to kill Aaron. And just like before, I am going to make you watch."

"No, I won't let you." Ryan made a fist and took a step toward his father. "You'll have to kill me first."

Lincoln laughed. "You foolish child. You don't have a say in the matter. When you're staring into the open eyes of his bullet-filled corpse, then maybe you'll realize the futility of friendship. In the meantime, stay here with the remains of what once was your butler. See what you did."

Lincoln stormed out the door.

Ryan heard a clink. The bastard locked it from the outside.

Ryan rushed the door. He slammed his fists against it. He screamed as he attacked the knob, but he couldn't get it open.

He had to get to Aaron. He couldn't let it end this way.

Aaron, Father Doyle, and Therese were led by the goons to the back patio.

Father Doyle looked to Therese. Then to Aaron. They both looked so scared. He couldn't let it end this way. Aaron deserved the chance to grow up. Therese deserved the chance to be a mother one day. They couldn't just give up.

They were led to the pool.

Lincoln stood by it. The cameras were already set up.

Two goons held Ryan prisoner behind him.

Ryan's eyes widened when he saw Aaron. This was real.

Aaron called out Ryan's name upon seeing him. "Are you okay?"

Ryan struggled in the goons' grip. "I'm fine. I'm sorry, Aaron. I'm so sorry. I tried so hard to get him to stop. I tried so hard to help you. I tried so hard." He began to cry.

So did Aaron. "It's okay. I'm scared, but I'm ready. Don't let him kill the good part of you. He can kill all of us. But only we can choose to be like him. Sometimes we've screwed up. But we can always change. Even if we did bad things before."

Ryan looked away.

Father Doyle looked at the surroundings. They were in the back. They'd never be able to run to the front without getting shot. Maybe if he rushed them all? Maybe he could hold them off just long enough.

Aaron took deep breaths as tears dampened his face. "I'm glad God let me meet you, Ryan. Even if I have to die now. I never had a real friend like you before. At least for a little while, I did. Just do me a favor. Remember me. Remember the stuff we talked about."

"I will."

Aaron smiled thanks.

Lincoln rolled his eyes. "I'd say get a room if I wasn't about to kill Aaron." He wiped his glasses with his shirt-sleeve. "Let's do this."

He ordered the goons to restrain the three of them.

Lincoln took out a large pistol. "Now, let's see who's going to get it first."

Father Doyle heard sirens in the distance. Growing louder. And louder. Was this an audio mirage? His desperate mind imagining a way out? He closed his eyes and prayed it was real. That God was finally granting his prayer. He had to chance it. It was now or never.

So he attacked the goon behind him.

Bang.

Wayne and Julie hopped out of the first police car of a team of ten. The officers prepared to storm the Prescott estate.

Julie clutched the warrant and took out her gun.

Wayne eyed the Glock. "I think I deserve a gun."

Julie grinned. "To the knees? I can do that."

"You know what I mean."

"I don't want you going in. You brought us this case. Let us finish it."

"I've been a part of this case from the start. I deserve to be part of the finish."

"Tempest, I can't have you getting hurt."

"I went through all the same training you did. I'm every bit as prepared for this as you are. I just don't have a badge."

"You think I'm going to give you my spare gun?"

Wayne grinned. "I wasn't asking for yours." He took out a gun. "I brought my own." He waved it. "I just wanted the lead detective's permission to use it. To confirm we got each other's backs."

Julie rolled her eyes. "You're an ass." She smacked him and smiled. "Let's go. Don't get killed. And don't blame me if you do." She winked.

Wayne smiled. "Fair enough." He loaded the gun. "Now let's go rescue people."

A bullet hit the dirt next to his feet.

Father Doyle wrestled the goon as police charged through the gate.

The other two goons fell dead.

Lincoln pointed his gun at Father Doyle.

Father Doyle turned the goon around to take the bullet. The goon crumpled to the ground.

"Whatever happens, keep faith. Now run."

Therese and Aaron took off. Gunfire between security and cops blocked the gate.

They ran toward the house.

Father Doyle lunged at Lincoln. He dodged a bullet and tackled Lincoln to the ground. He pounded Lincoln's face. Then again.

Lincoln lay there unmoving. Was he out cold or just faking to save himself? Father Doyle didn't have time to guess. He grabbed the gun from Lincoln's hand and turned to aim it at the goons who were holding Ryan.

They were gone.

"Go," Ryan said. "Go now."

"Be careful."

Father Doyle followed in the direction Therese and Aaron went. Getting through this house alive wasn't going to be easy. But at least now he had a gun. It wasn't much but it was something.

Therese found Bradford waiting for her inside with a gun pointed at her. She could see it in his eyes. He was there for her. Aaron was right behind her. She couldn't let this creep hurt him.

"Hello." Bradford stepped toward her. "Didn't think you'd be able to just walk out the front door, did you?"

She made a run down a hall.

Bradford chased her.

He fired. A picture on the wall shattered and smashed to the ground.

Therese screamed and kept running. As long as Aaron survived this, what happened to her didn't matter.

Aaron lagged behind. He couldn't run as fast as usual. It must've been the drugs from Maude still in his system.

He held out his hands as he burst through the doors to the Prescott mansion. He could hear footsteps above and all around. How many goons were there? And how many cops were here?

He couldn't find Therese. How did she disappear so fast?

He ran down a hall. It led to a dead end.

He turned back.

Then he felt a slimy hand swipe over his mouth and slam him back.

"Gotcha." Lincoln.

Aaron squirmed against Lincoln's bony frame but the man overpowered him and carried him out to the pool again. "If I kill nobody else, I'm killing you."

He threw Aaron on the ground.

Ryan rushed his father from behind. "I won't let you hurt him."

Lincoln knocked Ryan back. "Watch closely, son. Your father's about to teach you what it means to be a man."

He pointed his gun at Aaron. "The cameras are rolling. If they're coming for me, I'm having one last showdown. The climax of my story is now."

Aaron stared up at Lincoln's grimy eyes. They were full of pure malice.

"I'm not afraid of you." Aaron clenched his fists and prepared for the bullet. "Jesus." He didn't even know what to pray for. Strength? His life? It didn't matter. He just kept repeating that to himself. He closed his eyes. He wouldn't let Lincoln see the fear.

He heard Ryan scream for it to stop.

Two loud claps.

Aaron waited for the pain. Or a light. Was he hit in the chest? Or maybe the bullet went right through his brain and he was already dead. But he didn't see anything but the colored shapes from the sunlight hitting his eyes.

He risked opening his eyes, terrified he'd see his chest bleeding.

He didn't.

Ryan was standing in front of him. Two bloody holes in his stomach.

Lincoln's eyes were wide as he backed away.

"Ryan." Aaron's voice was a scream. He could hear it echo.

Ryan opened his mouth to respond but only muffled puffs of air came out.

He clutched the wound a moment. He pulled his hand back red. Slowly, he crumpled to the ground, hitting the grass with a thump.

Lincoln held his head and screamed. "Damn it! Ryan, why did you do that?"

The cops stormed the yard.

Aaron saw a woman and a man leading them with guns drawn.

Lincoln did too. He made a dash for the house.

The man shouted to the woman, "Go on without me."

"I thought you wanted to be a part of rescuing them," she said.

"That's what I'm doing."

The woman nodded and chased after Lincoln.

The man rushed over to the patio. "Oh my gosh." He eyed Ryan bleeding.

Aaron recognized the man from the restaurant where he was taken. He was a private detective. Wayne.

Aaron looked to Ryan. "He shot him. He shot Ryan. Please, you have to help him."

Ryan looked bad. His skin was becoming pale. The boy gasped for breath as blood drained from two bloody wounds in his lower chest.

Wayne pressed down on the wound. "Aaron, see what I'm doing? I need you to press down with all your might. We need to keep pressure on this. I'm going to call for help."

Aaron was crying. Hard. "Ryan, why'd you do that?" He pressed his hands hard against Ryan's wounds. The blood squirted onto his hands and covered them in red. "He was supposed to shoot me. Not you."

The creep shouldn't be shooting anybody.

"I needed to stand up to him," Ryan said.

"By taking the bullets meant for me?"

"Whatever gets the job done." Ryan cracked a smile.

Wayne flipped out his cell and called for an ambulance.

He stuffed his phone away and returned to putting pressure on the wound. "Ryan, just stay with me. Help is coming. You can pull through this." There was already so much blood pooling around Ryan on the patio. Too much.

Aaron grabbed Ryan's hand. "You hear that? The doctors are coming. You're not going to die. You're going to be okay."

Ryan smiled at Aaron and looked to Wayne.

Wayne could see it in his eyes. The boy knew.

Bradford chased Therese through the corridors into the kitchen. Then to the stairs.

The front door. Unguarded. Could it really be so easy?

Bradford blocked her way. "Were you planning to leave?"

She turned to the stairs and scurried up. Maybe she could find a way to lock herself in a room. It could at least buy her time. Especially with cops crawling everywhere.

She ran toward the prisoner's wing. A cop ran past her and pinned a goon to the wall. They didn't even see her.

Bradford's hands around her mouth. "You know never to run from me."

She screamed a muffled scream. She thought of Aaron. Of Father Doyle. She prayed they'd be able to escape. Even if . . .

Snap.

Kevin Martel made another wrong turn in the labyrinth of the Prescott mansion. He was the last one in. He hadn't seen any of the victims yet. Just a lot of underlings being shot or arrested by a lot of cops. Even the cook went down in a shootout. This was one quirky place. But still no sign of the bosses.

He decided to try upstairs to see if he could find any of the hostages or the honchos.

He slowly ascended the stairs, keeping his gun pointed outward.

Two of the underlings burst out of a room, guns drawn.

Kevin quickly took out each of them with a single shot.

"Why can't they ever just save us bullets?"

He stepped over their bodies. He opened the door they'd come out of. It was a fully furnished apartment. Luxurious, but less so than the rest of the house. Was this where the prisoners were kept? It couldn't be. It looked too clean. Too normal.

Then he saw something in the corner of the room. A woman. She was splayed against the wall. Her long blonde hair covered her face.

He rushed to her and checked her neck for a pulse. He was too late. He could feel her neck was snapped. Her body was still warm. She'd only been dead minutes.

He moved the hair from her face to see if he recognized her from Tempest's photos of the victims. Her shut eyes and drooping mouth made it harder but she resembled the blue-eyed smiling woman that brought Tempest into the case. Therese.

He sighed and turned his head down. Tempest wouldn't take that well.

He radioed it in to his men and proceeded to check the rest of the rooms. He still hadn't seen the boy. He prayed he wouldn't find him the same way. After all of this, they had to at least bring the kid back alive.

The rest of the rooms were empty. Normal, lived-in rooms.

He moved on. The floor had grown horribly quiet. He heard all the ruckus downstairs. But aside from some bodies of Prescott's men, there was no sign of anybody else.

He saw one of his officers dead on the ground outside an office. It was one of the rookies. Kevin cursed and pounded the wall and closed the young officer's eyes and moved to the next room.

He opened the door. Empty.

Another. A bedroom. A boy's room. Probably Ryan's. There was a man dead against the wall from a headshot. But he didn't have a gun on him. His men hadn't done it.

He turned to go and saw a small dot above the door. He couldn't shake the feeling that he was being watched. Did the bastard even record his own son?

He continued down the hall. There he found the master bedroom of the house.

He cautiously crossed the threshold. The room was an overbusy mess of seizure-inducing wallpaper and the radiating scent of overpriced cologne.

There was an office in the room,. The door was slightly ajar but he could see the light on.

Kevin inched toward it. He hesitated with each progression but his will pushed him forward until his hand made contact with the door. He pushed it open. The creak echoed in the silence of the room.

There was nobody behind the desk but the computer was on.

Another step.

The click of a gun about to be fired. A slow exhale behind him.

He spun around prepared to shoot an underling dead. "Bradford Prescott."

"Kevin Martel. I should've known you'd be the one to find me. Good to see you again. How's your daughter?"

The two steadied the barrel of his gun at the other's head.

Bradford smiled. "This was bound to happen eventually. If anyone would ever actually find a way to get to me, it'd be you. I can't say it's not my fault for allowing Lincoln to get away with so damn much, but if we're here, we both might as well enjoy it." He walked to his desk and held up a bottle of scotch and two shot glasses. "What do you say we have a drink for old times?"

A bead of sweat dripped down Kevin's neck. "Cut the crap, Prescott."

Bradford poured himself a drink. "Right down to business. Typical Kevin Martel. But where's my joke?" Bradford downed the shot of bourbon. "Kevin Martel always has a snappy one-liner ready."

"I'll write you a book full of them for your cellmate to read to you. Now you're under arrest."

Bradford smiled and prepared to fire his gun. "Now that's more like it."

Julie found a line of goons waiting for her in the house.

There were three of her men nearby. They all opened fire.

She emptied her clip.

The entire line of henchmen fell dead at her feet.

She quickly reloaded and proceeded further into the house. She had to find Lincoln. The house seemed to get very empty very quickly. Her officers had covered the floor well. She had to step over several of Lincoln's men.

"Where are you, Lincoln?"

She then noticed a small closet. It seemed entirely of unimportance. Too much so. She opened it. Just some cleaning supplies. It would've been fitting in a house a quarter of the size, like hers. But not here. It just stuck out. She decided to try the shelves.

The third from the bottom had a trick back. One press, and the closet opened to reveal a dark staircase. This wouldn't be the way to the basement. This was leading to something else.

"Why can't movie clichés stay in the movies?" She

held out her gun and slowly descended the staircase.

This chamber was almost pitch black. Toward the bottom, she saw a flickering light. A television.

She reached the bottom. Five screens sat atop a workstation of some kind. A man in a chair sat before it, typing away at a keyboard.

Julie clicked her gun. "Freeze. SPPD. Stand up slowly with your hands in the air."

"Sorry, officer. I don't think that's going to happen."

The man spun around in his chair. Lincoln Prescott.

He had a gun of his own in hand and wore a smirk on his face.

"Looks like this is the climax of my movie," he said. "Oh what fun."

"Sorry Lincoln, but your production is about to be shut down."

"Are you sure about that?"

Julie steadied her weapon at his chest. But she didn't want to fire yet. Lincoln was too calm. He was planning something and she needed to find out what that was.

CHAPTER 20

"Happy Birthday, Ryan." Ryan was six now. He was a big boy. And his father seemed happy. His father never hugged him like this.

"Thank you, Daddy." Ryan threw his arms around his father.

"I hope you're hungry, because I had the cook whip up all of your favorites for breakfast."

"Strawberry pancakes?" Ryan's kissed his father's cheek. "Thank you so very much."

Ryan ran to the kitchen table. Steak, sausage, eggs, the pancakes, orange juice. All for him. Ryan downed every bite. His stomach hurt a little but he was a big boy now. He could take it.

"Do you like everything?" Lincoln paced behind Ryan's chair at the table.

"I love it." Ryan wiped his face with a cloth.

"If you're done, I have something to show you." Lincoln waved Ryan on.

"What is it?" Ryan hopped out of his chair.

"Your present." He winked.

Lincoln led Ryan to the patio.

There was a teenager with him. On his knees.

A camera was filming them.

Did his father want to make him a movie? Maybe this

boy was helping him.

Ryan had seen the boy help his dad film other things. He lived in the part of the house that Ryan wasn't ever allowed to go to. The boy was named Leo. He had a muscular chest and long black hair. Leo seemed like he could give good piggyback rides.

Lincoln asked Ryan, "Do you recognize this boy?"

Ryan nodded. "Yeah, that's Leo. He's cool."

Leo cracked a smile.

"I'll bet he is cool," Lincoln said. "Another question, Ryan. Do you know what it means to die?"

Ryan froze. His father was turning scary again. He didn't like thinking about dying. "I guess so," he said. "What's going on, Dad?"

"Just watch closely. Do you see Leo now?"

Ryan nodded.

Lincoln took out a gun. He placed it against the back of Leo's head. *Boom.*

Leo fell dead on the floor.

Ryan screamed. "You killed him."

"Yes I did." Lincoln patted Ryan on the back. "Happy Birthday."

"What?"

"This is the best present you could get. A chance to see up close and personal how worthless the lives of other people are. Come closer and look at Leo now."

He turned Leo on his back.

Ryan kneeled down next to him. He had never seen a real dead body before. It felt weird to put his hand on a chest and not feel a beat or a slow rise and fall.

"Why are his eyes open? Everyone on TV who dies has their eyes closed."

"A lot of people die with their eyes open."

Ryan felt tears on his cheek. But why? He didn't really know Leo. But seeing him dead? It hurt so much.

"Everyone dies." Lincoln lifted Ryan to his feet. "That's why it's useless to worry about other people. They're going to die and be like this. You're going to die one day too. You'll be just like this. So enjoy your life while you're alive. Do what feels good. So when you end up like this, you don't have regrets."

"But why did you have to shoot him? He didn't do anything wrong."

Lincoln shoved Ryan. "I told you. I wanted to teach you. That's more valuable than any stupid toy. Stay with Leo a while. Study what a dead human body looks like. It'll help remind you of what's really important in life."

"No. You killed him. You killed him."

Lincoln walked away and locked Ryan on the patio. Just him and Leo.

Ryan remembered that day so clearly. Every painful second. His dad was right. He'd be just like Leo. But he never thought it'd be when he was still a kid.

Ryan felt Aaron's tears raining down on him.

He placed his hand on Aaron's. "Hey, don't cry. It's okay."

Aaron shook his head with squeezed eyes. "No, it's not. I should've been the one to die." He whimpered. "So many times in the past few days, I almost died and I should have. You shouldn't have gotten hurt. I'm so sorry I was so mean to you. I treated you like crap and now you take bullets for me. It's not fair."

"You showed me that I could be a good person." A gurgle of blood shot out of his mouth. Ryan hacked it into Wayne's face.

Wayne wiped the blood aside. "Hang on. The ambulance is coming. Just a few more minutes."

Ryan said, "I'm not one of the hostages. It's okay if I die, as long as Aaron's okay."

"Your life matters too, Ryan."

Did his life matter? Ryan wanted to believe that. If Aaron didn't want him to die, maybe his life did matter.

Ryan grabbed Aaron's hand. "Aaron, I'm going to die. It's okay. But I need you to help me do something. As soon as I met you, I knew there was something good in you. And now I know what that something good is. And I want it too. I want what's good in you to be good in me." Even for just a minute. "So you have to listen. I need you to baptize me."

"Baptize you?"

"You're a pastor's son, aren't you? Who better?" Agony pounded his stomach. Then nothing. It didn't hurt anymore. Ryan knew that was bad. "You can use the pool water. It still works, right?"

Aaron cried harder. "You can get baptized yourself when you get out of the hospital. I can take you to church and tell you about Jesus."

"Aaron, I'm not getting better." He tried to take a breath. Only a tiny puff escaped. Time was running out. "I don't know that much about Jesus, but I know you believe in Him. What I do know about Him, I see it in you. I want to be like that too. Aaron. Please. Baptize me?"

Aaron looked so confused. His eyes were so wet. Seeing Aaron in pain hurt him more than his own injuries did.

Aaron looked to Wayne.

Wayne gave him a nod.

Wayne picked Ryan off the ground. He carried him to

the edge of the pool.

Aaron cupped his hands and dipped them in the water.

"I'm ready." Ryan smiled.

Aaron slowly released the water from his hands onto Ryan's head and let it flow down his face. "Ryan, I baptize you in the name of the Father, and of the Son, and of the Holy Spirit. Amen." The last drop of water landed on Ryan's forehead.

Ryan closed his eyes as the water ran down his face, washing away his tears.

He felt something in his chest. A lightness. He didn't feel sad anymore about his father. Or even the things he did wrong. He was sorry for all of his regrets. Now it was like they were dripping away with the water.

Aaron turned his head down. "Welcome, Ryan."

"Thank you, Aaron. You did it. You're like a real pastor now."

"But you still have to hang on. You can't die, Ryan."

Ryan turned to Wayne. "Aaron needs a dad."

Wayne looked confused. But he'd get it after they were safe.

Ryan looked Aaron in the eyes. "I'm so glad I met you, Aaron."

He felt Aaron's grip on his hand tighten. The sun seemed to get brighter. But it wasn't blinding. It was a different kind of light.

Ryan felt somebody lift him off the ground. But it wasn't Wayne this time. He looked down and saw his own eyes looking back. Aaron was next to him. He was crying louder. But Wayne was there for him. Ryan could tell Wayne was a good man. He felt that he'd keep Aaron safe. It was okay to go now.

One final breath escaped Ryan's lungs. Then he went still in one horrible second.

Aaron screamed. He called Ryan's name. It didn't matter.

Aaron looked at Ryan's empty eyes. He wasn't in there anymore. His mouth was slightly open, like he was seeing something unbelievable.

Wayne felt for Ryan's pulse. He sighed.

Wayne put his hands on Aaron's shoulder. "He's gone, Aaron."

"No, he can't be gone."

"He was just a kid. His body couldn't take those wounds. I'm surprised he held on as long as he did."

"But he was my best friend." More tears. "He can't be dead. He just can't be."

Aaron fought the urge to throw up. Aaron buried his head on Ryan's chest and cried more. He didn't care that Ryan's blood smeared all over his face. Why was everyone dying? Why did everyone he cared about have to die?

Sirens blared out front. Ryan's ambulance. They couldn't have helped him anyway.

"So how did you find out about all my plans?" Lincoln rose to his feet.

"A little birdie told me." Julie kept her gun steady on him.

"A little birdie? Was that little birdie my son, by any chance?"

"Does it matter?" She raised an eyebrow. "It's over,

Lincoln. You're going away for a very long time. Oh, and by the way, you're under arrest."

"We'll see about that."

Julie then felt a gun pressed against the back of her neck. She froze and raised her hands.

"Thank you kindly, Lawrence." Lincoln clapped.

"My pleasure, boss. Do you want me to shoot her?"

"Yes, but not yet. I want her to see my work first."

Lawrence shoved her closer to the screens. He yanked her gun from her hand.

Lincoln pounded on the keyboard. "Sorry about my little bodyguard. I figured I should keep him on standby just in case."

Of course the scumbag had backup. She cursed herself for coming down without backup of her own. Rookie mistake that was beneath her. "You can kill me. But you're not getting out of this."

"Look at my screens." He pointed to each one. "The movies I've produced. Aren't they lovely?"

The death scenes of all of the previous victims began playing. Lincoln skipped ahead to the moment of death each time. Julie could barely stand to look at all the bloody last moments of the people. Shootings. Stabbings. A little girl pushed off a roof.

"Why are you showing me this?"

"I like an audience. I took videos of every moment of their lives. But most of it was so boring. This is where it all comes to life."

"You think these are movies? If you were really any good you wouldn't have to kill your actors to make it look real. Real directors can create emotion without killing their casts."

He rushed to his feet and punched her. "You have

the nerve to insult me when I hold your life in my hands? You foolish woman."

"I don't mince words to save my ass. If you're a fool, I'm going to call you a fool. And you, Lincoln Prescott, are a fool. You think you're some kind of director who likes good production value, right? Well, let me tell you something. I catch killers for a living. I've faced down some of the most depraved minds in the country. And they all thought they were justified. You're no different. That's why you leave those photographs at every scene. They're a signature. You did it as a calling card, because you are a serial killer. Your videos are your trophies. You're just like every one of them. I know what you are."

"Lawrence." He pounded his desk. "Shoot her ass, now."

Three shots rang out.

The man fell onto her, both of them hitting the floor.

"You damn cop." Lincoln took a step back.

Julie landed a kick to Lincoln's face. He fell to the ground.

"How are you alive?" Lincoln rose to his feet. His glasses fell from his face in pieces. "He shot you."

She swiped her gun from Lawrence. He was dead at her feet. She aimed at Lincoln. "Does it matter?"

A man in priest's clothes stepped into the room. A pistol was in his hands. Was he one of Lincoln's men in disguise? She looked at his face. She recognized it from the photos of the missing persons. Jake Doyle, Roman Catholic priest.

"A priest with a gun?" She shot him a smile.

"A priest with a mission."

Lincoln quickly made a run for it.

Julie fired at him. She missed.

She chased after him. The priest ran beside her.

"You're one of the ones he kept here, right? Where did you get a gun anyway?"

"I took it off one of the bodies."

"How come I didn't see you in the house?"

"I know hiding places. But we can interview later."

Lincoln scurried up the stairs. He maneuvered something in the railing. Then flames shot up in front of Julie and Father Doyle.

Julie forced herself to stop, falling back onto the priest, and down to the ground.

"Had a back-up plan, just in case." Lincoln slammed the door shut behind him.

The flames followed them down the stairs.

Father Doyle picked up a chair and threw it at one of Lincoln's monitors with a scream. The unit sparked and fell to the ground, shattered. "I can't let him get to Aaron. I should've watched them closer."

Julie scanned the room. There had to be another way out. A vent. A secret corridor. Something. She refused to come this far only to burn to death in a basement. She wouldn't leave Patrick an orphan.

The flames were quickly spreading. Smoke was beginning to choke them.

Father Doyle tried panels on the wall.

Julie said a quick prayer for God to bring them out safely. There had to be another way out. She'd find it.

Lincoln took out two cops as he ran for the patio again. He had to see if Ryan was okay. His son was tough. A few bullets wouldn't stop him.

He took out a thumb drive from his pocket. He kissed

it. "My greatest works. This house can burn as long as I have this."

He charged out the back, tearing through the screen. Toward the pool, he saw them.

Wayne touched Aaron's shoulder. Aaron had run out of tears for a minute. But he still looked broken.

The boy threw his arms around Wayne. Head to chest, he just wanted somebody to hold him.

Wayne embraced Aaron. He could feel the boy's heartbeat pounding. He'd been through so much. Wayne thought back to meeting Aaron in the diner. He knew more now. He knew why Aaron looked sad. But now Aaron's life was wrecked even more.

He looked down at Aaron. For the first time, he was able to touch one of the people he was trying to bring home. It felt good to not just know them through pictures.

He saw Lincoln approaching.

"Get back, Aaron." Wayne pushed the boy aside.

A bullet shot through his shoulder.

Wayne was thrust back and screamed in pain. He pressed the wound and felt hot blood on his hand.

Lincoln walked up and kneeled down besides Ryan.

He looked into Ryan's lifeless eyes and began to cry. "I didn't think I shot him that bad." He touched his son's face. "My little boy," he said. "It's so sad."

He then pointed his gun at Aaron's head.

Aaron froze in terror.

"It's your fault that my son is dead, you worthless little piece of crap. Well, now it's your turn."

Bang.

Lincoln grabbed his shoulder and screamed.

Wayne struggled to his feet, Glock aimed at Lincoln. "Leave the boy alone."

Lincoln refocused his gun at Aaron.

Wayne tackled Lincoln as the gun went off.

Aaron screamed.

"Aaron!" Wayne looked over at the boy. He was clutching his upper arm. Wayne saw a little blood but not a lot. It looked like just a graze.

The two fell to the ground. The guns flew from their hands.

Wayne wrapped his arms around Lincoln. "You're done killing."

Lincoln grabbed Wayne's wounded arm and yanked.

Through the sharpest of pains and throat-burning screams, Wayne did the same to Lincoln.

Lincoln let out a high-pitched screech as they rolled into the pool.

They landed with a splash and floated apart.

Wayne gasped for breath as he broke to the surface.

Lincoln made a dash for the ladder.

"You're not going anywhere." Wayne wrestled him back. "You've taken enough from them. I won't let you hurt Aaron anymore"

"Taken from them?" Lincoln punched him. "Don't make me laugh. Nothing they have is worth preserving. Least of all their lives."

Wayne punched Lincoln back. Then again. He slammed his head against the side.

Lincoln headbutted Wayne.

Wayne flinched just a moment.

Lincoln threw himself at Wayne and held him underwater. "Once I'm done with you, I'll finish off that bastard kid as payback for Ryan's death."

Wayne couldn't hold his breath long. He hated going underwater. His face burned, but he couldn't give in. He threw Lincoln off. "You murdered your son, you narcissistic son of a bitch. He's dead because you killed him."

"That's a lie." A retaliatory kick.

He tried to get out again.

Wayne grabbed him and pulled him back into the water.

The two then grabbed each other's necks as they flailed in the water. Wayne squeezed as tight as he could, hoping he could stay conscious longer.

"Wayne. Here." Aaron tossed Wayne one of the guns.

Wayne pounded Lincoln's head and caught it.

Lincoln tackled Wayne under the water again.

Then Wayne fired.

Stalemate. Kevin and Bradford kept eyes and guns locked at each other for several minutes. Both refused to give the other an opening.

"You had everything. You had more money than my entire force put together. You could have anything you wanted in life. Why let your son do this? Why hurt so many people?"

Bradford shrugged. "It made him happy. I never could give him what he wanted. Every year on his birthday, I tried. I'd get him a really expensive gift. He hated every one. Toys, video games. He didn't even like when I introduced him to a hooker." Bradford smiled. "Then I discovered what he did love, making movies. So when it seemed like a career in film wasn't in his future, I decided to look the other way when he found alternative methods. I could protect him and make sure he was never caught. I live to make my son happy and I did."

"Sounds to me like you just couldn't love him the right way and thought you could buy your way out of it. And when your son became a sociopath, the price tag got higher.'"

"I had the money and power to make his dream come true. My only regret is giving you an opening to get a warrant."

"Well, you'll have a long time to stew on that regret in solitary confinement. Why don't you make this easier on yourself and stop resisting?"

"Do you really think this is a standoff?" Bradford laughed. "I just wanted to savor this before I kill you." He then pressed a button on the back of his desk.

The light fixture above Kevin came crashing down.

Kevin rolled past it but it caught his foot and pinned him to the ground. "What the hell?"

"I had some insurance policies installed throughout the house. Rainy day plans."

Kevin aimed his gun at Bradford and fired two shots.

Bradford dodged both.

He returned fire.

Kevin dodged, barely. "Your aim sucks."

Bradford walked closer. "Let's fix that."

Kevin squeezed his foot out from the chandelier and rolled past another shot.

He fired a round into Bradford's firing hand.

Kevin charged Bradford and pinned him against the wall. "That's a wrap, Prescott."

"Fat chance."

Bradford pulled out a knife and slashed at Kevin.

Kevin jumped back. The knife made a gash at his arm. It stung but was superficial.

Bradford made a run for it.

"Damn it." Kevin clutched his wound. "Why can't anybody ever make this easy, just once?"

Julie and Father Doyle had struggled through a small crawl space found behind a hidden trap door.

Now they were outside.

The house was filling with smoke from the basement fire. She prayed everyone was out by now. They couldn't go back for anyone still inside.

She saw Lincoln and Wayne struggling in the pool. Lincoln was holding Wayne under the water. Her heart fluttered a second as rushed to the edge of the patio.

She fired a shot at Lincoln.

Two loud cracks.

Blood spread in the blue water. Lincoln stopped moving. His eyes were still looking back at Wayne.

Wayne rushed to the surface and gasped for air. He turned to Lincoln, floating lifeless in the water surrounded by a halo of blood.

Wayne looked to see Julie standing a few feet away with a gun. Father Doyle was a few feet behind her.

Had his shot done Lincoln in or was it hers? It didn't matter. Lincoln was finally gone. He couldn't hurt anybody ever again.

Wayne held up his hand to Julie. "You gonna help me out?"

Julie rolled her eyes. "No, I'm going to save your ass only to watch you drown." She held out her hand and pulled him out.

Her eyes widened. "Oh God, you're hurt."

Wayne held his bloody shoulder. "It's a flesh wound." He stuck out his tongue.

"It's a bullet wound."

He pointed to Aaron. "Check him out first. He got hit."

Julie turned to the boy with her Mom Panic Face on. She kneeled down next to him and rolled up his sleeve. A bloody gash ran across his upper arm.

"It doesn't look too deep. We'll definitely get him checked out, but he should live."

Wayne walked to her, dripping a red trail behind him. "I think I will too. But I want strong pain killers."

Julie rolled her eyes. "I saved your life, Tempest. Now you want to go and disappear on me?"

He winked at her and took a seat next to Aaron. "Very funny." Then he caught sight of Ryan again and his stomach turned. Making jokes didn't seem appropriate next to a dead child.

Lincoln was dragged ashore and laid next to Ryan.

Julie knelt down next to Ryan, a tear in her eye. "How did it happen?"

Aaron looked away. "He was aiming for me."

"Lincoln?"

Wayne nodded. "His own son. Bastard ran away to avoid seeing his son die. Coward couldn't even face what he did."

Julie caressed Ryan's hand. "He should've just stayed at the hospital." She shook her head. "I tried to get him to stay. He ran away. This is what I was trying to avoid."

Wayne took her hand. "We did what we could. He did what he had to."

Julie turned to Aaron. "You must be Aaron. Ryan talked about you a lot when he came to see me last night.

All he cared about was rescuing you. That's the only reason we're here. Because of him."

"He went to see you?"

Julie nodded. "He wanted to rescue you so badly. He got his wish."

"And it killed him."

She caressed Aaron's cheek and wiped aside some of Ryan's blood. "You're alive because of Ryan. That's a gift. I hope you use it for something good."

Bradford staggered out of the smoking house, one hand bleeding.

Wayne threw Aaron to the ground. "Julie! Behind you."

Julie whipped around and fired a round into Bradford's shoulder. "Stop right there."

Bradford kept walking undaunted.

Julie was on her feet. "I told you to stop."

Bradford gazed over the bodies. "Lincoln . . . Ryan. You killed a child?"

"Your son killed your grandson."

Bradford took another step toward them.

She fired into his leg. He stumbled but kept moving.

Bradford held up his hands. "They're my family. I just need a minute before you take me." He knelt down beside the bodies of Lincoln and Ryan.

He began to cry. He didn't say anything. What could he? This was his fault too, and he had to know it.

"They'd both still be alive if you put a stop to this a long time ago," Wayne said. "This is on you."

"I wanted to give them a full life. Was that so horrible?"

"Lincoln was taking other people's lives for his own sick pleasure. Nobody's entitled to do that for any reason."

Kevin followed out of the house, bleeding down his arm, but closing in quickly on Prescott.

Julie and her father exchanged a nod. They both had their guns drawn on Prescott.

Julie looked over Kevin. "You all right?"

Kevin nodded. "Been through worse."

Bradford turned to Kevin. "I'm glad you made it out. I wouldn't want you to miss this."

He pulled out a gun from his jacket and fired at Julie. She rolled away.

He turned to Kevin and did the same.

Kevin dodged.

Bradford looked down at his son. "I wanted better for you." He put the gun under his chin. In a flash, he was gone.

He collapsed to the ground, his face a bloody mess. Only his open eyes were left intact.

Julie and Kevin rose to their feet. They didn't need to check a pulse.

"Saved us the trouble of arresting him, I guess." Kevin walked over to the bodies. "Three generations."

Wayne looked over them. They were arranged oldest to youngest. All their eyes were open. The same shade of brown.

Julie helped Wayne and Aaron to their feet. "At least one of them showed he was a good person. It's not right that Ryan had to suffer for who his family was."

Father Doyle approached them. "Have any of you seen a young woman? Blonde? Her name was Therese. She was the only other captive still with us."

Wayne froze. He took out Therese's picture. "Is this her?"

Father Doyle nodded. "Yes."

"She's the one whose family first hired me for this case."

Kevin took the photo from Wayne. He looked it over and handed it back with a sigh. "I saw her inside. Prescott got to her."

Father Doyle froze. "No."

Kevin nodded.

Wayne shouted and kicked the ground. "She was alive all this time? Until today?"

Kevin nodded. "She wasn't gone fifteen minutes when I found her."

Father Doyle grabbed Kevin by the arm. "Where was she? Are you sure she was dead? Maybe she was like Aaron was earlier."

"Her neck was . . . she was gone. I'm sorry."

"I have to find her."

Wayne grabbed him. "Don't risk your life. You and Aaron are the survivors of this." All those victims and only two were left alive. "It's over now. There's no point in looking back."

They all turned away from the burning building as fire engines blared onto the court.

Aaron kneeled down to Ryan again. He reached over Ryan's face and slid his friend's eyes closed. At least one of the Prescotts made the decision to show love. Now he was being shown it.

Aaron made a fist with Ryan's limp hand and then with his own. He gave his friend one final fist bump before looking away. "You were my friend and you were a good person. Forever. I'll remember you forever, Ryan."

Aaron ran to Father Doyle and hugged him. And then Wayne. He was still shaking. He'd been through more than any child ever should. But the Prescotts were gone. Aaron was a survivor. Now it was time for him to heal.

The fire was out quickly. It hadn't spread as far as they'd thought. The house would survive, for the little that was worth.

Wayne and Aaron were both loaded into an ambulance and driven away.

Julie watched one of the paramedics try to stitch up her father's wound. He was fighting him every step of the way.

The victims were all carried out of the house. First the goons. Then the fallen officers. They were her men. They had families too. Sometimes she forgot just how much danger they all were in every day. She saluted them. They'd sacrificed everything for this case and she'd never let them be forgotten.

Father Doyle ran when he saw another body brought out. Somehow, he must've known. Therese. They unzipped her for a just a moment. He blessed her.

Julie walked up to him and put her hand on his shoulder. "I'm sorry we didn't get here sooner. Maybe if I didn't wait for a warrant . . ."

"Don't." He turned to her. "God doesn't hold us accountable for what we can't predict. You risked your life to save us. And because of you, Aaron and I are alive. We survived this. Thank you. I don't know where God plans to send me now, but if you ever need a priest for any reason, I'm there."

Officers told them about Lincoln's freezer. They couldn't even count all the bodies in there. It took an hour to remove them all. Small and large. Julie checked every one against the known victims. Every one was accounted for, and there were still ten others they didn't have a match for. How many years had Lincoln been doing this?

At least now they'd be able to rest in peace. Their families would have closure. Julie knew just how much that meant.

Ryan's body was taken out just before his father's. She cried as he was zipped up into a body bag. She was there when he woke up that morning. She didn't know him that time yesterday. Now her heart stabbed her at seeing him taken away like this.

Bradford and Lincoln were carried out last. Father and son, partners in crime.

Julie stayed until it was almost dark.

She watched the house, so elegant on the outside. So much horror had gone on inside for years. And nobody knew a thing. These people died in there. Now, for the first time since it was built, the Prescott Estate was empty. Only Aaron and Father Doyle remained to remember the lives of those who lived there. But it was enough. They'd rescued two people. Good people. She'd forever lament every one they'd failed to save, but even two lives made her glad Wayne had come to her with the case. Together, they ensured that Aaron would have a future. That was something priceless.

Wayne looked over at Aaron in the ambulance. The boy's eyes were cold.

"Are you all right?"

Aaron nodded. "What's going to happen to me? Dad's gone. Mom died a long time ago. We don't have anybody I know in the family. Therese was going to take care of me. Now she's dead too. Are they going to send me away?"

Wayne shook his head. "I won't ever let them take you away. We'll figure this out."

Aaron took his hand. "Just until I fall asleep."

Wayne smiled. "Of course."

He squeezed tighter. Aaron's hands were cold and small, but they were still strong. Wayne thought of all the people he failed to save. And here Aaron was, sitting next to him. Wounded, but still here. Like him. Maybe Aaron was the reason he'd been brought into this case to begin with. Maybe this is what God had planned for him all along.

CHAPTER 21

Aaron looked out the hospital window. Morning was coming but it was still dark out. He'd slept on and off through the night. His shoulder was bandaged up now. It hurt and itched a little but the doctors said he was lucky. It was going to heal. Might not even scar much. He could go home in the morning.

Where was home? He didn't know anymore. Probably somewhere with strangers and too many kids to even notice he was there. Would that really be much different from where he was? A strange bed with strange people and somebody telling him he can't leave.

He turned under the cold hospital covers and grabbed a fistful of sheets, trying to remember the coziness of his own bed and the safe sounds of his parents' lullabies.

Then he noticed Father Doyle seated next to him. "You're here."

The priest smiled. "I wanted to check up on you. We went through a lot and saw a lot of bad things. But we're alive, and we have to make that count."

Aaron turned away. "I don't know what to do. I'm not dead. They are. What does God want me to do?"

"Pray. Live. Help others. Talk to God. Be nice to people. Do your schoolwork." He smiled. "Sometimes it's living a normal life that is the best way to honor being alive. If God ever wants more from you, He'll let you know. And you can always talk to me if you ever need to. For any reason."

"Won't you be sent away?"

Father Doyle shook his head. "I asked the archbishop if I could be assigned to the local parish. He agreed. I'm going to be staying around for now."

"That's good." Aaron looked at a clock on the wall. Just past 4. "You haven't slept all night, have you? You should try to rest. You had a hard day yesterday too."

"You're worried about me after all you went through?"

Aaron shrugged. "I'm okay. You should go. If I need anything, I can call the nurse." He pointed over to the bed behind the curtain. "And Wayne's here. He was snoring really loud earlier but he stopped so I think he's awake."

Wayne snickered. "Kid's observant. He's right, though. You can go, Father. We're going to be okay. Plus, there's something I want to talk with Aaron about."

Father Doyle nodded. He blessed Aaron and turned to go. "God be with you."

When they were alone, Wayne walked over to Aaron, taking a seat next to Aaron's bed.

Aaron looked over Wayne's bandaged shoulder. "Sorry you got shot."

"Sorry you got shot." Wayne nodded to Aaron's wound.

"It doesn't hurt that much."

Wayne clutched his. "Well, neither does mine." He twitched.

"I don't believe you."

"I'm gonna live. Don't worry about me."

"So what did you want to talk about?"

Wayne took a deep breath. "You had asked about where you were going to go now? Where home would be."

Aaron nodded.

"I was thinking a lot. And I'm just going to come right out and say it. How would you feel about coming to live with me?"

Aaron sat up in his bed. "With you?" Why would Wayne want him to come live with him?

Wayne nodded. "I don't have a big house. But I have a nice apartment and it has an extra bedroom so you'd have your own space. And we don't have to call it 'adoption.' I can put in to be your foster parent and it can be more like I'm a friend making sure you're cared for. You don't have to call me 'Dad' or anything. I'm not trying to replace your father. I'd never do that." Wayne looked down a moment. "I just know what it's like to spend time in a foster home. It's not always bad. Sometimes the people are really nice. But a lot of the time, there were so many other kids. They couldn't really pay attention to all of us. And then somebody took me in. Somebody went above and beyond to make sure I was cared for. I can't pay him back. He's gone. But I can pay it forward to somebody else. To you. If you want. Only if you want. You could trust me. And you could feel safe. We'd get through each day together and you wouldn't ever fall through the cracks."

"Would they even let you do that?" Aaron looked away, terrified of getting his hopes up. His dad had tried to take in foster kids a few times but they never let him.

Wayne smiled. "I know people. I can make it happen. But it's up to you." He pointed at Aaron. "Is that something you would want?"

Aaron nodded. "I do. You're cool and nice. But why would you want to help me? What did I do?"

"When Therese's family hired me to find her, I didn't know just how big this thing would be. For three years, I've been obsessed with finding everybody that creep took. And then I met you and your dad. You were real people. I got to see a peek of your lives before you were taken. Then I saw them throw you into that car. I saw it happen. Now you weren't just faces and names to me. I had to bring you all back. No matter what. But I was too late to save most of you. Just you and the priest. Only you don't have a home now. So what good is saving you only to be thrown into a system where you're just a number? Another case? I don't have anybody to take care of. You don't have anybody to take care of you. So why not? I found you. But now I need to walk with you."

Aaron felt his heart ease a little bit. "You don't have to do that. You brought me back. It's okay. You can go."

Wayne shook his head. "I don't want to go. You're right. I don't have to do this. I could move on and it probably wouldn't even be wrong. You're strong. You'd probably be okay. I'm not obligated to take in every person I bring home. Not at all." Wayne took Aaron's hand. "But I'm choosing to help you. I want to help you. I see how good a kid you are and I want to give you a safe place where you can grow into the kind of man your father would be proud of."

Aaron felt his eyes welling up with tears. "Thank you, Wayne."

He shifted in his bed. Wayne's hands were strong. Aaron didn't have to pretend not to be in pain around him. Maybe God and his dad sent Wayne to make sure he'd be okay.

"Would it be bad if I cried again? I know I've done nothing else but cry since you found me. But . . ."

Wayne held up his hand. "You don't have to explain. I know. You do what you need to do."

Aaron smiled as a tear streamed down his face. He didn't need to wail this time. But as the tears fell onto his hospital gown, they didn't feel as heavy as before. Aaron didn't think he'd still be alive after all the horrible things he'd seen. But he felt safe now. He was going to be okay. With every tear, he seemed to feel just a little bit better. Maybe this time they weren't just sad tears.

Aaron went home with Wayne that afternoon. He was surprised everything moved so quickly, but he did hear that nice cop named Julie yelling at social services to make it happen fast. Maybe that had something to do with it.

Wayne went with Aaron to the funerals. Father Doyle presided over most of them, even if the deceased weren't Catholic. Nobody had any arguments. He even invited Aaron up to talk at a few of them. Aaron didn't say much but it felt right standing up there like his father would have.

Emily was buried by a rosebush. The beautiful pink flowers typically rained petals on her grave so that there wasn't a day that went by that her grave was left bare. Even in the winter.

Maude was laid to rest next to her brothers. Aaron was happy she could see them again after all those years.

Drake was buried beside his son. His wife came. Aaron had heard that she used to live in a mental hospital but was able to live on her own after that.

Dinah's family had her cremated. Her ashes were scattered over the river. Maybe now she could finally be free from her pain.

At Therese's funeral, her mother hugged Wayne and thanked him for never giving up on her daughter. She hugged Aaron too and thanked him for giving her little girl a child to care about, even for a few days.

Aaron's dad was buried beside his mom. Aaron spent five hours that day sitting by their graves. Wayne stood behind him the whole time. He understood.

Bradford and Lincoln were placed in a lavish family crypt per their arrangements. Nobody but the family attorneys attended the funeral.

Father Doyle raised money for Ryan's funeral and burial. Ryan was issued legal certificates of birth and death. Even the law knew he existed now. Julie made it so Lincoln wasn't mentioned as the father. The world didn't need to know of Ryan's ties to that horrible family. He deserved that dignity. Ryan's grave was in a sunny spot of the cemetery. A likeness of a young boy was carved on the front of the tombstone. Father Doyle told Aaron it was St. Dominic Savio, a boy who died not much older than Ryan but lived a holy life and was now one of God's saints in Heaven. Aaron liked that choice. Ryan deserved a grave that showed that he was a good person. That somebody remembered him.

It was almost Thanksgiving. Aaron had lost so much since the last year, yet he had so much to be thankful for. He was settling in at Wayne's nicely. He hadn't decorated his room yet. But when he thought of home, Wayne's place was starting to match the picture in his mind.

Julie's house looked nice and harvesty as Wayne

walked Aaron to the front door and rang the bell.

A boy opened the door with a smile. "Hey, Wayne."

Wayne fist-bumped the boy. "How you doing? Mom home?"

The boy nodded. "You two going to talk?" He raised an eyebrow.

Wayne snickered. "Did you plan another candlelight dinner?" He pointed at the boy. "Don't think we don't know what you're trying to do."

The boy's eyes shifted. "I don't know what you're talking about."

"Sure you don't."

Wayne eased Aaron across the threshold.

Aaron looked around. The house felt very homey. He saw Julie putting out a few snacks. "Your house is nice, Ms. Martel."

She walked to Aaron and hugged him. "Julie. You can call me Julie. And thank you."

Julie held out her hand to the boy. "Aaron, this is my son. He's just about your age. His name is Patrick. I think you two would have a lot in common."

Patrick held out his hand to Aaron. "Nice to meet you."

Aaron shook. "You too."

"Patrick, why don't you show Aaron your room?"

Patrick rolled his eyes. "You can just say you want to be alone with Wayne, Mom." He winked. "Come on, Aaron." He waved Aaron on.

Aaron followed Patrick upstairs. His bedroom looked nice. He saw a picture on the dresser. It was of a younger Patrick with another boy who looked just like him. He didn't see a second bed.

Aaron walked to the picture and picked it up a moment. He looked to Patrick. He could see it in the boy's eyes. "I'm sorry."

Patrick shook his head. "It's okay. Mom told me about all you've been through."

Aaron nodded. "It sucks."

Patrick took a seat on the floor and signaled for Aaron to sit next to him. Aaron did.

Patrick picked up a small book. "I had a bad summer. A lot of bad things happened. A lot of good people died." Patrick handed Aaron the book. "I made this after it all happened."

Aaron opened the book. On the first page was a picture of a man. "Dad" was written above it. Next to him a picture of that boy who looked like Patrick. "Petey" was written above it.

Aaron turned the page. A family and two boys, one a teenager and the other a curly-haired boy about Patrick's age. "The Greenes" was written at the top. "Milo" written next to the boy.

He turned the page. More faces.

"Is everyone in this . . . dead?"

Patrick nodded. He wiped aside a tear. "It still hurts to think about it."

"What do you do with it?"

"I flip through it every day and I pray for them." Patrick tensed his lips. "It helps sometimes."

"Why do you pray for someone who's already dead?"

Patrick curled up his legs. "Sometimes people die and they're still God's friends, but they have some things they haven't let go of yet. Things that keep them from shining as much as they could. God wants everybody to have the brightest shine possible in Heaven. So sometimes after we die, we need to be cleaned a little bit so we shine better. When we pray for people who died, we help them shine faster. And they know we're praying for them. They appreciate it and they pray for us back." He pressed his chest. "It keeps us connected forever. Until we can see them again." He pointed to the book. "Putting somebody's picture in the book helps me remember and it lets me sort of carry all of them with me."

Aaron closed the book and handed it back to Patrick. "That's so beautiful. I never thought of it like that."

Patrick opened a drawer and took another book out. "Mom told me about your dad and your friends." He handed Aaron the book. "I thought maybe you could have one of your own. So you could put their pictures and names in there."

Aaron took the book. He ran his hands across the cover. Images of all the people he'd lost in just a few days flashed in his mind. "I don't have pictures of anybody but my parents."

"My mom could help you get some."

Aaron felt tears and a smile on his face. He hugged the book. "Thank you. I never want to forget them. Not ever."

Patrick nodded. "You got it."

"Patrick? Does it ever stop hurting so much?"

Patrick put his arm around Aaron. "It still hurts for Petey and my dad. Even after five years. Everyone else in that book died just a few months ago. So it still really hurts."

Aaron thought as much. His chest began to ache.

"But . . ." Patrick turned to him. "I have a new friend named Jacob. He's cool. And if you want, I could be your friend too. And you could be his friend."

Aaron nodded. "Sure. That'd be cool. But what does

that have to do with how much it hurts?"

"Friends. And family. Sometimes Mom takes me to this restaurant and we get the best pizza in the world. It's like so good. And sometimes we go to the beach and I get to swim in the ocean. And sometimes we go to church and it's so quiet and peaceful and I just see Jesus. And sometimes we're just sitting together talking." Patrick exhaled hard. "It hurts every day. And sometimes it hurts less, and then it hurts again. But there are still good things. You're alive. And every day that you're alive, you can find a reason to smile. A reason to be happy. Even if you're still sad. The good things, and especially the good people help make the hurt not so bad."

Aaron prayed Patrick was right. Wayne helped make his chest hurt a little less. So did Patrick. Feeling a friend's arm around him reminded him of Ryan. And that hurt. But it also made him feel like he had a true friend again, that Ryan made sure he wasn't alone. That made it hurt a little bit less.

Wayne just stared at Julie for a moment. She'd gotten even more beautiful than he'd remembered. He hadn't even realized it until now.

She caught him eying her. "You okay, Tempest?"

He smiled. "I'm fine. I just . . . did you want me to stay or just come pick up Aaron later?"

Julie was silent a moment. She walked to the window without an answer.

"Julie?"

"That was a good thing you did. Taking Aaron in. He looks good."

"He is."

She turned to him. "I never got to thank you properly

for helping me when Patrick was sick."

He pocketed his hands. "Julie, you're fine."

"What I'm trying to say is . . ." She walked over to him. "We were so busy and I didn't have time to really process you being back. And how I felt about that."

Wayne went to say something but he didn't know what to say. Anything he could think of seemed inappropriate.

"Wayne, you were a great partner. A great friend. I was married and I loved Seth. I never felt anything else between us. But since you've been back, the feelings have felt different. I like it when you're around. I like having a partner again. And a part of me is just wondering if we should ever be more than that."

"Julie, what are you saying?"

"Seth's been gone a long time now. Patrick could use a good man to be a father to him. And my heart doesn't have to suffer alone forever. There's no reason we can't at least look. I guess what I'm saying is, I want you to stay. And I want you to come back. I want us to see if this could work. If we could work. You and me, the boys. As a family."

Wayne smiled. "Are you saying we should get married?" He raised an eyebrow.

She smacked his chest. "Gosh, Wayne. You're making this even more awkward."

"Well, I . . ." he backed away. "What you're feeling, I've felt it too. But I didn't want to say anything. I didn't want to pressure you. If you're not ready."

She leaned in and pulled him into a kiss. She held his face and he lifted his hands to hers. It was soft. Tender.

She pulled back. "Yes. If we court a while and we think we could work as a family, then yes. I'd like to maybe marry you one day, Wayne Tempest. But we need to do this right. We have to see first. I don't want to rush into something. I want to take the time to make sure we're all on the same page and we know this is what is supposed to happen."

Wayne looked her in the eyes. Her beautiful, majestic eyes. They were looking back at him with everything he felt right now. "That works for me."

They heard the boys coming down.

They quickly turned to them and tried to act natural. Wayne locked eyes with Patrick. He couldn't fool that boy. Patrick smiled and gave him a thumbs-up. Seems he already decided what he wanted.

Julie sat them down on the couch and put on a movie. Wayne didn't pay much attention to it. He couldn't take his eyes off of them. She was beautiful. And the boys were the best kids he knew. They would grow up to be such great men and he wanted to be a part of that.

Three years that case had taken of his life. And before that, he'd been coasting. Now Wayne Tempest had a purpose. A future.

He took a mental screencap of the three of them. He put his arm around the boys and met Julie's hand at the other side.

She turned to him and took his hand with a smile. There wasn't any doubt in his mind at that moment. But he'd wait until she was ready. It would make it worth more.

Aaron had the faintest smile on. Subtle, but real. Wayne prayed it would only grow if he was part of a real family again.

This was what he wanted. This was where he needed to be. Right here.

God had led him to amazing people. They had the

chance to be happy. Together. It was beautiful. He hadn't even realized he'd been dreaming about this for so long. A family. His family.

ACKNOWLEDGEMENTS

To God for continued inspiration, to my family for continued support and encouragement, and to everyone who bought a copy of *Blood Chain*, thank you from the bottom of my heart.

Thank you to Jansina for working another miracle with this book. It looks great. Really, you rock.

Thank you to Catherine and Sue for your thoughts, advice, and critique of this book.

Thanks to author Melanie P. Smith for providing some of the photos used on the cover. (And her nephew Devin for agreeing to model for them.)

Thanks to Cody, Chelise, Gina, Rebecca, Jana, Jessica, Father Sean, and to anyone who contributed in any way to this book. (A thousand apologies if I forgot to mention you specifically.) And to anyone reading it now, thank you. You make this possible.

MORE BY J.J. FRANCESCO

CONTACT THE AUTHOR

www.facebook.com/jjfrancesco
www.twitter.com/jjfrancesco

RIVERSHORE BOOKS

www.rivershorebooks.com
blog.rivershorebooks. com
forum.rivershorebooks. com
www.facebook.com/rivershore.books
www.twitter.com/rivershorebooks
Info@rivershorebooks.com

www.ingramcontent.com/pod-product-compliance
Lightning Source LLC
Chambersburg PA
CBHW051440260626
47162CB00001B/184

* 9 7 8 0 6 9 2 6 7 9 2 1 0 *